Susan didn't believe in love at first sight . . .

But there was such a thing as intuition, and she was feeling the same thing about Nicholas Claus that she had felt with Bill; that deep down knowledge that they were a match, that eventually after the right number of dates, the right number of kisses, the right number of shared dreams, she and this man would agree they were meant to spend the rest of their lives together. The feeling was so strong it was almost palpable. As he tooled the car toward the downtown area of Angel Falls, she glanced in Nick's direction, looking for some indication that he felt it, too.

"Cuddle up by the fire with a glass of eggnog and get ready to be immersed in the joy of the season with Suzi Christmas and Nicholas Claus."
> —*The New York Times* bestselling author
> Debbie Macomber

All I Want for Christmas

Sheila Rabe

JOVE BOOKS, NEW YORK

This is a work of fiction. Names, characters, places, and incidents are
either the product of the author's imagination or are used fictitiously,
and any resemblance to actual persons, living or dead, business
establishments, events, or locales is entirely coincidental.

ALL I WANT FOR CHRISTMAS

A Jove Book / published by arrangement with
the author

PRINTING HISTORY
Jove edition / October 2000

The Penguin Putnam Inc. World Wide Web site address is
http://www.penguinputnam.com

ISBN: 0-515-12925-9

A JOVE BOOK®
Jove Books are published by The Berkley Publishing Group,
a division of Penguin Putnam Inc.,
375 Hudson Street, New York, New York 10014.
JOVE and the "J" design
are trademarks belonging to Penguin Putnam Inc.

PRINTED IN THE UNITED STATES OF AMERICA

10 9 8 7 6 5 4 3 2 1

for Ben and Sam,
who know how to keep Christmas well

Acknowledgments

Does anyone besides me ever read these things? I hope so, because I have some serious acknowledging to do. Thanks to Lisa Hendrix, the human hard drive, for being such a great critique partner. Thanks, Susan Wiggs, for introducing me to Helen Breitweiser, the best agent on the planet. And thanks, Helen, for bringing me back to The Berkley Publishing Group and hooking me up with Gail Fortune, who is just as wonderful as her name. (Isn't that a great name for a heroine? Too bad Gail's mommy thought of it first.) I need to thank some lawyers here, too; and, after all those who have helped me, I swear I'll never tell another lawyer joke again. (Not that I ever did, guys. Really.) Big Bad John Dolesey answered more questions than a key witness. Kany Levine was both kind and helpful. Even Kristin Hannah, who has long since left the profession to become a literary star, took time to pull out some legal pearls from her past and help me with a plot problem. If I flunked the bar guys, it wasn't your fault. Thanks to Paula Willems for banking advice, Steve Hanberg for computer input and to Bob Jones at the Kitsap Mall for his input on sprinkler systems. Last, but not least, thanks to Joe Mooney at the *Seattle Post-Intelligencer,* who gave me insights into how a big newspaper is put out, and who said, "It's okay. You don't have to mention my name in a romance novel." What a modest guy! To one and all, my heartfelt appreciation.

One

Luke Potter edged his Lexus forward another foot and scowled. No wonder his renters had fled. This was nuts. Traffic was snailing along and he still couldn't see THE HOUSE. By seven o'clock at night a person ought to be able to zip down the street to his own garage, but here on the main drag through the Sylvan Estates housing development on December second, no one was zipping anywhere. It looked like a street fair with people strolling by him, kids in tow, and passengers hanging out of car windows, hooting and calling to each other. It seemed to Luke that all the kids coming from the direction of The House had candy canes sticking out of their beaks. He lowered his window and called to one, "Hey, kid, where'd you get the candy cane?"

"Suzi Christmas," hollered the boy.

Suzi Christmas. What a stupid name.

The cars moved forward again, and in another five minutes Luke caught his first glimpse of Suzi's famous house. Good God, he thought, they don't light up Times Square this much. Strains of canned music crept past his now raised window.

"Silent Night." What a joke! The night was anything but, what with all the people, cars, and that ticky-tacky music going. Up ahead, Luke could see cars jockeying for parking places and people lined along the white picket fence in front of the Dutch Colonial. Some were even opening the gate and walking inside the yard, like state fair revelers lining up to go see the pigs. Maybe the woman charged a fee. That had to be the only way she could afford to pay the electric bill on this monstrosity. Luke shook his head. All that was missing from the scene was the Ferris wheel and a cotton-candy stand.

Now he was within a block of the place and could see the whole mess close up. A glowing Santa waved at him from a sleigh on the roof, while lit mechanical reindeer pawed the shingles, anxious to be off. Farther down, a lit plastic angel hovered over the door as if guarding the fools who lived inside. White lights outlined the house, and blue ones twinkled their way along the picket fence. Not to be outdone, every bush in the yard modeled fat, red lights. A small fir tree in the front yard glowed with every color of the rainbow. Luke could now see that the people going inside the yard were depositing cans in a big, beribboned wooden crate that sat beside the tree. The other side of the yard was drawing the attention of several families with a nativity scene portrayed by live actors. Not content with humans, she'd added a sheep and even a donkey. Where the heck had the woman gotten a donkey?

Luke shook his head in amazement. If he hadn't seen the circus for himself he would never have believed it. His attention was next drawn to the action taking place beneath the two giant candy canes that met in an arch at the gate of the picket fence. There stood a woman in some sort of goofy Mrs. Santa outfit, handing out candy canes. Luke eyed her with disgust, taking in her pillow-padded figure, the fake white wig drawn back into a bun, and the silly, wire-rimmed glasses. That must be Suzi. So that's what a fruitcake looked like.

He let his gaze drift across the street to the neat, white house decorated only with a wreath on the front door. Now, that was tasteful. Yeah, his old lemon-sucking godfather who lived there had the right idea. Don't overdo, don't create a fuss, and don't inconvenience your neighbors. That was the true spirit of Christmas.

Luke didn't like to spoil anyone's fantasy, but Don was right. This Suzi Christmas person's holiday fun was affecting other people. Not only was she depriving Don and Aggie of their sleep, she was also depriving Luke of his rental income. Now that he'd seen the mess for himself, he couldn't blame his renters for moving out. Moving? Running would be a better word. Luke had never seen people vacate a house so fast. Granted, they'd paid him through the end of December. But who knew how long it would take him to get in new renters; and when he did, how long would they stay after finding out what lived next door?

He looked at his dark, vacant house and scowled. No wonder he'd gotten such a good deal on the place. The real-estate agent who sold him that holiday turkey last June must have known about Susan Carpenter and her holiday madness. Supposedly she'd been doing this for the last nine years. Luke had half a mind to sue the real-estate guy and the former owners, too. He'd talk to his lawyer about that first thing in the morning.

As soon as he was out of the housing development, he floored the gas, as if driving fast could put the whole unpleasant sensory experience out of his mind. Why did people go so nuts at Christmas, anyway?

Hey, he told himself, be glad they do. A lot of computers from your stores end up under their trees.

Still, it seemed like an overrated holiday to Luke. People did a lot of talking about the Christmas Spirit like it was a good thing. From what he could see, it only produced a frenzy of shopping for useless presents to take up space in someone's garage or basement, expensive office parties where some moron always got drunk and made a pass at someone else's wife, and disastrous family gatherings.

Well, maybe somewhere in America there existed a Norman Rockwell family who, every December twenty-fifth, sat around the tree in their bathrobes, unwrapping presents, listening to carols, and smiling at each other, but he doubted it. His family sure had never fit the bill. Their Christmases were always of the National Lampoon variety.

Luke still remembered the time that Uncle Harvey had too much Christmas eggnog and fell into the tree, managing to knock it over and trample Luke's model airplane kit in the process. Then there was the great turkey robbery, where the family dog got to the main course before the rest of the family. The capper, of course, was the big Christmas fight. Merry Christmas, kids. You're gonna get a second house this year, and one of your parents will be living in it. But don't worry, you'll see Daddy on the holidays.

Luke's jaw tightened with the memory. Christmas. Scrooge had it right: Bury all the fa-la-la-ers with a sprig of holly stuck through their hearts.

He got back to his condo with its river view and its elegant, treeless living room. This time last year he'd had a tree. His girlfriend, Lynette, had bought it and decorated it for him as a surprise. She'd expected to find a diamond ring under it. When she opened the little black box tied with the red ribbon and found only pearl earrings, she'd wished Luke a Merry Christmas and a Happy New Year, and split, leaving him to take down the blasted tree! Another reason to hate Christmas.

Well, it was only a few weeks of madness. He'd grit his teeth and endure it, and come January first, it would all be behind him like a bad dream. Everything except the problem of one empty rental house.

•   •   •

Susan handed her last candy cane to the little, redheaded boy. "You get the last one, Jamie."

"Oh, boy!" he whooped and went running off.

"Don't run with that in your mouth," Susan called after him. She smiled at the handful of people left lingering along the fence. "That's it for tonight, folks. Everything goes off at ten."

"It's so pretty," said one of the women. "You've added that angel this year, haven't you?"

Susan nodded. "I think angels and nativity scenes are just as important as Santas."

"Well, it's beautiful," said the woman. "This is our fourth year coming, and we look forward to it. It just gets prettier every season. Don't you ever stop."

"I don't plan on it," said Susan, her voice taking on a steely tinge. The Rawlinses could squawk all they wanted, but they'd lost their allies when the renters next door moved out; the rest of the neighborhood was on her side. She had started putting up her lights nine years ago, when she and Bill had first moved here, and she wasn't about to stop now.

The show over for the night, Mary and Joseph helped her load the donated goodies for the food bank into plastic bags and transfer them from the crate to the trunk of her car while her shepherd, a 4-H kid from a farm just outside town, headed off to bring his horse trailer around the front of the house to load up the four-legged actors.

"That has to be the most you've gotten yet," said Joseph, wedging the last bag into the trunk.

"Good," said Susan. "Anne told me donations have been down this year. This will put a smile on her face."

The shepherd returned, and he and Joseph loaded up the animals, then the actors left.

The local tourists were now long gone, leaving Susan to enjoy the last chorus of "Joy to the World" in solitude, and she gave her new guardian angel one final, admiring look before walking up her candy cane–lined front walk and around to the side of the house to turn off the lights.

Susan loved that angel with her golden hair and pale blue gown and those huge, silvery wings. Electricity gave her face and clothes a heavenly glow Susan found comforting, and she liked to think that, like her angel, Bill was looking down from heaven, watching her and Willie, and smiling. How he would have loved this latest addition to their Christmas display! He was always looking for new decorations, and he'd planned to add a mechanical Santa's workshop to the front corner of the yard to entertain Willie for his second Christmas. But he'd never lived to do it.

Susan sighed. Who would have thought he'd die so young? More people are killed every day in car accidents than in plane crashes, but that fact was small comfort when your husband was one of the few who died in a flaming plane. No unpleasant thoughts, she told herself firmly, not at Christmas. She shook off the grim memory and pulled the plug on her holiday fantasyland.

Inside the house, she turned off the music, then went upstairs to Willie's room. He lay curled up in the old easy chair by the window, sound asleep, his brown curls sticking out in all directions, a hand pillowing his freckled cheek. At six, his face still held that baby look when he slept, and watching him caused a painfully sweet, maternal swell deep in Susan's chest.

Next to the chair, Ralph, their rag mop of a dog, lifted his head and thumped his tail in greeting. She patted the dog, then touched her son's shoulder, whispering, "Time for bed."

It was the same every night. After giving out candy canes until eight, Willie would come inside, get into his red jammies, then take his post by the window, where he'd wave to friends and watch all the people coming to admire his Christmas lights. He'd fall asleep to their rainbow glow and the lullaby of Christmas carols. When he'd been smaller, Susan had carried him to his bed, but he weighed too much for that now.

He got out of the chair and tottered to bed. She tucked him in and kissed him on the cheek. "God bless us," she whispered.

"God bless us, everyone," he mumbled in return, smiled and rolled over with a sigh. Ralph jumped onto the bed and curled up at Willie's feet.

Susan smiled and tiptoed out, her heart as full as a Christmas stocking.

By ten the next morning, Susan's heart was pretty well deflated. She'd gotten Willie off to school, then sat down to go over the books for her singing telegram company, Yours-For-A-Song. Where was she going to get the money to pay her employees' Christmas bonuses this year?

For the last two years, it had come from her contract with the Angel Falls Mall. Starting December first, her singers dressed in Dickensian costumes and caroled their way around the mall every Saturday and Sunday; and the week before Christmas, they were there every night. While the carolers sang, her Santa's elves juggled and passed out candy canes, always a big hit with the families waiting to have their pictures taken with Santa.

For years she'd been providing the community with an opportunity to feel the Christmas Spirit, and this was the thanks she got! Susan still could hardly believe that Jack Williams, the mall manager, had listened to a small handful of complainers, sour old descendants of Ebenezer Scrooge himself, who had persuaded him not to hire her singers this season. Bah, humbug.

She scowled at the figures in front of her and chomped viciously on her pencil. Not only did she have to contend with the mall not renewing her contract, but she also had to endure another season of the Rawlinses trying to get the other residents of Sylvan Estates to side with them in their battle to end her tradition of lighting up her house and yard—the Rawlinses had moved in four years ago and had complained about her lights each of those four years. Having Mr. Rawlins in her face, shaking his finger at her was becoming nearly as much a Christmas tradition as lighting her house.

What was wrong with people these days, anyway? All they cared about was money and things. What happened to goodness and kindness and sharing, and remembering the reason for the season? Well, if she ever met that Luke Potter jerk who started the Scrooge disease at the mall she'd give him something to remember the season—sore shins. She'd gotten his name out of Jack, but before he'd coughed it up, he'd made Susan promise not to go running off and create a scene. Good old Jack, the wimp. Susan hoped he got a lump of coal in his stocking this year. He certainly deserved one. And a lump on the head, too. Confrontation wasn't her style, so she wasn't going to be the one to give it to Luke Potter. But she wished someone would.

Look how he'd messed her up! Her contract with the mall had not only provided nice Christmas bonuses for her employees, but had gone a long way toward paying her whopping electric bill in January. Without that money, how was she going to pay that bill?

For a moment she thought of borrowing from her dad, but he was just recovering from paying all the hospital bills left from Mom's final bout with cancer two years ago. And anyway, Susan liked being independent, able to take care of her own needs and solve her own problems. So Dad was really not an option. Dipping into Willie's college fund was as impossible as it was unthinkable. She supposed she could turn on her display only on weekends. That would save a bundle.

But no, she wasn't going to do that. Then the grinches of the world—like the Rawlinses and the Luke Potters—would win. The shine would be rubbed off the season just like they wanted, and everything would be black and gray like the scenes in the movie *Joe Versus the Volcano* before Joe got a life. Besides, those lights were one of the ways she kept Bill's memory alive for herself and Willie. Bill would never have buckled under to the Rawlinses, and neither would she.

"It'll work out," she told herself firmly. "Christmas is the season for miracles, and I'll get mine, somehow."

Luke's intercom buzzed and his secretary, Martha, said, "Mr. Rawlins is holding for you on line two."

"Thanks," said Luke. He punched the speaker button on his phone and went back to signing letters. "Hi, Don."

"Well, did you see the house?" demanded a gruff voice.

"Yes, I drove by last night."

"Crawled by, don'tcha mean?"

"It's pretty bad."

"You should try living opposite it," snapped Don Rawlins. "I told you you'd lose those renters."

"Yeah, well, I wish you'd told me that before I bought the house," said Luke.

"You should have come to me before it was a done deal. If you had, I'd have warned you, because we've been trying to do something about that woman for the last four Christmases. You know Aggie's not a well woman. She needs her rest, and that music blares every night until ten."

Actually, ten seemed a reasonable enough time to shut down. Didn't the Angel Falls cops give people until ten-thirty to quiet down on weekdays? Luke caught himself. *Whose side are you on, anyway? Would you want to listen to that every night?*

"So, do we have a deal?" persisted Don.

He'd be a fool to pass up the deal his godfather was offering. The no-interest capital would keep Luke's new PC Edge, his third computer store, going and allow him to put in that video arcade at the Angel Falls Mall a whole year earlier than he'd originally planned.

Of course, Don wasn't loaning Luke money out of the goodness of his heart; he had precious little of that commodity. Luke was a hired gun, the weight Don intended to use to tip the scales his way in his battle against his neighbor. Although Don could sell and move out of Sylvan Estates—the old coot could afford to buy twice, no, three times the house he had now and pay cash—that would be admitting defeat, and Luke knew his godfather didn't like to lose at anything. Don would leave his present neighborhood only after he'd put his stamp on it.

Well, the sick and convoluted workings of his godfather's mind were none of Luke's business. Helping Don unplug the ding-a-ling, who'd driven away Luke's renters, in exchange for liquid funds to pour into his own growing empire was too sweet a deal to pass up. And, even though Luke had been keeping Don waiting for his answer, he'd known what side he was going to come down on and had already put the arcade deal in motion. "I contacted Melville about it half an hour ago," said Luke.

"Good. At least someone in this town has some sense."

"Let's hope we can get some action," said Luke.

"I should say," agreed Don. "You know the light shines right into our bedroom window."

Luke frowned. He really didn't have time for Don's complaints. "We'll put an end to it, don't worry. I'm sure we can move fast on this."

"I want that lawyer of yours to move faster than fast," snapped Don. "If Melville tries to drag his feet on this, you hold them to the fire."

"Don't worry," Luke assured him. "Suzi Christmas will get her present from us before another week goes by."

"Good. And we'll get that money in your account today."

Luke envisioned another piece of his growing financial empire falling into place and grinned. Ho, ho, ho. Merry Christmas.

• • •

"Oooh, artichoke dip."

The reverent tone in her younger sister's voice made Susan grin as she took the casserole dish from the oven. "It's the least I could do, knowing how much you hate wearing that wig."

"Almost as much as I hate waddling around with all that padding," said Nicole, dumping crackers onto a plate. "But, hey, it's for a good cause. I can't let the real Mrs. Santa miss her own son's winter concert."

"You're right. And somebody needs to be here tonight to pass out the candy canes and make sure people know where to put their donations for the food bank."

"As if people don't know by now," scoffed Nicole.

"I get more visitors every year. You'd be surprised how many people asked me where to put their cans last night, even though the crate was sitting right there in plain sight."

Nicole shook her head. "To think I gave up a cozy evening in front of the fire with Hot Toddy for this."

"You should have made him come over, too. We could have dressed him up like Santa."

"He wouldn't want to miss Monday night football. Anyway, I think Todd prefers to do his Christmas good deeds in a less public way. We're not all born hams."

"Well, Miss Piggy, don't try to pretend you're not. You know you love doing this."

"If any of my customers see me, I'll die."

"They won't make any connection between Mrs. Santa and the Marilyn Monroe clone who sells them makeup during the day, trust me," said Susan. "And Todd will survive without you for one night."

"Well, he'll still get part of me: my voice." Nicole dug in her purse and produced a cell phone. "Ta-dah!"

"When did you get that?"

"Just today. And about time. I swear I'm the last woman on the planet to get one of these. Todd's going to call me tonight and help break it in."

Susan smiled indulgently and shook her head. "You're

not exactly a high-powered businesswoman. Why on Earth do you need a cell phone?"

"It will come in handy if my car ever breaks down, or if you have an emergency. In fact, you really should get one. It would help you with your business, and if Willie got sick at school, they could reach you."

"Well, I'll give them your cell phone number. Then if Willie gets sick at school they can reach you," joked Susan.

Nicole rolled her eyes. "Yeah, I can stretch him out under the perfume counter. I'm serious, Suz. This is one case where you shouldn't be a techno-dinosaur. You really should have one. I'm only paying twenty bucks a month."

"Well, if you want to know the truth, it's on my list of things to get after Christmas."

Nicole plopped her new toy back in her purse, muttering, "About time."

"You know, I really do appreciate you filling in for me," said Susan, returning to the business at hand.

Nicole grinned. "And you know I really don't mind. I just like to give you a hard time."

"Well, I haven't completely forgotten what it's like to be in love. And just remember, by giving up an evening with Todd to do this good deed, you won't have to worry about getting a lump of coal in your stocking."

"I wasn't planning on it, believe me. In fact, I'm thinking more along the lines of a diamond."

"That's some lump of coal," teased Susan. "Speaking of presents, I hope you weren't planning on spending a lot on me this year."

Nicole dredged a wheat cracker through the artichoke dip. "With the discount I get on perfume now? You've got to be kidding."

"Good, because I won't be able to spend much on you. All my Christmas money may be going to pay my electric bill."

"Oh, yeah. No money from the mall this year," said

Nicole sympathetically. "Well, don't worry about me. You can promise me a year's supply of this stuff and I'll be happy."

"Boy, you're easy."

"That's not what Todd says."

"Good girl. Hold out for that diamond."

Nicole's expression turned serious. "Are you going to be able to do Christmas for Willie?"

"Of course. That's what plastic is for, right?"

Nicole popped another dip-laden cracker into her mouth. Ralph thumped his tail and looked at her hopefully. She dropped him a cracker, which he devoured with a snap and a gulp. "You know, it's hard to believe there are people like Luke Potter out there, isn't it? Imagine complaining about having carolers in the mall at Christmas. The guy's mother must have screwed up his potty training or something."

"Or else someone told him there was no Santa."

"Well, he'll get what's coming to him," predicted Nicole. "Bad guys always do." She helped herself to another cracker, then said, "Okay, I'm fortified. Let's get those pillows on me."

"At the rate you've been going through the dip, you won't need them," observed Susan.

"I wouldn't want to hurt your feelings and not eat it."

It took less than half an hour for the two sisters to get Nicole in costume, the house lighted up, and the music going.

"You know, you could save money by not giving out these things," said Nicole, picking up the shopping bag full of candy canes.

"I wouldn't save that much, not with the discount the store gives me. Anyway, just because I got hit by someone with Scrooge disease doesn't mean I have to pass it on to anyone else."

"You've got a point there," agreed Nicole, unwrapping a candy cane.

Susan watched her sister stick the cane in her mouth. "It's a good thing you go to the gym every day, that's all I can say."

"Just getting into the Christmas Spirit."

At that moment Willie came down the stairs, resplendent in his new black slacks and white shirt.

Nicole let out a whistle. "Studly Dudley."

Willie grinned, ran to his mom and held a clip-on, red necktie up to her.

"What are those funny white things?" Nicole teased, lifting up the end of the tie for a closer look.

"Candy canes!" supplied Willie.

"You don't expect the son of Suzi Christmas to show up for his winter concert in just a plain tie, do you?" said Susan, putting it on him.

"Of course not," said Nicole.

Willie was now eyeing Nicole's candy cane. "Can I have a candy cane?" he asked.

"No," said Susan. "They'll have cookies after the program."

"Oh, come on, Mom. It'll make his breath smell good," put in Nicole.

Susan gave up the fight. "Oh, okay."

"Alright!" he exclaimed and dove his hand into the bag.

"Just one," said Susan, seeing him come up with two. She put a hand on her son's shoulders. "Now, let's go, Willie Winkie, or we're going to be late."

With a whoop, Willie was out the door, his mother and aunt following him.

Nicole watched them drive away, then made her way to the candy cane arch, clapping her mittened hands together for warmth. Something small and white drifted by her nose. Then another something. "Oh, great," she muttered, "snow."

It was a Monday night, and almost seven o'clock, time for all good commuters to be done with work and tucked snugly into their suburban homes, but cars were already inching by, and two teenage boys stood waiting for their candy canes. "Yo, Mrs. Santa!" called one. "Your boobs are lopsided."

Nicole frowned. Of course, the younger kids in the neighborhood would be over at Angel Falls Elementary, right now, getting ready to take part in the concert, which meant that she'd see mostly smart-mouthed juvenile delinquents like these two. "Don't get cute, little boy, or Mrs. Santa will have to stick this candy cane someplace besides your mouth," she said sweetly.

This brought a hoot of laughter from the boys. Nicole gave them their candy canes and sent them on their way, discreetly adjusting her padding as they sauntered off. Her enhanced chest refused to cooperate, shifting to a new, unnatural angle and making her scowl. She tried using both arms to straighten the padding and wound up with a worse mess. "Great. Cyclops boob." She turned her back to street and did some serious adjusting and finally achieved a more natural look.

Natural? That was a joke. She did enjoy the spotlight, but she wasn't sure if waddling around in the cold like a human pillowcase, making a fool of herself qualified as a great performance.

Although the candy cane business was slow, Nicole had plenty of visitors who wanted to contribute to the food bank, exclaim over the house, and tell her how cute she looked. Between helping them and waving at the steady stream of cars rolling by, she was soon warm and enjoying herself. Just enough snow fell to give the yard a fairyland look, and surveying her domain, Nicole decided that first thing tomorrow she'd write a letter to the mayor, suggesting he give her sister some kind of award for everything she did to make Christmas special for the community. This really was great!

She'd tucked her cellular phone in the pocket of Mrs. Santa's apron, and now it rang, making her start. Feeling the same way she had when she got her first Barbie doll, she fished the phone out of her pocket and fumbled it open. "Hello?"

"Ho, ho, ho. This is Santa, looking for my woman."

"She's stuck in the great outdoors, trying to stay warm."

"Stop by here on your way home. I can unfreeze you."

His promise lit an instant fire inside Nicole, making her only mildly aware of the short, stocky man in the overcoat, who was coming through the front gate.

"So how does my light-stringing job look?" asked Todd.

"*Our* light-stringing job," she corrected him. "It looks great, especially considering the fact that we got it up in record time. It takes Suz and Dad twice as long."

"Listen," said Todd, "John just called. He and his wife have got tickets to *The Nutcracker* over in . . ."

Suddenly the short man in the overcoat was in front of Nicole, talking. She caught the words "Susan Carpenter."

People were always asking her if this was Susan Carpenter's famous house. She nodded absently, trying to concentrate on what Todd was saying, and held up a friendly hand so the stranger would know she would be with him in just a minute.

The man nodded and placed a manila envelope in Nicole's hand and turned to walk away. She looked at it. What was this? "Excuse me?"

No answer. Instead, the man strode briskly away.

"Wait a minute," she called, but he ignored her and hurried back out through the front gate. "Well, if that wasn't about the rudest . . ."

"Hey, babe, are you with me?" demanded Todd.

"Some man just dropped off something for Susan. "Where were we?"

"*The Nutcracker.* Do we want to go see it?"

"Sure."

"Okay, then. Don't make any plans for the fourteenth. See ya a little later, huh?"

Todd hung up, and Nicole slipped her new toy back in her pocket. Curious, she turned the envelope over in her hand. It was very official looking. Maybe someone was a step ahead of her and had decided to honor Suz. Perhaps this was some sort of proclamation.

Nicole craned her neck, looking for the man who delivered it, but he was long gone, melted into the night. Unable to resist the temptation to snoop, she opened the envelope and began to scan the papers. The words jumped off the first page and scared away her earlier euphoria. " 'Public nuisance'?"

She read on. " 'Mr. Luke Potter, a single person, and Mr. and Mrs. Don Rawlins, a married couple . . .' " Swallowing the painful growth in her throat, Nicole shuffled through the papers. " 'You are summoned to appear . . .' Oh, my gosh. Oh, my gosh!" She dropped the pages as if they were on fire and clapped her mittened hands to her cheeks.

"What is it?" asked one of Suz's neighbors. "Bad news?"

Nicole blinked at him. "I just . . . no, no, nothing." She knelt down and, working as best she could around her pillowy chest, scooped up the papers. "Everything's okay. Really. Excuse me."

Clasping the shameful, legal poison to her chest, she hurried inside the house.

Like a choir of wicked fairies, voices from the speaker on the front porch seemed to pursue Nicole, warbling about needing a little Christmas this very minute.

"No," she wailed. "We need a lawyer."

Two

Still wailing, Nicole fished her phone out of her pocket and dialed with trembling fingers. Todd had barely answered when she said, "You've got to get over here right away!"

"Nicki, whatsa matter?"

"We're being sued!"

"What!"

"Just get over here."

"Okay, okay. I'm on my way. Try to stay calm."

Stay calm? He had to be kidding. Nicole paced around the entryway and found it too confining. But going outside and seeing the smiling people waving at her was too much, too. She gave them a weak wave from the front porch, then retreated back into the house and made a beeline for the kitchen. By the time Todd arrived she'd downed the entire casserole dish of artichoke dip.

His glance went to the empty dish. "Oh, boy."

"Oh, boy is right." Nicole grabbed the sheaf of papers, which was already beginning to look manhandled, and shoved it at him. "The Rawlinses are suing Suz to make her take down her Christmas lights."

"You gotta be kidding." He scanned the pages. "My God, I can't believe it."

"First the mall, now this. What are we going to do?"

"Bump off this Luke Potter. Isn't that the same guy who got everybody all stirred up over the carolers at the mall?"

"Oh, my gosh, you're right. Oh, Todd. What are we going to do?" Nicole repeated, her voice rising.

"Get a lawyer."

Nicole rubbed her forehead. "Suz doesn't have money for that, and I sure don't have that kind of cash. Buddy and Jan could maybe scrape together a couple hundred."

"How about your dad?"

Nicole shook her head. "I don't know. All the bills from when Mom was sick wiped out most of his savings. He's good for a couple hundred, maybe five, I guess."

Todd was chewing his lip, a sure sign of creative genius at work. Nicole looked at him hopefully.

"There's gotta be a way to work this out," he said.

Nicole felt as if she'd been dropped on cement. This was the best her genius reporter boyfriend could come up with? "That's all you've got to say?"

"Give me time. I'm still thinking."

"Well, think fast. My sister will be here any minute."

"And a partridge in a pear tree." Susan and Willie finished the song on a double forte note.

"That was definitely your best song," she said.

"I wouldn't want any of that stuff for Christmas," said Willie. "I just want Luke Skywalker's X-Wing."

As if I didn't already know, thought Susan. "And I bet Santa's working hard to find it for you right now," she said.

They turned onto Sylvan Boulevard, bringing up the rear of the slow procession passing their house. Even from here Susan could see the welcoming glow of the lights. Bill would have enjoyed this so much.

Susan was willing to bet that by now her sister was having the time of her life. Nicole had helped her for the last five years, and while Nicole was making a tradition of complaining all the way into the Mrs. Santa costume, it never took long for her to forget her embarrassment. As they got closer, Susan expected to see her sister highly visible and waving at the passing cars like the little ham she was, but Mrs. Santa was nowhere to be found. And whose Jeep was that parked in her driveway? It looked like Todd's. Something was odd here.

"Where's Aunt Nicki?" asked Willie.

"Maybe she had to go into the house to get more candy canes," said Susan.

"Can I have one?"

"You already had one earlier, remember? And Christmas cookies at school. I think that's enough for tonight."

Concern nibbling at the back of her mind, Susan turned into her driveway.

One woman called a hello to her as Susan got out of the car. The woman pointed to the angel on the roof. "We like the new addition."

"Thanks," Susan replied, and hurried into the house, Willie close behind her. "Nicki!"

Her sister came out of the kitchen, her boyfriend, Todd Shelburne, behind her. Todd normally had a big smile on his boyish face. Tonight he wasn't smiling, and Nicole looked about to cry. Susan felt suddenly sick. The dog was dead.

"Todd!" Willie squealed and ran to his idol.

"Hey, man, give me five," said Todd, holding out his palm for Willie to slap. Now he was smiling, but it was a halfhearted one. Oh, Lord!

"Willie," Susan said, trying to keep the panic out of

her voice. "I want you to go upstairs and get your jammies on."

"Can I still watch out the window?"

"Yes, but jammies first, and brush your teeth. Then I'll come and hear you say your prayers."

"Okay," said Willie. "G'night, Aunt Nicki."

"Goodnight, Willie," said Nicole. Her voice broke and she turned her back.

"Is Aunt Nicki crying?" asked the child.

"Yes," said Nicole in a wobbly voice. "The artichoke dip is gone."

"Don't worry. Mom will make you some more," said Willie.

Now Susan was really scared. If it wasn't the dog, it had to be Dad. "Upstairs, Willie Winkie," she commanded, grabbing her sister by the elbow and propelling her into the kitchen. "All right," Susan said as soon as the door had shut behind them. "What's happened?"

Nicole looked to Todd, who had followed them in.

"Somebody tell me!"

"We're being sued," announced Nicole, handing Susan the legal papers.

"What?" Susan stared at the sheaf of papers in her hands.

"A process server came while you were gone," Todd explained. "They're calling your lights a public nuisance, citing increased traffic . . ."

Susan was already skimming the papers. The name jumped off the page at her. "Luke Potter. Him again!"

"What's his connection with the Rawlinses?" asked Todd.

"All grinches stick together," said Nicole.

"It has to be more than that," said Todd. "I mean, I can see the Rawlinses bitching. They've been personally affected by the lights and traffic."

"Whose side are you on?" demanded Nicole.

"Hey, I'm just trying to think reasonably," he said.

"This guy has to have some reason for his actions, something that makes logical sense to him—like the Rawlinses not wanting the traffic and noise."

Susan shook her head. "The Rawlinses are the only ones who ever griped about that. Well, them and the renters next door," she added. She sighed. "Why couldn't the Rawlinses be like those people and just move? He's got tons of money. He could buy a house somewhere far away from everyone."

"Because it's more fun to stay here and ruin your life," said her sister bitterly.

Todd was chewing his lip again.

"What is it, Toddy?" asked Nicole hopefully.

He adjusted his glasses. "What about whoever owns that house next door? He'd be losing rental income. Could Luke Potter be that guy?"

"Gosh, I was at the lake with Buddy and Jan when the house sold, and the Steubings never did tell me the name of the person who bought it," said Susan. "Then the renters moved in, but I'm afraid I never talked with them very much."

"They got off to a bad start," Nicole explained. "Ralph got loose one day and dug up their flower beds."

"Well, I'll lay odds that this Luke Potter is the one who owns the vacant house next door," said Todd.

"Oh, great. What are we going to do?" asked Nicole, her voice rising.

Sit down, thought Susan, that's what we're going to do. She dropped onto a kitchen chair saying, "*We* don't have to do anything. It's only me who's being sued."

"Oh, and we're all going to sit around and watch those old prune faces across the street make you take down your Christmas lights?" retorted her sister. "You were here first. Don't you have squatter's rights or something?"

"That might be a good defense," mused Todd.

Susan was shaking her head. "To have a defense you

have to be able to afford a lawyer. Where am I going to get the money for a court battle?"

Sudden inspiration lit Todd's face and he snapped his fingers. "A legal defense fund! Oh, yeah."

Susan blinked. She felt like every gear in her brain was clogged with sand and molasses. "Gosh, I don't know," she said. "I suppose some of the neighbors might kick in something."

"No," said Todd. "You gotta think bigger than that." He tapped a finger on his chest. "You don't know a man with media connections for nothing."

"That's right!" agreed Nicole. "Hot Toddy can write about this and raise money for you. Think how many people read the *Angel Falls Clarion.*"

Not as many as read the *Chronicle* thought Susan. The *Clarion* only serviced the town of Angel Falls, while the *Chronicle* was sold in all the towns within a hundred mile radius. But Nicole was right. Even though he wrote for a small paper, Todd did have something of a readership. And any exposure was better than none.

"This won't hurt the paper any, either," Todd was saying. "In fact, if I play my cards right I might just land myself at the old *Chronicle.*"

"Todd!"

"And you might just get that diamond ring yet, baby."

"Todd! We're talking about my sister's fate here."

Todd's fair skin turned red. "Sorry, Suz. I got carried away. But hey, if I can get this story out and picked up by some of the larger papers, it won't just be me who benefits. You'll have the money you need in no time."

"I knew you'd come through," said Nicole, throwing her arms around him.

She gave him a big kiss, and he grinned and said, "Hold that thought." Then he grabbed his coat and started out of the kitchen.

"Hey, where are you going in such a hurry?" demanded Nicole.

"To write my first Pulitzer winner," he called back as he pushed through the door.

Nicole grinned at her sister. "Well, our worries are over."

Susan sat silent, thinking.

"Suz?" prompted Nicole.

"It's great of Todd to want to help me and everything, but I'm just wondering if there isn't some other way to solve this."

"Like what?"

"Well, maybe we could talk this out, settle out of court."

"You've tried talking to the Rawlinses before, remember?"

"Yeah, but I've never talked to this Luke Potter," said Susan. "He's probably only heard the Rawlinses' side. If he came and saw the house, I could tell him about the good it does. About our donations to the food bank, how much people love it."

"Everyone but his renters. Anyway, even if you talked Luke Potter out of suing you, you'd still have Mr. Rawlins after you," Nicole added practically.

"Maybe not. They haven't tried to sue me before. Maybe they won't go to court by themselves. If I take Luke Potter off their team, they may back off."

"Fat chance of that. I like Hot Toddy's idea better."

"I should try handling things my way first," said Susan, jumping up. She went to her kitchen junk drawer and pulled out the Angel Falls phone directory.

"He's probably unlisted," said Nicole, still trying to discourage her.

"Ha!" gloated Susan. "Here it is. L. Potter. Ooh. He's over on River View Drive."

"Yeah, he got there by suing helpless widows."

"I'm not helpless," retorted Susan, grabbing for the phone.

• • •

Luke let the phone ring. Whoever it was, he could call them back after this last quarter of the game was over.

"Mr. Potter?"

The delicate voice on his answering machine caught his attention and he punched the mute button on the TV remote.

"This is Susan Carpenter. I hope I have the right Luke Potter. Are you the one who's suing me? I thought, perhaps, I could talk to you for a few minutes. If it's not too much trouble, maybe you could call me . . ."

Oh, hell, get it over with now. Luke snatched up the phone. "This is Luke Potter."

"Oh." She sounded startled. "I hope I'm not bothering you."

Right. "Look, Ms. Carpenter. I appreciate the diplomatic gesture, but I don't know what good you think it will do for us to talk. I'm not going to change my mind."

"But . . ." she began.

Luke didn't let her get started. "I've got nothing against you, personally. This is just business."

"Just business?" she bristled. "Mr. Potter, what I'm doing has nothing to do with business. It has to do with the joy of the season. I know if you just came by and saw my house . . ."

"Lady, I've seen your house. Thanks to you I've lost my renters. Now, I'm sorry to have to settle things this way, but you've got to get a grip on reality and realize there are other people being affected by your fun and games."

"Fun and games!" she sputtered.

Their conversation was escalating into an emotional scene, and Luke hated playing those scenes with women, either in person or on the phone. He softened his tone. "I'm sorry about this, really, but I think we'd better leave it for the court to settle. That's what the system is there for." Feeling a little like a heel, he hung up, cutting her off in midprotest. Well, he reasoned, there was no sense in talking anymore. They'd just have done that Mars-Venus thing and gone in circles.

Susan stared at the phone. "He hung up on me. I can't believe it."

"The jerk," sympathized Nicole. "Well, don't worry. Todd has things under control."

On Wednesday, December tenth, Luke grabbed his morning paper and his cup of coffee and headed for work. He plugged in a motivational tape and listened to it as he drove. By the time he pulled into his parking slot in the underground garage of the Angel Falls Towers, he was feeling pumped and ready to take on the fierce animal that is the world of business.

He tossed Martha a good morning. She nodded at the paper under his arm as he passed her desk and asked, "Have you read that yet?"

"No. Why?"

"Better be sitting down when you do," was all she'd say.

Luke went on into his private office, hung up his overcoat, then settled at his desk. He couldn't imagine what horrible news—short of the stock market collapsing—Martha thought would upset him. He took a sip of coffee and unfolded the paper. The headline hadn't changed since he'd grabbed the thing. The president was still fighting with the senate.

He let his eyes travel farther down the page. IS SCROOGE ALIVE AND WELL? Luke's brows knit. What the heck was this?

"We all thought Ebenezer Scrooge was a fictitious character invented by Charles Dickens," the article began, "but Angel Falls's own Suzi Christmas might tell you differently."

The sick rumble deep in his gut warned Luke of worse things to come. Jaw clenched, he read on.

"Susan Carpenter, nicknamed 'Suzi Christmas' because of her good deeds for the community and the festive way she has decorated her house every December for the last nine years, often has people coming to admire her handiwork and sing along with her Christmas music from as far away as Rockhaven.

"Although both Mrs. Carpenter's lights and music are off by ten o'clock every evening, Mr. and Mrs. Don Rawlins and Mr. Luke Potter, all Angel Falls residents, are suing her, citing Suzi's Christmas house as a public nuisance. The Rawlinses moved into Mrs. Carpenter's neighborhood four years ago, five years after her, and live across the street. Mr. Potter owns the house next door to Mrs. Carpenter but is not living in it. At the time of this writing, Mr. Potter was unavailable for comment, but Mr. Rawlins talked with this reporter. 'My wife is in poor health, and the traffic, noise, and lights bother her,' said Rawlins. What about you, Mr. Potter? Are the lights bothering you over there on River View Drive, or do you just have aspirations to become Angel Falls's very own Scrooge?"

Luke crumpled the paper in a rage and stormed out of his office.

Martha looked up from her desk. "I see you read it."

"What's this 'unavailable for comment' crap?" he stormed.

Martha was a sturdily built woman almost old enough to be his mother, and she'd been with him since he first went into business for himself. His anger didn't phase her. "Someone from the Angel Falls *Clarion* came here yesterday. You were over in East Moline, building your empire."

"So you said?"

Martha shrugged. "That you were unavailable for comment. If this guy calls or comes by do you want to talk to him?"

People needed to hear his side, but the person who

wrote that article already had his bias set in cement. Anything Luke said would only be misquoted and twisted. That was the freedom of the press for you. "No. Tell the guy to stay away from me or I'll sue him, too."

"If I were you, I'd back out of this lawsuit and quick," said Martha.

"Thank you for your advice," snapped Luke as he headed back into his office.

He took a huge gulp of coffee, scalded his throat, and coughed out an oath.

Luke's mood didn't improve when he learned he was going to have to pay through the nose to get the cash registers in time for the grand opening of the new PC Edge store he was opening in the Twelve Oaks Mall, thanks to his goof-off brother's having forgotten to order them. He stabbed the intercom line for Ben's desk, but got no answer. He looked out his office window to see that little brother's desk was, as yet, unoccupied. Eight-forty and no Ben. Luke scowled. This was what happened when you let your irresponsible brother work for you.

He buzzed Martha. "If my brother ever decides to come to work today, send him in."

"Yessir," she said crisply.

"And quit using your Luke's-a-dictator voice," he growled. "If this was any other office, Ben would have been out on his ear months ago."

Luke cut the connection before his smart-mouthed secretary could reply. He should have hired a sweet, young thing with no opinions, he thought, scowling. Martha was always saying she'd love to put him and Ben in a bag and shake them up a little in the hopes that each would pick up a few of the other's characteristics. Ben could use a little more drive, and Luke needed to loosen up.

Loosen up. Right. Someone in the family had to be responsible. What with Dad hitting him up for loans every time he had a hot new stock tip, and Mom going through boyfriends like they were panty hose, and Ben thinking life was just one big ball game . . . Good grief, it was a good thing Luke had some drive.

At eight fifty-nine the door to Luke's office opened and a hand reached in, fluttering a lady's white handkerchief.

Luke rolled his eyes. "Oh, very funny."

Ben's head poked around the door. He was grinning. "Martha thought so. Hey, sorry I'm late, but . . ."

Luke cut him off. "That is the least of your problems. Do you know what I'm going to have to pay to get those cash registers in time?"

Ben shook his head. "No, and I'd rather not."

"Are you sure? It's going to be coming out of your paycheck."

"What?"

Luke smiled smugly. That got his attention. "Listen, little brother, I'm tired of carrying the team while you goof off. Either you do a better job of pulling your weight around here or you're history."

"Hey, man. I said I was sorry about the cash registers."

"And I'm going to be sorry if I have to fire your ass, but it's getting to be an expensive one to keep around."

"Yeah, and the dollar is the most important thing to you, isn't it?" retorted Ben, his handsome face looking a little mottled.

"It is important, because without it we don't have a business," said Luke sternly. "I'm the one who's responsible for keeping this boat afloat."

"Yeah? Well, I'm the one who talked old man Wells into lowering our rent for the new location, which is going to save you a lot more than the cost of a couple of cash registers. I may be a screwup, but at least I'm not a Scrooge. How many people do you think are gonna want to do business with us when they find out that the owner of PC Edge is the Scrooge of Angel Falls?"

Luke felt a sudden overwhelming desire to grab his brother by the collar and choke him. But Mom wouldn't appreciate having her baby choked to death, so instead, he took a deep, calming breath. "Look, Ben. I just want you to take this business seriously. That's all."

Ben was still looking mutinous, but he managed a surly, "Okay." Then, "Anything else?"

"Yeah, if you mention the word Scrooge again I'm going to pop you one."

Ben swallowed a spiteful grin and left. Luke sighed and leaned back in his chair. He picked up the *Clarion* again and looked at the name of the reporter responsible for his new nickname. Todd Shelburne was a thorough little devil. He'd already learned that Luke owned the house next door to Suzi Christmas, and he'd somehow ferreted out the location of Luke's office, as well as where Luke lived. Great. Would he go home tonight to find reporters on his doorstep?

Martha stuck her head in Luke's door five minutes before he was about to go to lunch. "The vultures are gathering. Two men are lurking around the hall, and one of them has a camera."

"Great," said Luke. "Do me a favor, Martha."

"Pretend I'm you?"

"No." He went over to the brass coat tree standing by his door and dug his car keys out of his overcoat. Giving them to her, he said, "Go down to my car and get my sunglasses out of the glove compartment."

"Camera shy, are we?"

"I haven't had my picture taken since high school graduation. I don't think this is the time to start."

"If you're going to be a business tycoon you'd better get used to it."

"Well, right now I'm only a business tycoon in the

making and this kind of publicity won't do my stores any good."

"Your name's not on them," said Martha. "You should be safe enough. Just be glad you went with PC Edge and not Potter's PCs," she added, and left.

Luke raked his fingers through his hair. His name wasn't on his office door, but the twerp from the *Clarion* had tracked him here, which meant if he didn't know already, he had to be close to making the connection between Luke and PC Edge, the cornerstone of his company, Bad Boy Enterprises. How long before the guy printed that information? And when he did, what would it do to Luke's business?

By ten o'clock, half the neighborhood had called Susan to commiserate with her, and she finally had to let her answering machine take over so she could get the next day's assignments for her employees done.

At eleven, her father's voice came over the speaker. "Susan, it's Dad. I called to see if you're all right."

She picked up the phone. "I'm here. I guess you read Todd's article."

"I sure did. I tried to get through to you for an hour this morning."

"A lot of people have called."

"I'll bet. I hope they've all called those Rawlinses."

"Knowing Mr. Rawlins, the more calls he gets the more determined he'll be to unplug my lights."

"I oughta come over and punch that guy in the nose. And who is this Luke Potter?"

"He owns the house next door."

"Well, don't you worry. I've still got some money. We'll find you a good lawyer."

"You just hang on to your money, Dad. Todd is going to set up a defense fund for me, and half the neighbors have already pledged to contribute."

"Really? That boy might just prove himself worthy of my daughter yet."

Susan laughed, then said goodbye and hung up.

That afternoon her brother called to check in and offered to dip into his savings to help the cause. Susan gave him the news about her defense fund.

"Well then, I'll be the first contributor," said Buddy.

"I'm afraid you're too late for that distinction. Dad, as well as half the neighborhood, already beat you to it."

"Okay, so I'll be the hundredth. Let me know what else we can do. We don't live so far away that we can't be over there in under an hour if you need us."

"I know."

"I mean it, kid. And you or Nicki let me know where to send my check."

Susan smiled as she hung up the phone. Thank God for her family and friends.

She had just given Willie an after-school snack when the ever-ringing phone started again.

"Suzi?" came a hoarse whisper that sounded vaguely like one of her employees.

"Tina?"

"I can't sing."

Susan moaned inwardly. A nasty bug had hit the community during the last week, including a good many of its musicians, and her sub was already booked solid, covering for one of her other employees. Now it looked like another singer was biting the dust. And just when she had new orders to fill. "You sound awful," Susan said.

"I don't feel as bad as I sound, really. I'm almost over this, but what's left has settled in my throat, and I've got that five-thirty to deliver. . . ."

Susan had already grabbed the schedule. "Yeah, I see it. A twenty-first birthday. Well, don't worry. I'll get my dad to watch Willie, and I'll cover for you. Stay in bed and drink lemon juice and honey. You can do that, can't you?"

"I had my last final yesterday."

"That's probably why you're sick. Are you going to get all A's again this quarter?"

"I hope so," said Tina.

"I do, too. Meanwhile, you've got a day and a half to get your voice back. I need you up and running by day after tomorrow. I've got a ton of orders for birthdays and Christmas greetings. You're booked all morning and evening."

"Don't worry, I'll make it. I need the money."

Susan hung up. So much for getting any paperwork done today. Look on the bright side, she told herself. With the money she was saving by not having to pay Tina, she might at least be able to give her employees boxes of candy for a Christmas bonus.

Susan switched on the answering machine for the business line, then called her dad and made arrangements to drop Willie over for dinner. Then she went to her bedroom and dragged her black tuxedo from the closet.

She'd been a one woman operation when she first started Yours-For-A-Song, but singing telegrams had caught on in Angel Falls and the surrounding communities, and she'd quickly expanded to hire first a man, then a college girl, then a third, part-time employee who pitched in when someone was sick, and a quartet who caroled for her at Christmas. Next she'd added her elves, a couple of college kids who happened to do a little bit of juggling. Her business was still a small one, though, and she often had to don a tuxedo when an emergency arose. On Valentine's Day, which was a biggie, she always worked a full day right along with her employees. She didn't mind really. It was fun to get out once in a while and sing. She might not have majored in music in college to write ditties for special occasions and hand out flowers, but it was a creative outlet, and her customers appreciated her efforts.

After putting on her tux, long pants, and black heels, she popped her black top hat on her head and struck a pose in front of the closet mirror. In the summer she and her female singers wore cute little black shorts with their tux jackets, but Susan thought the long pants actually looked smarter. She had to admit, she didn't look bad for a woman who'd just hit the big three-zero.

She bowed to her reflection. Then, with Willie in tow, left the house for the flower shop, where she'd pick up a pink carnation boutonniere. Yours-For-A-Song customers got their money's worth: a card and a long-stemmed carnation resting in a bed of baby's breath and ferns for the ladies, or a boutonniere for the men (pinned on at no extra charge—the older men loved it!). Her troubles temporarily forgotten, Susan burst into song, and Willie joined her, "Here we come a caroling . . ."

Other than the fire escape, there was no back way out of Luke's third story office. He'd never considered himself a coward, but he didn't relish going by those two clowns in the hall, and he knew he was only postponing the inevitable by holing up in his office.

The door opened and Martha poked her graying head around the door. "Everybody's gone, and I'm getting ready to take off, too. You want a bodyguard?"

"No. I've still got some more work to do here."

"Okay. Good luck."

Half an hour later, Luke sat drumming his fingers on the desk.

This was ridiculous! He'd already ordered lunch in, and that was enough. He'd be hanged if he was going to let those bozos out there keep him a prisoner in his own office. He got up, pulled on his overcoat, whipped his sunglasses over his eyes and, with briefcase in hand, left his office.

With no people to give it life, the outer office of Bad Boy Enterprises made Luke think of ghost towns. Would the sort of bad publicity the *Clarion* was concocting turn his operation into the business equivalent? No, he told himself firmly, people will buy from the devil, himself, if he gives them a good enough deal. I'll survive. And if I don't, I'll make sure I take the *Clarion* down with me.

The two vultures came to life as soon as he stepped out the door. "Are you Luke Potter?" asked the red-headed one wearing glasses.

There's a reason you're wearing those, thought Luke, his free hand clenching into a fist. "Are you the guy who's printing libel about me?"

"Libel's pretty hard to prove," said the reporter, adjusting his glasses.

The other man, a slope shouldered bean pole with a camera, snapped Luke's picture and Luke glared at him from behind his shades.

"Is it too bright in here for you, Mr. Potter?" asked four eyes. "Or do you have something to hide?"

With great difficulty, Luke resisted the urge to punch his tormentor. "If you really wanted to know my side of this story you'd have contacted me before going to press. You're just looking for something sensational to make your career."

The guy gave him a cocky look and stepped in front of him, pencil poised over his notepad. "Can I quote you on that?"

"Yeah, if you've got the guts." Luke brushed past him.

"Hey, Mr. Potter! Do you believe in Santa Claus?" the reporter called after him.

If it hadn't been for his friend with the camera, Luke would have grabbed the twit by the neck. He entered the elevator in a black cloud of rage. That Carpenter woman and her fun house had deprived him of income, and he was the being made the bad guy. What was wrong with this picture?

Ben sat at his regular booth at the bar of the Spuds 'n Suds looking into his beer as if it held the keys to the universe.

"He ain't never gonna be like you," said Ben's former linesman, Otto. "It's that birth order thing, ya know. He's the oldest. The oldest is always responsible."

"The oldest doesn't have to be a jerk," said Ben. "Man, you should have heard him."

Their friend, Greg, shrugged and said, "Big brothers are always jerks. Mine hit me over the head with the family Christmas tree one year." Both Otto and Ben stared at him and he added, "It was before the ornaments were on it."

"He needs to lighten up," said Ben, returning to the subject at hand. "I know he's thirty-four, but that's not that old. He needs a hobby."

Otto's face lit up. "There's what he needs," he said, nodding toward the entrance to the bar.

The other two followed Otto's gaze, and Greg let out a low whistle. "Whoa, Mama."

Ben watched as the stacked blonde in the tuxedo and top hat strutted into the bar. The bartender pointed her toward a corner table where a bunch of college kids sat. She started over with a shimmy that left Ben's mouth dry, singing at the top of her lungs, "Hey, hey, baby, it's your birthday."

He craned around the booth and watched the whole performance. The woman was great. She had a voice that should have been on Broadway, and if the voice hadn't qualified her, those long legs sure would have. After the woman was done, everyone in the bar burst into applause, and she bent and pinned a flower on the blushing birthday boy.

"Too bad it's not your brother's birthday," said Greg.

"A present like that would sure get you out of the dog-house in a hurry."

Inspiration surged through Ben, lighting him up like a pinball machine. "Who says it's not?"

Three

Ben intercepted the singer at the bar. "Hey, that was great," he said, surreptitiously checking her left hand for a ring. *Good, not taken.*

She smiled. *Wow, what a smile!* "Thanks," she said.

"I've got a brother with a birthday tomorrow, and I've been trying to think of something special to get him. Have you got a card?"

"Sure," she said. She fished into the breast pocket of her tux, and Ben had to force himself not to stare where those fingers were foraging.

She handed him an embossed, cream-colored card, and Ben read it. "Yours-For-A-Song. Susan Carp—Carpenter," he stuttered, and looked up in amazement. "You're not the Susan Carpenter I read about in the paper?"

"Guilty as charged."

"Suzi Christmas." Ben chuckled wickedly. It got better and better. "Pretty amazing. So you work for this company?"

"I own it."

"Really? You must be one clever lady."

She beamed on him. The girl had a killer smile that

38

could melt a polar ice cap. Could she melt Luke's flash-frozen ticker? "How much do you charge to come and sing to somebody?"

"Thirty-five dollars, and that includes a boutonniere."

Thirty-five dollars to get his brother off his back, to distract Luke from the bottom line with a pretty bottom. Cheap at twice the price. Ben fished his wallet out of his back pocket. "Sold."

"Good, I'll be happy to send someone out. . . ."

"No!" She looked startled by the force of his reply, and he softened his voice. "My brother's been under a lot of pressure lately, working hard, been a little depressed. You know, sometimes the season does that to people. You've got such a great smile. I know you'd be just what he needs." She hesitated. "Please, Suzi Christmas? You could consider it your good deed for the day."

Her smile told him he'd won. "Okay," she said. "I can probably fit him in sometime tomorrow afternoon."

"Great," said Ben.

"What's your brother's name?"

Ben blinked. "Name?" he echoed.

She nodded. "I need to know who I'm singing to."

"Oh, yeah." *Name. Quick! Think of a name—something other than the name of the man who's suing her.* Ben's gaze darted frantically around the room in search of inspiration, then was caught by a plasticized poster sitting on the bar. There stood a smiling, red-nosed Santa holding a glass of the real thing. "Baccardi and Coke: A Real Great Christmas," it read. Scrawled across the bottom, like an autograph, he saw *St. Nick.* "Nick," he blurted, then soaring to new heights of inspiration, he added, "Nicholas, Nicholas Claus."

She blinked and Ben's heart rate picked up. She hadn't bought it. He'd overdone it.

"Nicholas Claus, like in Santa Claus, Saint Nick?" she said, and looked at him as if to say, *You're pulling my leg, right?*

Ben, the consummate poker player, nodded and looked back at her with an expression that said, *I'm not pulling your leg, even though I would like to.*

"That's his name, really?" she said.

Again, Ben nodded, and gave her his imitation of an honest smile.

Now she was grinning, regarding him as if he had just given her good news. "How amazing! What a wonderful name!"

"Yeah," said Ben. "My mom thought it was a good idea. He fits it, too," he added, warming to his theme. "We call him Saint Nick." *Ha! That was a good one.*

"Oh, how cute!" she gushed.

Cute was not really a word in Ben's vocabulary, but he smiled and nodded as if it were. Handing over the cash to Suzi, he said, "I really appreciate this. It's gonna make Nick's birthday."

"Do you want me to deliver the telegram at your brother's home or where he works?"

Work. Why not? Martha would love it. "At work would be great. Here's the address. . . ."

Five minutes later, Ben sauntered back to his friends.

"Man, you were over there long enough," said Otto. "What was that all about?"

"I'm so brilliant, sometimes I even amaze myself," said Ben, sliding back into the booth. He raised his glass of beer. "Here's to old Saint Nick and a very merry Christmas for his brother, Ben."

By the time Susan had picked Willie up from her dad's and gotten home it was well after six-thirty, and time to get into her Mrs. Santa outfit. She'd just finished stuffing her padding into her skirt and blouse when the doorbell rang. She grabbed her wig and hurried down the hall, already knowing who her visitors were.

Sure enough. Nicole swept into the room in a cloud

of perfume, followed by a grinning Todd. "So, how'd you like it?" he asked.

Good question. Susan had felt vindicated when she read his article in the *Clarion*. She knew it had done exactly what he'd intended; made her look like a victim in need of protecting while making the Rawlinses look petty and turning Luke Potter into an arch villain. So why did she feel just a little like an accomplice to a crime? "It was a great article," she said, turning to the entryway mirror and tucking her blond hair into the white Mrs. Claus wig.

She could see her sister's reflection studying her, head cocked. "But?"

Susan felt her face growing warm, saw her cheeks turning pink. She shrugged. "I don't know. I feel like we're being kind of . . . manipulative."

"You're kidding, right?" said Nicole, her voice thrumming with shock.

Susan gave her a what-can-l-say shrug.

"You're not kidding." Nicole shook her head and went into the living room. She plopped onto the couch and helped herself from the candy dish on the glass coffee table.

"We've got to stir up sympathy for you, otherwise no one will contribute to your defense fund," said Todd. He joined Nicole and she popped a green peanut M&M into his mouth. Crunching on it, he added, "Which, incidentally, I set up today at the Angel Falls branch of the Illinois Mutual."

"Thank you," said Susan. "You know I really appreciate everything you're doing for me."

"Hey, you deserve it. And these people who are trying to take you down need to be jailed and forced to eat fruitcake for the rest of their lives."

Nicole snickered, and Susan grinned. Todd was right. She shouldn't feel even the tiniest bit bad about that article. After all, she wasn't the one trying to ruin Christmas for the community.

"I did something else today," Todd announced.

"What?" demanded Nicole. "You didn't tell me."

"I was saving it until I had you both together, as a surprise." He looked at Susan. "You, Suzi Christmas, are going to be on the radio."

"What!" squealed Nicole. "Oh, Toddy, that is so great!"

Todd nodded. "I just happen to know Jack Bane, the host of *Talk of the Town,* and he called me at the paper today. He wants you to come on his show tomorrow morning, Suz. His producer should be calling any minute to give you all the details."

"Oh, my gosh," said Susan. "But that's all the way over in Moline. I can't go there. My business . . ."

"You don't have to go to Moline. They'll call here and interview you by phone."

Susan shook her head. "I don't know what to say."

"Just say, 'Brilliant, Todd.' "

"Brilliant, Todd," said both sisters in unison, and he leaned back against the couch and grinned.

Luke dumped the morning newspaper into his office wastebasket. It was a rehash of the first story; the only new addition being the picture of him outside his office and the mention of a defense fund having been started for the martyr. This latest story had evidently made the *Chronicle* as well, for his mother had called before he left for work to find out what on Earth was going on. He'd tried to explain to her that it wasn't as bad as it looked, but she hadn't sounded convinced. She'd then told him she loved him no matter what—as if he were going to jail or something. The picture of him in his sunglasses had made him look like a Mafia criminal, and he vowed if he ever saw that newspaper photographer again he'd break the guy's camera over his head.

"Want more bad news?" asked Martha as he stopped by her desk on his way to a morning meeting.

"Frankly, no, but give it to me anyway."

"They're discussing you on KYDD."

"Great. What next?"

"*Oprah*?"

Luke made a face. "Ha-ha. If anyone calls, I'll be back in by one-thirty."

Once in his car, Luke turned on the radio to see what horrible new thing was being said about him. The same soft voice he'd heard on his phone only a couple of days ago was speaking. "I've been doing this for nine years now. Of course, I realize Sylvan Estates was a much smaller development then, and traffic is a bit of a problem."

"But people love it, don't they?" prompted Jack Bane.

"Oh, yes. Well, except for the Rawlinses, who moved in across the street four years ago."

"Let me get this right," said Bane. "These people moved in five years after you and they want you to change a tradition you've been doing for nine years?"

"I'm afraid that's true."

"And what about Angel Falls's Scrooge?" asked Bane. Luke winced.

"I know Mr. Potter blames me that his renters moved out, but maybe they weren't the right family for our neighborhood."

"Yeah, you need somebody in there who's had a lobotomy," snapped Luke.

"Well, you're being pretty gracious to a guy who sounds like a jerk to me," said Bane. "I mean, come on folks. It's Christmas. Hey, this is KYDD talk radio, *Talk of the Town*'s the show, and the question we're asking today is: What ever happened to the Christmas Spirit? We'll be right back to take your calls, so stay tuned."

Luke fumed through the commercial. Jack Bane had a lot of nerve judging him without even talking to him to hear his side of this story. Instead he had Little Orphan Annie on, singing about sunshine while the rest of the world was trying to unsnarl the traffic messes she created.

Jack Bane cut in on Luke's thoughts. "Okay, we're back with Susan Carpenter, also known as Suzi Christmas. How'd you get that nickname, Suzi?"

"You know, I'm not sure. I've had it for quite a few years."

"You probably made it up yourself," muttered Luke.

"You've had some bad luck this Christmas season on more than one front, haven't you?" continued Bane.

"You might say that," said Suzi.

"I'll bet some of our listeners have shopped at the Angel Falls Mall in Christmases past and enjoyed the Dickens carolers and those jugglers dressed up like elves. But hey, you folks up there in Angel Falls won't be seeing them this year. Those people work for Suzi, and the mall canceled their contract. What happened, Suzi?"

"Well, some of the store owners complained about the increased traffic and confusion."

Luke knew exactly who those store owners were. He'd been the one behind The Great Mall Christmas Revolt last year. He'd only wanted that nonsense stopped because he'd had complaints from his customers. Between the carolers and those goofy elves, they'd managed to attract enough of a crowd of lookey-loos to block store entrances and keep away paying customers. "Now I have to take the rap for trying to oblige my customers?" he fumed.

"What's the world coming to?" asked Bane.

"Oh, yes. God forbid anyone should point out a practical problem," sniped Luke.

"Got a comment?" said Bane. "We're at 726-46-46. Ha! I never noticed it before. Our producer just pointed out, that's 726-ho-ho. Good one, Tom. Jane, you're on the air."

A nasal female voice said, "My family goes to see Suzi's house every year. It's a regular family outing."

"Good for you," grumped Luke.

"The kids love the live nativity scene, and we use it to tell them the story of Christmas. And, you know, she even collects food for the food bank. I'd hate to see Suzi have to stop what she's doing just because of some sour old Scrooge."

"I am not a sour old Scrooge! That does it." Luke grabbed for his cell phone.

Bane's screener answered after three rings. *"Talk of the Town.* Who's this?"

Luke's real name sat on the tip of his tongue. An image of himself in tar and feathers came to mind and he opted for the safe haven of anonymity. "Lee."

"What do you think about all this, Lee?"

"I think you guys are being kind of hard on this Luke Potter."

"Oh, yeah? Well, Jack's gonna want to talk to you. Just hold. We'll put you on right after Jane. And turn off your radio."

The conversation continued to play at Luke through his phone for another two minutes. Then Jane was gone and it was his turn to talk.

"Lee, you're on the air," said Jack Bane. "I understand you think we're being too hard on this Potter guy, but I've got to tell you, Lee, I think he's a jerk. So, how're you going to defend him?"

"I shouldn't have to. This is America. A man's supposed to be innocent until proven guilty."

"Hey, he already proved himself guilty," said Bane. "Why do you think he's picking on this woman?"

Picking on . . . ? Oh, this guy was a master at twisting things. "I don't think Luke Potter meant to pick on your guest. If she's creating a public nuisance, maybe something needs to be done about it. And by using the kind of inflammatory language you're using, you're making someone who's just trying to be practical look like . . ."

"Scrooge," cut in Jack Bane.

"Yeah," agreed Luke. "How do you think that guy feels having had that label slapped on him?"

"I'd say he deserves it," said Bane. "What do you think, Suzi?"

"I don't know if he deserves that nickname, but I do think he needs to take a step back and examine what it is about Christmas that we celebrate. I suspect he doesn't have much joy in his life."

Luke felt his blood pressure soaring. "The lady has reached that conclusion thanks to the articles in the *Angel Falls Clarion.* Now we've got a man who's been labeled a Scrooge and a jerk, and who has to live with that, thanks to the media."

"Well, we're not here today to examine the media," said Bane, cutting Luke off.

He blinked in amazement, then swore as he shut off his phone and slammed it back into its cradle. He flipped his radio back on.

Suzi was talking now. "I feel badly about what that last caller said. I want people to know I didn't label Luke Potter a Scrooge, although I think he's acting like one. I'd like to have a chance to meet Mr. Potter and show him the joys of the season. I think then he'd see what I do in a different light."

"Well, there you have it," said Bane. "Luke Potter, if you're listening, this lovely lady is offering to be your ghost of Christmas present and show you the true meaning of the season, and if I were you I'd take her up on the offer."

"Yeah, right," said Luke, and snapped off the radio. Enough was enough.

"Happy birthday," called Martha when Luke returned from lunch.

"You know it's not my birthday."

"Does that mean we don't get to eat the cake?"

"What?"

"Go look," said Martha, and Luke went into his office to find a small, round, bakery cake sitting on his desk.

Propped among the red frosting roses sat a florist card and Luke plucked it out and read it. *Don't say I never did anything for you. Happy birthday, Nicholas Claus from your loving bro.* "Nicholas Claus?"

"Well, I couldn't give the woman your real name. She'd deliver you a bomb instead of a singing telegram," said a voice from the door.

Luke turned to see his brother grinning at him. 'What is this all about?" he demanded.

"I heard them talking about you on the radio," said Ben, ignoring his question. "Heard you talking, too. You were Lee, weren't you?"

Luke felt his cheeks warming, and his embarrassment at being discovered irked him nearly as much as this bizarre birthday gag. "Never mind that. Tell me what this cake is for?"

"Let's just say I'm doing you a favor. I really do love you, bro, even if you are a grinch."

"I'm not a grinch," said Luke between gritted teeth.

"No? How'd you like a chance to prove it?"

"I don't have to prove it," snapped Luke.

Ben ignored this. "How'd you like a chance to prove it to Suzi Christmas herself?"

"That woman . . ."

A sweet, feminine voice drifted in to them. "I'm looking for Nicholas Claus."

"Hey, here's your birthday present, now," said Ben, moving away from the door. "In here," he called.

The space he vacated was suddenly filled by a leggy blonde in tuxedo and top hat, carrying a small, plastic box with some sort of flower in it. "Are you Nicholas Claus?" she asked.

This must be what angels looked like. She had a small, delicately chiseled nose, lips that were full but not over-stuffed like the current look that was so popular, and eyes the color of a blue topaz. And her voice, soft and sweet . . . What was it about that voice? Why did it sound famil-iar?

"That's him," said Ben as Luke stared stupidly at the woman.

"I have a singing telegram for you for your birthday, Mr. Claus," she said.

Luke raised his eyebrows. *Mr. Claus? What the heck is going on here?*

"Happy birthday to the man of the year," she sang. "You grow more classy with each passing year. So what's to hesitate? Let's celebrate. Your birthday's something great to cheer!"

She threw her arms up in the air and spread her legs in a Broadway dancer's pose. Luke found himself wish-ing she was wearing shorts so he could actually see those great, long legs. Imagination showed him soft thighs and calves, delicately curved as a Vega painting. Now she was kicking those intriguing legs in a chorus line kick. "Break out the champagne, balloons, and the band. And we'll all toast to a man who is grand. . . ."

Luke found himself smiling stupidly. He couldn't help it. This woman made him want to smile. She was the most alive, joyous person he'd had ever seen. He felt a sudden urge to run up and hug her and try to suck up some of that warmth into his own needy soul.

Needy? No, he wasn't needy. He was doing just fine, and if he ever saw little Suzi Christmas he'd tell her so. But his life did lack a certain spark, and this woman had it.

He looked at her left hand. Nothing there, but he did notice a glint of gold on the third finger of her right hand that sure looked like a wedding ring. Wrong hand, though.

Well, maybe she was divorced. It happened—a lot in his family.

"Happy birthday to you!" She took off her top hat and brandished it in the air for her big finish. Then, amid the hoots and applause of Ben and Martha and Roxy, the bookkeeper, who'd been standing in the doorway behind her, she walked up to Luke. She opened the little box and pulled out a boutonniere and pinned it on Luke's lapel. He caught a whiff of her perfume, some sort of floral scent that reminded him of his mom's backyard in spring. "I hope you have a wonderful birthday," she said in that soft voice. "And so does your brother."

"How can I not, after all that?" he said, and smiled down at her. Her cheeks turned rose-petal pink, and it took all of his restraint not to take her in his arms and kiss her.

She gave him a final smile, then turned and headed out of his office, nodding politely at his employees as she went.

Luke just stood there like a dope, watching her, vaguely aware of the goofy grin on his face.

His brother came to stand by him and whispered, "Do you know who that was?"

No, but as soon as I do I'm asking her out. Wait a minute. Why was Ben asking him this question? If Ben knew her, something had to be fishy. "Should I?" Luke countered cautiously.

"That, dear bro, is Suzi Christmas. The woman who would like a chance to show you the joys of the season. You gonna take her up on the offer?"

Luke felt his blood taking a fast elevator ride from his head to his toes. That little angel was Susan Carpenter? The ditz? "You're kidding!"

"Nope. And here's your chance to prove to her you're not Angel Falls's new Scrooge."

Luke scowled. So much for fantasy. "Yeah, right."

"Hey, as Luke Potter she wouldn't give you the time of day. But I've fixed that . . . Nick."

Luke looked at his brother with new understanding.

"She thought you had a great name, by the way. Maybe old Saint Nick can prove to her that Luke isn't such a jerk. Maybe Nick can even talk her into taking down a few strings of lights. Then Don will be happy, and you won't be a Scrooge anymore. And," Ben added, "business will stay good and we'll all have a Merry Christmas."

"Lie about who I am?"

"Well, sure. That Zorro guy did it."

Luke gave a snort of disgust. "What a bunch of crap. Anyway, he was a good guy."

Ben cocked his head. "So are you. At least, that's what you keep telling me. Besides, you don't have to stay Nicholas forever. Just long enough to show her you're a nice guy and get her to listen to your side of the problem."

Luke stood, chewing his lip. Maybe his brother had something there.

"She's probably at the elevator by now," said Ben casually.

Luke took the hint. He got into the hallway just as she was about to step into the elevator. "Wait!" he called. *What was he doing? This was insane.*

She turned, her eyebrows raised, a questioning smile on her face.

Too late to back down now. *Okay, then go tell her your real name right now.* That would really be insane. Luke caught up with her in a few quick strides. "That was great," he said, and smiled.

She smiled back. So far so good. "Thanks," she said. "I'm glad you enjoyed it."

"Do you have a business card?"

"Oh, sure." She dove her fingers into the breast pocket of her tux, inadvertently making Luke salivate like one of Pavlov's dogs. Then she pulled out a cream-colored card and handed it over.

Luke read it. "Yours-For-A-Song, huh?"

She nodded.

"It says you'll help me celebrate any occasion."

"That's right."

"What if my cat just died?"

She gave him a playful grin and a dimple popped out in one cheek. "If your cat just died then we'd send you a telegram to cheer you up."

Luke was grinning, too. "What if I never really liked my cat?"

"Well, then I guess you could save yourself the thirty-five bucks."

"Is that how much one of these costs?"

She nodded. "That includes the flower and card."

"My brother spent that much on me?"

"He thinks a lot of you. I could tell that when he placed the order."

"Good old Ben," said Luke, sure that the bill for his birthday telegram would show up on Roxy's desk as a business expense.

"And you're Susan Carpenter?" he asked, tapping the card.

She nodded and looked at him as if expecting him to make some comment on her name. Better to play dumb, he decided. "You've got a great voice, Susan Carpenter. Maybe I'll see you singing on TV or something some-day."

She looked flattered. "Probably not. I'm pretty happy singing right here in Angel Falls." Another elevator car had arrived and the door opened in front of them. "Well, happy birthday," she said, and stepped in.

Luke got in after her. "I'll ride down with you," he offered. Her smile faded a little, a sure sign that he was making her nervous.

"Thanks," she said, her voice not quite so friendly.

"Don't worry, I'm not dangerous," said Luke.

She gave him a polite smile.

"My secretary can give me a character reference," he added.

"Working at a company called Bad Boy Enterprises, maybe you need a character reference."

"Don't let the name fool you. We're really good guys."

"With a name like Claus you'd have to be, wouldn't you? Are you any relation to Santa?" she teased.

He smiled stupidly, then wondered why he was smiling so much, especially at the woman who was making him the villain of Angel Falls. No, he corrected himself, not her, just that stupid reporter.

"Cousins," he said. "And actually," he added, we pronounce our names differently. Mine is pronounced Closs, like floss with a hard 'C.'"

"Oh." She nodded and said nothing more.

The momentary silence felt awkward to Luke, or was it his discomfort with this deception he'd started? "So, this is your business?" he asked, struggling to make his tone of voice relaxed.

She nodded. "One of my employees is sick today. I'm filling in for her."

In all the right places, thought Luke. "You must work up quite a thirst doing all that singing. Could I buy you a cup of coffee?" His little angel looked as if she were searching for a polite way to refuse. "Coffee comes with no strings attached. It's only dinner you have to worry about."

She relaxed visibly and smiled. "You're pretty funny. If I ever need a stand-up comic, I'll remember you."

The elevator door opened, and, taking her words for a form of acceptance, Luke stepped out with her. She stole a look at him, then blushed. Cute. And certainly different from his last girlfriend. The only pink Luke had ever seen on Lynette's cheeks had been put there by a brush.

The little angel walked with him to the espresso stand outside the building and allowed him to buy her a mocha. "Thanks," she said, and took a sip.

"No. Thank you."

She looked questioningly at him.

"For brightening my day. It can get a little dark up there in the salt mines."

"Does your boss work you hard?"

"He's a slave driver, but I don't mind."

"If he works you all the time you should quit and go somewhere else," said the angel firmly. "I mean, I believe in hard work and all, but there's more to life. You have to balance that work with some play or you're just not living."

No one could accuse this lady of not being alive. "I'll tell that to my boss."

"You should hire me to bring him a singing telegram," she said, gesturing with her cardboard cup. "And since it would be for a good cause, I'd even give you a discount. What's his name, anyway?"

Luke grinned, enjoying the game. "Luke Potter."

"Potter." She made a face as if just bringing the name out of her mouth had left slug slime on her tongue, and her rejection stabbed Luke.

"You know him?"

"I know of him, and that's enough."

"He's not as bad as people are making him out to be," said Luke in his own defense.

"Oh, I'm sure he has his good qualities," she said, but she sounded doubtful.

"Yeah, he does."

"Well, you seem like a nice man. Don't let him infect you."

"Infect me. With what?"

"With Scrooge disease." Luke's eyebrows shot up and she blushed. "That was tacky of me. Forget I said it."

She checked her watch. "I've gotta go. Thanks for the coffee."

"Wait."

She turned, a question on her face.

"Look, you can't just drop a bomb about a guy's employer on him like that and then walk off. Don't you think you owe me something?"

She looked at him, her pretty face a picture of confusion. "I'm sorry?"

"You should be. Make it up to me for insulting my boss and have dinner with me tonight."

"Oh, I don't think . . ."

"Hey, what I said back there at the elevator about the strings, I was only kidding. If you'd feel more comfortable, we could come in separate cars. Chez Rory's, seven o'clock?"

Her eyes grew wide, and he knew he'd picked the right carrot to dangle. There wasn't a woman living anywhere near Angel Falls who didn't love going to Chez Rory's, with its linen tablecloths, expensive food, and strolling violin player. To top off the evening, the waiters presented every female diner with a long-stemmed rose. And for all this, a man paid enough money to fill his fridge for a month. Yeah, old Rory had a racket going.

Now Susan was shaking her head slowly, "Oh, I don't think . . ."

"Don't worry, my boss pays me very well. We won't end up washing dishes."

She smiled shyly and said, "Okay. And you don't really look like a Ted Bundy, so I guess if you'd like to pick me up. . . ."

Luke grinned. He liked getting what he wanted, and right now he wanted this woman to himself for a whole evening. "Sure," he said. He pretended he didn't know where she lived, and she gave him her address. "I'll see you tonight then," he said.

She nodded. "I'll be looking forward to it. Nicholas."

She tossed her cup in the nearby garbage can, then with one last smile, turned and walked away.

Luke stood, watching her. He liked the way her hips swayed when she walked. He liked that smile of hers, too. And he liked the way she talked. Heck, he liked everything about her.

What was he doing, anyway? As soon as she learned his real name she'd hate his guts. But maybe not, not if he could show her that he really wasn't a Scrooge. With all of Angel Falls hating him, he'd wanted a chance to explain himself. His brother was right. Who better to do that to than Suzi Christmas herself? He'd prove to her he wasn't a jerk and then reveal his true identity.

He turned and went back up to the office. Ben was waiting for him, perched on Martha's desk. They both turned and looked questioningly at him.

"Well?" said Ben.

"We're going out to dinner tonight."

Ben chuckled. "This is great. Somebody ought to make a movie out of this."

"Yeah," agreed Martha, her voice teasing. "What would you call it?"

"I'm not listening to this," said Luke, heading for his office.

But he couldn't help hearing his brother's words, "I've got the perfect title: *Suzi Christmas Meets Scrooge.*"

"The name is Claus," Luke corrected.

"Yeah. Good old Saint Nick," said Ben.

Knowing what a dirty trick he was playing on little Suzi Christmas made Luke feel like anything but a saint. It's just for one night, he told himself. *Saint for a night.* Oh, boy. What had he done?

Four

As Susan walked away she had to fight the urge to dance a jig. After all, Mr. Gorgeous might be watching, and she didn't want to look like a complete fool. She did allow herself to let out a little squeal and do a quick shimmy as soon as she rounded the corner of the building.

She had no sooner done that than guilt landed on her shoulder and took a peck at her euphoria. How could she be so disloyal to Bill's memory, thinking of another man?

But Bill had been gone for four years, now, and he wouldn't have wanted her to continue mourning him the rest of her life. That was what everyone had been telling her. To shut up her well-meaning family and friends, she had dipped a toe into the dating waters. She'd encountered one cheapskate, two sex maniacs, and one nice, but very boring, man, and had concluded that dating was more trouble than it was worth. Bill was a tough act to follow, and she hadn't met anyone who even held out a hope of coming close. Until today.

There had been something about this man. Her fingers had barely been able to resist the temptation to reach up and trace the strong line of his jaw, then take a walk through those long, brown locks, swept back from his forehead. Then there had been his eyes: hazel colored and laughing. She had heard it said that the eyes were the window to the soul. Peeking in those particular windows, Susan was sure she had caught sight of strong emotion and laughter and something else she couldn't quite put her finger on, something that tickled her maternal instinct and made her want to cradle him in her arms and whisper, "There, there." And the man's name had to be a sign that he was going to be important in her life. If it was a sign, then she didn't have to feel guilty for being so attracted to him. Surely Bill would approve of her going out with someone whose name made you suspect he was related to Santa.

She got inside her car and checked the visor mirror to make sure she had looked okay. Her makeup was still in place; no mascara spots under her eyes, no lipstick on her chin. Obviously Nicholas Claus had liked what he'd seen. He'd asked her out to dinner, hadn't he?

The image of her well-lit house and a line of children waiting for their candy canes suddenly pushed away the picture of herself seated at a fancy table at Chez Rory's.

No, no. That was a small hurdle, not a major obstacle. She'd get Dad to come over for the evening. He and Willie could eat dinner together, then Dad could don the Santa suit he'd had for so many years and go mug it up. He pulled Santa duty a few times for her every December and loved it.

That hurdle jumped, she turned her car toward downtown to deal with the next one: nothing to wear. She had some time now. She'd indulge herself with a new dress—from the boutique downtown, not the mall. If the Angel Falls Mall didn't need her carolers, she didn't need their clothes. Petty behavior, she supposed, but satisfying nonetheless.

Susan returned home with her new, updated version of the classic little black dress to find her answering machine blinking. There was just one message, from Todd.

"Hey, Suz, it's Todd. You'll never guess who wants to take your case: Andrew Hawkinson. He's the best lawyer in the whole county, and we've got an appointment to see him tomorrow at ten. I can come by and get you if you want. I'll be there by nine-thirty. See ya."

A black cloud sailed across Susan's bright horizon, making her frown. She should not have to be dealing with lawyers and lawsuits. She'd never done anything to anyone her whole life. At least not anything to deserve getting sued for.

And of all the times to be sued, and of all the things to be sued over! December had always been her month of celebration: shopping, parties, decorating, delivering telegrams, going to the mall to enjoy her carolers, and soaking in the feeling of peace as she sang "Silent Night" at her church's Christmas Eve candlelight service. But from the first year the Rawlinses moved in, Mr. Rawlins and his wimpy wife had been nibbling away at her joy like Hansel and Gretel picking apart the gingerbread house. How she wished she could strangle Don Rawlins with a string of lights, and his nasty friend, Luke Potter, too! Now, that would be poetic justice. But not very noble, and hardly befitting of the season that proclaimed goodwill toward men.

Don't think about it, she told herself sternly. She pulled her dress out of its box, and ran a hand over the soft, sateen material. So some jerk was suing her. Everything in her life wasn't bad right now. She'd just think about the good things, like dinner out tonight with a handsome and charming man.

After carefully laying the dress on her bed, Susan hurried downstairs to find an after-school snack for Willie. She had just set out a glass of milk and small plate of oatmeal cookies when he slammed the front door and hollered, "What's to eat, Mommy?"

While Willie wolfed down his snack, she dialed her

father's number. He answered the phone on the fourth ring.

"Hi, Daddy."

"Susan, you caught me just in time. I was headed out the door."

"Going to run some errands?"

"You might say that."

"Do you think you'll be done by dinnertime?"

"I'm afraid not, sweetheart."

"Oh." Susan brushed the disappointment out of her voice. "Where are you off to? There isn't anything going on at the Eagles Club this early in the week, is there?"

Her father cleared his throat. "Well, actually, I'm headed over to Deer Grove to see someone."

"An old friend?"

Susan could hear him clearing his throat again. "A new one, actually."

All this throat clearing and evasiveness could only mean one thing. "Daddy, have you got a lady in your life?"

"Well, I have met someone. We're just friends, though."

"You're sure being mysterious for 'just friends,'" teased Susan.

"Don't worry Sherlock. When the time comes, I'll clue you in," said her father.

"Where'd you meet her?"

"At the Deer Grove Eagles."

"Is she a widow?"

There went the throat thing again. "Actually she's divorced. Been divorced a couple of times."

A couple of times? What sort of flake was her father getting involved with? "Twice?"

"Now, I know what you're thinking, Susan, but she's a real nice woman. If this goes anywhere, I'll introduce you."

"That would be appreciated. I'd like to know if I'm getting a new mother for Christmas."

"Like I said, right now we're just friends. This house gets lonely. I'm sure you know about that."

Susan felt her own throat constricting. She swallowed. "I do, Dad, and I'm happy you've found yourself a new dancing partner. She does dance, doesn't she?"

"You bet. Almost as good as your mother."

Susan chuckled. "Well, you have a good time tonight, but take things slow, okay? Come straight home. No stopping to—what was it the Fonz called it?—watch the submarine races."

"Straight home. Scout's honor," said her father.

"What are submarine races?" asked Willie as she hung up the phone.

"It's something grown-ups go to," said Susan.

"Can I go sometime?"

Susan ruffled his hair. "I'm sure you will one day, when you're older."

"Can I go see if Reid is home?"

"Sure."

Willie was already bounding out the room. "But you be sure to tell Reid's mom you need to be home by four o'clock," Susan called after him.

"Okay," his voice echoed from down the hall.

Susan leaned her elbows on the white-tiled work island and stared out the kitchen window at the weak blue, December sky. She hoped her father wasn't getting sucked into a relationship with someone who wouldn't be right for him. She still remembered her Aunt Lila's hasty marriage only a year after her husband's death. And the divorce that followed six months later. Of course, she wanted her father to be happy, but who was this woman? She dismissed her foolishness. Daddy was a levelheaded man, and he would be fine. And she would just have to find another Willie-sitter.

So, who could she get? She didn't want to call Nicole. If she suckered her sister into doing Christmas patrol again so soon, she'd have to explain why, and she wasn't sure she wanted to. Not that Nicki wouldn't be thrilled to see her sister going out, but Susan somehow felt like she'd jinx things if she told about the amazing Nicholas Claus too early. Besides, he could turn out to be a dud, then she'd really feel stupid. Well, she'd get Mrs. Murphy down the street to come over and keep an eye on Willie. He and Mark, her 4-H volunteer shepherd, could pass out candy canes until Susan got home from dinner.

She smiled as she dialed Mrs. Murphy. Funny to think of both herself and her dad going on a date tonight. Maybe sometime they could double date.

Hank Appleby tooled his Buick toward Deer Grove, humming along while the King crooned a sad song. Now, that was music!

The King asked if he was "lonesome tonight."

Nope, thought Hank, and smiled. Not tonight.

He ran a palm along the side of his head to remind his hair to lie flat. He'd been a lucky devil. His hair might be gray, but he still had it, and at sixty-five that was saying something. In fact, he didn't look half bad for his age. Almost all of his hair and hardly any gut—that was more than most of his buddies could boast.

He did have more than his share of wrinkles. Coping with Beth's illness had done that for him. Cancer had taken his wife of forty years and carved his suffering on his face. For a while there, he had felt every one of those deep creases. Oh, he'd put a good face on things for the girls, especially Susan. Bad enough to lose a husband, then a mother. He didn't want her having to worry about her old man.

Old man. He shook his head. If only he and Bethie could have gotten it right and had their kids earlier, the girls wouldn't have an old man for their dad now, and they'd have been able to enjoy their mom an extra ten years. And Willie would have had a grandma.

Hank scowled. There was no sense trying to remake

the past. He couldn't bring back Beth any more than he could buy back his business.

Not that he wanted to, he reminded himself. He'd gotten a good price for the hardware store and had been able to finally pay off the last of his bills. His investments, such as they were, were doing well, and he might just take that part-time job that Jim at Good Sports had offered him. He wasn't ready to sit around and wait for his monthly social security check, anyway. In spite of playing Mr. Fix-it for Susan every time her plumbing acted up, time had hung way too heavy on his hands this last year. He should do pretty darned well working in his friend's store; there wasn't that much difference between selling hammers and tennis shoes. And he sure knew enough about soccer equipment from the girls' soccer days. As for fishing gear? Piece of cake.

Hank looked at his future and grinned. Money in the bank again, a job, a cute grandkid, and a pretty woman to share dinner with him tonight. Ho, ho, ho, Merry Christmas.

He pulled up in front of Celeste Knight's powder blue rambler promptly at five. White shutters lovingly hugged windows adorned with matching white window box lips that right now stood empty. He could imagine those window boxes in the summer, filled with geraniums. He grabbed the single red rose he'd picked up on the way, then got out and headed up the front walk.

He saw the curtain at the front window twitch, and by the time he got to the front door she was standing in the doorway, smiling at him as if he were Santa, himself. He'd take this lady on his lap any day. "You look good enough to eat, Celeste."

She blushed like a schoolgirl. She almost looked like one with her slim body and her blond-gray hair cut all short and wispy around her cheeks. At fifty-eight, she was still one fine-looking woman.

"Well, I hope you're going to live up to that promise," she quipped as she stepped aside for him to enter.

Hank's grin turned wolfish. "I aim to please." He held out the rose and she put a hand to her chest and gasped as if she had just now noticed it."

"Oh, you darling, romantic man."

"I heard somewhere that a single rose is a good thing to give a woman."

"Did you treat your wife like this?"

One thing that had amazed Hank about this woman right from the start was the unabashed way she talked about things. Other women he'd met tiptoed around the subject of his deceased wife, afraid to broach it, as if Bethie had never existed. Not this lady. "I tried," said Hank humbly, almost certain Beth would agree. Funny thing how when the one you loved was alive, you thought you were doing everything you possibly could for them, but after they were gone you thought of a million more things you could have done.

"She was a very lucky woman," said Celeste, her face suddenly serious. She changed the subject before he could get sentimental and make a fool of himself. "I have a beautiful, lead crystal vase that will show this off perfectly. Come on in and sit down. As soon as I've given my rose a drink, I'll see about getting you one."

He followed her into the sunken living room and settled on her couch, watching her walk on into her dining room. She was wearing a black dress that clung to her bottom, and he watched that bottom appreciatively as it wiggled off toward the buffet. Yes, Celeste Knight was one fine-looking woman. And black was a good color for her. Watching her bend over to pull a vase from the side door of her antique mahogany buffet, Hank found himself wondering if Celeste owned a black nightgown.

Black was a good color for Susan Carpenter, thought Luke as Jacques, the maître d', led them to the corner table

Luke had requested. When Luke had helped her out of her coat at the coatroom door, he had felt like a kid opening a present. It had taken all his willpower not to let his eyes bug out at the hint of cleavage peeking over the black, scooped neck of her dress. Her shoulders, in contrast to the soft, shiny material had looked like cream, or a spring moon, warm and luminescent. She had swept her hair up into some sort of roll at the back of her head, and the faint smell of roses had wafted up from her neck and danced about his nose, teasing him to lean down and kiss her right below the ear and see if the skin would feel as warm and soft to his mouth as it looked to his eyes. Now, walking behind her, he let his gaze travel her legs, those gorgeous, long legs. Her nylons made them shimmer in the candlelight, reminding him of the inside of an oyster shell.

Jacques settled her into her seat, wished them both *bon appétit,* then made himself scarce. She turned to face Luke, the smile still fresh on her face. He smiled back, and her cheeks took on a pink tinge. She broke the eye contact and suddenly took a great interest in examining her surroundings. "This is lovely. I've never been here before."

"I can't believe it. A beautiful woman like you?"

Her cheeks bloomed pinker still, and she caught her lower lip between her teeth for a moment, then braved another look at him. "When my husband was alive we never could afford this place. Now . . ." She shrugged.

Now it was Luke's turn to feel a warmth burning beneath his skin. "I'm sorry."

She shrugged. "It happens."

"You just don't think about it happening to you when you're young."

She shook her head, then lowered her gaze again. A kid in a white jacket came and filled their water glasses. She grabbed hers and took a sip.

Before Luke could say anything, their waiter appeared to ask if they wanted a drink.

Luke raised questioning eyebrows at Susan. "Would you like something?" She definitely looked like she could use a big slug of brandy.

"White wine, please."

"Vodka on the rocks," said Luke, and the waiter left them sitting in an uncomfortable silence.

What do I say now? wondered Luke. He couldn't just pretend the subject of her deceased husband had never come up, although he wished he could.

Thoughts bounced around in his brain like clothes in a dryer. What would he do if she started crying? He didn't have any experience to draw on that would comfort her. Compared to what she'd been through, his own life had been a picnic. Don't make a big deal of this, cautioned his logical businessman's mind. Most women have men in their pasts. This one's just happens to be dead.

And probably enshrined forever. Ex-husbands were a pain in the neck, but they at least had faults. A woman couldn't turn an ex into a saint.

"Do you want to talk about it?" he asked, hoping she didn't, then feeling like a rat for hoping.

She shook her head. "It's water over the falls."

It was going to be two for dinner, after all. Luke breathed an inner sigh of relief. "Over the Angel Falls," he corrected, his voice lightly teasing, and it brought back the ghost of her smile.

"Over the Angel Falls," she agreed. "And anyway, I'm not totally alone. I have a son."

A kid. Luke always avoided women with kids. Too many vines to wrap around a man's legs. Well, what did it matter? He wasn't going to marry Suzi Christmas, just use her to improve his image. "How old?" he asked politely.

"Six."

A widow with a six-year-old. This was not the kind

of woman he normally took to dinner. He nodded, while behind his suave facade, his mind stalled at a conversational crossroad, frantically asking, *Where to now?*

He suddenly realized she was studying him, and her scrutiny made his shirt collar shrink. With difficulty, he resisted the urge to tug at it.

"You really don't look anything like Santa," she observed. "How did your mother come to name you Nicholas?"

If there was one subject Luke didn't want to get into, it was this phony-baloney stuff his brother had saddled him with. "She thought it would be cute. The way I pronounce my last name, most people don't really make the connection. And I usually go by Nick."

"Nick," she said the name experimentally, as if she were seeing how well it rolled off her tongue. "It fits you. But your brother pronounces your last name just like Santa would."

"He can afford to. He doesn't have the same first name," said Luke. All this talk about his fake name was making him sweat. There must be some other subject they could talk about. Why couldn't he think of it?

The waiter arrived with their drinks, and Luke realized that now he was the one who needed to grab his glass.

As he reached for it, she said, "I think you have a wonderful name. Does it embarrass you?"

There was an understatement. "I'm no Saint Nick," said Luke. *And if you knew my real name, you wouldn't be sitting here across from me.*

"No one's a saint," she said.

"Not even you, Susan Carpenter?"

"Not even me. I'm as flawed as the next person." She raised her glass to him. "Well, then, here's to those flaws that make life so interesting."

"To flaws," he said, and drank deeply.

• • • •

Hank took one last drink of coffee to wash down the apple pie, then leaned back against the faded, red leather of the banquette with a contented sigh. "Great place," he observed.

The Little Red Hen was packed with people. Families crowded around tables, devouring fried chicken and biscuits, senior citizens and young couples alike sat at the small tables scattered around the room, and although it was nearly nine, two couples still hovered hopefully in the tiny waiting area by the entrance.

Celeste dabbed at her lips with her red-checked napkin. "Their pie is almost as good as mine."

"You can top that?"

"With my eyes closed. You should have let me make dinner for you."

Hank shook his head. "I'm an old-fashioned kind of guy. When I'm courting a lady I like to take her out."

"Is that what you're doing, Hank? Courting me?"

She was watching him, her head cocked to the side like an inquisitive robin. He felt his cheeks turning warm. Why had he said that? He hadn't meant to, had he? "You know, I'm not sure."

She smiled, making the skin at the side of her eyes crinkle. "That's what I like about you, Hank, you're so honest. No games."

"I think that's one of the things I like about you, too. You're a beautiful woman, Celeste, both inside and out." Now it was her turn to blush. He reached across the table and covered her hand with his. "I want to be with you. You like to have fun and you make me laugh. It's been a long time since I've laughed. I've been so lonesome since Beth died."

"I know," she said, and patted his hand. "Even though my first marriage wasn't the greatest, I found myself so lonely after the divorce I just rushed into the arms of the first man who smiled at me. It wasn't until after I said 'I do' that I realized I didn't."

"I don't want to rush into anything, either," said Hank, understanding the underlying message, but I suspect it's going to be hard not to."

She smiled. "I suspect you're right."

There was a small combo playing in the restaurant's lounge, and as they danced, Hank realized how right he had been. It was going to be harder than hard not to lose his heart before his head could have time to make any rational decisions about a future with Celeste. She felt so right in his arms, and she followed his lead as if they had been dancing together for years. He felt incredibly comfortable with her, free to be himself.

So, had what he'd said at dinner about courting her been a statement of fact or a slip of the tongue? Something in him, somewhere beneath the level where his mind functioned must know he was ready to have a woman in his life. Surely the fact that he was starting to get out again had already proved that.

And Beth would have approved. Even before she died, she was throwing out suggestions for women she thought would make good replacement wives. Every time she had brought up the subject, Hank had ground his teeth, not wanting to even talk about his wife's death, let alone think beyond it.

A year after her death, the emptiness in the house and the great waves of loneliness that his daughters couldn't fill had finally driven him back to his friends, his old haunts, and, when those had proved too painful, to some new ones.

He had met Celeste at one of those new places. She had been all energy and life and laughter, the dream of every man over the age of fifty at the Deer Grove Eagles Club. But when Hank had walked in the door, she'd only had eyes for him. He had felt the same about her. What was the sense in denying it?

Now he pulled her a little closer to him and she looked up into his eyes and smiled as if she knew exactly what he had been thinking. He twirled them and almost laughed out loud just for the heck of it.

Still, he had no intention of kissing her when he took her home. He was just going to shake her hand and thank her for the good company and the great dancing. But she caught his hand as they walked up the front walk, and when she turned at the door and looked up at him with that same wonderful smile, she seemed to be commanding him to kiss her. So he obliged, just a quick one, a soft touching of the lips, an experimental dipping into the pool to test the waters. The water felt fine. Dive in!

But before he could, she pulled back, still smiling, and said, "That was a wonderful evening, Hank. Shall we do it again soon?"

Tomorrow! Hank suddenly found himself as tongue-tied as a seventeen-year-old kid with his first girlfriend and unable to string two intelligent words together. He nodded.

"Good. How about Friday? And this time I'll come to your side of the world. You choose the restaurant, and I'll pick up the tab." He started to protest, but she held up a hand and said, "This is not the fifties, and we women have come a long way, baby. Dinner won't break the bank."

"All right," he said, his voice betraying how uncomfortable he felt with her offer.

She seemed to know it, too, for her smile was teasing. "Call me," she said, then slipped inside the front door, leaving Hank with a thousand balloons dancing inside his chest. Driving the car home would be a mere formality. God knew he didn't really need it; those balloons would carry him all the way back to Angel Falls.

Celeste leaned against the door and let a soft sigh escape. What a romantic evening! First that lovely rose, then dinner at her favorite quaint, little roadhouse. And the last dance they had shared, when Hank had drawn her close to him, that had certainly set the butterflies loose in her stomach. But his kiss had been the topper. She could already tell, this was a man who knew how to curl a girl's toes with his kiss.

It was hard to think of such a romantic man having such a mundane name. Hank Appleby. Hank. As far as Celeste was concerned, cowboys and country singers were named Hank. Men who drove trucks were named Hank. This man was more like a Gregory or a Martin or William. He had polish, and he was no ignoramus about the world outside his hardware store. She'd learned that much just visiting with him at the Eagles Club and listening to him talk with the other men. He was knowledgeable on everything from politics to business investments. But it wasn't his mind she had thought about when he spun her around on the dance floor at The Little Red Hen. She caught her lower lip between her teeth and started to hum the tune to "Some Enchanted Evening." That was how it had happened when they met, and she had a good feeling about this man.

You had a good feeling about Andrew Knight, too, whispered her oft-ignored, practical side. But Andrew had been different from Hank. Andrew, she had learned to her regret, had been all flash and no substance. Andrew, with his fine name and wonderful looks had been superficial and selfish. Once he'd won her, he'd lost interest in keeping her, rather like a child who wheedles for a toy that goes forgotten once he possesses it.

Celeste already knew Hank had substance. And heart. She could tell by the way he smiled, by the way he made sure no woman at the club sat out all night without getting a whirl around the dance floor.

This last thought brought her back full circle to their last dance. What a man, what a wonderful, delightful man! Strong, yet not having to prove himself, a man willing to take time to enjoy life, a man very different from her first husband. And her son.

Well, maybe if this romance developed between herself and Hank . . . She smiled at the thought of some of Hank's easygoing nature rubbing off on her son. Heaven only knew the poor boy needed it; he got more like his father every day: driven, materialistic, and cynical. And this time of the year seemed to bring out the worst of that cynicism in him. But surely her boy was still young enough to change. And maybe, with Hank for inspiration, this Christmas would be different from so many of the Christmases past that her son loved to harp on. Maybe this one would transform Luke from the Scrooge of Angel Falls back into the warm and happy boy he had once been.

Hank for husband number three and a chance for her son to feel, once again, the holiday spirit—was it too much to ask for Christmas? Celeste didn't think so.

Five

Susan settled against the black leather seat, luxuriating in the experience of riding in an expensive car. Not that there was anything wrong with her Honda. It was only seven years old, and she kept it well maintained. Still, it wasn't . . . this. The interior, with its only light coming from the glow of the instrument panel, made her feel like a baby in its mother's womb, and the soft rock music drifted into her mind as if filtered through thick, soft walls.

Next to her, Nicholas Claus sat with his hands on the wheel, his eyes on the road, and a tiny smile playing on his face. As Phil Collins began to serenade them, Nick turned his head to give her a full on smile, and she suddenly felt shivery, nervous almost. Or was it excited? Whatever it was, it was the same thing she had felt the first time she went out with Bill.

She smiled back, then said, "I love this song."

"Me, too."

"What's your favorite song?" she asked.

"That'd be too hard to answer."

"Okay," she said, "how about favorite group?"

"Fleetwood Mac."

"Favorite movie?"

"*Die Hard.* How about you?" he added.

"Guess." Susan kept her voice light, trying to sound sophisticated and at ease, instead of adolescent and fidgety.

Nick grinned over at her. "It's gotta be something sentimental. How about *Titanic*?"

Susan shook her head. "Too depressing."

"Okay. Let me think. There was one that my bookkeeper and secretary both love to watch on video. Something about clouds. A day in the clouds . . . a stroll . . ."

"*A Walk in the Clouds,*" said Susan. "That was a wonderful movie, but, actually, it's not my favorite. Want to try again?"

"Hmm," he said. "Wait a minute. You're Suzi Christmas, so it's probably *A Christmas Carol.*"

Susan's nervous energy erupted in a giggle. "No, but you're getting warmer. It's the other movie they show this time of year."

"*It's a Wonderful Life.*"

Just thinking about that movie brought a warm glow to Susan's heart. "George Bailey is the most wonderful hero ever invented, and that movie is, without a doubt, the best ever made."

"Not better than *Field of Dreams,*" said Nick.

"With a name like yours, how can you say such a thing?" protested Susan, mock scolding. The genuineness faded from his smile, leaving behind a sickly imitation and Susan felt like a stupid, thoughtless idiot. "Sorry," she said. "I suppose you do get teased about your name a lot."

"Well, what's in a name?" he said with a shrug. "Unless," he added, "it happens to be a name that fits the person. Like yours. You look like a Susan, sweet and warm."

His voice felt like a caress. "Thanks," Susan murmured, feeling fresh shivers.

"I'm glad you took a chance on having dinner with me," he said.

"Thanks for asking."

"I hope you had a good enough time to want to do it again."

Do it. Those words conjured up an image of entwined, naked legs and long, fevered kisses that set Susan's cheeks simmering. She blinked. "I'd like to go out with you again, Nick," she said, assuring herself that the reason she wanted to go out with Nicholas Claus again was not purely sexual, but because he was kind and charming.

And the thought of him kissing her made her whole body feel like warm taffy.

She pulled her mind back to the moment at hand. "I think so."

"Even though I'm from the enemy camp?" he asked, his voice teasing.

"That's right. For a while there, I'd forgotten who you work for."

"I read about you in the paper today," he said. "You are the Susan Carpenter my boss is suing, aren't you?"

"Guilty as charged," said Susan. "What would your boss say if he knew you were out with me?"

"This is America. No one is guilty until proven so, not you or Mr. Potter."

"Oh, please, let's not spoil a perfect evening by talking about him," said Susan.

Nick looked slightly pained by her request, but he said, "All right." Then, "Your friend, George Bailey, is at the Movie Palace this week."

The old Movie Palace. It had the smallest big screen in the state, and ancient wooden chairs with gum stuck to the bottom, and with the price Mr. Mullinex charged for popcorn he could have been selling bags of gold nuggets. But Susan loved the place. It sported an old-fashioned marquee that proudly displayed whatever movie was showing, much like an elderly woman wearing her diamonds. And the ceiling had a Milky Way's worth of stars painted on it, stars she'd tried to count when she was a kid. Back then the theater had shown B movies, and double-feature Disney matinees for the kids on Saturdays. Now they showed old classics and art films, and she went whenever she got the chance. "I love that place," she said.

"How about tomorrow night?"

Out again tomorrow? Who could she get to mind the house? On a Friday night Dad would surely be doing something with his new girlfriend. Nicole and Todd always went out on Friday nights. Which one of the neighbors could she bamboozle?

"I'll throw in clam chowder at Matey's," added Nicholas. "Well, if you like it, that is."

"I love clam chowder, but I'm not sure I can get a sitter. I do have a son, remember?"

He fell silent and Susan, watching him ponder this dilemma, admired his profile. That chin was like granite. And he had such nice cheekbones. He reminded her a little of the Marlboro Man. She could see Nicholas Claus looking very at home on a big, chestnut stallion, wearing a leg-hugging pair of jeans. Suddenly aware that drool was collecting at one corner of her mouth, Susan swallowed and pulled herself together with a stern reminder to quit sliding into these adolescent fantasies.

"I've got an idea," said Marlboro Claus.

She cocked her head and looked expectantly at him.

"My brother is great with kids."

"But won't he have plans for tomorrow?"

The granite jaw jutted out. "He'll change them. He owes me."

Susan detected some secret meaning behind those words. Having siblings of her own, she imagined Nick's younger brother must owe him a big chunk of money to get volunteered like this. It was sweet of Nick, but his younger brother was barely more than a face in the crowd from last night. And she barely knew Nick, himself, for that matter. Willie was too precious to entrust to strangers. "That's okay. I'm sure I can work something out."

He nodded, taking no offense at her refusal, and thus unknowingly scoring himself yet another point.

It was quarter til ten when they pulled up in front of her house, and there was barely any traffic left on the street, but the few cars crawling by and the actors on her front lawn precluded a goodnight kiss. Nick opened the car door for her and walked her to her front door.

The Virgin Mary waved at her as they headed up the walk, and Joseph called, "You got a lot of donations for the food bank again."

"Great," she called back.

"The food bank, huh?" said Nick.

"Christmas isn't very merry when there's nothing in your cupboard," Susan replied.

"You can have a full cupboard and still miss out on a Merry Christmas," he observed.

Something in his voice made her suddenly defensive. "Well, as soon as I get hunger licked, I'll start working on the peace on Earth."

This produced a lopsided grin and a question. "How about goodwill toward men?"

Susan took* the proffered olive branch. "That would depend on the man," she said, making her voice light.

They were at her front porch now. "How about one who needs it real badly?" he asked, moving close enough to make Susan very aware of him. She suddenly felt like she'd been caught in some sort of magnetic force field, and her body thrummed with the contact from it.

Nicholas smiled down at her and gave the tip of her nose a teasing tap, jump-starting her heart into high gear. "With that cold, red nose, you could be related to a certain reindeer I know. Better get inside."

Susan felt her cheeks making an effort to color coordinate with her nose. She nodded, and slipped inside her front door, feeling sixteen all over again. If just a tap on the nose brought on this kind of reaction, what would she do when Nick kissed her? *Oh, Bill, it feels so right, and I never thought it would again.*

Luke sauntered back to his car, feeling like a man who had just closed a million dollar deal. *Well, little Suzi Christmas, old Scrooge has you eating out of the palm of his hand. It won't be long before I've got you begging me to take down a few strings of lights for you. Yessir, you've been without practical advice far too long. All you need is a man to open those pretty blue eyes and show you the facts of life.*

The facts of life. There were more important facts to master than how many Christmas lights a person could decently string up on her house, and just thinking about giving Susan Carpenter some one-on-one instruction was enough to make Luke's mouth go dry. She wanted him as much as he did her, he was sure of it. If he played his cards right, he could end up with a very Merry Christmas.

Back in his car, a remake of the old song, "Can't Help Falling in Love" was playing, and Luke started singing along.

Can't help falling in love? Oh, no. He wasn't falling in love. He was doing PR, trying to improve his image. That was all.

Luke frowned and switched channels. He was no fool, and he had no intention of falling helplessly in love with anyone, especially Suzi Christmas.

Susan had awakened on a cloud of euphoria, until she remembered her appointment with the lawyer. Then the euphoria dissolved into the same nervous stomach she always got on the morning of her annual pelvic exam.

The uneasiness was still with her when she and Todd walked into Andrew Hawkinson's swank office. Looking around at the expensive furniture and the original art on the walls of his reception area, she wondered if the money in her legal defense fund would be enough to cover his fees.

"Mr. Hawkinson will see you now," said his secretary, and she rose and opened the door to the inner sanctum.

This room, too, reeked of success, thought Susan, as her feet sunk deep into its oyster-colored carpet. A large window bathed the room in light. Books occupied an entire wall, a wet bar another, and off to the side, Susan saw a small door to what she suspected was Mr. Hawkinson's private bathroom.

Andrew Hawkinson rose from his desk to greet them. He fit his name. In spite of the fact that he was of average height, he exuded power. Or was that an illusion produced by the navy-colored, three piece suit? His hair was prematurely gray, his eyes were deep-set and came together over a beak of a nose and thin lips. In short, he looked the human equivalent of a hawk, and was unnerving to behold. Until he smiled. Then he was terrifying. "Have a seat," he said, indicating two black leather chairs opposite his desk.

He didn't appear to terrify Todd, who was his usual animated self. "Hey, we really appreciate you taking on Suz," he was saying.

The way Mr. Hawkinson was assessing her, Susan wasn't sure whether he was contemplating defending her or eating her. "I caught the end of *Talk of the Town,* Mrs. Carpenter, and your situation interested me. I suppose most neighborhoods have a man like this Rawlins character, someone with a sour temper who finds his greatest pleasure in quashing others' enjoyment. It is my opinion that men like him should all be gassed. They're a blight on society. But," he added on a world weary sigh, "they are also the way men like me make our living, and it is their right within the law to protest your behavior if they feel it is adversely affecting their life." Susan frowned, and he continued, "To win their case, however, both Mr. Rawlins and Mr. Potter must prove to a judge that you have done them irreparable harm."

"I haven't done anything to hurt them," protested Susan. "Well, not Mr. Rawlins, anyway."

"What about Luke Potter?" asked Hawkinson.

"He bought the house next door for a rental," said Todd. "His renters have moved out."

Hawkinson leaned back in his chair and steepled his fingers under his chin. "Did Mr. Potter purchase this house before or after you began your decorating, Mrs. Carpenter?"

"After," said Susan. "I've been living in my house nine years. Mr. Potter only bought his house last summer."

"And Mr. Rawlins has been in residence . . . ?"

"Four years," put in Todd.

Hawkinson pulled a legal tablet in front of him and began to scribble. "And you were served?"

"Well, it wasn't me, exactly," said Susan. "My sister, Nicole, was over visiting and she took the papers."

"Visiting? Your sister doesn't live with you?"

"No."

Hawkinson smirked. "Not even a legal serve."

"What do you mean?" asked Todd.

"Papers don't have to be served to the person who is being sued, but they must be served to someone of legal age—eighteen or older—who is in residence at the defendant's domicile."

Todd chuckled wickedly. "Oh, I love it."

"You have the papers with you, Mrs. Carpenter?"

Susan nodded and handed them over.

"Let's see what Santa brought," said Hawkinson.

Susan and Todd exchanged glances while her new lawyer scanned the sheaf of legal papers, and Todd smiled encouragingly at her.

"Well," said Hawkinson, "this looks like just the sort of battle I enjoy. Although I wish I had a more worthy opponent. Melville is, in my opinion, a moron."

"So, what happens now?" asked Todd.

"First, I notify Mr. Melville that his process server goofed. He will send out another man pronto. You can expect to be served by tomorrow, or Saturday at the latest. By next week, we'll be in court, arguing against the injunction."

"I told Susan she didn't have to turn her lights off just because she was served," said Todd. "That is correct, isn't it?"

In spite of Todd's assurances, Susan had been nervous about leaving her lights on after receiving such important legal papers. Now she felt herself tensing. She wet her lips.

Hawkinson shook his head. "You don't have to unplug your lights until the court orders you to do so."

"What do you think the chances are of that?" asked Susan.

"With me defending you? Nil. This is a clear case of first amendment rights, and it's not as if this type of thing is a new holiday tradition, either with you or in our society in general. Do you have a nativity scene?"

Susan nodded. "A live one."

"Freedom of religion," said Hawkinson.

Todd flipped through his notepad. "Rawlins claims his wife is in ill health, and the traffic and noise, combined with the lights, makes it difficult for her to sleep. What do you think about that?"

"I think she'd better have a heart condition or an equally serious problem to make that one stick," said Hawkinson.

But what if they did make it stick, Susan worried as Todd drove her back home.

As if reading her mind, he said, "Don't you worry,

Suz. Hawkinson is the best. He won't let these guys take you down."

Susan shut her eyes and sighed.

"You sound like I feel," said Todd. "I think I'm coming down with something. Here, let's have some Christmas music to cheer us up," he added, slipping a tape into the car's cassette player.

The car suddenly turned into an orchestra pit, surrounding Susan with the sounds of strings and woodwinds. Then came the voices, singing, "Deck the halls with boughs of holly." Four part harmony: "Fa-la-la-la-la, la-la-la-la." Booming male voices: "Tis the season to be jolly. . . ."

Bah, humbug, thought Susan sourly, and wished the scariest of Dickens's Christmas ghosts would visit Mr. Rawlins and line his bed with holly leaves.

It took Susan a long time to quit stewing about her legal problems, but she was finally able to set them aside and turn her attention to the task of finding a babysitter for the evening. She had just hung up from a disappointing conversation with Mrs. Murphy when Nicole called on her lunch break. "So, how did the meeting with the lawyer go?"

Her sister's reminder of what she had worked so hard to ignore made Susan feel like she'd taken a bite of something rotten. "Didn't Todd tell you?"

"He wasn't in a very talkative mood when he called. He thinks he's coming down with something. I heard more about his symptoms than what the lawyer had to say. By now poor Toddy's probably in bed, tucked under a pile of blankets."

"He was looking a little pale by the time he dropped me off," said Susan.

"So, what did the lawyer say?" prompted Nicole.

"He seems to think we can win."

"Good," said Nicole. "Todd says he's the best."

"Well, I wouldn't want to be the lawyer battling him, that's for sure."

"Guess where I'm calling from?" said Nicole, jumping the conversational track at her usual lightning speed.

"Jamaica?"

Nicole ignored the quip. "I'm sitting here in the break room, calling from my . . ."

"Cell phone," Susan finished with her. "I see the novelty hasn't worn off yet."

"This is not a novelty," insisted Nicole. "It is a necessary tool in a high-tech, fast-paced society."

"Impressive," said Susan. "You could write brochures for this company."

"I could, but somebody already beat me to it," Nicole admitted.

Susan grinned. "You had me scared for a minute. I thought some evil scientist had given you a brain transplant and turned you into a consort for Bill Gates."

"Ha-ha," said Nicole.

"So is that the only reason you called, to make sure your high-tech tool was in good working order?"

"No. I called to see if you want to do a chick flick tonight after you're done with Mrs. Claus patrol."

Hmm. Todd was sick, and Nicole was wanting to do something. What a fortunate coincidence. Now, the big question was, should she go ahead and tell her sister about Nicholas? "I'd love to, except . . ." Susan paused, trying to decide how to word her request.

"Except what?" prompted Nicole.

"I've got a date."

"A date!"

Susan pulled the receiver away from her ear, hoping her hearing hadn't been permanently damaged.

"Well, I might have a date, if I can get a baby-sitter. I suspect Dad has plans, and Mrs. Murphy is sick."

"Oh, I'll baby-sit," said Nicole in a resigned voice. "With Hot Toddy out of commission I haven't got anything else to do. But I'm not playing Mrs. Santa any later than eight. It's cold out, and there's talk of snow. And anyway, I'm dying to curl up on your couch with a roaring fire and some of your microwave popcorn."

"It's a deal," said Susan.

"So, now, what about this date? Don't tell me you finally told that bozo at the garage you'd go out with him."

"No," said Susan. "This is someone new, someone I just met."

"You just met? Where could you have met him? You don't do anything this time of year. Wait, let me guess. You met him at the store, in the produce department. I saw something on *Oprah* once . . ."

Susan cut her off. "I didn't meet him at the store. I did a singing telegram for him."

"Oooh. Is he gorgeous?"

"Yes," said Susan, feeling all fluttery just talking about her great adventure.

"And is this your first date?"

"Well, no."

"You mean you already went out with somebody and didn't tell me?"

"Well . . ."

"If you hadn't needed a sitter would you have even told me about tonight?" Nicole's voice sounded suspicious and slightly accusing.

"Actually, no. I know it sounds silly, but this man is almost too good to be true and . . ."

"You didn't want to jinx it," Nicole finished for her.

"Well, yeah."

"It's not like you to be superstitious."

"I know. It's just that this is so amazing. I can't believe that after Bill I could meet someone so perfect."

"Wow," said Nicole, her voice filled with awe. "So, what's his name?"

"You're not going to believe this. It's Nicholas Claus."

"Nicholas Claus? Claus, like in ho, ho, ho?"

"Yes," said Susan, "but he doesn't pronounce it quite like that. It's more of a German pronunciation thing. Closs, like floss with a hard 'c.' But still, when I heard his name, it was like . . . a sign."

"You're right," said Nicole flatly. "I don't believe it."

Susan blinked. "What?"

"Something is weird here, Suz. I mean, nobody is named Nicholas Claus."

"Well, this man is. His mother thought it would be cute, considering their last name. Anyway, I told you, he pronounces his last name different, and he doesn't go by Nicholas. He goes by Nick."

"Well," said Nicole in a dubious tone that irritated Susan. "I guess. Does Daddy know about this?"

"I think I'm old enough to make a date without asking permission from Dad," said Susan, insulted.

"Sorry," said Nicole humbly.

"He really is a nice man," Susan insisted.

"You deserve a really nice man," said her sister firmly. "So, what are you going to do?"

"He's taking me to see *It's a Wonderful Life.*"

"You have the video. And didn't you just watch the thing last week?"

"Yes, but I love that movie," said Susan. "And there's something so nostalgic about watching it at the old Movie Palace."

"Those hard, old seats. Yuck," said Nicole.

"I don't care. I love the place."

"So, what time do you want me over?"

"Why don't you come on over after work? I've got homemade chicken soup in the fridge and french bread."

"Great. And Suz."

"Yes?"

"I really am happy for you, you know that. I just don't want to see you get hurt, that's all."

"I know," said Susan. "But he really is wonderful. And

so gorgeous. I'm glad you've already got Todd or I'd never even let you see Nick."

"Don't worry. A man who is crazy enough to sit on those hard old seats at the Palace and watch a movie he could see on video is no one I'd want," said Nicole. "See you later."

Susan smiled as she hung up. She supposed she'd better call her father before Nicole and her handy cell phone got to him and told him his oldest daughter was going out with a nut.

He answered on the third ring. "Were you going out the door again?" she teased.

"Not just yet," he said, and didn't offer any more information on the mysterious new woman in his life.

"Not talking yet, huh?" guessed Susan.

"Not yet."

"Then maybe I won't tell you about my date, either."

"My daughter the hermit going on a date? This is news. Anyone I know?"

"Nope, but maybe if you're real nice I'll introduce you to him someday. After I've met your new girlfriend."

"Where'd you meet this guy?" asked her father suspiciously.

"Oh, I went to a bar and picked him up, and we spent last night together."

Her father let her little funny pass without remark, instead saying, "I don't suppose it's that fancy lawyer you went to see today."

"No. He scares me."

"Good. Let's hope he does the same to Rawlins. So, if it's not the lawyer, who is this man you're going out with?"

"He's perfectly legit, Dad. Don't worry. I sang happy birthday to him at work."

"He works. That's good."

"He seems to earn a pretty good salary, if his car and where he took me to dinner last night is any indication."

"All right. I'll bite," said her dad. "Where'd he take you?"

"Chez Rory's."

Her father let out a low whistle. "Impressive. Good girl. Marry a rich man and support your old dad in his golden years."

"As if you'd ever let me."

"So, seriously. You like this guy?"

"More than anyone I've met since Bill," said Susan.

"That says a lot," said her father. "I'll be prepared to like him when you finally bring him around to meet me."

"Well, we'll see if it gets that far," said Susan. "The only reason you're hearing about this so early in the game is that I figured I'd better beat Nicole and her little cell phone to the draw. With that new toy of hers, she's a real menace."

Nicole stood at her perfume counter, chewing her lip. She supposed somewhere in the world there could be a man named Nicholas Claus. Suzi Christmas and Nicholas Claus—if this guy was legit, it would be the perfect match. But what were the chances? What would Todd think of this?

She dove into her purse and pulled out her cell phone. After five rings, Todd's answering machine picked up. "Don't bother to pick up the phone, Toddy-O, but here's something for your fevered brain to think about. Susan just met a guy and is teetering on the edge of plunging into a mad, passionate affair. But the weird thing is his name: Nicholas Claus, as in Santa. Am I crazy or does Suzi Christmas meeting someone with a name like that sound like just too much of a coincidence? Anyway, I'm going to baby-sit for her tonight while they go out, so I'll have a physical description of him for you, then maybe you can find a way to tail this guy or something. Love ya."

She hung up feeling better for having taken some step

toward protecting Suz. Two customers later she was awash in guilt. What had she done? Suz would be furious if she found out her sister had set Todd the bloodhound on her dream man's trail.

And probably all for nothing. People couldn't help their names. Look at her poor dentist, Dr. Rencher, and her best friend in grade school, Sonny Shine. Still, what could it hurt getting Todd to see if he could dredge up anything on Nicholas Claus? And there was no need to tell Suz Todd was snooping. If he didn't turn up anything, Suz never needed to know. If he did find out the guy was a flake, they'd be protecting her from a world of hurt. And if there was one thing Suz didn't need any more of, it was pain.

Nicole went back to work, her mind at ease and a smile on her face. Suzi Christmas needed more than just a plastic angel watching over her, and Nicole intended to see she got it.

Susan had a hard time finding just the outfit for eating clam chowder. When Nicole arrived, she found her sister in her bedroom, surveying the pile of pants and sweaters on her bed.

"Here," said Nicole, picking up a pair of black wool slacks and a long, pink, cashmere sweater. "This will make you look good enough to eat."

Susan pulled on the suggested combination and Nicole surveyed her critically.

"Now, pull your hair back and wear those pearl earrings, and Grandma's locket.

Susan did as she was told and turned around for her sister's inspection.

Nicole nodded. "You look perfect."

Susan turned to survey herself in the mirror. She did, indeed, look pretty darned good, she thought, smiling at her reflection. The pink sweater brought out all the right skin tones.

Willie knocked on the door, calling, "Mommy," then entered the room, followed by Ralph.

Willie's eyes grew wide at the sight of Susan, making her realize it had been too long since she'd dressed up.

"Are you going to a party?" he asked.

"No, but I am going out."

Willie looked far from thrilled for his mother.

"Hey now, what's this?" she teased, tapping his protruding lower lip.

"You went out last night."

"Yes, I did," agreed Susan. "And tonight while I'm gone, Aunt Nicole is going to keep you company."

"And we're going to stay up and watch a great chick flick," added Nicole.

Willie's scowl deepened.

"And then tomorrow, you and I are going to see Santa," said Susan.

Chief Thundercloud vanished, replaced by an excited little boy. "And can we go and have peppermint milkshakes afterward?"

"Of course," said Susan.

"Oh, boy! Oh boy!" Willie gave a leap in the air and landed in the pile of clothes on Susan's bed. Ralph, sharing his young master's enthusiasm, yipped excitedly and joined Willie.

"So, you'd better be good for Aunt Nicole tonight," warned Susan, tickling him, and he let out a screech.

It wasn't until the din lessened that Susan realized the doorbell was ringing. "That's him. He's early!" She checked her watch. "Oh, I'm late. My teeth, I have to brush my teeth." She ran to the bathroom, calling, "Go let him in."

"Sure," said Nicole, and hurried down the stairs.

The man was tall, a good head taller than Todd. He was wearing a parka over jeans and some sort of faux hiking boots. He seemed to fill the door. And he was gorgeous.

Totally, darkly, make-you-go-soft gorgeous. Nicole blinked and swallowed, trying to get past gauche to cooly sophisticated.

The man was blinking, too, looking slightly disoriented. "I'm looking for Susan Carpenter."

"That's my sister," said Nicole. "She'll be down in a minute."

His face cleared and he smiled. What a smile!

Nicole smiled, too.

He motioned with his hand and asked, "May I come in?"

"Oh." Nicole giggled like a maniac and stepped aside, and he came in, still smiling politely. "My sister tells me she met you when she was doing a singing telegram."

He nodded. "She came to my office. She has a wonderful voice," he added.

Nicole nodded. She was just about to see if she could trap him with some clever question about his name when Suz came running down the stairs, Willie and Ralph behind her. He looked up, and at the sight of her, his face lit up more than Suz's house.

Suddenly Nicole felt very stupid. Rumplestiltskin, Blue Beard, who cared what the guy's name was? It was plain to see he was crazy about Suz, and Nicole had been a fool to worry.

"Sorry to keep you waiting," said Suz.

"No problem," he said. Then to Willie, "Hi."

"Hi," said Willie. "I'm going to see Santa tomorrow."

"Cool. What are you going to ask him for?"

"I want Luke Skywalker's X-Wing."

"Good choice. I like Luke Skywalker."

"You know who Luke Skywalker is?" asked Willie.

"Oh, yeah."

Suz pulled out a coat from the hall closet. Nicole saw that her date was quick to take it from her and help her on with it, which was more than Todd did.

"I'll try not to keep her out too late."

"Hey, no hurry," said Nicole. "Have a good time."

There was no need to say it. From the shine in her sister's eyes, it was evident they would.

As Nicole realized she hadn't seen Suz like this since the days when she was dating Bill, a fresh shower of guilt over her earlier call to Todd washed over her. It was tacky to be working behind her sister's back to spoil her happiness.

I'm not spoiling her happiness, she reminded herself. I'm protecting her. If this guy turns out to be okay, great; but if he's some kind of weirdo, better to find it out now before Suz falls in love.

Susan didn't believe in love at first sight. But there was such a thing as intuition, and she was feeling the same thing about Nicholas Claus that she had felt with Bill; that deep down knowledge that they were a match, that eventually after the right number of dates, the right number of kisses, the right number of shared dreams, she and this man would agree they were meant to spend the rest of their lives together. The feeling was so strong it was almost palpable. As he tooled the car toward the downtown area of Angel Falls, she glanced Nick's direction, looking for some indication that he felt it, too.

As if pulled by her thoughts, he turned his head and smiled. "I hope you're hungry."

"I'm always hungry for clam chowder."

"Me, too," he said. "You know, someday I want to go to the beach and dig my own clams for chowder."

"You've never made it to the beach?"

"We went to the ocean once when we were kids, but we didn't dig clams. I loved that vacation though. My parents were still together then. It was one of the few times my dad really relaxed and played with us, one of the few times he and Mom didn't fight."

"Your parents are divorced?"

"Yeah."

"How old were you when they got divorced?"

"Almost ten. "Dad moved out two days before Christmas."

Susan heard someone gasp and realized it was her.

He nodded. "Pretty tacky, huh?"

"I'd say."

"For years I wanted to throw up every time I heard the song, 'I'll Be Home for Christmas.' "

"Is that why you don't like Christmas?"

"Did I say that?"

"Not directly."

He shrugged. "Not all my Christmases were that bad. I remember the year I got my first bike. That was a biggie. Then there was the year our dog, Whitey, got to the Christmas turkey before we could." He chuckled. "We caught him bellied up to the kitchen counter with his snout buried in the thing. Dad tried to get it, but old Whitey had gotten pretty attached to that turkey. By the time Dad had chased him all over the house and Whitey had drooled all over it, Mom wouldn't have any part of the thing."

"I don't blame her."

"The stuffing was already out before Whitey got the turkey, though, so we had stuffing and hamburgers for Christmas dinner. Ben and I loved it. Mom wasn't too happy."

"So, what do you do now at Christmas?"

"It varies. The last couple of years I've taken my dad out for dinner on Christmas Eve. He got married this year, so I may not see him. Christmas Day, my brother and I spend with my mom. You'd like my mom."

"What's she like?"

"She's one of a kind. There isn't anything she wouldn't do for her kids. And she's the eternal optimist. She goes through men faster than I go through socks, and with each one, she's sure she's found Mr. Right. So far she hasn't, but she's kind of a gambler, always convinced that she's going to win the love lottery."

"She sounds great," said Susan wistfully.

"She is." Nicholas grinned at her. "I'll bet your mom is great, too."

Susan felt her throat tightening, but managed to squeeze out, "She was."

"Was? Don't tell me."

Speaking had become impossible. Susan had to settle for nodding her head.

"Man, I'm sorry. You've had some tough breaks."

There was a pity-party invitation if ever she'd heard one, but Susan refused to accept it. She'd had her dark times and her long cries, but life's sky was too big to stay forever under a black cloud. You moved on. "I've had some really good times, too," she said. "Still do. As a matter of fact, I'm having a very good time right now."

"You'd have a better time if I found another subject. What would you like to talk about?"

Susan couldn't remember any man, not even Bill, ever asking her that question. This Nicholas Claus was truly amazing. "Gosh, I don't know. That's kind of like having a genie pop out of a bottle and tell you that you've got three wishes."

"Well," he said, turning the car into Matey's parking lot, "I'll give you until we get seated to think about it."

Matey's was a fast-food joint decorated with life buoys, plastic driftwood, and thick ropes. The servers behind its counters wore blue shirts and sailor hats, and Susan noticed that one of the sweet young things was looking at Nicholas like he was the catch of the day.

They ordered deep-fried halibut and french fries and clam chowder, then carried their treasures to a plastic booth by one of the small building's many windows.

"I know what I want to talk about," said Susan, sliding into the booth opposite Nicholas.

"Okay. What?"

"You. What do you do for a living?"

"I push pencils."

"That is a very evasive answer," Susan observed.

"What I do for money isn't half as much fun as what you do."

"You probably make more."

"You're probably right. Let's talk about something else."

"Okay. You choose."

"You."

Susan felt a blush coming on. For someone who spent a lot of time in the spotlight, it never ceased to amaze and irritate her that she so readily blushed under scrutiny.

"Favorite book," he prompted.

"Georgette Heyer's *The Masqueraders*."

"Sorry. I never heard of it."

"I'm not surprised. It's old. It's all about a woman masquerading as a man, and her brother, who is a political fugitive and is pretending to be a woman."

"Victor-Victoria?"

"Not exactly. It probably sounds stupid, but it's really very romantic. Of course, the woman meets this wonderful man, who protects her, and they eventually marry and live happily ever after." He nodded, and Susan could tell from the look in his eyes what he thought of that sort of drivel. She shrugged. "What can I say? I'm a big fan of happy ever afters. So, what's your favorite book?"

"I like stuff by Tom Clancy and John Grisham, but I think my favorite book is still *The Count of Monte Cristo*."

"Oh, yes. That is a wonderful book. I love its underlying message: Things will eventually work out if you just hang in there."

Nick cocked his head. "I always thought the message was that if you wait long enough you'll get your revenge."

Susan blinked.

"It is a book about revenge," he pointed out.

"Well, yes," she said, "I guess it is." Suddenly, she felt

chasms apart from this man, and could think of nothing more to say. She turned her attention to her clam chowder.

"Okay, favorite food," he said, obviously trying to repair the breach he'd created.

"Definitely pizza."

"I wish I'd known. We could have gone somewhere for pizza."

"Oh, but I love this, too," said Susan quickly. Was she sounding too eager to please? She shut herself up with a spoonful of chowder.

They ate for a few moments in silence, and Susan felt the sudden urge to fill it, but couldn't seem to think of anything to say. As if feeling her need for talk, he said, "They're threatening snow tonight."

"I love the snow," said Susan.

Nick grinned. "Somehow, I thought you would."

"Don't you?"

"Yeah. It's a blast to drive in."

"That's the one thing I don't like about it," confessed Susan. "I never drive on a white street."

"You're missing a great adventure," said Nick.

"I had my great adventure two years ago. I slid down a hill. Backward."

"That would be a little scary," he agreed.

She shook her head. "I just don't like that out-of-control feeling."

He was studying her now, wearing a hint of a smile, and she felt herself growing warm from the intensity of his gaze and knew he was thinking about something that had nothing to do with driving in the snow. Her heart rate quickened as she imagined herself lost to the world in his embrace. She lowered her gaze and stared at her bowl of chowder, forcing herself to focus on her present surroundings.

He didn't talk about what she knew they were both thinking. Instead, he said, "You've already had some pretty major times in your life where things were out of your control, haven't you? Yet it looks like you've managed to survive them."

"I don't like to take chances," said Susan.

"Don't you?" he said softly. "You took one on me."

She shrugged, trying to ignore her burning cheeks. "You looked more like a sure thing than a chance."

His expression was unreadable. "Thanks. I appreciate that." He consulted his watch. "We'd better get over to the Palace or we won't get a good seat."

The theater was nearly two-thirds full by the time the movie started. A half dozen people had stopped to say hello to Susan and eye the man sitting with her. Nick had seemed rather uneasy under so much scrutiny, so she had only introduced him as "My friend, Nick." Now, with the lights off, he settled back into his chair, his shoulder resting comfortably against hers, and stretched his long legs out into the aisle.

The pressure of his body against hers was a big distraction, and for the first time in years, the on-screen adventures of the Bailey family didn't get Susan's full attention. Her mind kept wandering to the concerns of the flesh and blood man sitting next to her and the conversation they'd had in his car. He had tried to make light of it, but she was beginning to see that his childhood hurts had never quite healed, and although the scab over them was rock hard, underneath that scab was a soft and tender heart, a heart that needed love and security just like every other human being. Nicholas Claus needed an angel to help him see how wonderful life was just as much as—no, even more than—the hero up there on the movie screen. Could she be that angel?

Romantic fool that she was, she kept hoping he would put an arm around her, but Nick kept his arms to himself. Well, he was being a gentleman. Darn.

When George grabbed Mary and kissed her, Susan found herself filled with such yearning, she could hardly stand it. Bill had never in their entire life given her an embrace so full of passion and surrender.

Of course, he had had nothing to surrender, They had been high school sweethearts, and their marriage had been one more logical step on Bill's calm and happy life path. There was nothing wrong with calm and happy, but just once Susan thought she would like to feel the passion of high drama, where a man grabbed her like she was his lifeline and kissed her with every ounce of passion he could beg, borrow, or steal. Just once.

How would Nick kiss a woman? She felt suddenly warm and self-conscious, as if he could read her thoughts and was looking at her. Don't be ridiculous, she told herself. Still, she was glad when the scene ended and the plot moved on.

She felt Nick straighten in his seat when George Bailey suffered his moment of crisis. Something had obviously struck a nerve.

Susan found herself tensing, too. This was the one part of the movie that always made her grit her teeth, watching her hero crack under the strain, turn viciously on his uncle and snarl at his family. She stole a look at Nick, and saw that his jaw was clenched. In sympathetic anger?

The following scenes where George Bailey saw a different world without his good influence were stark, and made Susan want to weep for the cruelty of mankind, but, as always, at the final scene, she wept for the goodness of which people were equally capable, for the love of God and the joy of the season.

Fresh hope infused her with the belief that her own story would end as happily as the Bailey family's, and that she would find a way to triumph over the real-life Mr. Potter, who was trying to ruin Christmas for her and everyone else in Angel Falls.

She turned, misty-eyed, to Nick as the lights came up and smiled at him.

He grinned back at her. "And they lived happily ever after."

She caught the cynicism behind the statement. "A lot of people do."

"In this day and age, the ones who do are walking miracles."

"I believe in miracles," said Susan softly.

"I'd like to," he said, and this time his voice held no cynicism. "How about some hot chocolate?"

They followed the crowd outside and found the streets and sidewalks disappearing under a blanket of sparkling white, and more fat flakes swirling around them and dancing in the beam of the streetlights. "Oh, it's so lovely!" cried Susan. "Like being inside one of those little globes that you shake."

"I can't think of anyone I'd rather be in there with," said Nick.

She smiled up at him, took a step and nearly lost her balance.

Laughing, he caught her. Then with his arm around her, he led her to the car, starting those shivers again.

The rest of their evening together, Nicholas Claus was charming, attentive, and perfect, as if aware that he'd betrayed his less perfect side earlier and was now determined to balance the scales. He was thoughtful, funny, and ready to discuss everything from politics to favorite TV shows.

"I had a great time tonight," she said as they drove toward her home. "In fact, with everything that's going on in my life right now, you'll never know how much I needed this."

"Oh?"

She shook her head. "I don't want to spoil a perfect evening by talking about my troubles." He pressed his lips together as if chewing over a meaty problem, and she added, "Don't worry. I'm not going to bad-mouth your boss."

"You know, he could have a point. When I was coming to get you, it took me ten minutes to drive one mile. Would it really be so bad to take down a few strings of lights?"

Susan's jaw clenched. It was a long moment before she could speak. "My husband and I started this tradition together," she said finally. "It keeps his memory alive for my son. Not only that, but it provides enjoyment for the whole community. The only reason I'd take down so much as one string would be to wrap it tightly around Luke Potter's neck. I know that doesn't sound very charitable," she added, sorry to sound as mean as the men who were suing her.

He shrugged. "It's honest. And you're right, we shouldn't spoil a perfect evening talking about it."

They pulled up in front of the house. Mary and Joseph and the livestock were gone and the music was off, but Nicole had left the lights on, and now the snowflakes swirled around Susan's house, making it look like something magical. Well, it was. She stood a moment after Nick helped her out of the car, just admiring the sight and listening to the soft whisper of a world burying itself under the snow. Turning to Nick, she said, "Have you ever seen anything more beautiful?"

"Never," he said, and the way he was looking at her, she knew he wasn't talking about the house.

At her door, he took her face in his hands and brought their lips together, oh so tantalizingly slowly, then gave her a kiss as soft as a snowflake. Little elves were still dancing around inside her when he pulled away to smile at her.

"You're an amazing woman, Susan Carpenter," he whispered, and she felt sure he meant it.

"Thank you," she whispered back. "You're pretty fabulous yourself."

This dulled his smile, and he just shook his head and turned to go.

She caught his arm. "Aren't you?"

He cupped her cheek with his hand. "I'd like you to think so."

"I do," said Susan.

Those two words put the shine back in his expression. "Goodnight, Suzi Christmas," he whispered.

He turned and walked down her front walk with an easy grace. Susan watched him and sighed. Now, there was a beautiful sight. She had never met a man so suave and sophisticated, yet gentle. And so capable of lighting a roaring fire inside her with one small, soft kiss. What would he do to her if he ever got down to business?

She hugged herself as she remembered all the little flatteries he had used to tickle her self-esteem. She liked this charming Nick Claus, but the one that fascinated her was the Nick who was hiding behind the mask of perfection, the one that sometimes made his smile look so sad.

You can't hide in there forever, thought Susan as she slipped inside the front door. I'll find you sooner or later, and when I do we'll pull off that hard scab on your heart and dress the wound properly.

Six

Luke was halfway across town before his brain emerged from the pleasant anesthesia of Susan Carpenter's kiss. Why are you feeling so smug? he asked himself. You're not really making any progress here.

Boy, that was an understatement! Hearing Susan talk about strangling him with her Christmas lights hadn't exactly made his day. Well, it was obviously going to take longer than he had originally thought to win Suzi Christmas over to the side of common sense. For that matter, could she even be won over?

Like an ostrich looking for sand, his mind returned to the more pleasant subject of their goodnight kiss. He had kept it short and sweet, a sample of things to come, but the memory of how soft her lips had felt still clung to his own, along with traces of her pink lipstick.

Sitting in such close contact in the theater for two hours, he had worked up an appetite for a kiss. Well, he'd worked up a much heftier appetite than that, but he wasn't about to rush things and blow his image. He'd come close to losing ground a couple of times during the evening, but he felt confident from the dreamy look on Susan's face, after he ended their close encounter, that he was, once again, Saint Nicholas.

Saint Nick. Luke felt his stomach souring. What sort of head games was he playing here? What did he really hope to gain from this stupid charade he had stepped into?

He had only to remember the way Susan looked at him back there on her front porch to know what he wanted.

And all he had to do to get it was make her see that old Saint Nick and Luke Potter were the same man, and that Luke Potter was no more a villain than Saint Nick was a saint. Once she understood that, then maybe it wouldn't matter what his name was, what their differences were. Maybe they could find some middle ground where they could come to a compromise on the meaning of Christmas. Meanwhile, he had to steer clear of any places where he would be likely to encounter anyone he knew.

Meeting her friends in the theater had been a little discomfiting, but, thankfully, his hunch had been correct. Going to see that sappy, old movie had been a safe bet. None of his business associates or racquetball buddies had been present. Luke had been fairly sure that they would consider it an extreme waste of time to go to an old dump of a theater and see a movie that was freely offered them on television several times every Christmas. In fact, he doubted anyone he associated with would even watch the thing on TV.

If they did, they would certainly snicker at some of those corny scenes. Like that ending one where the whole town crowded into George Bailey's living room to give him thousands of dollars in spare change and sing about angels. Gag.

Unasked for, the scene where George came home, bringing the specter of financial and social ruin with him, flashed into Luke's mind. There was Mom, baking Christmas dinner, talking about wreaths, there were the kids, playing Christmas carols and running around in goofy

Santa hats. And there was Daddy, going mad. *You've really had a wonderful life. . . .*

Luke gave a start like a man waking up from a nightmare, and realized his heart was pounding as if he'd been running home instead of driving. Those were his parents he'd been watching on the screen tonight: his mom, playing Donna Reed, trying to make their house a home; while his dad fought to build his fortune, cut his deals, and make his name. Christmas holidays had always been eventful, but the night of the big fight was forever burned into Luke's memory. Even now, he could clearly see himself, huddled at the top of the stairs, peeping down toward the living room, at first unable to see anything more of his parents than flickering shadows, their raised voices lifted like ghosts to where he sat clinging to the bannister. Then he had seen his dad, Luke Senior, stride out into the hallway looking like a giant bird with his raincoat flapping, head for the door, and yank it open. He turned and Luke caught a glimpse of his face contorted with rage. There came his mother in her soft, red bathrobe, shrieking, "We won't miss you. You're never here, anyway!"

She'd been partly right. As Dad's real-estate empire had grown, so had the number of times his chair at the dinner table sat empty. He was always out showing property, or on the phone trying to save a deal. But as for the not missing him part, Mom had been wrong. Maybe she hadn't missed Dad all those years, but Luke had.

Christmas morning had been as exciting as an ornament that had lost its glitter. Mom hadn't been interested in joining Luke in playing with his new train, and without Dad there, he himself had lost interest. Feeling foul, he'd taken his new jackknife and carved his name into the staircase bannister. Ben had ratted on him and Mom had spanked his butt. Dad had showed up after dinner— the one year the dinner was perfect, wouldn't you know, and Dad missed it!—and told them he was moving out, but they could come and stay with him on weekends. Dad had forgotten to add, "Once in a while."

Luke sighed. Well, the old man had tried as much as guys of his generation were capable. He'd pop by the house sometimes, and he and Mom would stand around and look awkward. He'd rumple Ben's hair, ask how school was going and when Luke's next Little League game was, then he'd be gone. Sometimes he'd actually make it to a game, but the few times he did, Luke struck out. Was there some symbolism in that?

Luke scowled. Here he was, mutating into his dad and working all the time. Well, now he knew why Dad had worked so much. A man had to. You couldn't just drift through life like Mom and Ben and Suzi Christmas, singing carols. Someone had to provide the money to pay for the big, drafty house to decorate with Christmas wreaths, someone had to bring in the bucks to put the Christmas turkey on the table. Life was more than fun and games.

You've really had a wonderful life.

"My life hasn't been so bad," Luke muttered. "No worse than anyone else's. And thanks to me, little brother is having a great life."

That sounded just a little bitter. Luke gave a mental shrug. Not so much bitter as real. It seemed to be the lot in life of all older brothers to bust their backsides paving a nice, smooth road for their younger siblings. Maybe that was why so many George Baileys didn't see the magic under the tree anymore; they were just too tired.

Too tired for Christmas? Little Suzi would be shocked.

Was she right? Was he a Scrooge, miserable and wanting everyone else to be miserable, too? "I am not miserable" he growled. "And I'm not a Scrooge. And I'll prove it to her."

Before they got to court?

Luke felt a dull ache creeping up the back of his head. How had life gotten so suddenly complicated? The answer to that was simple: It was because he was seeing this woman. What did he really think he was going to accomplish here anyway? Dating her wouldn't bring back his renters.

It didn't matter. He wanted her. And he wanted her at his feet, begging his forgiveness for the way she'd allowed his name to be slandered all over town. He wanted her lifting up her arms in supplication, begging him to hold her, kiss her, love her. He wanted justice and understanding, and new renters who wouldn't have to live next door to Times Square. And before he was done with Suzi Christmas he'd have it. All of it!

Todd Shelburne woke up Saturday morning, wondering if he should start to make arrangements for his funeral. The flu medicine he had taken the night before had worn off, and he ached all over. He had developed a nasty cough, his nose was stuffed fuller than a Christmas stocking, and he had the energy of a ninety-year-old man; but he knew by Monday he'd be ready to take on the world again. Had to be. He couldn't let his story get cold. He dragged himself to the bathroom and emptied the contents of the medicine cabinet down his throat, then headed to his phone to check his messages.

Nicole was second to come on, after a message from one of his poker buddies. "Am I crazy," she asked at the end of her story, "or does Suzi Christmas meeting someone with a name like that sound like just too much of a coincidence?"

"Yeah, baby, it does," Todd muttered. The girl would have made a great reporter. She had the instincts.

He opened his junk drawer, pulled out his phone book and thumbed his way to the C's, barely aware of Nicki's voice. There was no Nicholas Claus here. No N. Claus, either. Of course, the guy could have an unlisted number.

Todd rubbed his stubbled chin thoughtfully. This could

be something. He grinned. Stuffed up as his nose was, he could still smell a good story in the making, and this one smelled better than a bayberry candle. But it would have to wait until he at least had the strength to stand up for more than five minutes. Meanwhile, back to bed and medicated oblivion.

Susan was standing at the stove in her ratty, blue bathrobe, flipping pancakes when the doorbell rang, sending Ralph, the Doberman wanna-be, into a barking frenzy.

"I'll get it," volunteered Willie, hopping down from his chair.

"Willie," began Susan, but her son was already out of the kitchen, the barking Ralph galloping after him. Her new lawyer had warned her, and a caller at eight-thirty on a Saturday morning could mean only one thing. Feeling queasy, Susan hurried after her son.

"Let Mommy get it!" she commanded, catching up to Willie at the door. "Ralph, be quiet!"

Ralph sat on his haunches with a final yap and a whine. Willie stepped aside, hovering at her elbow, ready to help his mother greet their visitor.

With his crew cut and square shoulders, the man in the doorway was a cement block with a human head. He looked unsmilingly at Susan and asked, "Are you Susan Carpenter?"

She saw the envelope in his hand and felt the corners of her mouth sliding down. "Yes. Give me that junk and get out of here."

He handed over the legal papers, saying, "I'm sorry, Mrs. Carpenter. It's my job." Was that what the executioner told Marie Antoinette before he lopped off her head?

"Merry Christmas," said Susan, and shut the door in his face. She opened the manila envelope and there they were, the same nasty papers Nicole had received.

"What are those, Mommy?" asked Willie, standing on tiptoe and craning to see.

"These are legal papers. Grown-up stuff."

"Can I see them?" asked Willie.

Susan stuffed the papers back in the envelope and tossed it on the entryway table. "They're really very boring reading for a little boy. Let's have our pancakes instead. Then we'll get dressed and go see Santa."

"Yippee!" cried Willie, heading back toward the kitchen.

Susan sniffed at the odor dancing beneath her nostrils. Smoke! "Oh my gosh, the pancakes!"

She nearly trampled Willie as she tore into the kitchen, which was now filling with smoke. Coughing, she yanked the offending pan from the back burner, then went to open the kitchen window. Process servers, burnt pancakes. Susan felt a sudden desire to pitch the pan out the window. Instead, she sighed and opted for Plan B. "Well, I'd rather go get doughnuts for breakfast, anyway. How about you?"

Her son was off and running toward his room before her last words were even finished, the yapping Ralph at his heels.

Susan followed at a more sedate pace. As she passed the hall table, she snatched up the offending legal papers and stuffed them in the drawer, determined to leave her worries there, too.

Across the street, a man with a body like a pear and a hairless, long head watched the process server climb into his car and speed off down the slushy street like a criminal leaving the scene of the crime. The man let the curtain of his living room window fall back in place and chuckled. It ended in a hacking cough, and he pulled a crumpled package of cigarettes from the pocket of his blue plaid bathrobe. He pulled one out, lit up, and took a comforting drag.

"What are you doing, Don?"

He turned to his wife, his near twin except for the addition of a pair of prunelike, sagging breasts and the presence of gray hair on her head. She was pulling her pink, terry-cloth bathrobe more tightly across her scrawny chest and looking at him suspiciously.

"Just seeing if our man got it right this time." His wife's mouth slid into a sideways frown, and he waved her away as if the movement of his hand would make her disappear. "Don't go making that face at me, Aggie. You know you don't like those lights any better than I do."

"But I never wanted everyone in Angel Falls to hate me," she said.

"They don't hate you," said Don Rawlins. "They hate me, and I don't care. Merry Christmas, Susan Carpenter," he added in a mutter. "You dingbat."

For the third time, Luke wandered past the line of mothers and children waiting to see Santa in his red, plywood shack, wondering how long he'd have to hang out at this scene of holiday robbery before Susan showed. A yard of fake snow surrounded Santa's workshop, and plastic candy canes grew in its flower beds. Skinny, teenage elves ran the customers through like cattle. What a racket. And what a waste of money! He shook his head as he thought of the pictures Mom had of him and Ben. Half of them showed one or the other of them crying. Some keepsake.

And Santa had often proved a real dud when it came to delivering the goods, especially the year Luke had asked to have his daddy come home. "Sorry, kid," Santa had said. I only do toys." The store should have fired that jerk.

Well, most men weren't cut out to be Santas. Women would probably make better ones, but they would take too long fussing over each kid and the photographers wouldn't make any money, so that would never happen.

Luke ambled past a bed and bath supply store, and the manager called hello to him. He stopped long enough to hear about how good her business was doing this year, then moved on, scanning the mall for a pretty, blond woman with a small boy in tow. He hadn't tried to accidentally run into a woman since he was fourteen. He felt stupid and conspicuous, although in this crowd he was nothing more than an ant on an anthill. Well, she had to show up eventually. A mother like Susan wouldn't promise to take her kid to see Santa and not deliver the goods.

As Luke looked around, it occurred to him that, in spite of Santa and his elves, the mall seemed rather lackluster this year. A nasty thought that it was due to the lack of Suzi Christmas's carolers stole into his mind, but he kicked it out. They were a nuisance, and since they weren't a moneymaker for the mall like Santa, who boosted business for both Portraits Unlimited and Toys 4 Kidz, there was no reason to have them.

He stopped in front of a Fredericks of Hollywood store to contemplate the frilled and transparent candy wrapping on the mannequins. How would Susan look in one of those things? The image that sprang to mind made his heart rate pick up. He continued his tour of the mall and stopped at the Candy Shoppe. White fudge. He'd be willing to bet a steak dinner that Susan liked white fudge. He bought some. His pal, Betty, winked from behind the counter and slipped in a couple extra pieces, then Luke headed back toward Santa again.

He spotted her instantly. She was wearing some purple and green lady version of a letterman jacket, and those fabulous, long legs were lovingly hugged by blue denim jeans. Luke smiled, admiring the soft, perfect curve of her hips. Susan Carpenter truly was a work of art.

Next to her, her boy hopped up and down like he had

to hit the bathroom. Luke remembered when he had felt that same uncontainable excitement himself. Yeah, he had to admit, he'd enjoyed the visit to Santa once. Or twice.

He came up behind them and positioned himself just in back of her right ear, then whispered, "Ho, ho, ho."

She gave a start and turned, and at the sight of him her cheeks turned that delicious shade of pink. "Hi."

"Hi." Luke smiled across her at her son. "Hi."

"Are you going to see Santa?" asked Willie.

Luke shook his head. "I was just here buying some fudge." He held out the bag. "Want some?"

"Yeah." Willie's hand dove into the bag and came out with a piece.

His mother's eyes widened. "White fudge."

Luke smiled at the near reverent tone in Susan's voice. "I kind of figured you for a white fudge sort of woman." He tipped the bag toward her.

"Oh, gosh, I shouldn't. I already had a doughnut."

"Go ahead," urged Luke. "It's Christmas."

She smiled and dug out a large piece.

Luke watched as she bit into the fudge. She ate it slowly, wrapping her lips lovingly around it with each bite and savoring it, causing Luke to swallow hard. He stood mesmerized as a candy-covered finger disappeared into her mouth. As if suddenly realizing the reaction she was having on him, she blushed and pulled out her finger, then hid it behind her back as if to make sure he wouldn't see it.

Luke held out the bag. "More?"

"I think I've had enough."

Her face still flushed, she turned the direction of the Santa shack.

"What are you going to ask Santa for?" asked Luke.

He watched those soft lips press together, as if holding in some strong emotion. It seemed an eternity before anything came out, and he began to wonder if she'd even heard him. He was just about to repeat himself, when she said, "A miracle."

"I'm not sure that's his department," Luke teased, trying to make his voice gentle. She turned her face toward him again, and he caught the glisten of tears in her eyes. "What is it?"

She pressed her lips together again and shook her head.

"Suzi Christmas unhappy this time of year? There's something wrong with that picture."

"I'm afraid you can blame your boss for that."

Luke suddenly felt like his belly was made of cement. Of course, she'd have gotten served by now. *Merry Christmas, Susan Carpenter, from Mr. Scrooge.*

"I'm sorry," she said. "He is your boss, and I'm sure he must have some good points. . . ."

"He'd like to think so," said Luke.

"But it's a good thing he's not here right now. I'd . . ." Her hands curled into fists, and if it weren't for the fact that she was talking about him, Luke would have laughed, because she looked as threatening as a kitten. "It's just that I got all the legal papers today, and it's so depressing," she said. "You have no idea how awful it is to be sued for trying to do something good. I've never done anything to this man. Or Mr. Rawlins."

Luke found himself suddenly glad he was nowhere near a mirror because he didn't think he'd like what he saw. "Don't you think he has his reasons?"

"I'm sure he does. But he won't talk to me about them. I tried to call him, you know. He hung up on me."

Luke turned away, unable to look into that trusting face. He really was a monster. No, not a monster. Greedy, stupid, maybe, but not a monster. If he just hadn't wanted to expand so fast, take advantage of that big chunk of interest-free money, he wouldn't be standing here feeling like the Christmas version of Benedict Arnold.

The line moved forward another foot. Now they were

almost to the money-grabbing elf. Luke could hear her asking the woman two customers ahead, "Will that be cash or charge?"

"I'm not going to let him spoil my Christmas," said Susan firmly. "Somehow, this will all work out, so I'm not going to ruin my day by worrying about it. I'm going to see Santa and enjoy myself." The smile she gave Luke was pitiful in its forced brightness. "I think you should see him, too."

Luke shook his head. "No, that's okay. I'm not into sitting on guys' laps."

"How about getting our picture taken together?" she pressed.

"Yes, yes," chanted Willie, looking like a human spring.

She was kidding, right? No, judging from the mischief that had suddenly surfaced in her eyes, she wasn't. "Oh, I don't think so," said Luke.

"Come on," she urged. "That looks like a pretty sturdy Santa. I think he can bear your weight."

A grown man sitting on Santa's lap? Stupid. Ridiculous. But Susan was grinning up at him, her troubles temporarily forgotten.

Luke capitulated. "All right." He fished in his back pocket for his wallet.

"I'll pay," she said, stepping up to the elf before he could stop her.

Now he felt doubly uncomfortable. Coming here today had been a dumb idea. One in a long chain of dumb ideas, he added miserably.

Susan's next words broke in on his thoughts. "Where would you like yours sent?"

Not to his house, that was for sure. She'd looked up his phone number once, and reciting his address might jog a memory he wanted left alone. "Er. Bad Boy Enterprises," he said.

Her sunny expression darkened.

Improvising, he said, "I'll show it to my boss: Part of my campaign to expose him to the joys of Christmas."

"It won't work," she said. "He's been inoculated."

The bitter words and matching expression on her face made him feel like he'd been slapped. Well, he had, and maybe he deserved it.

Willie was already rushing into Santa's lair, and Susan hurried after him. Luke studied her face as she watched her child chatting animatedly with the old coot in the red suit and fake beard. Old Santa looked the part with his blue eyes and deeply lined face and snub nose, a nose, Luke noticed, that bore the shade of red one could only acquire by many years of imbibing. "We can get you that, son," he said, after Willie finished with his request. They smiled for the camera, then Willie hopped down.

Susan stepped up next, Luke reluctantly following, and Santa chuckled. "Well, well, what have we here?"

"One of your biggest fans," said Susan, settling herself.

She held out a hand to Luke, and he felt the warmth of a blush prickling all the way from his neck to his forehead. This must be how a chameleon felt when it changed colors, he thought, sure he now was a perfect match for old Santa's suit. "I'll just stand here next to Santa," he said.

The old man chuckled. "Santa won't hurt you, young man."

"Ha-ha," said Luke.

"Come on, boy, you got to get close enough to get in the picture."

Luke frowned and knelt down by the man's knee, watching while Santa tightened his grip on Susan and pulled her firmly onto his lap. *Dirty, old man.*

"And what would you like this year, young lady? A diamond ring, perhaps?" teased Santa.

Now it was Susan's turn to blush. "No, I just want to be able to keep my Christmas lights up."

"Well, why shouldn't you?" demanded Santa.

"I'm being sued."

Luke caught the tremor in her voice and felt his face go hotter.

"Sued!" roared Santa. "Wait a minute. You're not . . . are you Suzi Christmas?"

Susan nodded.

"I read about you. I'd like to get my hands on those jackasses who are suing you. I'd rip 'em limb from limb."

"Santa," said picture-snapping elf, "are you ready to take a picture?"

"Oh, yeah," said Santa, getting back into character. "Smile young fellow," he said, then produced a cheezy grin for the photographer, and picture-snapping elf did her quick and dirty duty. Santa gave Susan a hug, saying, "I'm sure you'll get to keep your lights, Suzi. We're all pulling for you."

"Thank you, Santa," said Susan, giving his cheek a pat. As she stood up, she said, "You didn't ask my friend what he wants for Christmas."

Santa cocked his head at Susan, then gave Luke the conspiratorial wink of one lecher to another. "I know what he wants. Get outta here. Ho, ho, ho!"

Luke took a scarlet faced Susan by the elbow and propelled them out of Santa's lair.

"Can we go to the toy store now?" asked Willie.

Susan nodded, and he whooped and ran ahead of them.

"You've got a sweet kid," Luke observed.

Susan nodded. "He takes after his dad."

Luke felt the shadow of unbeatable competition hovering over him. "It's hard to be raised by a ghost dad."

She nodded. "I know. Willie started baseball last spring. He was the only one who never had a father at the game. My sister and her boyfriend came to see him, and Todd is great, but an almost uncle is not the same as a dad. And, anyway, Todd is so busy working at the paper he can't make it to all of the games."

Paper? Luke's brain went on red alert. "Your sister's boyfriend works for a newspaper?"

Susan nodded. "He wrote that story about me in the *Clarion.*"

"I read that story," said Luke, trying not to let his anger bleed into his voice.

"What did you think?"

Here was dangerous ground. "It was very well written," he hedged.

"But?"

"We weren't going to spoil your day by talking about any of this, remember?"

"How could what you think about Todd's article spoil my day?"

"My opinion on it might not make you happy."

"All right, you've given your proviso. Now, you can safely share your opinion."

Luke sighed. "I know you love your Christmas lights, but the story your sister's boyfriend wrote was pretty one-sided. He painted Luke Potter with a villain's brush, and now everyone in Angel Falls thinks he's some sort of monster."

"Well, isn't he? What would you call someone who does everything he can to ruin Christmas for everyone else? He's as close to Dr. Seuss's Grinch as a human can get."

"Aren't you being a little hard on him?" asked Luke, trying to sound like an unbiased observer.

Susan gave a snort of disgust. "You may not know this, but your boss is also the man most responsible for my Dickens Carolers being out of work this month."

Boy, did he know it. His words last year came back to haunt him like the ghost of Christmas past: "This is a shopping mall, not Broadway. People come here to shop." That remark had made perfect sense at the time.

Why did it sound so rotten now? Get your bearings, Potter. "I'm sure there was a logical reason for that decision," he said, feeling like a prime turkey even as he said it.

"What?"

She was getting hotter under the collar by the minute. Why had he let her lure him into this discussion? "I knew you wouldn't like my opinion," he muttered.

"You're right, I don't. And do you know why? Because this man, your boss, wasn't even willing to talk to me. He just slapped me with a lawsuit. And he wasn't willing to talk to me about my carolers, either, just assassinated them without thinking of anyone but himself and his store."

"Maybe he'd talk to you now," suggested Luke, hoping against hope that her answer would be something on which he could hang some small ray of hope.

"Well, it's a little too late for that, isn't it, now that this thing is going to court. My only consolation is that I've got my legal fees paid. I hope this costs Mr. Scrooge Potter and his big ugly, Don Rawlins, a bundle."

Having delivered that tirade, she swept into the toy store, leaving Luke to either follow or go back to the traitors' camp from whence he sprang. He followed her in, feeling like hanging was too good for him.

He found her standing before a rack of *Star Wars* toys, swiping at her eyes. "They're out of Luke Skywalker's X-Wings." The tremble in her voice betrayed barely repressed emotion. "I'll have to go to Deer Grove to get one."

"My mom lives in Deer Grove. I'll bet she wouldn't mind running out and picking one up."

Susan turned to him. "I'm sorry I took my frustration out on you. You haven't done anything to deserve that."

Feeling slightly ill, Luke put an arm around her and pulled her against him. "I'm really sorry this has happened, Susan. You've got to believe me."

She nodded, and he knew her throat was too constricted by emotion to allow her to speak. It was a sure bet she'd find her voice when she learned who he was. What the hell was he going to do?

Seven

Luke observed that it only took twenty minutes of browsing the toy store with her son to help Susan recover most of her smile, confirming his earlier suspicions that she was one of those people who found it hard to let a sunny disposition stay clouded for long. When Willie asked to go see his aunt Nicki, she showed Luke she had forgiven him his earlier disloyalty by inviting him along. "Unless you had plans to meet someone here?"

I met the person I was looking for," he said, and was rewarded with a pleased expression.

Entering the cosmetics department, they caught sight of Nicole, manning the counter for a high-priced line of products. Willie was about to dash up to her when his mother put a staying arm on his shoulder. "Aunt Nicki's with a customer. We have to wait until she's done."

He remembered her sister from the night before, a younger, more heavily made-up version of Susan, not quite so tall and, Luke suspected, watching her sweeping hand gestures as she talked with a customer, a little more flamboyant. A word, a nod, and a confidential giggle, and Nicole's customer produced her charge card and Nicole loaded a bag with several bottles of mysterious potions. The transaction finished, Nicole smiled and scanned the shoppers for another victim. That was when she spotted Susan and waved. Willie was off like a shot, leaving the adults to follow at their unbearable adult pace.

Nicole leaned over the counter and said, "Hey, Willie Winkie. How're you doing?"

"I went to see Santa," Willie announced.

"Awesome." Nicole smiled at Susan. "Hey, Suz. I've got some new samples."

"Great," said Susan. "You remember Nick Claus?"

Nicole nodded and gave Luke a smile he found hard to label. If he didn't know better, he'd swear she was somehow suspicious of him. "Did you see Santa, too?" she asked him.

"Your sister made me," said Luke.

"You can't hang around with Suzi Christmas and not end up going to see Santa," said Nicole. "Gosh, I wish I could have come and had my picture taken with you," she said to her sister. "Sometimes, I really hate working Saturdays." She looked assessingly at Luke, and he had no trouble labeling the smile she was wearing now: sly. "I guess in your line of work you don't have to work Saturdays, huh Nick?"

"Nope," said Luke.

"Where did you say you worked?"

Playing detective, are we? "I work downtown," he answered.

Nicole nodded. "I don't think I got the name of your company."

Luke didn't tell her. Instead, he smiled cordially and nodded at the old bat on the other side of the counter who was clearing her throat.

"We'd better go," said Susan. "Talk to you later."

•   •   •

Nicole dealt with her customer in a manner as plastic as the woman's Visa card, and as soon as the woman had left, she dug under the counter for her purse and fished out her cell phone.

"Hello," croaked Todd.

"Oh, you're still sick," moaned Nicole.

"I'm getting better," he insisted.

"You could have fooled me. You sound awful. Are you in bed?"

"Yeah, but it's lonesome here all by myself."

"Poor baby," said Nicole unsympathetically. "You'll never guess who was just here."

"Liz Taylor."

"Suz and Mr. Nicholas Claus. If that guy's name is really Nicholas Claus, then I'm Cindy Crawford."

"Okay, so what's he look like?"

"Tall, dark hair, nice, square Superman chin, broad shoulders. He's a hunk."

"Humph," grunted Todd.

"But not as cute as you, Toddy," Nicole added quickly.

"Did you happen to find out where he works?"

"No. I tried to get that information out of him, but he's tight as a clam, and if that isn't suspicious I don't know what is. What man doesn't love to talk about his job?"

"One who's unemployed."

"I don't think that's the case here. But there's something not right about this guy, and I'm getting worried."

"Well," said Todd, "I'd have to say I agree with you. I looked in the phone book, and there are no Clauses listed."

"I knew it!"

"He could have an unlisted phone number," said Todd.

"I don't know," said Nicole doubtfully.

"Well, if he's at your sister's next time you're there, try and get his license plate number."

"You going to check with the D.M.V., just like they do on TV?" asked Nicole excitedly.

"John Tanner works the police beat. I'm sure he'll know somebody."

"Excuse me."

Nicole looked over her shoulder to see a slender, middle-aged woman in an expensive, wool coat, tapping the glass counter with her plum-colored acrylic nails. "Oops, gotta go."

After treating Willie and Susan to hamburgers, Nick left them, and Susan found herself feeling oddly empty after they parted. It seemed so right, being with him. Strolling the mall with him and Willie, she had felt like a family.

Tears she hadn't shed in many years now stung her eyes, and she realized she wasn't just crying because she missed Bill, she was crying because she'd found someone to help her fill her empty heart. He wouldn't take Bill's place—no one could—but Nicholas Claus had found a new corner and claimed it for himself, and she was very happy to have him there. Yes, very happy.

Luke showed up at his mother's house on Sunday in time for lunch. Humming as she worked, she fixed him a fat sandwich loaded with every imaginable kind of cold cuts, thick slices of cheese, tomato, and lettuce; and the expensive brand of dijon mustard he loved but never found in her fridge.

He examined the creation and said, "You've got enough cold cuts here to stock a whole meat department. You haven't kept this much meat since Ben moved out."

Celeste gave her tea bag one more dunking in her mug of hot water and smiled impishly at him over her shoulder. "Maybe I've developed a sudden fondness for baloney."

"Baloney," said her son. "You've been dancing around this kitchen like you're seventeen again. What gives?"

She joined him at the kitchen table, her face looking like she'd swallowed a sunbeam. "If you must know, I've met someone."

Oh, boy. He had to ask. Luke sat back in his chair and eyed her warily.

"I know what you're thinking, so don't say it," she commanded. "This man is different. He's kind and sensible and . . ."

"Divorced?"

"He's a widower, smart guy."

Luke nodded. "Respectable enough," he admitted, and attempted to get his mouth around the sandwich.

"I'm so glad I have your approval," said his mother tartly. Luke rolled his eyes and chewed. She leaned across the table and patted his arm. "You'll like him, I know you will."

"So, when do I get to meet Mr. Wonderful?"

"Sometime, soon. Maybe I'll have a party."

"Just don't make it a Christmas party."

This brought a scowl to her face. "If you're going to go poisoning the air in my home with your holiday cynicism, you can just leave. I'll give you a doggie bag."

"Hey, I'm here to help you pick out a Christmas tree. Would a cynic do that?"

"It does give me hope," said Celeste. "I'll go put on my face while you finish your sandwich."

Ten minutes later, they were in Luke's Bronco, on their way to Grandpa's Great Trees, the same tree lot they'd been hitting ever since Luke could remember. "Do you mind if we make a quick detour by Toyland?" he asked.

"Toyland? Why on Earth do you want to go to a toy store?"

"I have a friend who's trying to find a certain toy for her son for Christmas and the mall was sold out."

"Friend?" said his mother, pouncing on the word like a beggar on a coin. "As in lady friend?"

"As in friend," said Luke firmly.

"Too soon to tell?" she guessed.

"Too soon to tell," Luke repeated.

"Want to talk about it?"

"Not particularly." Or maybe he did. Why else would he have been stupid enough to run this errand with his mother present?

He kept his eyes on the road, but he could feel her studying him and knew she was bursting at the seams with questions, none of which would be comfortable to answer.

"Darling, your life is your own," she said reassuringly. "If you don't want to talk about this woman, I won't force you."

He knew that was a bald-faced lie. His mother, bless her heart, was a hopeless romantic. The day she stopped taking an avid interest in her sons' romances would be the day she was standing at the pearly gates, introducing Saint Peter to some nice girl she'd met on the way up. Luke shook his head. "I don't even know where to begin."

"You could try a name."

"Does the name Suzi Christmas ring a bell?"

His mother's eyebrows shot up. "Suzi Christmas? It rings a silver bell. But you're . . ." She ground to a halt.

Luke nodded. "Scrooge."

"And you're . . ."

"Suing her. Geez, Mom, I wish you could finish a sentence here."

"This makes no sense to me."

"I'm not seeing her as Luke Potter. She doesn't know my real name."

"What does she think your name is?"

Luke steeled himself for uncontrolled laughter. "Nicholas Claus."

"Nicholas Claus!" She shook her head in disgust. "What on Earth were you thinking of?"

"It wasn't me, it was Ben."

"Luke," said his mother, in the clipped tones he remembered from his childhood, "I think you had better explain."

So he did, and when he was done she let out a long sigh. "This does not look good, my son. Your only hope is if she falls totally and completely in love with you before she finds out your real name. Once she really knows you, she won't care."

"Don't you think you're slightly prejudiced?"

"Maybe slightly," she conceded. "It would help matters immensely if you backed out of this unholy alliance with Don Rawlins. What you were thinking of when you allowed that man to talk you into this, I cannot imagine."

"Money, Mother, pure and simple. I was being greedy, and like the monkey caught with its hand in the jar, I can't seem to get free."

"Let go of the banana," said his mother.

"The banana is now nearly gone. I spent it on my new store and a video arcade. I can hardly give Don what's left and say 'deal's off.'"

Celeste shook her head and looked out the window. "There's a man who changed over the years. Well, maybe not so much. He was always rather self-centered. I think going bald turned him bitter."

This psychological analysis produced a guffaw from Luke, and she said, "Well, I do. He hasn't had any other tragedies in his life to excuse his beastly disposition." She tapped her lip thoughtfully. "He and Aggie never had children. Maybe he's impotent, maybe that's why he's become moneygrubbing and power-hungry, to satisfy some unfulfilled paternal urge by producing money since he can't produce children." She turned to Luke. "What do you think?"

"That you've been listening to Dr. Laura too long."

"I don't listen to Dr. Laura, I listen to Dr. Joy. Have you talked to your father lately? Maybe he could help you out."

Luke shook his head. "He's been skating close to the

edge ever since that housing development deal fell through three years ago."

"When was the last time you talked to him about finances?" Celeste persisted.

Luke shrugged. "I don't remember, but I'm sure they haven't changed. Otherwise, he would have offered to help me out."

"Maybe he doesn't know you're in trouble."

"I'm not in trouble. If this doesn't work out, it doesn't work out."

"Um-hmm," she said knowingly. "Well, I guess you're back to Plan One. Win the lady over, and maybe, once you've won her heart, she'll feel inclined to negotiate, and you won't have to go to court."

"That's what I'm hoping, but the more I think about it, the more I realize how hopeless this whole Nicholas Claus masquerade is. I mean, it seemed like a great idea at first, but now I can't find the right time to tell her who I really am. I didn't mean for it to go on this long. I was just going to prove to her that I was a normal human being and not a monster, but now . . ."

Now, what? What did he want? He wanted Susan, yes, but he wanted more from Susan than an apology, more than her body. More even than her love. Greedy monkey that he was, he realized that he wanted her respect. After everything he'd done, respect was too much to hope for. Could he get forgiveness, absolution? Would she give him that?

"But now your heart has become involved, and you're on dangerous ground," his mother finished for him. He realized she was right and felt sick. "You know, you're going to have to make a clean breast of the whole thing," she said.

"I will, but not yet. If I tell her now, she'll never see me again."

"She won't feel any different if she discovers your true identity in court. It would appear to me, my son, that you have until your court date to make Susan Carpenter fall in love with you. When is that, by the way?"

"This coming Friday," said Luke, feeling like he had a belly full of lead.

"You know, if there's anything I can do to help I will," said Celeste, "but I wouldn't set my heart on this girl if I were you, darling."

Suddenly his throat felt tight. He nodded and managed to squeeze out two words. "I know."

Luke knew his mother was right. It was completely senseless to pursue Susan, but he couldn't seem to help himself. He felt so good when he was with her, and if there was such a thing as Santa (which Uncle Hal had informed him there wasn't that Christmas his folks split), he'd have told the old guy, "All I want for Christmas is Susan. Just put her heart under my tree."

He looked over at the tree, propped next to his living room window and wondered what had possessed him to buy it. The Spirit of Christmas? No, just plain, old insanity, with a little help from his mother. As if getting her floor covered with needles wasn't enough, she had to make sure his got messed up, too. What was he going to do with a ten-foot Douglas fir?

He suddenly knew exactly what he was going to do with the thing and why he'd bought it. He wrestled it out the door and headed back to his Bronco.

Half an hour later, Luke stood on Susan's front porch. The lights were on, as usual, and the speakers sent the strains of "It Came Upon a Midnight Clear" out to the few cars slowly driving by. Mary and Joseph and their entourage were missing, and Luke supposed that, it being Sunday, they had the day off. He hadn't heard Susan's doorbell chime over the noise of the music, and was just about to try it again when the door opened.

There she stood, his little Christmas angel, framed by light and looking like she'd just stepped off a sun ray.

She wore a fuzzy, cream-colored sweater that begged Luke to touch it and a pair of matching pants. The smell of gingerbread wafted past her and out to him, beckoning him inside. Or was the smell coming from her?

She smiled. "Nick, what a surprise!"

Feeling like a cheat, Luke forced a smile and said, "I got myself in an embarrassing situation, and I'm hoping you can help me out of it."

"I can try.. Come on in."

"Well, first, I need to know where to unload that tree." He gestured to his fir-topped Bronco parked on her street.

Her eyes widened. "Oh."

"I took my mom shopping for a Christmas tree, and she talked me into buying that. But I probably have a grand total of six ornaments to my name."

"It's lovely! But we couldn't."

"Well, I can't use it, and I know my mom is going to ask me how it looks. If we put it up here, I can tell her it looks great. Be a sport. Take it."

She tried to bite back a smile and a dimple appeared. It was all Luke could do not to reach out a gloved finger and touch her cheek.

"We hadn't gotten a tree yet."

"You've got one now."

"Then you must let me pay. . . ." She turned to get her purse.

"No!"

She looked at him, obviously surprised by the vehemence of his answer. He softened his voice. "For all you know I could be some mean old Scrooge who needs to buy someone a Christmas tree in order to redeem himself."

She smiled and shook her head. "Yes, anyone can tell what a Scrooge you are just by looking at you."

Luke forced another smile and tried to pretend what she had said was funny.

"Willie Winkie," she called, "come see what we've got."

Luke heard Willie before he saw him. The tiny thunder of little, stockinged feet, accompanied by a yapping dog, took Luke back to the early years of his childhood, when the season was magical and a scraped knee was the only reason for a little boy to cry.

"Look what Mr. Claus brought us," said Susan, directing her son's attention to the Christmas tree on Luke's truck.

"Oh, boy!" He whooped. "Can we put it up tonight?"

"Only if Mr. Claus will stay and help get it into the tree stand," said Susan. To Luke, she added, "My dad usually helps me. On my own, I'm hopeless."

On her own, she is anything but, thought Luke, and marveled at the strong spirit that could not only overcome personal loss, but also revel in life in spite of it. "I'd love to help," he said.

Susan turned back to her son. "Let's get our shoes and coats and we'll help Mr. Claus bring it in."

"Christmas tree, Christmas tree, we've got a Christmas tree," Willie sang as he ran back down the hallway in search of his shoes.

Susan had slipped into a pair of fur-trimmed black boots and now dug a powder blue parka out of her closet. Luke took it from her and helped her into it. He was no expert on women's clothes, but even he could see that this coat was no longer a fashion statement. Susan didn't seem bothered by the fact that she wasn't wearing the latest thing. She thanked him for his help, then headed out the door. He wondered how many other out-of-style clothes hung in her closet. She probably didn't have a huge amount of money to live on. If someone hadn't set up a legal fund for her, how would she have paid her court costs? He pressed his lips firmly together over the anger and frustration that made him want to yell and hit something, and followed her out the door.

Falling into step with her, he said, "I got that other thing you wanted. It's in a bag on my backseat."

Her eyes sparkled. "Oh, thank you. And I *will* pay you for that."

"Okay, I'll let you," he said, and started to unrope the tree.

They hauled it off the truck just as Willie came out. "Wow!" he breathed.

"We haven't had a tree this big in, well, ever," said Susan.

"You've got a nice, high ceiling," said Luke. "It should look great."

"We'll put it in the corner by the window, where people can see it from the outside."

They trooped back in the house with the tree, Ralph hopping and barking at it all the way, and then, to the accompaniment of Christmas carols, set it in its stand. It only tipped once, completely burying the coffee table and sending Ralph running for shelter with a yelp and making Willie applaud as if he were watching clowns in a circus. At last the tree stood secure. They draped it with multicolored lights, hung ornaments on every available space, and drowned it in tinsel. When they were done, it was a gaudy, glorious thing of wonder. Susan turned off the living room lights and the three of them stood and admired it.

Smiling, she turned to Luke. "It takes my breath away."

"I was going to say the same thing," murmured Luke, "only about you."

She pinked and made a self-conscious face.

"If you could see yourself right now, standing here in the glow of all those lights. I don't think you're real. I think you're an angel masquerading as a mortal."

"I'm very mortal," she said softly.

"Can we have our hot chocolate and frost gingerbread boys now?" asked Willie, tugging on Susan's sweater.

"Good idea," she said.

"Yippee!" cried Willie, and bounced off toward the kitchen.

Susan turned to Luke. "Would you like to join us?"

He nodded and followed her down the hall.

Willie had already scrambled up onto a stool and now hovered over the rack of cookies setting on the white tile work island. "Do you like gingerbread boys?" he asked Luke.

"Love 'em. I always eat their legs off first so they can't run away."

Willie laughed uproariously and grabbed for the bowl of raisins as his mother began drizzling icing on the little figures. "We put raisins on them for their buttons," he said, pressing one onto the top of a sugar-icing jacket, "then we give them red candy eyes. The red candies are hot."

Luke watched mother and son at work and realized that although he was here and they were trying to include him, he was very much an outsider. These two shared a wonder of the holiday season he had long ago lost. He could buy all the Christmas trees he wanted, but it wouldn't make any difference. He was still a Scrooge who had started a nasty snowball rolling, and soon it was going to roll right between them, and once done, it would leave an uncrossable chasm. He had to stop that snowball. He'd get a loan, pay Don back, get out of this mess. And tonight he'd confess to Susan, before this ridiculous charade went any farther.

Willie had his gingerbread creation now and was stuffing it in his mouth. Susan held one up to Luke, and he took a bite. She had icing on her finger, and he caught it and licked the icing off, watching her face as he did. She licked her lips as if her mouth had suddenly gone dry. He grinned and said, "Delicious." That brought out the blush he so loved and his grin grew into a broad smile.

"I'll get our cocoa," she said, turning toward the stove and presenting him with a view of her well-rounded backside. He picked up the cookie she'd abandoned on the counter and bit off the gingerbread boy's legs. "Now he's caught," he said to Willie, "and he can't run away." *Like me.*

While Willie gobbled cookies, Luke and Susan drank their cocoa and talked of everyday things. Luke was well aware that this ordinary moment was poised over something very big and tumultuous, and that they both knew it. Susan's facade of calm was belied by the way her hands kept finding things to do. Like butterflies, they flitted from perching on the edge of her mug, to rearranging the gingerbread boys on the rack, to sponging off the same spot on the counter she'd wiped down only minutes before.

"Can we watch a movie?" asked Willie.

She shook her head. "No, it's too late for that. In fact, it is already past your bedtime, and you have school in the morning."

"But I'm not tired," protested Willie.

Luke looked at the boy's pink-tipped ears and knew what was coming next.

"Oh, yes, you are," said Susan. "Your ears are red."

Luke couldn't help smiling. He doubted there was any scientific data to support the equation of red ears with exhaustion, but obviously it was one of those Dr. Mom symptoms that women watched for. "My mom used to say that to me all the time when I was a kid," he told Willie. "And you know what?"

"What?" asked Willie hopefully.

"She was always right."

"Aw."

"Come on, let's go brush your teeth," said Susan, putting a hand to his back and giving him a gentle push. "Say goodnight to Mr. Claus."

"Goodnight, Mr. Claus," said the child, sounding sullen.

Luke remembered feeling exactly like Willie felt just

now, facing an undeserved exile, banished from the land of grown-up fun. "Goodnight, Willie," he said, letting his empathy show in his voice.

"Make yourself at home on the couch if you want," said Susan as she exited.

After fetching Willie's present from his Bronco, Luke took Susan up on her offer. When she came back downstairs, he was settled into a corner of the couch, his arm resting on the back. "Join me?"

She smiled and sat down on the opposite end.

"You can see the tree better from here," he said.

She caught her lip between her teeth and looked at her lap, and for a moment he thought she was going to successfully fight free of the unseen current that was now carrying them along. Instead, she scooted over, inserting herself under his arm. She looked up at him, eyes trusting, smile tremulous.

He had planned to say something seductively clever. But he found he could only manage her name, and that burst forth as though some unseen assailant had punched it out. He pulled her to him as if he was a drowning man, and she was the only thing that could save him—making contact with that soft sweater, with the soft body underneath. He kissed her, and her lips were as fabulously soft as the rest of her. She slipped a hand up around the back of his neck, and every nerve in his body went on red alert. Hungry for more, he pulled her tightly against him, deepening their kiss and tasting gingerbread and sugar. Now his head was swimming as if he'd been drinking. He let his fingers get lost in her silky hair, and her soft moan begged him to explore further. He broke the kiss to whisper, "Susan, do you have any idea what you do to me?"

"If it's like what you're doing to me, we're in trouble."

He was skimming her chin with his lips now. "Trouble? I thought it was called something else."

"It's probably too soon to tell what this is," she murmured, "but I've got to confess, it feels pretty wonderful."

Confess. The word fell like snow on Luke's soul, instantly cooling his ardor, and he pulled away a little. "Susan," he began, not sure how he was going to word what he had to say.

"Mommy!" Willie's frantic call from upstairs jerked her out of his arms. "Mommy, come quick. I'm sick!"

Eight

❄

Susan was up from the couch like a shot. "I knew I shouldn't have let him eat all those cookies. Excuse me, I need to . . ."

"Of course you do," said Luke.

She was already halfway out of the living room, throwing her parting words over her shoulder, "I'm really sorry, Nick."

"I'll call you," he called after her, and then wondered if he would. He'd lost his window of opportunity, and he wasn't sure he had the courage to open another.

He let himself out the door, feeling sick. If only the kind of sickness he felt was as easily cured as Willie's.

It took Susan an hour to get Willie cleaned up, settled, and to sleep. But she knew that was nothing compared to how long it was going to take her to find sleep.

She lay in her bed, reliving every second of her encounter with Nick that evening. He had hauled her into his arms with such passion, such need. It had left her reeling. And now, reliving it stirred her afresh.

What had prompted it? It wasn't purely sexual, she

knew that. There was some deeper need in him that had cried out to her. It was as if he had wanted to possess her very soul.

Soul mates. Were they?

She touched her fingers to her lips, remembering the feel of Nick's touch on them. It had been a long time since she had been this happy. Maybe she would go see Santa again. This time she would tell him, "All I want for Christmas is Nick."

By Monday morning the frustration and angst resulting from his aborted attempt at confession, coupled with little sleep, had Luke's head pounding, and he entered his office wearing a frown.

"What's the matter? Don't tell me you blew it with Miss Christmas already?" teased Ben.

"No, I didn't," snapped Luke, "and I wish I'd never listened to your half-baked, moronic idea in the first place."

"Boy, have you got it bad," said Ben.

Luke shook his head. "What a mess. I'd give anything to get out of this."

"Tell Don to take a hike."

"I can't. I already took his money."

Ben shrugged, "Give it back."

Luke fixed him with a killing glare. "And where am I supposed to get the money to do that? If you can't come up with something helpful just keep your mouth shut."

"Dad," said Ben, ignoring his brother's request. "Have you tried him?"

"He doesn't have any money."

"I don't know," said Ben doubtfully.

"Just get out of here, will you?" said Luke, and grabbed for his phone.

His racquetball friend, Keith, loan officer at First National, was out of the office and wouldn't be back until the following week. Great, thought Luke as he hung up.

He reached for the pile of paperwork that had been building up on his desk and tried to concentrate on it, but the image of Susan Carpenter kept interposing itself. What would it hurt to see her one more time?

Susan was sitting with Mrs. Murphy, enjoying a cup of coffee, when the phone rang.

"How's the gingerbread boy this morning?" asked the now-familiar voice.

Just hearing Nick's voice brought back the memory of his kiss, making Susan's pulse pick up. "He made a complete recovery from his gluttony and went to school. I think he just had a little too much excitement last night." *Didn't we all!* "Thanks for asking. I'm sorry about the rotten timing."

"Me, too. I suppose you have to play Mrs. Santa tonight."

"I should," said Susan, and was surprised to find herself wishing for the first time that she hadn't started that particular tradition.

"Well, then, how about lunch tomorrow?"

"That sounds wonderful. I need to get downtown and do some more Christmas shopping anyway."

"Great. How about Lilleth's Tea Room?"

Susan was surprised Nick would suggest a restaurant with such an ultrafeminine setting, but after a moment's consideration, she realized she shouldn't be in the least. Nicholas Claus was such a thoughtful man. Why should she be surprised that he'd think of a restaurant she'd be sure to like? "I love that place, but you don't see very many men there. Are you sure you want to go?" she asked, giving him an out.

"They have good food, don't they?"

"The best."

"Well, then. That settles it. Can you meet me at eleven-thirty?"

"Sure."

"Great. See you tomorrow."

Susan realized she was grinning and hanging on to the receiver as if it were his arm. "Bye," she said, and forced herself to hang up.

"Well," said Mrs. Murphy, "it may be winter but something is in bloom here, and it's not Christmas cactus."

"I think I'm in love," said Susan.

Mrs. Murphy gave a sniff. "And about time, I'd say. And who is this Mr. Wonderful?"

"You won't believe this, but his name is Nicholas Claus, like in Santa. Only he pronounces it a little different, and he's absolutely gorgeous and sweet and . . ."

"And, yes, I think Bill would approve," Mrs. Murphy said, as if reading Susan's mind. "You can't mourn the dead forever. Bill would have been the first to tell you that. And he'll be there in spirit, dancing at your wedding."

"Well, we haven't gotten that far," said Susan, imagining herself in a lacy, cream-colored tea-length gown, holding a bouquet of pink tea roses.

"Yet," added Mrs. Murphy. "But you will. Mark my words. And now I've got to get home. I'm sure my cinnamon rolls have finished rising by now. Let me know if you need me to stay with Willie."

Susan saw her neighbor to the door, and then leaned against it and hugged herself. How funny life was! One moment everything was just awful, the next you were riding on a rainbow. Who would have thought singing a birthday greeting to someone would lead to this?

She closed her eyes, savoring the memory of Nick's kiss and all the pleasant sensations that had gone along with it. She had come alive at his touch, every part of her humming and throbbing. It didn't seem to matter whether he kissed her softly or hard. Either way, her body begged for more.

What a great kisser Nicholas Claus was, and no wonder. With that face and body, he had to have had more than his share of girlfriends and plenty of practice. Seeing him tomorrow would be wonderful, but Susan found herself regretting they only had a lunch date. There would be no kisses in broad daylight in downtown Angel Falls.

The next day, as they sat tucked away at a back corner table, half hidden by a long lace curtain and surrounded by silk roses, Susan quickly learned that it wasn't just Nick's kisses that could send fairy-sized lightning bolts zinging through her body. Holding her hand, he traced her fingers and caressed the top of her hand as she babbled mindlessly. Well, who could concentrate when slow ripples of pleasure were lapping their way up her arms? The waitress came with their food, and he released her hand, sliding his over the top of it, like a lover leaving his partner with reluctance.

Over their meal, they talked of nothing and everything, and all Susan could think of was what he said with his eyes: I want you. She wanted him, too, and the thought left her stomach feeling like a cage full of hummingbirds.

At last the waitress came and took away Susan's barely touched food and asked them if they wanted dessert.

"I'm sure the lady does," said Nick.

Susan hesitated. "The servings are so huge. Will you split something with me?"

"Sure. What do you want?"

"I love the white wedding cake," she said, then felt like she'd spilled some dark secret. Feeling the betraying warmth she hated so much on her cheeks, she bit her lip and grabbed for her water goblet.

She heard him chuckling and looked up again. "I like wedding cake," he said.

Susan shook her head. "I feel like I'm sixteen."

"Is that such a bad thing?"

"I had zits when I was sixteen."

"You don't now. In fact, I can't find anything wrong with you."

"What a coincidence! I can't find anything wrong with you, either."

His smile shrank and the light in his eyes faded. Susan wondered what painful nerve she hit every time she said something good about him. "Susan," he began. "I'm not Nicholas Claus. I'm not the male counterpart to Suzi Christmas."

Now it was she who reached out to take his hand. "I know," she said.

The waitress reappeared, set down two forks and a plate with a huge piece of white cake surrounded by a froth of white frosting and buried under a mound of freshly whipped cream. Susan stabbed a piece of cake with her fork. He still hadn't reached for his. She smiled encouragingly and said, "It really is good."

He nodded and took a bite, but his expression said, I'm chewing sawdust.

"What is it?" she prompted.

He shook his head. "Nothing. I'm just not sure you're going to want to see me when you get to know the real me."

"I thought that was what I've been doing."

"Well, yeah. This is the real me, but there's another me, a past me."

"Did you kill someone?"

He rolled his eyes. "No, of course not, and I'm not a woman beater or a pervert. I'm just a hard-nosed, aggressive businessman, that's all."

"I own a business, remember?" said Susan. "I know what it is to be a business person."

"Do you, Susan? Do you really?"

There was something so fiercely sad behind his eyes, it almost scared her. "Yes," she insisted, "I do. I don't know what horrible things you think you've done, Nick, but they can't be that bad. I know you. You're a good man."

His smile was sardonic, and suddenly Susan thought

of Harrison Ford playing Linus Larrabee in *Sabrina*. She smiled tenderly at him and thought, I'll save you, Nick.

Now he was shaking his head. "Not when it comes to business. In fact, I lied a moment ago. I'm not aggressive. I'm ruthless."

His jaw was tight with suppressed feeling, but Susan suspected that whatever he was feeling, it was nothing compared to what this last remark had just aroused in her. "You don't know what ruthless is, although if you stay with Luke Potter for very long you'll learn in a hurry. That man is the lowest of the low and the meanest of the mean. Suing people for hanging Christmas lights, for crying out loud! Maybe your Luke Potter should come with me to the food bank sometime and see how happy those people are to get the food I collect. Maybe he should be there to see the children's faces light up at the sight of Mary and Joseph and the donkey."

"Susan, don't."

The sight of Nick's pained face brought Susan's tirade to an end. She imagined how ugly her own expression must look right now as she spewed venom. She sighed. "I'm sorry. It just makes me so mad every time I think about a bully like that getting his way and spoiling the season for everyone else. Did you ever see my Dickens Carolers?"

He nodded, still looking pained.

"Weren't they wonderful?"

"They were very good."

"But they didn't bring business to any of the mall stores, so Mr. Scrooge Potter put pressure on the mall manager and made sure they didn't work this Christmas. I suppose Luke Potter would have gotten Santa booted out, too. All that congestion he causes! Lucky for Santa somebody in the mall makes money off him, or Luke Potter would have had the Angel Falls cops in there, putting a parking ticket on his sleigh." Susan realized she was at full steam again, and put on the brakes. She shook her head. "I'm sorry."

He covered her hand with his, then let out a world weary sigh. "Don't be. You're justified."

She shook her head. "No. I don't want to sink to your boss's level of meanness. It's just that he makes me so mad. I mean, I know business is important, but it isn't everything." She pushed away the cake, her appetite dead. "Maybe it takes losing someone precious to you to make you see how much more there is to life. Maybe Luke Potter has never had that particular lesson."

"Maybe he has," said Nick, "but maybe he didn't get it right. I can tell you, Susan, he's learning some hard lessons now. He's really changing."

Susan shook her head, her expression doubtful. "I hope, for his sake, he can."

"Well, it looks like a white Christmas again this year," said the waitress, returning with their check. "It's really starting to come down out there. I just heard on the radio we can expect six to eight inches."

"Great," grumbled Susan. "There go a dozen customers."

Nick was fishing in his wallet. "Good thing there's more to life," he quipped.

She scowled at him. "Very funny. I still have to make a living."

"None of your employees have snow tires or four-wheel drive?"

"One of them does," said Susan. "But when it gets this bad, none of them has it easy. I'll either have to pick up the slack or cancel my orders, and I can't afford to cancel a single one. Thanks to your boss losing me my contract at the mall, I need all the business I can get."

"But you don't like to drive in the snow."

"That doesn't mean I can't do it," said Susan stoutly. Already the thought of crawling around on slippery streets was making her muscles stiffen in dread.

"I've got four-wheel drive and snow tires. I'll play chauffeur for you tomorrow."

"You have a job."

"I can make up the hours," said Nick, rising. "And besides, my boss owes you. This is one way you can make him pay."

Susan stood. He helped her on with her coat, and ended the process with his arms wrapped around her. She leaned her head back against his shoulder and he brushed her cheek with his lips, then kissed her ear, sending a message of pleasure spiraling downward to leave her weak-kneed.

"You know what I want for Christmas?" he whispered.

She shook her head.

"To stand like this forever."

She turned and smiled up at him. He pulled her against him and kissed her right there, setting off such a fire inside her that she thought the conflagration must catch the lace curtain, too. Then he turned her loose and smiled down at her. "Out into the cold, cruel world," he said, and she caught the note of regret in his voice.

"Can I walk you to your car?" he asked, outside the restaurant.

"I took the bus."

"Then I'll walk you to your bus stop."

They waited at the bus stop, Nick holding her against him, sheltered from the cold. She could smell his after-shave. "What are you wearing?" she murmured.

"Brut."

She smiled up at him. "I don't think you're one of those."

His answering smile didn't reach his eyes. With his hand, he gently pressed her face back to his shoulder and laid his head against hers. She felt the light touch of his lips on her hair. "Here's your bus," he said.

With reluctance, she stepped out of the circle of his arms and onto the bus.

Luke stood with clenched fist and watched the bus rumble off. *Coward! You should have told her.*

Well, he might be a coward, but he wasn't a fool. Back there in the restaurant had not been the moment to warble, "Surprise!" and reveal his true name. She'd have tried to run him through with a butter knife. He had to find the right moment, when he had time to explain his metamorphosis, when she had seen he had a good side. Tomorrow? At least he'd have been playing Good Samaritan. She'd look on him in a more favorable light tomorrow.

I'll think about it tomorrow, Luke smiled grimly. Scarlett O'Hara had the right idea.

And what if tomorrow doesn't turn out to be right, either? came the nasty thought. Their first court date was December nineteenth. Three days away.

Tomorrow. He had to tell her tomorrow.

Willie had gotten out of school early due to snow panic, and Susan barely beat him home. She was just feeding him cheese and crackers when her sister called.

"Are you snowed in yet?" asked Nicole.

"No, but I will be by tomorrow."

"That'll be good for business," said Nicole sarcastically.

"Well, as it turns out I won't have to cancel on any of my customers. I'm going to pick up the slack for my singers."

"If you knew it was going to come down like this you could have told me," complained Nicole. "I'll be lucky if the bus gets me home tonight. Hey, wait a minute. I thought you didn't drive in the snow anymore."

"I'll be riding, not driving. I just happen to know someone with snow tires and four-wheel drive who wants to play white knight."

"Oh, don't tell me, let me guess. Mr. Santa?"

"Good guess."

Nicole grunted. "It must be nice to be able to take off

work whenever you want. Um, where does he work, by the way? You never told me."

"Oh, gosh, I can't believe I never mentioned that. This is so ironic. He works at Bad Boy Enterprises, and you won't believe who owns that."

"Oh, try me."

"Luke Potter."

"The Scrooge of Angel Falls?"

"Yep. That's why Nick has no guilt over driving me around tomorrow. He says his boss owes me."

"That's for sure. Well, I've gotta go. I'll talk to you later."

Nicole rang off and immediately called Todd.

He still sounded raspy when he answered the phone.

"Aren't you well yet?" she demanded.

"Hey, I'm working on it. Are you going to brave the snow and come over here and feed me chicken soup?"

"If I ever get home tonight, I'm staying put and opening up my own can. My sister is going to be out in the stuff tomorrow, though, with guess who."

"So, did you find out where he works?"

"He works for Luke Potter."

"Luke Potter!"

"Yep. How's that for a strange coincidence?"

"That's strange, all right. Thanks, baby. You've just given me another lead to follow."

"This is not for a story, Toddy," warned Nicole. "We're helping my sister here."

"Hey, just leave everything to me. I know what I'm doing."

"Okay," said Nicole, and hung up, wondering if he did.

Todd suddenly felt like a new man. He had already made some calls, pulled some strings, and he had his suspicions. But this newest bit of information, oh, this was great!

A little more research and those suspicions hardened into proof. This was too good! Todd pulled on boots over his wool socks and a parka over his sweats and headed for his Jeep. He'd find himself a couple of props, then take a little drive over to Bad Boy Enterprises before the snow got any worse. He looked at the darkening gray sky and shivered. Well, adventure called. Anyway, this would be a short, quick trip. It shouldn't take him too long to pull off Potter's mask, maybe even get a juicy comment. Then he'd curl up in a blanket with his laptop and write yet another Pulitzer winner.

This is not for a story, Toddy. Nicole's words came back like some sort of Jiminy Cricket to nag him. Well, he wasn't just doing this for a story. He was doing it to help Susan. And the only way he knew to help Susan was to do what he did best: write. Besides, if he was ever going to be able to support a wife—a certain cosmetics peddler with expensive taste—then he needed to move on to a bigger paper. This story might just be his ticket into the *Chronicle*. Nicole would understand, especially when he saved her sister from certain heartbreak. And, anyway, with what Potter was up to, didn't Nicki want to see him pay? What better way to pay than by public humiliation!

There was even more here at stake than protecting Susan. The public had a right to know, and he had an obligation to tell them. Todd thought of Gary Cooper in *High Noon* and nodded. Yep, a man had to do what a man had to do. And he just had time to do it before Bad Boy Enterprises closed up shop for the day.

He climbed into his Jeep and eased out onto the street. He'd gotten two miles when some idiot skidded into him, crunching both vehicles. By the time they'd exchanged insurance information and the tow truck had arrived, Todd was chilled to the bone and his teeth were chattering. The Jeep was still drivable, but he looked at the mounds of snow forming like igloos over the bushes in nearby yards, checked his watch, and knew he'd lost the battle. But not the war, he thought, smiling grimly. *I'm coming, Potter. See you soon.*

Something is stinking here, and Hot Toddy is going to dig it up. Very soon.

"How about another piece of pie?" asked Celeste.

Hank patted his middle. "I'm stuffed. It was great."

"Yes, it was, if I do say so myself. And I finally got to pick up the tab, which is more than you let me do on Friday night, you naughty boy."

I tried," he said. "I really did. I just couldn't bring myself to let you. And anyway, with my senior citizen discount, it didn't cost that much."

"So, when I reach sixty-two, I'll pay," she teased.

"Maybe."

She poured him more coffee and changed the subject. "Tell me more about this new job. When will you start?"

"I'm putting in a few days here and there already— sort of a training period— but I won't officially start until after the holidays. I'm looking forward to it."

"I'll have to come to Angel Falls when I need camping gear and Rollerblades."

"Do you like to camp?" Hank asked.

Celeste could see the eagerness on his face and was tempted to lie. She resisted and said, "Not if it means lying on the hard ground, freezing in a tent, or dragging around a trailer that I would have to cook in and clean. That doesn't sound like much of a vacation to me."

"Oh."

He looked so disappointed she couldn't help but smile. "But a rustic, little mountain cabin sounds pretty wonderful," she added. "As long as we import plenty of ready-made food and Chinese takeout."

His face lit up. "Cabins are good. A cabin on a lake, where we can fish."

"You fish and I read," she amended. "And you clean the fish."

"Celeste. Do you hear what we're saying?"

Her heart rate skyrocketed as she nodded. "We weren't going to rush."

"I know," he said, nodding. "But let's not go too slow, either. Life is short."

She reached out to cover his hand. "I know, and I don't want to be lonely, but I don't want to make another mistake."

"Do I look like a mistake?"

His voice was gentle, no insult taken. Which was good, because she hadn't meant any. "No, you don't in any way resemble a mistake." He lifted her hand to his lips, and she smiled on him. "My boys are going to love you."

He laid down her hand and patted it. "I hope so, because I intend to marry you whether they like me or not."

Celeste gave him a scolding look. "There we go again, rushing things."

"It's getting hard not to," he said. "But no ring for Christmas, I promise. I can make it til Valentine's Day."

"And I hope I can," she said. "My oldest son thinks I've gone around the bend. I told him about you, and he's curious."

"I'll bet he gave you a regular third degree."

Celeste nodded. "That he did. You know," she added thoughtfully, "I've got two sons and you've got two daughters. . . ."

"*The Brady Bunch* on a smaller scale," he said, not following her train of thought.

"Wouldn't it be delightful if our kids hit it off?"

"Amazing, more likely," said Hank. "Let's not spoil the holiday by introducing them."

Celeste shook her head at him, and they left the dining room for the living room. She looked at the display of fat snowflakes outside, framed by her picture window and exclaimed, "When did that start?"

Hank walked over to the window for a closer look. "Looks like we've already got a couple inches. Want to take a walk in the snow?"

"Oh, Hank, it's really coming down. Maybe we'd better call it a day so you can get home in one piece."

"I've got studded tires. Anyway," he added, waggling his eyebrows at her, "if I delay another hour or so, I might just have to spend the night on your couch."

She smiled at the vision of herself and Hank curled up in front of a blazing fire, listening to Johnny Mathis. "I'll get my coat."

The turgid, gray clouds finally finished unloading their cargo by evening, then moved off, leaving the residents of Angel Falls buried under over six inches of snow. Most of Susan's customers postponed their birthday surprises, but several hardy souls held firm, leaving her date with Nick for the following day intact.

She suddenly realized she would have had no way to tell him if they canceled, as she didn't have his home phone. Well, that would have been an easy enough problem to solve, she thought, pulling out her phone book. She thumbed through it and scanned the C's. Funny, no Claus. He must have an unlisted phone number. In this high-tech age that seemed almost a waste of time. Surely anyone who wanted to track a person down these days could do so.

The town of Angel Falls prided itself on its efficiency, and the snowplows had already been busy, clearing the downtown arteries and side streets, and leaving miniature mountain ranges of dirty snow along the curbs. Martha had made it in to Bad Boy Enterprises with no problem. Roxy, who lived outside of town, was still snowed in, and Ben, who had an apartment only a mile away, was missing, but Martha had expected to find Luke in his office, hard at work. Instead, she'd found a message from him on the answering machine, informing her that he'd be tied up all day and asking her to hold the fort. "Catch up that filing, then leave early if you want," he'd added. That was a first.

Now Martha eyed the young man standing in front of her. It was the reporter from the *Clarion* again. He must have thought she wouldn't recognize him hiding under that deliveryman cap. He'd lost his glasses and put a rinse on his hair—black, which, combined with his fair skin, made the boy look like a vampire—but she wasn't stupid.

That was the trouble with the youth of today, they thought they were so smart. And did he think he could rattle her by asking for Mr. Claus? Whatever game he was playing, he'd get no help from her. Luke had asked her to hold the fort, and that was just what she intended to do. "Mr. Claus isn't in today," she said, the picture of brisk efficiency. "I can see that he gets that," she added, nodding at the package the man held.

She could see her news had disappointed him, that he had hoped to get a glimpse of the mysterious Mr. Claus. It was a struggle, but she managed to keep her expression innocent. She raised her eyebrows expectantly.

"Er, sure," he said, and forced a smile.

He handed over a book-sized package, then gave her a clipboard with an official-looking paper to sign. The paper even had names. Very good, she thought, except real deliverymen had gone much more high-tech than this. Maybe little Rockford Junior had come by this prop by digging it out of somebody's Dumpster. She signed her name and handed it back.

"Thanks," he said. Then he tipped his hat and left.

Martha studied the package and wondered what was in it. Had the reporter, somehow, known Luke wouldn't be coming in to the office today? And what new theory was he testing out, asking for Nicholas Claus? One thing Martha knew for sure, Luke didn't want his cover blown, and he wouldn't squawk about the way she'd handled the reporter this time. In fact, after saving his hide, her obsessed, young employer owed her a very big Christmas bonus.

"This is so sweet of you," said Susan as Luke's Bronco tooled easily down an icy residential street, toward downtown Angel Falls.

One moment of kindness. Was it enough? "I do have my good points," he said, and hoped she'd remember that when the time came for his big confession.

He stole a glance her direction and saw she was smiling. And there was that dimple in her cheek. If only life was like a video. Luke would rewind it, edit out those scenes where he had behaved like an arch villain and tried to ruin Christmas, and now he and Susan would be riding around like any other couple in love, maybe even on their way to look at rings.

He sighed inwardly. Only ten o'clock in the morning and his gut was churning acid. It was going to be a long day.

"I'm just glad not all my customers canceled."

"Because then you wouldn't have been able to see me?" he quipped.

Her smile grew, but Luke noticed she barely blushed this time. Past the self-conscious stage of the relationship, which meant she was feeling comfortable with him, which meant she trusted him. Luke's hands tightened on the steering wheel. His confession was going to shatter that trust into a million pieces. How had he let himself get into this mess?

"There is that," she said. "But I also couldn't have gotten ahold of you last night to let you know not to come. I don't know your phone number."

"I'm unlisted," he improvised.

"I figured that," she said. "I looked for you in the phone book."

"I used to be," he lied on. "But with a name like · mine . . . too many prank calls."

She nodded her understanding.

"Remind me and I'll give you my pager number," he said. "You can reach me anywhere on that." That seemed to satisfy her, and he loosened his death grip on the steering wheel.

They pulled up in front of her first destination, an office building in the same block as his. As Luke went to her door to let her out, he prayed he wouldn't see anyone he knew. The banks of snow at the curb presented a barricade, and just as he'd done at her house, Luke picked Susan up and carried her to the door of the building.

"You're better than Sir Walter Raleigh," she teased.

"Cheaper. Carrying you saves me money on the dry cleaning. Anyway, I wore out my cape on my last girlfriend."

This made her look at him speculatively, and he knew exactly where their conversation would be headed once she came back.

Sure enough, as soon as he started the Bronco in motion again, she casually said, "I can't imagine any woman ever wanting to let you go."

"We parted by mutual consent."

Susan nodded and kept quiet, obviously waiting, hoping he'd say more.

"We couldn't agree on what to get her for Christmas."

"Oh?"

He shrugged. "I gave her pearls. She wanted diamonds."

"As in a ring?"

Luke nodded. "I'm a little cautious about marriage."

"I suppose most men are," said Susan.

"Maybe. I never wanted to end up like my folks."

"Not every marriage ends in divorce," she said softly.

He reached across the seat and took her hand. "I'm beginning to understand that."

Marriage to Susan would be great. And, unless Luke could work out his finances and lose Don, impossible. He had thought he could confess today, tell Susan everything. But he knew now he couldn't. The disappointment and hate in her eyes would kill him. He hadn't wanted to cry like this since his folks split up. He stuffed down his emotions and kept his face a smiling mask until Susan disappeared inside another office building, then he marched back to the Bronco and slammed his fist into the hood. Looking at the dent, he smiled bitterly. Merry Christmas, Scrooge.

She invited him in for coffee when he brought her back home, but he declined, saying he had to get going. He held his breath, sure she was going to remind him to give her his pager number, but she didn't. Of course, Susan was too polite for that.

It was better that she didn't have it, better that she didn't see him again. Ever. He gave her a kiss goodbye, forcing himself to keep it light although he wanted to stand on her porch and kiss her clear into the New Year, wanted to hang on to her like a lifeline. He broke the contact, forced one last smile, then hurried down her front walk and out of the snow-covered yard. Tonight this place would look like Disneyland, with the snow reflecting the colored lights.

Luke glanced across the street to his godfather's house. The curtain at the living room window twitched. Don was probably watching him right now, and he'd hear about it when they met at Melville's office tomorrow. Luke got in his vehicle and slammed the door after him. He wished he could punch Don Rawlins in the nose. He had to settle for punching the gas and feeling the Bronco fishtail off down the street.

Susan chewed her lip as she watched the Bronco roar off. Something was wrong. Nick hadn't given her his pager

number, and their kiss had felt more like goodbye than
see you later. What had happened?

She shouldn't have been so polite. Instead, she should
have asked him what was wrong the minute she felt the
wall going up between them. With a sigh, she turned into
the house. Nicholas Claus was fighting some demons, and
although Susan had a stake in how it came out, it looked
like he preferred to wage his battle without her help. At
this point, there was nothing she could do but wait. But
what if he lost the battle? What then?

"Your father called," said Mrs. Murphy as Susan
shrugged out of her coat.

"I'll call him back."

Mrs. Murphy shook her head. "Don't bother," she said,
trying to make herself heard over a rambunctious Willie,
who was dancing around his mother in his stocking feet,
holding up a Picasso-like rendition of a reindeer. "I asked
him if he wanted you to and he said not to bother since
he wasn't at home right now. He just wanted to make
sure you were okay."

"Not home, huh?" said Susan thoughtfully, scooping
up her son and planting a kiss on his neck. So, if Daddy
wasn't home and there was six inches of snow on the
ground, where was he? It wasn't a difficult question to
answer. She could almost see her father parked in his new
lady friend's kitchen, enjoying a second cup of morning
coffee. Of course, she was happy for her dad, but she
wished she had been home when he called so she could
have asked him about Nick's strange behavior.

Thinking about that was a waste of time. She poured
herself some coffee and a fresh cup for Mrs. Murphy and
resolutely forced herself away from the puzzle that was
Nick Claus. Right now there was nothing she could do
to solve it, and if there was nothing she could do, it was
a waste of time to think about it. So why couldn't she
help thinking about it?

Luke arrived home to find his answering machine blinking. He punched the play button and heard his dad's rich baritone. "Hello, Lukester. We haven't talked about Christmas yet. How about coming over Christmas Eve? It won't be much, just Sandy and me and the kids, but I'd really like to see you." The talking stopped as his dad cleared his throat. "I know there were a lot of Christmases and other times where I blew it in the dad department, but I've got something for you this year that I think you'll appreciate. I know you're not wild about Sandy, but please come. It would mean a lot to your old man."

Luke sighed. Good, old Dad, still trying to make up for lost time. Maybe the old man was planning on giving him a train set.

He picked up the phone and dialed. He got his stepmom, who dutifully promised to tell Luke Senior that his son would be joining them.

He hung up and walked over to the window to look at the view below. He could see house lights twinkling, their reflection coloring the snow and dancing on the river, and wondered about the people living in those houses. Right now, he'd change places with any one of them.

That thought brought a mirthless laugh. No one would want to trade places with the Scrooge of Angel Falls. He was stuck in his own skin.

On December eighteenth, Luke walked into Melville, Armor, and Bouie wearing his Brooks Brothers navy suit, his camel-hair overcoat, and a frown. He saw Don Rawlins, slumped at one end of the reception area's black, leather couch, and his frown deepened.

"You're late," said Don, tossing a magazine on the glass-top coffee table.

Luke shrugged. "Melville is never on time himself."

"Was that you I saw over at the dingbat's house last night?" demanded Don.

Luke let out a sigh. "I own the place next door. Remember?"

"Yeah, but you don't seem to. That wasn't your porch I saw you standing on."

At that moment, Melville's secretary appeared to usher them into his office.

Luke had only seen pictures of Teddy Roosevelt, but every time he saw Jack Melville, with his short, stocky body, his curly, dark brown hair, his ruddy complexion, and his wire-rimmed glasses, he felt the urge to clap the guy on the back and say, "Bully for you, Mr. President."

Jack shook hands with both men and all three took seats, Jack behind his desk, and Luke and Don in two comfortable leather chairs.

"Well, gentlemen, things are progressing," said Melville. I think we have a good chance of winning our case, but Hawkinson isn't the sort of man to let his opponent get by without a few blows." Melville turned to Don. "He's subpoenaed your wife's doctor, Mr. Rawlins."

"What!" Don glared at Melville as if this latest development was his fault.

"As I said, our worthy opponent has no intention of laying down and letting us steamroller over him."

"I don't give a damn about him," said Don. "I want those lights gone."

"Why?"

Don turned to Luke in surprise. "What do mean by that? You know why. You lost renters thanks to her. Can you imagine having to live across from that?"

"You could afford to live anywhere. Why didn't you sell and move, Don?" asked Luke quietly.

"Why the hell should I? It's my neighborhood, too. And what are you getting at?"

"I'm thinking I was wrong."

Don twisted in his seat to glare at Luke. His face was reddening, and Luke wondered for a moment if the old coot was going to jump up and pop him one. "I know what's changed your mind: long legs and a cute butt."

Luke was halfway out of his chair when he felt Melville's hand on his arm.

"Gentlemen, please," said the lawyer. "This is hardly civilized behavior. May I remind you that you are allies and not enemies?"

Don gave a snort. "You think I didn't see you kissing her yesterday? I don't know what sort of game you're playing, kid, but you're playing it with my money. Now, I don't like those lights. I want them gone, and that's what's going to happen, one way or the other."

"You have a lawyer. Why the hell didn't you sue her by yourself? Why did you have to drag me into it?" demanded Luke.

Don looked at him as if he was crazy.

"I'll tell you why," Luke continued. "Because you didn't want to be the only jerk in town. You figured if you suckered me into your little war you wouldn't look so bad. Might makes right. Well, I don't want to play war anymore."

"Make love, not war, huh kid? Well, that's fine. You give me back my money today, and I'll go on alone."

"You know I can't do that. You know how much I've already spent."

Don shrugged. "A deal is a deal, Lukie. You're a businessman. You know that. I'm not letting you off the hook just because you've got the hots for this little cutie."

"She won't want anything to do with me once she finds out I'm in league with you, you devil."

"That's your problem, my boy, not mine. Use your influence on her, talk her into taking down those lights and shutting off the music. Get the cars off the streets. We don't have to sue her if she'll cooperate. Maybe if you talk to her she'll come to her senses."

Luke fell back into his chair, shaking his head. "She won't. She feels too strongly about this."

"So do I," snapped Don.

Luke glared at him. "What the hell did my dad ever see in you?"

Don smiled maliciously. "The same thing you do. Himself."

That was it. If Luke sat there anymore, he was going to do something very violent to his godfather. He shot from his chair and marched toward the door.

"Where are you going?" shouted Don. "We've got a meeting going here."

"You keep it."

"Luke," Melville's voice stayed Luke at the door. "We're due in court tomorrow. We still have things to discuss."

"Not me," said Luke. "I'm done talking."

Nine

"Luke!"

Luke shut the door on Don and left. He wasn't going through with this. He'd get the money to pay off the old buzzard, and as soon as he had it and Don was out of his life, he'd confess everything to Susan. He'd make it up to her. He'd contribute to her legal defense fund, get her carolers back at the mall, whatever it took to prove to her that he could be the kind of man she respected.

He punched the elevator button and leaned his head against the wall. It would be a miracle if he got a loan from First National. They were a conservative bunch with an ultracautious loan policy. Keith had told him as much when he was first looking for more expansion capital. He should have put together a package anyway or gone to another bank. Instead, he'd snapped up Don's offer, which had been quicker and easier.

Somebody once told him there's no such thing as easy money. Probably, Don himself, now that Luke thought about it. He smiled bitterly. How true.

Don't think negatively, he told himself. The bank could still come through. And if the bank copped out, what liquid assets could he sell to make a pile of cash big enough to save himself? He cast about frantically in his mind. His Lexus? That wouldn't work. He was upside down on it, with the car worth less than he owed. He'd find no profit there. Okay, so what else? His condo? Why not? He could move into his rental, move next door to Susan. Luke chuckled bitterly. Old Don would love that. But condos were sometimes hard to sell. If only he hadn't cashed in those stocks last year. He'd offered them up to his ambition, plowing that money into his business, which had swallowed it whole just like it had his life. Well, he'd think of something. He had to, because he didn't want to lose Susan. Nothing even came close in value to what he had found with her. Any deal in the world could slip away, but not this. Please God, not this.

Luke headed for his office, determined to start working on his escape Plan A and get together facts and figures to impress the stodgy powers-that-be at First National Bank.

Martha was at her desk, sorting through the mail, and, she smiled at him as he walked through the door. "You're getting as bad as your brother. Where were you all day yesterday?"

"Out trying to grow a heart," said Luke, heading toward his office. "I guess you made it in okay."

"Oh, yes. I had a visitor while you were out tending your new heart, Pinnochio."

Luke stopped, slipping off his overcoat and draping it over his arm. He turned cautiously, as if expecting to get a pie in the face.

"That reporter was here again."

Luke's heart gave a sick flop. He'd rather have had the pie. "Oh?"

"This time he was in disguise: dyed hair and a UPS outfit. He had a delivery for a Nicholas Claus."

Nicholas Claus? How did the reporter come to link Nicholas Claus with Bad Boy Enterprises? Then Luke remembered: Todd Shelburne was practically part of Susan Carpenter's family. An invisible vise gripped Luke's heart and squeezed, sending painful tingles out to the end of his fingers. This was how a hunted animal felt when it heard the bloodhounds baying.

Luke smoothed his coat and noticed his hand was trembling. "Oh?"

"Don't worry," said Martha. "I covered for you. I told him Nick wasn't in and took the package. It's in on your desk."

"Thanks, Martha. I owe you."

"You certainly do."

Luke went into his office and shut the door behind him. He looked at the package sitting on his desk and felt a wild desire to lunge at the thing and rip into it.

Instead, he forced himself to go to the coatrack and hang up his coat, forced himself to walk slowly to his desk and sit down behind it. He picked up the package and examined it. It was the size of a book and wrapped in brown paper. The address read Nicholas Claus in care of Bad Boy Enterprises, and there was no return address.

He ripped off the paper and found himself staring at a dust jacket bearing a portrait of Charles Dickens. He read the title: *A Christmas Carol and Other Stories by Charles Dickens.* There was the pie in the face. No, worse. This was a brick.

Luke dropped the book. It was like staring at a murder weapon.

What did this mean? What the hell did this mean?

Of course, it could only mean one thing: That reporter was getting closer, closing in on him like a mad killer. Did he know for sure that Nicholas Claus and Luke Potter, a.k.a. Scrooge, were one in the same or was he still just guessing? Just guessing; had to be.

Luke let out a slow, calming breath. Bless Martha's middle-aged heart, she had sent Shelburne away and bought Luke some time. He only hoped she had bought him enough.

Susan threw her purse on the hall table and hung her coat over the banister, then trudged wearily into the living room to collapse on the couch. Puzzling over Nick's mysterious behavior yesterday had already weighed down her Christmas Spirit. Meeting with her lawyer today had brought it down the rest of the way and squashed it flat. Of all the bad things she could have imagined happening to her, being sued had never been one of them.

She looked at the Christmas tree Nick had brought her and felt her eyes tearing up. She wished he was sitting next to her, taking her in his arms and kissing her, making her feel secure and protected. It had been a long time since she'd felt this alone and vulnerable, not since Bill's death. And now that aloneness pressed in on her. How hard it was to fight life's battles by yourself!

You're not by yourself, she reminded herself firmly. You have a beautiful child, and Nicole and Dad and Buddy and Todd to help you. But much as she loved them all, and good as they all were to her, they weren't enough anymore. Now that she'd met Nicholas, she wanted more. *Oh, Nick, please call.*

Wait a minute. Why was she just sitting here, waiting for him to call? She knew how he felt about her. She was a modern woman, she could do something about this. So what if she didn't have his pager number? She knew where he worked. A quick glance at the clock told her she still had plenty of time until Willie got home from school.

Susan launched herself from the couch, grabbed her purse and coat and hurried out the door. The streets were slushy but drivable, and Susan took it as a sign that she was doing the right thing. Maybe she could help Nick fight his battle, whatever it was, even as he helped her face her moment of crisis.

•   •   •

Todd sat, coughing, on his couch, and punched one final key on his laptop. He read what he'd just written and chortled with glee. Oh, this was good stuff. Old bogus Nicholas Claus was about to have his sleigh tipped over. "I'll bet you're scared by now, man," he muttered. "Did you like my little present?" Still grinning, Todd shut down the computer, then reached for his phone.

It took a few rings for Nicki to answer her cell phone, and Todd envisioned her digging frantically through that saddlebag she called a purse, searching for it. Her voice was breathless when she answered, and it made his chest tighten just to hear her.

"Hey, Sugar Lips," he said. "Feel like going out for Mexican tonight?"

"Oh, yes. It seems like forever since I saw you, and I'm going through withdrawal."

Todd's grin widened. Nicole sure knew how to make a man feel like a man. "Good. I'll pick you up at work. I've got something to show you that I think you'll find interesting."

"About Nicholas?"

"Yep."

"Is he a fake?"

"He's worse than that."

"Oh, dear."

"Oh, dear is right," said Todd. "But the sooner your sister knows what scum this guy is, the easier it will be for her to get over him."

"Yeah, you're right," said Nicole, but there was something in her voice that made him feel like she wasn't so sure.

"You bet I'm right," said Todd forcefully. "I'll see you at six." He hung up and settled back among the couch cushions. "I've almost got you, guy," he murmured. "By this time next week, the whole story will be front page news. And what a story it will be!"

• • •

Luke glanced up from his work to see Ben darting past his office window like the building was on fire. What the devil was he up to now? Luke left his desk and opened his door and nearly stumbled over Martha, who was heading his way, nervously glancing over her shoulder. She turned, saw him and jumped. "What's going on?" he demanded.

Then he could hear Ben's voice from the reception area. "I think he's in Mr. Potter's office. Martha will get him for you. Can I get you a cup of coffee? Tea? How about a Coke?"

Luke peered around Martha's shoulder to see Ben turning Susan toward a chair. She was looking up at him like he was a lunatic, and if there hadn't been more than one lunatic in this office right now, Luke would have laughed.

His heart thundering, he slipped past Martha and hurried across the room, all the while wondering what on Earth Susan was doing here, hoping desperately it had nothing to do with a certain book laying on his desk. He forced a smile and said, "Susan, what are you doing here?" She turned to look at him, her cheeks blooming pink, and he realized that his greeting hadn't exactly sounded welcoming, so he added, "This is a great surprise."

Now she relaxed into a smile. I hope you don't mind me coming down. You forgot to give me your pager number."

Luke felt his cheeks warming, and was sure they now matched the color in hers. Out of the comer of his eye, he could see Ben looking on avidly and wanted to kick him. Turning his back to his brother, Luke said, "Can I buy you a coffee?"

She looked back to Luke's office as if hoping for a view of her archenemy. "Are you sure you're not too busy? Your brother said you were with Mr. Potter?"

"No, it's okay. I was just leaving some papers in his office," said Luke, and steered her toward the door. To his brother he said, "When Mr. Potter comes in tell him I'll be back in half an hour."

Ben grinned broadly. "Sure. Nick."

The last Luke saw of his brother, he had his hands stuffed in his pockets and was rocking back and forth on his feet and wearing a Cheshire Cat grin. This was providing Ben with more entertainment than a boxing match. Luke vowed that if little brother didn't stop bugging him, that was exactly what Ben was going to find himself in the middle of. Maybe he wouldn't have so much to smile about with a couple of teeth missing.

"Are you sure you can get away?" asked Susan, taking Luke's mind off his mischief-making brother.

"I can. And I'm glad you came."

"Are you? Really?"

Maybe not. Maybe he didn't want to see Susan until he'd cleaned up his mess and could come to her as a new man, one she'd be willing to share toothpaste with for the rest of her life.

But it was so good to see her face, to smell her perfume, to feel her arm cupped in his hand like it belonged there. "I'd have to be crazy not to want to see you," he said honestly. They got to the bank of elevators and he pushed the down button. "But I must admit, I'm surprised."

"I guess I was looking for some moral support," she said. "I saw my lawyer today."

So did I. Luke felt his skin burning under his shirt collar, and his stomach began to churn. He should have told Susan he couldn't get away, should have remembered an urgent phone call he had to make. The elevator opened, and he followed her into it.

"I'm going to court tomorrow," she was saying. "The judge will be deciding on whether to grant a temporary injunction against my lights. I was hoping, well . . ."

Luke watched her stumble over her words, knew what she was going to ask, and now his insides had switched from churning to spin cycle. The elevator walls began to close in on him, and he found it hard to breathe.

"I wondered if you could get away to come hold my hand."

"I wish I could, but I'm going to be out of town tomorrow. My boss is opening a new store over at the Twelve Oaks Mall and . . ." Luke ran out of steam and let the sentence fade away unfinished. He saw the disappointment on her face and hated himself.

She nodded. "Of course. I understand. I'll be fine. My dad's coming."

That would have been all Luke needed, to meet her dad under those circumstances. *Hello, sir. I'm in love with your daughter, and as soon as I'm done suing her I'd like to marry her.*

"My lawyer said I don't have to be there for this," Susan was saying, "but I can't stand not knowing what's going on. Anyway, I know Don Rawlins will be there, and your boss, I suppose."

And half the population of Angel Falls, thought Luke, all come out to boo and hiss at their resident Scrooge.

The elevator opened onto the lobby, and Luke found himself rushing them outside where he could take a deep breath of fresh air. It didn't help. Even out here the air around him stank.

He concentrated on ordering their coffee, on paying the barista, hoping the simple action would help him pretend he was just a normal man spending a few moments with the woman he loved. He watched her smile at him before sipping from her steaming cup and reminded himself that soon he'd have this whole mess cleaned up. Things would work out. He'd make them. "Are you nervous?" he asked, and then wondered what sort of masochist he was that he wanted to keep this topic alive.

She nodded. "I guess I shouldn't be. It's not like I'm on trial for murder, although if Mr. Scrooge wins this suit I could be by this time next year."

Mr. Scrooge. The name made Luke wince. "Maybe you and my boss could work out a compromise, then you wouldn't even have to go to court." Even as he said the words, he knew they were a waste of breath.

Sure enough, she was shaking her head vehemently. "I tried that. It didn't work."

"It might now. Anyway, it's the popular way to settle problems these days."

"It's not always the right way," said Susan. "Everyone isn't like you, Nick. I'll admit, I don't really know your boss, but I do know Don Rawlins. The first year he moved into the neighborhood, he was on my porch, demanding I take down my lights, and when I refused he went to the housing development's association board and made the same demand. Every year he's raised a stink at the association meetings, and when he couldn't get his way, he finally resorted to this. He's a selfish bully, and there's no negotiating with men like that. And since your boss is in cahoots with him, I can only assume that he's the same kind of man. Bullies don't negotiate. They only win or they lose."

Luke nodded. "You're right." And she was, except for one thing: He was not like Don Rawlins, not anymore.

"I didn't mean to get so intense," Susan apologized. "But thanks for letting me. I guess I just needed to let off some steam. I hope I didn't scald you in the process."

. *Only my heart.* "It's okay."

"Can I ask one more favor?" she said shyly.

"Sure."

"Well, Willie's in the Christmas play at church this Sunday night—he's a wise man—and I'd love to have you come."

Right now, feeling like the dirtiest, rottenest sneak who ever lived, church was the last place Luke wanted to be, but he'd already turned down one of Susan's requests. He couldn't bring himself to refuse another. "It's been a while since I've been in church," he said, hoping that would, somehow, let him off the hook.

"That's okay," she assured him. "This won't be painful."

This would be more painful than she could imagine, but Luke forced a smile and said, "Sure."

Now her delighted expression was like the sun, and its warmth penetrated deep into his soul, shedding the faintest glimmer of hope into the darkness.

"It's the Angel Falls Community Church," she said. "The one on the corner of Main Street and Maple."

The little, white church with the steeple, the one that always reminded Luke of Norman Rockwell. "I know the one," he said. Then inspired, he added, "How about if I take you and Willie out for Sunday dinner first?"

"That sounds great."

"I'll pick you up at one."

"The play isn't until seven," said Susan.

"Good. Because the place I have in mind is over in Deer Grove."

"Deer Grove?"

Luke nodded, and hoped fervently his mother didn't have plans for Sunday.

He saw Susan to her car and kissed her goodbye. Her lips were soft and she tasted like coffee, and he wished he could stand there all day holding her to him. But public streets weren't the place for long kisses, so he released her, promising himself that as soon as he was a new man he'd have her with him on his couch, curled up in his arms, with Michael Bolton serenading them via compact disc. "Drive carefully," he said. "The streets are still slushy."

"I will," she promised, and she sounded as breathless as he felt.

She waved at him from behind the wheel. He waved back. She pulled into traffic and he watched her drive away until she was completely out of sight, then he turned and hurried back into his office building.

When he entered the office, Ben was waiting for him, perched on Martha's desk. "Well, we've saved your hind end again, Mr. Claus," Ben called. "But who's going to save you tomorrow when it's time to go to court?"

"I won't be going," said Luke. "I'm planning on being sick."

"Don't you have to testify?" asked Martha.

"Yeah," put in Ben. "Won't your lawyer want you to explain about the missing renters?"

"I'm not necessary at this point. Anyway, they have a written statement from me, and Don will have enough gripes of his own to keep them busy for hours."

"So when are you going to tell her? You can't keep playing this game forever," said Martha. "I know I can't. My poor heart can't take much more strain."

Neither can mine, thought Luke. "I'll tell her as soon as I get the money together and can pay Don and get my name off those legal papers."

Ben shook his head. "You have got it bad, bro."

Luke ignored him and went into his office. He picked up the phone and called his mother. He didn't waste words when she answered. "Mom, I need a home-cooked meal and a great reference."

Todd picked Nicole up at six and took her to Carlos's Hacienda, their favorite restaurant. Also, the only one he could afford that didn't have a pair of golden arches over it. From the moment she'd gotten into the car, she'd been anxious to know what he'd found, but he waited until they were seated at a comer booth, fortified with margaritas.

"Okay, spill," said Nicole.

He started out humbly, saying, "Well, I made some phone calls, put some friends to work, surfed the net . . ."

"Todd, just tell me," commanded Nicole.

"Nicholas Claus's real name is Luke Potter."

"What?" she gasped.

"No doubt about it," said Todd. "I've got everything on Luke Potter from his driver's license to his business license. I even know where he went to college and the year he graduated. Now, you know what I've got on Nicholas Claus?"

She shook her head.

"Nothing. Zip. Nada, as they say here at old Carlos's place. And you know why?"

Nicole didn't say anything. Instead, she downed the last half of her margarita, then blinked owlishly at him.

"I'll tell you why," Todd continued. "It's because Nicholas Claus doesn't exist. He's bogus. Remember how you felt when your sister first told you about him? Well, babe, your instincts were right on."

"But none of that proves that Nicholas Claus and Luke Potter are one in the same," argued Nicole.

"Ah, but I'm not done yet," said Todd. "Our Nicholas Claus just happens to work at Luke Potter's business, but you never see him. And there's a reason for that." Todd pulled out the old high school yearbook that he'd gotten ahold of, saying, "Observe." He flipped to the C's. "Carlson, Chang, Collins. No Claus. But when we turn to the P's, what do we find?" He flipped the pages, then stabbed the picture of a Luke Potter. "There's our boy. Younger face, but the same color hair, same Superman chin you described. Dead ringer for your Nicholas Claus, I'll bet."

Nicole studied it, chewing her lip. "It kind of looks like him," she said at last.

"It is him," said Todd.

"How can you be so sure?" demanded Nicole. "You only saw him with sunglasses on. And I've only seen him a couple of times," she added.

Todd fell back against the fake red leather of the banquette and stared at the love of his life, hardly able to believe his ears. What on Earth was going on in that convoluted mind of hers?

Nicole stared into her empty glass like a gypsy about to read his fortune.

"Nicole, this is the guy," said Todd. "I know it and you know it."

"No, I don't," said Nicole, "and I don't want to risk my sister's happiness on a guess."

"A guess! This is first-class detective work and logical deduction," Todd protested.

"It's a guess."

Todd felt a sudden ache behind his eyes that had nothing to do with his cold. He took a swig of his drink. "Nicole, do you want this guy to take advantage of your sister?"

"No, but Susan is in love with Nick, and I want to be positive we've got the right man before you go ruining her life."

"Ruining? Wait a minute. How did I get from, 'Toddy help me.' and 'Toddy, you're brilliant,' to being the person who's ruining your sister's life?"

"That's not what I meant. I just want to be sure."

Todd held up a hand. "Okay, fine. We'll know soon enough when he shows up in court."

"And until then we don't say anything, not until we're one hundred percent sure," said Nicole. "Agreed?"

"Agreed," said Todd. *And when he does show up, we'll be sure, and Larry and his trusty camera will be there to capture it all. Old Scrooge will have no place to hide.*

Ten

Susan's dad arrived ten minutes after Willie's bus had left for school. "How are you feeling, honey?" he asked, putting an arm around her shoulder.

"Like I'm headed for a firing squad," she said.

He gave her a squeeze, then tucked a finger under her chin. "Chin up, kid. You've faced worse than this."

He was right, of course. Compared to Bill's funeral this was nothing. The thought of her dead husband brought tears to her eyes. "We have to win this, Dad. For Bill."

"We will. Now, let's go teach old man Rawlins a lesson."

Her father's comforting words settled the Mexican jumping beans in her stomach. Susan grabbed her coat, and they headed to his car arm in arm.

The Angel Falls courthouse was a small, brick building built in the thirties. Stepping inside it and seeing its worn, wood floors, its staircases with carved banisters, and elevators with fancy grillwork on the doors was like climbing inside an old movie. Courtroom A was small, with a jury box and witness stand ringed with carved rails, and the judge's bench stood high above all, looking like the judgment seat of God. The long tables for the lawyers and their clients were old and scarred, and the chairs were sturdy and thick and looked hard. Susan saw that the only concession to modern times was the padded chairs in the jury box and the equally comfortable-looking chairs provided for witnesses and the legal opponents' rooting teams.

She saw Don Rawlins standing next to one table, talking to a short man who looked like Teddy Roosevelt, and hardened her jaw. She hoped Don spent a fortune on the guy and lost this case. He was just like Mr. Potter in *It's a Wonderful Life,* and she hoped Don got every ounce of misery he deserved. And speaking of Mr. Potter, where was the mysterious Luke Potter? Running late? Or maybe he'd stopped along the way to take some little kid's candy cane from him. Well, she was no little kid, and she wouldn't be easy pickings for those two buzzards.

Her lawyer, Andrew Hawkinson was seated at his table, tiny, neat piles of papers laid out in front of him. He was jotting something on a legal pad, As if sensing her presence he looked up and turned in his chair, and she was struck again by how well his name fit him. He rose and started toward her and she half expected him to sprout huge wings and fly across the room.

"That your lawyer?" asked her dad.

"That's him."

"Impressive."

Hawkinson held out a hand to Susan. "Mrs. Carpenter, how are you doing?"

"I'm a little nervous."

"There's no need to be nervous." Andrew Hawkinson turned his attention to Susan's dad. "And this is?"

"My father, Hank Appleby."

Hawkinson nodded and shook her father's hand. "Mr. Appleby."

"Thank you for taking my daughter's case."

"My pleasure," said Hawkinson.

Susan suspected that almost any case was this man's

pleasure, that he enjoyed a fight. Good. That was the kind of man she needed to take on Don Rawlins.

"Susan!"

Susan turned to see Nicole rushing toward her. "Nicki, what are you doing here?"

"I called in sick. I couldn't let you be here by yourself." Now Nicole was looking at Hawkinson with rounded eyes. "Is this your lawyer?"

Susan had just finished introducing her sister when a familiar voice called, "Andrew, how's it going?"

Todd edged himself into the circle, and Susan saw a man with a camera dangling from his neck hovering behind him.

"Hello, Shelburne," said the lawyer, shaking hands with Todd.

"I hope you've got some good lines prepared," said Todd. "I want something hot."

Hawkinson's thin lips stretched into a smile, and Susan could see the light of battle in his eyes. "Don't worry," he said, "you'll get them." He turned to Susan. "You'll probably want to sit next to me." Motioning to a row of gray padded seats behind his table, he added, "Your family will be comfortable there."

Susan nodded. As everyone took their seat, she could hear Nicole's stage whisper, "What's that photographer doing here?"

Todd's reply, "Hey, this is news. People have contributed to Suz's defense fund. They want to know how it's going."

Susan suddenly felt exposed. She looked nervously over her shoulder and a flash from the photographer's camera momentarily blinded her. Little spots danced before her eyes, and she squinted through their shimmering curtain to see several of her neighbors filing through the door and filling up the seats reserved for witnesses and observers. Mrs. Murphy waved at her, and she smiled weakly and waved back.

She stole a glance at the opposition. Don had elected to seat himself next to his lawyer, and was looking at the man's legal notes as if he were a second-chair attorney. Don's wife sat behind him. She turned her head Susan's way and their gazes met. There was something almost pleading in Mrs. Rawlins' expression, but Susan couldn't be sure, because the older woman quickly turned away. Embarrassed to be here, thought Susan, embarrassed to be married to a monster. Poor woman.

Susan felt a touch on her shoulder and turned to see a tallish man bending over her, a man in his mid-thirties with blue eyes and a quickly receding hairline. "Buddy!" She jumped up and hugged him.

"Hey, sis," he said, "I told you I'd be here."

"You shouldn't have come all this way."

He smiled affectionately at her. "Don't be an idiot."

A door off to the side of the judge's bench opened, and the court bailiff intoned, "Court is now in session, Judge Emil Hawthorne presiding. All rise."

Susan stood and watched the man with the white hair and thick, matching eyebrows head for his throne, his black robe flapping. He had a jaw like a bulldog and wore a scowl that looked permanent pressed, and Susan felt her heart sink. This man did not look impartial; he looked like Don Rawlins's soul mate.

"Be seated," he growled, and everyone sat.

Someone cleared their throat, and Susan realized that someone was her. The room seemed overly warm, and she looked longingly at the bank of closed windows, wondering if anyone would care if she tiptoed over and opened one. Looking again at the judge, she decided it would be best to sit stone still and keep quiet. This judge probably didn't even allow sneezing in his courtroom, let alone wandering around.

The proceedings had begun, and now the Teddy Roosevelt look-alike was explaining to the judge what a hardship Susan had created for her poor, old neighbors with her lights, noise, and confusion. "My client has had access to his home nearly cut off due to the large amount of traffic that has ensued as a result of Mrs. Carpenter's excessive display."

"Objection," said Hawkinson calmly. " 'Excessive' is a very subjective term, which Mr. Melville has yet to prove."

"We intend to prove that, Your Honor," shot back Melville. "Mr. Potter's former renters are here and ready to testify as to why they vacated their home, which is right next door to Mrs. Carpenter's house."

The judge was jotting something on a legal pad and didn't look up at either lawyer. "Until such time as they do, I'll sustain Mr. Hawkinson's objection."

Susan smiled. First point to the good guys.

Melville adjusted his suitcoat and continued, "Also, Mr. Rawlins's wife's health has suffered due to an inability to sleep, which has been exacerbated by the lights on Mrs. Carpenter's house and the noise coming from the Christmas music Mrs. Carpenter broadcasts to the neighborhood. Until such time as this matter can be legally settled, we're asking for a temporary injunction to stop Mrs. Carpenter from displaying her lights and playing her music."

On hearing Luke Potter's name, Todd had searched the entire courtroom, but had seen no sign of the guy. He leaned over to Nicole and whispered, "Luke Potter's not here. Does that strike you as more than a little odd?"

"No," Nicole whispered back. "From what Susan said, he didn't have to be."

"But Susan's here. So is Rawlins. Maybe our Mr. Potter doesn't want to meet Susan face-to-face."

Nicole caught her lower lip between her teeth and said nothing.

Todd motioned over his shoulder to Larry, who was seated in back of him on his other side, and the photographer leaned forward. When he did, Todd whispered, "Go on over to Bad Boy Enterprises and see if you can catch our guy hiding out."

Larry nodded and exited. Nicole leaned over and hissed, "What did you say to him?"

"That he's wasting his time here," Todd replied.

Nicole nodded and turned her attention back to what the lawyers were saying, leaving Todd to wonder about her irrational behavior. Here he was, trying to help her sister and expose this Luke Potter for the slime he was, and Nicole was turning sentimental on him. It didn't make sense. Well, sure Suz would be hurt once she learned this guy's identity, but that wasn't Todd's fault, for crying out loud. He was just trying to do his job. He flipped the page in his tablet and started to take notes.

He had a great deal to note. The first hour was spent wrangling over traffic. Each side brought in an expert, one to testify that Susan's Christmas display was hopelessly clogging the streets, another to show two alternate routes through the housing development. It took even longer to discuss Mrs. Rawlins's mysterious ailment. Under Hawkinson's grilling, her doctor admitted that he had sent her to a sleep specialist before the Rawlinses ever moved in across from Susan. Melville produced the sleep specialist, who theorized that the noise from across the street could be exacerbating Mrs. Rawlins's sleep problems. But Hawkinson made mincemeat of him in short order when he pointed out to the judge that Susan's lights and music were always off by ten o'clock at night.

"Mrs. Rawlins is not currently employed," concluded Hawkinson, "so she is well able to make up for lost sleep by sleeping in mornings."

"The bus stops to pick up middle-school students almost in front of their house at seven-thirty in the morning," protested Melville.

Judge Hawthorne raised a bushy eyebrow at Melville, whose ruddy complexion turned the color of the courthouse bricks. "Mr. Melville, surely you can do better than that."

Todd chortled and the judge glared his direction. "I'll have order in my courtroom or see it cleared," he snarled. Todd's smile did a quick vanishing act.

The lawyers wrangled some more and finally ran out of steam at eleven-fifty. The judge glanced at the clock on the wall. "We'll break for lunch and resume at one-thirty,"

Todd set down his pen and stretched his cramped fingers. This was great stuff. He wondered how Larry was faring.

Larry Broom had found no one worth bothering with at Bad Boy Enterprises, but having almost as much initiative as Todd, he got creative, stopping by a pay phone booth on his way to his car and looking up Potter in the phone book. River View Drive, eh. Maybe he'd just take a little drive over to the other side of the tracks and camp out. Luke Potter might just decide to come home for a visit.

Luke spent the morning working at the new store, helping the manager, Steve, and his two new employees set out the last of the inventory for the grand opening the following day. Luke was pleased with the job Steve was doing. The man was dedicated, hardworking, and knew computers.

Steve's very pregnant wife, Jenny, had stopped by, and the way the two of them had looked at each other had made Luke's heart catch. If he got his act together, that could be Susan and him.

At noon, he'd left a message with Melville's secretary, instructing the lawyer to call him as soon as he got back from court. Now he drove home, the burger he'd had for lunch sitting on his stomach like a whole side of beef. He turned onto River View Drive and decided to call

Melville's office one more time. It was nearly two. Surely it didn't take that long to decide whether to allow a temporary injunction or not.

"I'm sorry, Mr. Potter," said the secretary. "He hasn't checked in yet."

"Okay," said Luke. "Thanks." He shut off his cell phone and pulled into the condo's parking garage.

He didn't think much about the strange car in the space next to his, not until he was out of his car and halfway to the elevator and someone called his name. He turned to look and, too late, noticed that the car had an occupant, and the occupant had a camera, and the camera was flashing.

"Hey!" hollered Luke.

The man gunned his engine and shoved the car in reverse as Luke ran toward him. Then he peeled out and swerved past Luke like a stunt driver in a B movie.

Luke slammed a hand on the trunk of the nearest car and swore. That reporter from the *Clarion* had finally nailed him good. Once Susan saw his picture in the paper minus his sunglasses it was all over.

Judge Hawthorne didn't look any happier for having had a lunch break. He frowned down equally on both lawyers from his Olympian perch, and Susan found it impossible to tell whose side he would take. "In spite of everything you've told me, Mr. Melville," he said, "this does not strike me as an emergency. Your temporary injunction is denied. I'm going to set a date for a hearing on the motion for a permanent injunction for January fifth, at ten o'clock."

Susan barely heard the rest of the judge's words. "Denied" was ringing through her head, making her nearly dizzy.

"All rise," intoned the court's bailiff, and it was all she could do not to jump up.

"We did it!" squealed Nicole after the judge had left,

grabbing Susan by the shoulders and jumping up and down.

Then Dad was hugging her, and Buddy was pressing in to give her a squeeze, saying, "I never doubted it for a minute, sis."

Mr. Hawkinson turned around and stepped forward. Susan grabbed his hand and shook it. "Oh, thank you."

"Don't thank me yet. This is only the first round."

"But we have a good chance, don't we?" pressed Todd.

"Yes, I think so," said Hawkinson, "but don't quote me."

"I wasn't sure with that judge," said Susan.

The lawyer smiled, and his expression looked positively sly. "You might like to drive by Judge Hawthorne's house sometime this Christmas. He has rather an impressive display himself."

"Did you know that?" asked Nicole.

Hawkinson didn't answer. Instead, he said, "Merry Christmas, Mrs. Carpenter."

"Thank you," said Susan, "and Merry Christmas to you, too."

She and her entourage stood silent for a moment, watching Hawkinson wind his way through the press of people. "Who was that masked man?" joked Todd, making the others grin.

"I'd say this calls for a celebration," said Susan. "How about everyone coming over to my house for eggnog punch?"

"Good idea," said Buddy. "I haven't had a chance to see Willie in ages."

Susan consulted her watch. "He's probably at his friend's house by now, but I'll bet once he hears Uncle Buddy is over he'll be home in a shot."

It took some time to exit the courtroom, as Susan had plenty of friends and neighbors who wanted to congratulate her. Out of the comer of her eye, she saw a glowering Don Rawlins slipping out the door with his wife in tow. She noticed that the woman's lips were pressed so tightly together the skin around them was white, and she suddenly felt very sorry for Mrs. Rawlins. It couldn't be easy being married to such a bitter, grumpy man. Susan couldn't help but wonder why the woman stayed. Money, she supposed. People did a lot of dumb things for money.

Susan's speculation on the Rawlinses' relationship was interrupted by Mrs. Murphy, who grabbed her by the arm and gave her a hug. "I'll bet Santa's celebrating at the North Pole right now!" she declared. "This proves the Christmas Spirit is alive and well in Angel Falls."

"May I quote you on that?" asked Todd.

Mrs. Murphy nodded. "You sure can."

At three-thirty Luke finally heard from Melville. "We didn't get our temporary injunction," he said, "but I suppose that doesn't bother you."

"It doesn't bother me at all," Luke admitted. "As soon as I get the money to pay back that old miser I want my name off everything."

"All right, Luke, but I really think we can win this. Hawthorne isn't about to make a decision that will show him in a bad light this time of year, and all anyone wants to think about right now is their office Christmas party, but it will be a different story come January."

"I hope you're wrong," said Luke. "You'll be hearing from me."

He hung up and phoned Susan. When she answered, her voice sounded so light she could have been dancing on the ceiling.

"Well, how did it go?" he asked.

"No temporary injunction. I wish you could have been there. My lawyer was fabulous. He tied the other man up in knots."

Luke breathed a sigh of relief, then made a mental note to switch lawyers. "So your lights stay on?"

"For this Christmas anyway. We don't go to court again until January."

"I thought about you," he said.

"All those good thoughts must have helped."

Luke could hear a burble of background voices. "Sounds like you're celebrating."

"My family's over," she said.

He could picture her there, surrounded by her loved ones, her face flushed with happiness. He thought of the photographer, and saw his picture plastered in tomorrow's paper and then felt the bowling ball in his gut settling deeper. "I'd better let you go," he said.

"Okay. See you Sunday?"

"Sure," he lied. After tomorrow she'd never want to see him again.

"Another well-wisher?" asked Todd.

"It was Nick," said Susan. "He called to see how things went."

"I kinda thought he'd be in court today to offer moral support."

Susan shook her head. "He couldn't. He had business out of town."

"Too bad. I was hoping to meet him."

"You will," she said. "He's coming to Willie's Christmas program Sunday night."

"Cool," said Todd.

Luke tossed fitfully most of the night. When he finally entered dreamland, it was to find a host of Christmas characters waiting for him at the gates. The plastic angel from Susan's roof shook her head at him and told him that she was very disappointed in him. Marley's ghost, looking twice as horrible as Dickens had described him, staggered up to Luke and draped a heavy chain over his neck that brought him to his knees. Santa was there, too, and beaned him on the head with a lump of coal. And in a corner was Dr. Seuss's Grinch, doubled up with laughter. Ebenezer Scrooge came up to him and clapped him on the back, saying, "They've got a new whipping boy now."

"No," cried Luke, trying to tear off the chain. "No!"

He woke up to find himself sitting up with his blanket over his head, his bedsheet wrapped around his legs. He threw off the blanket, wiped his wet forehead, and ran his fingers through his hair. It felt like he'd just toweled off from a shower, and his heart was pumping as if he'd finished a marathon. He looked at the clock. Five A.M.

He swung his legs over the bed and took a deep breath. Coffee was what he needed. Coffee laced with brandy. Maybe then he could face the morning paper.

At six he drove to the local convenience store and bought a copy of the *Clarion*, opening it as soon as he got in his car. As he'd expected, Susan's day in court had made the front page. THE SPIRIT OF CHRISTMAS IS ALIVE AND WELL IN ANGEL FALLS proclaimed the headline.

Luke quickly scanned the article. It covered the legal beagles' battle in great detail, and next to it was a picture of Susan in the courtroom, looking over her shoulder. She looked a little dazed, but beautiful. Luke bit his lip and searched for his mug shot. Nothing on the front page. "See page six for related story."

He flipped to page six, tearing the paper in his haste. There was no picture of him there, either, just interviews with Susan's friends and well-wishers. He searched the rest of the paper and found nothing.

He rubbed his chin thoughtfully. The guy who took his picture was the same photographer who had harrassed him earlier, no doubt about it. So, why didn't he make the morning paper? Other than one sentence saying that he hadn't been in court, there was no mention of him.

Something was fishy here. What was that reporter up to?

It didn't matter. He was going to Susan's right now. He'd find a way to explain everything to her so it made sense, so she understood how he'd gotten caught by Don. He'd explain that, like Scrooge, he'd changed and knew how to celebrate Christmas. And she'd understand, no matter what that cretin at the paper wrote.

He was reaching for his cell phone to let her know he was coming over when it rang. Who would be calling him at six A.M. on a Saturday? Feeling like a man who had just picked up a live snake, he, activated the phone and said a cautious hello.

"Mr. Potter," said a sober voice, "this is Andy Wells over at the Twelve Oaks Mall. I'm afraid we've had some trouble."

Eleven

"Trouble?" stammered Luke. It had to be big trouble if the manager of the mall was calling him at this hour of the morning.

"Grandma's Cookie Jar had a fire early this morning," said Wells. "The way our sprinkler system is set up, your store is in the same zone as theirs, and I'm afraid the heat set off its sprinklers."

Luke felt sick. PC Edge was right next door to the cookie place, the first store shoppers saw as they left the food area. A prime location, normally. "My computers," he said weakly. Oh, Lord. All that work, all that money. All those plans, gone up in smoke. Literally.

"Just be glad you're insured," said Wells. "I know you had your grand opening scheduled," he continued, "but, well, I'm just real sorry. If you can get out here as soon as possible, we'll start taking care of the necessary paperwork."

Now? Now, when he was having the biggest personal crisis of his life? Business emergencies were like animals; they didn't understand boundaries, especially when no boundaries had ever been set before. Anyway, this was more than an emergency. This was his life unravelling. He took a deep breath in an effort to calm himself. "Okay," he said. "I'll be there as soon as possible."

He hung up and drove a hand through his hair. He could just imagine the mess at the store. And what was that going to do to his chances of getting the money he needed to get free of Don?

He phoned his manager. Steve answered on the fourth ring, his voice sounding panicked. Wells must have already gotten to him. "Steve, it's Luke."

"Luke?" Steve sounded distracted. "Oh, Luke. Hi. Listen, I've got a problem."

"I know," said Luke. "I just talked to Andy."

"Wells?" Steve sounded puzzled. "What's wrong at the mall?"

"You haven't heard?"

"I've been a little busy. Jenny's gone into labor, and we're on our way to the hospital."

"Great," muttered Luke.

"What's the matter?"

"There was a fire at the Grandma's Cookie Jar, and it set off the sprinklers.

"Oh, no," said Steve, his voice sounding even more hysterical. "Somebody's got to get over there."

And Luke knew who that somebody was going to be. "Don't worry. I'm on my way out. You just get your wife to the hospital."

"Thanks," said Steve. "I'll come help out as soon as everything's under control."

"Don't worry about it," said Luke. "Ben and I can handle things for a few days."

He hung up, then punched Ben's number. He would have to get to the mall and deal with insurance reports and paperwork, but there was no reason why little brother couldn't come out and push around a Shop-Vac.

After six rings, a recorded voice said, "Hi. You've

reached Ben Potter. Sorry I can't come to the phone right now, but you know what to do. Call ya later."

Luke waited for the long series of beeps to come to an end, drumming his fingers on the steering wheel. "Ben, are you there?" he demanded. Stupid. Of course Ben wasn't home. "Look, as soon as you get home, get out to the new store. We've got major trouble, and I'm going to need your help."

He hung up the phone and slammed the steering wheel with the palm of his hand. There was no way he'd be able to talk to Susan now. Well, if he hurried, maybe he could get over to her place by dinner. He'd stop and pick up Chinese food on the way. He punched in the number of his insurance man and floored the gas.

In spite of what the manager had told him, nothing had prepared Luke for the mess he found at his new PC Edge store. Smoke from next door still hung in the air like a ghost. Inside, mall employees were already trying to deal with water that was standing two inches thick, the crepe paper streamers Luke's employees had draped carousel style on the ceiling had fallen and now hung straight and lifeless, dripping green and reminding him of a Florida swamp. And his computers, all his beautiful computers. Luke ran a shaking hand through his hair. He wanted to sit down and cry. Instead, he yanked the sopped GRAND OPENING SATURDAY sign from the window and threw it on the floor.

Okay, Potter, just get to work he told himself. Setting his jaw, he pulled off his jacket and tossed it over the counter next to the cash register. The sooner he got done, the sooner he could get to Susan.

The morning was filled with reports to write, people to talk to, and ruined inventory to check. At eleven, Luke still hoped to see Ben, but by noon his hope was fading fast. By two o'clock, it was dead. At three o'clock, he finally left the store, feeling like a climber nearing the top of Mount Everest, barely able to breathe or put one foot in front of the other. He climbed into his car, rolled the window down and turned the radio up full blast to keep himself awake and headed for home.

When he finally dragged through his front door, his answering machine was flashing. He punched the play button and Ben's voice said, "Hey, bro. I'm at the store. Where are you? It smells, but it doesn't look bad. I guess that means you got everything taken care of, so I'm heading over to Chuck's place to watch the game. I'll check in with you tomorrow and see what else needs to be done."

"Thanks," muttered Luke, and headed for the shower.

As soon as he got out, he called Susan, but got her baby-sitter instead. "She just left for her office Christmas party," said the girl. "Can I take a message?"

Great. With a baby-sitter there was no need to come home early, so who knew when Susan would be back. Still, how late could she stay out? "Tell her Nick called," said Luke and hung up. He'd give her until midnight, then he'd try again.

Hank was at Celeste's house promptly at five-thirty, whistling as he walked briskly up her front walk. He felt like he was seventeen again, like he could run a marathon. And now, with Susan's troubles well on the way to being settled he could enjoy his courtship of Celeste with a clear conscience.

He rang the doorbell and heard a muffled, "Just a minute," from the other side.

Celeste met him in her bathrobe, a sight that made visions of the sugar plums—the big boy version—dance through his head.

"I'm almost ready," she said. "I just need to slip on my dress. Come on in and make yourself at home."

Hank supposed that invitation didn't extend to helping her out of her bathrobe, but right now he couldn't think of anything he'd rather do. Celeste was already halfway down the hall, so he settled for sauntering into the living room toward that comfortable recliner chair in the corner he'd claimed on his last visit.

He stopped to pick up the double picture frame from the fireplace mantel. Two young men smiled out at him. Handsome boys, thought Hank. One had a square chin and dark hair, and looked a little like a candidate for a television Superman, the teen version. The other one's coloring wasn't so dark, but his features were perfect, and something about his smile said mischief-maker.

"There. How's that for speedy?"

Hank set the pictures back and turned around. He liked what he saw. Celeste had changed into a turquoise dress made of some sort of knit fabric that gently held her curves, just like he wanted to do. She wore a silver chain around her neck and silver earrings glinted in her ears. The whole look was elegant and sophisticated. "You look great," he said simply.

She walked over to him and linked her arms through his. "Thank you. I see you've met my boys. Those are their high school graduation pictures."

"Good looking kids," said Hank.

"They're good kids, too," she said proudly.

"They'd have to be, considering the mother they've got."

"Well, they're not perfect," she admitted.

"Who is?" said Hank. "I'm starved. Shall we go?"

She nodded and headed for the closet to get her coat. Hank helped her into it and found he couldn't resist the urge to wrap his arms around her and plant a kiss on her neck. *Chanel Number Five, the sexiest perfume ever made.* "You smell good enough to eat."

"Not before dinner, you'll spoil your appetite."

He chuckled and opened the door for her.

They found plenty to talk about at dinner. Hank had put in a couple of days at his friend's store, and already had a wealth of stories to tell. Sporting events, he called them. "My favorite event so far," he said, breaking off a piece of a crusty, sourdough roll, "was the lady who took a practice swing with one of the tennis racquets and almost took off some poor guy's nose following through on her backhand."

Celeste put her hand to her mouth and laughed, a good hearty laugh that warmed Hank's soul. "Sounds like a dangerous place to me," she said. "I hope you've got liability coverage."

Their waiter appeared to ask if they wanted dessert.

"Not me," said Celeste. "I've been eating too much of my Christmas baking. And none for you, either," she told Hank. "I've got a whole plate of cookies waiting at home for you."

Home-baked cookies, he thought, and grinned. *You know a woman's in love with you when she bakes for you.* But, of course, he'd already known that for some time. They both had.

From the restaurant, they headed for the Eagles Club, where they danced away the next three hours. "Would you like to take the long way home and look at Christmas lights?" asked Hank, starting the car.

"That sounds wonderful. I haven't done that since the boys were little."

"We used to go every year," Hank said. "And after the girls moved out, Bethie and I . . ." Unexpectedly, strong emotion grabbed him by the throat, leaving him unable to finish his sentence.

Celeste reached across the seat and laid a comforting hand on his arm. He patted her hand with his. "If you'd rather, we can just go back to my place," she said.

He shook his head. "No. I'd really like to do this. I've kind of missed it, you know?"

"There's a neighborhood just a couple of miles to the west that has some lovely displays."

In less than ten minutes they were driving slowly past houses decked in red and green lights. Santas waved at them from rooftops, and one house had lit candy canes strung all along its fence.

"That one's nice," said Hank.

"Look down there," said Celeste, pointing to a house trimmed with tiny gold lights. The trees in the yard shone with the same small lights, and the picket fence was hung with cedar bows and plastic red ribbons.

"Yeah, that's nice," Hank agreed. "You should see my daughter's place. She really goes all out, has people coming from all over just to see it."

"Really."

"Yeah. She's even got a live manger scene in the front yard."

"My goodness! She really does get in the spirit."

"Oh, yeah. They call her Suzi Christmas."

"Suzi Christmas?"

"You've probably read about her in the papers," said Hank. "She's the woman who's being sued."

"I have."

Hank shook his head. "I know it sounds prejudiced since it is my daughter, but I can't imagine somebody going and doing something like that to a woman, and a widow, too, for crying out loud." "Mmm," said Celeste, her voice distant.

Hank stole a glance at her and saw she was looking out the window. He supposed he'd gone on enough about Susan. After all, it was still too early in the relationship to bring the kids into it. Anyway, he didn't want to talk anymore. There was only one thing he wanted to do.

He parked the car under a huge maple, facing the house with the gold lights and turned off the engine. "But enough about our kids, huh? Here we are alone, the luckiest man in the world and the most beautiful woman." He reached over and put an arm around Celeste's shoulder, drawing her to him.

She came, and he could tell by the tears sparkling in her eyes that she felt as lucky as he did. She cupped his chin in her hands like he was something precious. Him, Hank Appleby. He felt like he'd swallowed the moon. Two wonderful women in one lifetime. God had been good to him.

He kissed her with all the tenderness he could muster, but it wasn't long before he was pushing past tender and ready to deepen the kiss. It seemed like he'd just gotten started when she pulled away. "What is it?" he asked, confused.

"I'm so sorry, Hank," she said.

"What? Aren't you feeling good?"

She shook her head. "I think you'd better take me home."

"Sure," he said, and started the car. Maybe the salmon she'd had at dinner was bad. "I hope it wasn't the dinner," he said.

She shook her head. "No, it's not my stomach." She pressed her fingers into her forehead.

Headache. Poor kid. Hank reached over and rubbed her shoulder, then started the car.

A profound silence seemed to have settled over the car, and Hank felt himself at a loss for how to fill it. He glanced over at Celeste. She had her head laid back against the headrest and her eyes pressed shut. He could see lines of strain around her eyes, as if she were fighting off pain. He'd never seen a headache come on so suddenly. "Do you get these headaches often?" he asked.

She didn't really answer him, and he gave up the idea of bothering her and, instead, slipped a cassette of Christmas music in the tape player.

Back at her house, he walked the still silent Celeste to her front door. "Get a good night's sleep," he whispered, then kissed her on the cheek.

"Thanks," she said, then stumbled into the house and shut the door.

Hank slowly walked back toward his car, fighting off the selfish disappointment at having their evening together so abruptly ended. There'll be other evenings, he told himself.

Hot tears escaped from the corner of Celeste's eyes, and she rubbed her throbbing forehead. A good night's sleep? That was going to be impossible. Oh, Luke, of all the people in the world, why did you have to pick Hank Appleby's daughter to sue?

As if Hank might still, somehow, be able to hear her, she walked into the kitchen, attempting to keep the sea of emotion dammed up by allowing only a whimper out, and grabbed the spare bottle of aspirin she kept in the cupboard. When she turned to get a glass she saw the plate of Christmas cookies she'd made for Hank sitting on the counter and the dam burst.

Nine-thirty. Luke hadn't felt a night drag by this slowly since that blind date he'd had with the nine-foot-tall basketball queen in his sophomore year of high school. His eyes felt like someone had poured ground glass in them, and a dull ache was starting behind his eyeballs. He slumped down on the couch, settling his head on the cushions and letting the mindless noise of the action movie on the television wash over him. He wouldn't wait until midnight to call Susan, he'd try at ten. Meanwhile, he'd just rest his eyes. Just rest . . . just . . .

Susan hummed as she pulled into the driveway. The babysitter had long since turned off the lights and music, and the street was quiet. Susan hoped not too many kids had come looking for Mrs. Claus to give them a candy cane.

Her company party had been a success, thanks to the uncle of one of her singers, who managed Wellington's, a new restaurant in town with a British pub flavor. He had given them a private room for free, and a good deal on drinks and hors d'oeuvres, and in return Susan and her employees had serenaded the customers with Christmas carols in four-part harmony. He had been so pleased, he'd talked with her about hiring her Dickens Carolers for the weekends next December. After consuming the fancy cake Susan had brought for dessert, they'd all stayed and danced.

She had told the baby-sitter she'd be home by eleven and here it was midnight. Hopefully, Megan wouldn't mind.

She found the girl asleep on the couch in front of the TV and shook her gently by the shoulder, whispering, "You can go home now, Megan."

Megan shot up. "Oh, my gosh. Mrs. Carpenter, you scared me."

"I'm sorry I'm so late," said Susan, digging in her wallet. "I hope an extra ten will make it up to you."

"You bet," said the girl, taking the money and stuffing it in her jeans pocket.

"How was Willie?"

"Great as always. And a man called for you."

"Oh?" Susan kept her voice casual, but her heart was thumping excitedly.

"Somebody named Nick."

"Did he leave a message?"

Megan shook her head. "Just said to tell you he called."

"Okay, thanks."

Susan smiled as she watched the teenager climb into her car. She was going to see Nick tomorrow, so there was no reason for him to call. Unless he'd just wanted to hear the sound of her voice. She knew she wanted to hear his. Tomorrow seemed a hundred years away, just like Christmas morning had when she was a little girl. Tomorrow will come soon enough, she told herself, and remembered her mother telling her those same words on Christmas Eve. She sighed happily and headed off to bed, hoping for pleasant dreams.

Luke slowly climbed out of the gray fog and rubbed his eyes. The local station was displaying a test pattern, which made him sit up and look at his watch. Three A.M.! He punched a sofa pillow. Of all the rotten luck! That paper would be on Susan's porch this morning, this time with his picture in it for sure. And he still hadn't seen her, hadn't had a chance to explain.

But he would. He'd get over there and steal the damned newspaper off her front porch, then he'd wake her up and tell her everything. He went to his bedroom, set his alarm for five A.M., then laid down hoping to find a little sleep before his big ordeal. Instead, he tossed and turned, and checked the clock every twenty minutes.

At five-thirty, eyes still feeling gritty, he was parking his car in front of Susan's house. He opened the door and got out, shutting it quietly behind him. Feeling a little like a burglar, he let himself through the front gate and stole up to her porch.

No paper. She either didn't have it delivered, or the paperboy hadn't come by yet. Luke decided not to take any chances. He went back to his car and settled down to wait.

Fifteen minutes later, he was wakened from his doze by a flashing, blue light. Wide eyed, he turned to see a face in his car window—a frowning face with a blue policeman's cap sitting on top of it. The cop tapped on Luke's window, and he let it down.

"Are you having a problem, sir?" asked the nice policeman.

"Uh, no. No, officer. I just fell asleep."

"Fell asleep? I see. Step out of the car, sir. I'd like to have you take a sobriety test."

"Sobriety? I haven't been drinking. I was just . . ." What did he say now? *I was just waiting for the paperboy to show so I could steal my neighbor's newspaper?* "I have not been drinking, officer. I just came by to check on my rental property." He pointed to his vacant house. "I own that place."

The cop jerked his head in the direction Luke had pointed. "That place next to Suzi Christmas's house?"

"Yes."

Now a look came over the officer's face that Luke didn't like at all. "Wait a minute. Are you that Scrooge character?"

"Umm."

The cop looked like he'd just bitten the head off a chicken. "I ought to give you a ticket just for breathing. Get out of here before I run you in."

Luke clamped his lips shut and started his car. He pulled away from the curb slowly, driving like a model citizen. As he did, he saw the paperboy coming down the street from the opposite direction. Okay, he'd circle the block and come back.

But circling the block was not an option, because the nice policeman followed him all the way home.

Fuming, Luke pulled into his parking garage, wishing that he had the morning paper delivered instead of getting his news off the Internet. He almost shut his car off, then changed his mind and pulled back out. The cop would be gone by now. He'd try again.

He'd barely gone a block when the blue lights flashed behind him once more and he had to pull over.

Mr. Nice Policeman came to his window and asked, "Are you lost?"

"This is police harassment," said Luke.

"I hope you're not on your way back to bug Mrs. Carpenter again," said the cop.

"No. I'm on my way to get a paper. I hope that's not against the law."

"No law against that," agreed the policeman. "I'll just follow you to make sure you find your way."

"Thank you, officer," said Luke with as much dignity as he could muster.

The policeman not only followed Luke to the convenience store, he came inside and bought himself a cup of coffee as well. "I hear your case isn't going real well," he said as Luke paid for his paper.

Luke glared at him. "This is harassment."

"Hey, I'm just making conversation."

"Well, I don't like to talk until I've had my first cup of coffee in the morning."

The cop shrugged. "Maybe you should stay home and drink it."

Luke marched back to his car, aware of Officer Friendly strolling along behind him. "Policemen are your friends," his mother used to say. Well, this cop was somebody's friend all right, but not Luke's. He threw the paper into his Lexus, climbed in after it, and headed back to the condo.

As soon as he had his car parked, he had the dome light on and the paper open. He stared at page one in shock. Nothing. He flipped through the thing, searching for the telltale picture of Mr. Scrooge caught entering his lair, but it was nowhere. Maybe it hadn't turned out.

A slow smile grew on Luke's face. He was out of the woods. At least for today. He'd be able to take Susan to meet his mom. Mom would put in a good word for him, tell Susan what a great son he was. Then they'd go to Willie's Christmas play, and, afterward, he'd take her home, and as soon as Willie was in bed he'd make his confession to Susan.

Larry Broom searched the *Clarion,* but his picture was nowhere to be found. Todd had loved it. He had said Larry's picture, combined with the hard-hitting exposé he was writing, would be Pulitzer material. They could both write their own ticket after this came out. Well, that was Friday, and there was nothing in Saturday's paper, and now nothing in today's. What was going on?

He picked up the phone and dialed Todd.

"Hello?" said a sleepy voice.

Larry didn't waste words on greetings. "Where's the story?" he demanded.

"Wha . . . Larry, do you know what time it is? This is Sunday morning, for crying out loud."

"Yeah, it's Sunday, and I still haven't seen my picture."

"You'll see it, don't worry. The story's in my computer at work, ready to go. I think I'm going to be catching our boy with his pants down tonight, and I want to see if I can get a quote to go with it."

"Okay," said Larry reluctantly. "That's a great picture, Todd. I had to wait three hours to get it."

"I know, Lar. Patience, okay? It'll be worth the wait. I promise."

"Okay," said Larry, and hung up. He'd give Todd until tomorrow. Just tomorrow.

Twelve

Luke knew he was a full fifteen minutes early when he rang Susan's doorbell, but nervous energy had finally driven him out the door, making him unable to wait any longer to see her.

She opened her door, wearing a cream-colored, knit dress. Her jewelry was simple: a gold chain and matching bracelet, and her hair was drawn back with a tortoiseshell clip to show small, pearl earrings in her ears.

She looked so feminine and soft and enchanting, Luke wanted to scoop her up in his arms and carry her off to her bedroom right then and there. He could imagine what the room looked like: lace curtains at the windows and a floral spread on her bed, and lots of fancy, lace-trimmed pillows. He could picture her laying among those pillows, her arms stretching up to him, her hair spread out like a golden ribbon, waiting to curl around his hands.

"Hi, Nick," piped Willie, dragging Luke out of his daydream and into another, one that pictured him and Susan and Willie, the perfect family, tooling down the road in a minivan to pay his mom a Sunday afternoon visit.

He smiled at the pleasant image and rumpled the boy's hair.

"I'm going to be a wise man in the Christmas play tonight," said Willie, jumping up and down.

"I know," said Luke. "I'm coming to watch you."

"I have a line to say," Willie volunteered. "I bring gold, man's greatest treasure," he intoned, his childish voice attempting a man's baritone.

"Sounds like you've got your part down real well."

"And we're going to have cookies and hot chocolate afterward," Willie continued. "And candy canes. Mom said I can stay up late."

Great, thought Luke. He had a vision of himself trying to make his confession to Susan with Willie bouncing off the walls and all around them.

"Not too late," said Susan, and Luke breathed in inward sigh of relief. She smiled at Luke. "Maybe you wouldn't mind bringing us back home before the play. That way I can get Willie's costume."

"No problem."

"We can take two cars if you like," she offered, "then you won't have to bring us home after the play."

"But I want to," he said. "There's something I need to talk to you about."

She looked at him questioningly, but there was no way he was going to ruin a perfect day by fessing up now. Besides, he needed one more opportunity to show himself in as good a light as possible.

"It can wait," he said, wishing he could keep the nasty moment that loomed in his future waiting forever. If only he hadn't been such a greedy, hard-hearted snake, he wouldn't be in this mess now.

"Okay," said Susan. "If you're sure."

"I'm sure."

"Well, then, maybe we'll just take the costume with us. That way I won't have to inconvenience you."

"Nothing you could ask would be an inconvenience," said Luke, and she blushed.

It made him smile. How he loved seeing her cheeks tinged that delicate shade, loved to watch the play of thick lashes on creamy skin when she lowered her eyes in embarrassment.

He fished in his pocket and pulled out an ornament-sized box. "I brought you something."

"You shouldn't have," she said.

"I wanted to," said Luke, proffering it.

Willie was dancing from one foot to the other. "Can I open it?"

"No," said his mother firmly. "You may watch." She opened the little box, then fished in the tissue paper and pulled out a small, ceramic angel with a blue gown and gold-tipped wings. "Oh," she breathed. "It's lovely."

"It looks like the angel on our roof," said Willie.

Susan looked up at Luke, and he tried to memorize that adoring expression. "It reminded me of you," he said.

They stood there looking at each other, the moment hanging in time like a golden Christmas ball.

Willie broke it. "When are we going?"

"Right now," said Luke, and opened the door for them.

The ride to his mom's was an experience. Willie squirmed in his seat and kept up a steady chatter all the way. Luke wondered if he'd been this wired at Willie's age. He decided he probably had, especially at Christmas, because when he was Willie's age Christmas was still a magical time of hope and dreams come true. As they drove, Luke found himself catching Willie's excitement. Okay, so the last twenty or so Christmases hadn't been great. That could change. Anything could happen.

Celeste met them at the door, dressed casually in jeans and a sweater. Luke noticed that her eyes were red, and she seemed subdued. He hoped she wasn't sick.

She held out a hand to Susan. "Hello, Susan. I've been hearing wonderful things about you. It's nice to meet you."

"It's nice to meet you, Mrs. Claus," said Susan.

His mom's smile flickered, and for a moment Luke thought it was going to die, but she rallied. "Please, call me Celeste." She bent to put her face at Willie's level. "And who is this?"

"This is my son, Willie," said Susan.

"Hello there, Willie. You're a handsome fellow."

"Are you Nick's grandma?" asked Willie.

"No. I'm his mother, and he was once as small as you."

Willie looked up at Luke as if he found the concept hard to fathom.

I know," said Celeste with a sigh. "Sometimes I can't believe he's all grown up, either." She straightened and said to Susan, I hope you like ham."

"Love it," said Susan.

They trooped into the living room, Willie bouncing with every step. Once settled on the couch, Susan reached into the satchel she'd been carrying and pulled out one of those tablets like Luke had played with as a child.

"A Magic Slate," he said. I didn't know they still made those."

Willie was already hard at work with the red, plastic pencil, drawing faces. As if feeling the need to demonstrate how his toy worked, he flipped up the transparent top sheet and the faces disappeared. Luke wished it could be that easy with his past. Just flip the sheet, and no more Mr. Scrooge.

They visited for awhile, then his mom disappeared into the kitchen, and Susan called, "May I help you with something?"

Celeste's head appeared around the doorway. "Perhaps you wouldn't mind putting ice in the glasses."

"Sure," said Susan, and left Luke for the kitchen.

He could hear them out there talking, and was dying to know what they were saying, but he forced himself to stay seated and keep Willie company. He hoped his mom was putting in a good word for him.

Susan appeared with a tray of glasses filled with ice and began setting them on the table.

"Luke, would you like to come cut the ham?" called his mom.

Luke's stomach tightened into a steel ball. Susan looked questioningly at him, and he felt sweat beads forming on his forehead. He shrugged helplessly. "It's my middle name," he improvised.

"Poor man," she said.

He got off the couch, forced himself to walk calmly toward the kitchen. "Why do you say that?" he asked, already knowing the answer.

"Because that nasty Luke Potter has contaminated your name."

Luke heard a thump come from the kitchen, followed by a cry of dismay. He hurried in to find his mother, bending over their dinner ham. She looked up at him, her eyes bleak. "It just slipped . . . off the platter," she finished as Susan came into the room.

"It's okay, Mom," said Luke.

"We can rinse it off and no harm done," added Susan. "It looks too good to waste."

Luke helped his mom scoop up the ham and carried it over to the sink for her.

"If you've got a damp towel or something, I can do mop patrol," Susan offered.

His mother was looking flustered. "Oh, yes, of course.

She wet a towel and squirted it with dish soap, handing it over to Susan, who smiled and said, "You have no idea how at home this makes me feel. Things like this were always happening in my family."

Celeste gave her a distracted smile. "Yes, of course. Thank you."

Willie put in an appearance. "What happened?"

"That ham just didn't want to be eaten," said Susan.

"It tried to get away by jumping off the platter, but we caught it."

Willie giggled, then said, "I'm hungry."

"Well, as soon as . . . Nicholas slices the meat, we can eat," said Celeste.

Once they were settled at the table, Celeste said to Susan, "I hear you're quite a celebrity."

Luke looked at his mother in amazement. What was she doing bringing up this topic? Here she was supposed to be singing his praises, and instead she was leading them down the path that led to his dark side.

Susan's cheeks were turning rosy. "Well, I'm not sure I'm famous in a very positive way lately. All this squabbling at a time when we should be celebrating has been hard." She smiled at Luke. "Your son has made it all easier."

Luke was aware of his mother studying him, and felt his own cheeks warming.

"My son is a good man, really. I'm afraid the holidays weren't always good to him when he was a boy. His father and I separated at Christmas."

This was doing no good whatsoever, and it was downright embarrassing. "Mom."

She raised innocent eyebrows at him. "Yes, dear?"

"I'm sure Susan doesn't want to hear all this."

"Perhaps not," said his mother. "I guess I only brought it up because sometimes knowing about a person's past experiences can help you better understand that person's present behavior." She looked to Susan. "Don't you agree?"

Susan nodded.

"Can I have some potatoes?" asked Willie, and Luke reached for the bowl, hoping the interruption had derailed his mother from that particular conversational track.

"Nicholas was a Boy Scout," Celeste observed casually.

"Really?" said Susan, smiling at Luke.

He smiled back weakly. Maybe bringing Susan here hadn't been such a good idea after all.

"All that Boy Scout training must have stood him in good stead, because he still follows the Boy Scout motto today," said his mother.

Oh, Lord. Don't quote it.

"Yes," continued Celeste, "he's given his brother a job, loaned his father I don't know how much money over the last few years, and helped me . . ."

"Mom!"

His mother blinked in surprise and Luke lowered his voice.

"Could I see you in the kitchen a moment?" he asked sweetly, and was aware of Susan, across from him, biting back a giggle.

"Certainly. You can bring those empty plates while you're at it."

Once in the kitchen, he hissed, "What are you doing?"

"Only what you asked me, " she hissed back, "which is more than you deserve. If you weren't bigger than me, I'd spank you."

His mom wasn't a sports fan, but somewhere along the way she'd learned that the best defense is a good offense. Luke blinked in surprise, trying to gather his wits. He looked over his shoulder to make sure Susan wasn't standing in the doorway. "What are you talking about?"

Her mother raised her chin a notch and announced in a whisper, "You are suing the daughter of the man I love."

Luke stood staring at her, trying to comprehend what he'd just misheard. He'd try again, but first, to make sure his mother's radical statement didn't reach the other room, he flipped on the dishwasher. It started whirring and swishing, washing invisible dishes. "What?"

"Susan Carpenter's father is Hank Appleby, the man I've been seeing," Celeste informed him. "And I don't want to lose him . . . *Nicholas.*" She spat out the name with distaste. "So, you had best do whatever it takes to make things right with this young woman, because if you ruin my chance for happiness I am going to kill you."

Luke sighed heavily. How was he ever going to be able to make things right with Susan? The mere mention of his name turned her from a sweet-natured lady to a snapping she-wolf. And now, to make matters worse, here was his mother's happiness riding on the outcome of his confession. She swept past him, and he followed her back into the dining room feeling like Atlas with the weight of the world bearing down on his shoulders.

He was barely aware of the rest of the conversation, hardly noticed when they moved from the dining room to the living room. His mind was too busy trying out, then discarding, various confessional styles. He watched his mother build a fire in the fireplace, Willie handing her the kindling while devouring a cookie, and wished he could regress right here and now back to those safe, early years of his childhood and just stay there.

That thought made him frown. He had never considered himself a coward before, but here he was, thinking about his upcoming confession to Susan and quaking in his boots, wondering what on Earth he could possibly say to explain his stone-hearted behavior. His mother was right: His cynicism had started the Christmas his folks separated. But that had been years ago, and it seemed whiny and gutless to blame his current behavior on something that had happened so far in the past. And all those Christmases between then and now, had they really been so bad? Okay, some of them were definitely National Lampoon material, but under all the chaos and mishaps hadn't there been some fun and laughter? Had every present really been useless, every office party so bad?

All this brought him back full circle to the ever-present question: What was he going to tell Susan? The answer was simple: He'd been greedy, he'd been wrong. But that wasn't much of a confession. What would Susan think? He looked to her end of the couch and found her smiling expectantly at him.

"What do you think?" she said.

"What?"

"Do you think we should be starting back pretty soon?"

Luke looked at his watch. How had it gotten to be so late? "Yeah, I guess we should." He rose and went to the entryway closet to get their coats.

"Can I have another cookie?" asked Willie.

"I think three is enough, Willie," said Susan quickly. "I'm afraid he has a terrible sweet tooth," she added apologetically.

"Please," Willie pleaded.

"There'll be cookies tonight after the program. You remember what happened last time you ate too many cookies."

Willie looked crestfallen and mumbled, "All right."

"How about if I put two in a sandwich bag for you," offered Celeste. "Then your mommy can put them in your lunch tomorrow."

Willie brightened at that suggestion and nodded eagerly.

"Thanks," said Susan.

"I'm big on compromise," said Celeste.

"Since when?" teased Luke.

"Since your father left," she said softly, and turned to go to the kitchen, leaving Luke to sort through a jumble of negative feelings.

He'd only been joking. Why had she reacted like that, opening up old wounds? Dumb question. She was unhappy about this rotten coincidence. There was no way Susan would know, but Luke had felt every forced smile his mother gave like an arrow to the heart. Him being the monster who ate Christmas was not only ruining his life, it was ruining hers, too, and she was miserable.

She came back with the cookies and handed them to

Susan, saying to Willie, "We'll let your mommy keep them so they don't get lost, okay?"

"Okay," he said.

"What do say?" prompted Susan.

"Thank you."

Celeste smiled, another one of those awful bittersweet things, and said, "You're welcome."

Luke kissed his mother's cheek and whispered, "Don't worry. I'll fix it." Then added, "Thanks, Mom."

She patted his cheek. "You're welcome, darling." Underlying message: I love you anyway.

That only made him feel worse.

Once in the car, Luke popped in the tape of children's songs Susan had brought along, then switched it to the back speakers, and while Willie sat singing along contentedly, Luke began to lay the groundwork for his big confession. "You know, you don't seem like the kind of person to carry a grudge or form an opinion about someone without meeting him."

He could see her stiffen and even though he hadn't said the words "Luke Potter," they hung between them like a bad smell.

"I have met Mr. Potter, by phone, said Susan. "He hung up on me."

Luke winced at the memory. He hadn't hung up on her, not really. He'd simply terminated the conversation. But she was still negotiating when he terminated the conversation. He had hung up on her.

"Maybe he wouldn't now. Maybe, with everyone calling him a Scrooge, he feels bad. Maybe Don Rawlins tricked him into that lawsuit."

Susan gave an uncharacteristic snort. "And maybe Santa rides a broom."

Luke felt like he'd been slapped.

She softened her voice. "I know he's your boss, and it's obvious you like him. It's not very nice the way I'm acting, but just hearing the man's name makes my blood pressure rise." She sighed. "Kind of tacky, isn't it? I'm on my way to church and talking about how much I hate Luke Potter."

"As much as Don Rawlins?"

"Let's just say I'd love to put them both in the stocks and throw rotten fruitcake at them," said Susan. "Or better yet, tie them up with Christmas lights and force them to listen to Alvin and the Chipmunks singing, 'Christmas, Don't Be Late' for hours on end."

"And what if, after all that, they said they were sorry? Would you forgive them?"

She grinned teasingly at him. "Is your boss paying you to soften me up?"

He smiled back. "Maybe."

"Tell him to drop his lawsuit."

"He's trying, Susan."

"Yeah, I could tell that on Friday," she said bitterly. "Nick, you don't mind if we change the subject, do you? This is really depressing me."

"No problem," said Luke. Strike one.

They got to the church twenty minutes early, but it was already nearly full with parents and grandparents, aunts and uncles. Their progress through the foyer was slow, as many people wanted to say hello to Susan and be introduced to her escort. Even under normal circumstances, Luke would have felt like a new puppy on display, but carrying his guilty secret, every kind greeting scalded his soul.

At last they made it to the sanctuary, and Luke scanned the crowd, checking for anyone he might know and need to avoid. He spotted Susan's sister in a side section pew, an older man seated next to her, a couple of coats and a purse reserving spaces on the other side. Luke looked at the deep blue cushions. At least the seats were padded; there was something for which to be thankful.

Nicole caught sight of them and waved eagerly. Luke

touched Susan's elbow and nodded toward Nicole. "There's your sister."

Susan's face lit up and she waved and hurried Luke over to where her sister and the man sat.

The man rose at the sight of Luke. He wasn't especially tall, but he was in excellent condition, with a firm gut and a strong chin, a chin that looked hard and unforgiving. He was studying Luke as if trying to place him.

"This is my dad, Hank Appleby. Daddy, this is my friend, Nick."

"Hello, sir," said Luke, extending his hand.

"Susan's told me about you," said Appleby. He took Luke's hand in a firm grip and smiled at him. "It's nice to meet you."

"Thank you, sir," said Luke, trying to ignore the sudden uncomfortable rise in both his pulse and his body temperature.

The older man sat down, and Luke followed suit, grateful to be off legs that suddenly felt too weak to hold him.

"You remember Nicole," said Susan.

Was he imagining it, or was there something assessing in the gaze Susan's sister was leveling at him? He hoped his smile hid his nervousness. "Nice to see you again, Nicole."

"Nice to see you, too," she said, but her tone of voice added, I think.

Oh, Lord, what was he doing here?

"Where's Todd?" he heard Susan ask.

"The men's room," said Nicole. "Oh, here he comes."

Luke's blood froze, turning him into a statue unable to turn around and look at Nicole's reporter boyfriend, the bloodhound who had been on his trail, the one person who could point a finger at him and cry, "Imposter!" He had a sudden wild idea to duck his head inside his coat like a turtle, but knew that would be completely idiotic. Some invisible force finally made him turn.

There came Todd Shelburne, Luke's nemesis, the same

little carrot-haired bantam rooster who had taunted him outside his office. The guy was wearing a happy-go-lucky smile as he sauntered down the aisle, but the moment his gaze locked with Luke's, it turned hard. Luke could see his eyes narrowing, could almost feel the little badger's heart rate pick up in anticipation of sinking his teeth into Luke's ankle and drawing blood. Ankle? Who was he kidding. Old Todd was no longer a badger, he was a Rotweiller, and he was going to go for Luke's jugular. The guy stopped next to their pew and looked assessingly at Luke, who gave him a flinty smile in return.

"This is Nicole's boyfriend," said Susan, "the one who started my legal defense fund. Todd, this is Nick Claus."

Todd's upper lip lifted in a sneer as he held out his hand. "Nice to meet you . . . Nick."

Luke knew his hand felt cold and clammy, like a dying man's, but he forced his handshake to be firm. "I've been following your articles, and I'd like to talk to you after the program. I have some information on Luke Potter that might interest you."

"I'll bet you do," said Todd.

The lights were lowering, so Todd clambered across Susan and Luke and took his place between the two sisters.

Luke found himself praying for the first time in years. *Please, God, don't let him say anything to Susan. Please.*

An adult choir started off the evening with a rousing, if slightly off-key rendition of "Joy to the World," and Luke clasped his hands tightly together in his lap to keep himself from drumming his fingers.

They finished, and a little boy in a suit who looked a couple of years younger than Willie scrambled up to the stage and craned his neck toward the microphone, which had been lowered to kid level. He cleared his throat and the sound reverberated around the room, followed by a few adult chuckles. The child looked down into the audience and waved at someone and whispered, "Hi, Mommy," producing more isn't-that-cute laughter.

The woman kneeling directly in front of the stage whispered something at him, and he nodded and got on with the program. "Christmas is a good time," he recited, "a time for giving cheer to lonely ones and sad ones, and those we hold most dear."

The audience applauded as he backed away from the mike, and a little girl in a red ruffled dress approached. The child's hair was a mass of blond curls. Luke could imagine Susan as a little girl looking like that, standing on a church platform, reciting a poem.

"So welcome everyone, we're glad that you are here," she said, her voice lifting and dropping in a singsong cadence, "to help us all rejoice, and share the Christmas cheer." She beamed on the audience, then left to more applause.

But her words remained to haunt Luke. Share the Christmas cheer. Now Luke knew how Ebenezer Scrooge had felt when visiting his nephew's home in the company of the Ghost of Christmas Present, looking on, wanting to participate, yet being an outsider.

Like Marley, Luke had forged this chain himself. He had haughtily pulled away, stepped outside, away from the light and laughter and slammed the door firmly shut behind his cynical self. Now, here he was, cold and miserable and wanting back in. And until he knew the door would open, he didn't want to stand at the window looking in a moment longer. He needed air, he had to get out of this pew, this room.

Just then the wise men made their entrance, all wearing bathrobes and homemade crowns, encrusted with dime-store jewels. Susan laid a hand on Luke's arm and snuggled next to him and he couldn't move. So there he sat, trying not to look like a man whose lungs were growing too big for his chest, whose heart was growing increasingly agitated. You can do this, he told himself, and took a deep breath.

He watched Willie make his way up the aisle, his little spray-painted, gold box held before him, his gaze looking straight ahead. The wise man in front of him tripped over his robe and dropped his bottle of frankincense, and the parade halted while he recovered it and hiked up his robe, but Willie never lost his cool. He stopped at the microphone and said his one line with great dignity before going to lay his box by the manger with the baby doll. Luke stole a glance at Susan. Her eyes were glistening.

He recognized that look: He'd seen it on his own mother's face when he had played a shepherd so many years ago at a similar event. He patted Susan's hand and she smiled up at him and his heart ached.

The play moved on. Little angels with tinsel halos sang "Away in a Manger," a prepubescent Mary and Joseph looked solemn, and the adult choir sang "It Came Upon a Midnight Clear." Then everyone sang "Silent Night."

"All is calm, all is bright," sang Luke, and knew that there was not a single calm nerve in his body, nor was there anything bright in his future. Despair hung over him like a shroud. He wanted to cry and hated himself for it, and hated himself even more for what he'd done to reach this sorry point.

The lights came up and the pastor took the stage. "That concludes our Christmas program for the year, folks. Our ladies have been busy baking, and those of you who have been here in years past know what good bakers they are. We hope you'll all stay and join us for cocoa and cookies."

The room filled with the burble of voices as parents filed out of the sanctuary, congratulating each other on their children's performances, the high-pitched, excited voices of those children inserting themselves like punctuation marks.

Willie came bounding up to his mother. I didn't forget my line!"

"You did wonderfully," said Susan.

"But I saw you trip that boy," teased Nicole.

I didn't trip him," said Willie. "He fell all by himself."

Like me, thought Luke. Don may have laid the trap that got me into this mess, but I put my greedy paw into it.

Willie had Susan by the hand now and was tugging. "Come on, Mommy, let's go get some cocoa."

Susan looked expectantly to Luke.

"You go ahead," he said. "Todd and I will catch up." He saw a hint of worry in Nicole's expression, and knew that she knew his guilty secret. She obviously had refrained from telling Susan so far. Luke hoped she'd be able to contain herself a little longer.

The women headed out to the foyer. Hank Appleby nodded pleasantly at Luke and followed them. As soon as Hank was out of earshot, Luke turned to Todd. "I need to talk to you."

"I ought to punch your lights out," Todd growled through gritted teeth.

"You've already done me enough damage, believe me," said Luke.

"Well, you ain't' seen nothing yet. Come out to my car. I've got something to show you."

Todd played forward to Luke's quarterback, making a path through the milling throng. Luke swam after him, smiling politely and agreeing with everyone who asked that, yes, the kids did a great job. By the time he got out to the parking lot he could barely breathe. He gulped in a deep breath of the frosty night air and followed Todd to his car, which was parked on the opposite side of the lot from his. They got in. Todd turned on the dome light, then handed over a manila file folder.

Luke opened it and saw the hard copy of what he knew was going to be THE STORY, the one that would go with

THE PICTURE. He read the opening sentence: "Since the denial of the request of Luke Potter and fellow claimant, Don Rawlins, for a temporary injunction against Susan Carpenter that would force Mrs. Carpenter to take down her Christmas lights, Mr. Potter has been seen squiring Mrs. Carpenter around town. It is still unknown why he has chosen to see Mrs. Carpenter under the name of Nicholas Claus."

Luke felt the blood drain from his face. He shut the folder, feeling too sick to read any more. "You can't print this."

"You watch me. This is my girlfriend's sister you've been messing with. By the end of this month Nicki and I will be engaged, which makes me family. Nobody hurts my family."

"I don't want to hurt Susan, I want to marry her."

Todd glared at Luke. "Get out of my car."

"I will, but not until you shut up and let me explain."

"All right, smart guy. Explain."

Susan craned her neck, trying to spot Luke in the chattering throng. Where was he?

Her dad came up beside her and handed her a disposable cup filled with hot chocolate. "Our boy did great," he said.

Willie was missing, too, Susan realized. "Where is he?"

Hank motioned to the serving table set up on the other side of the room. Susan saw her son leaning over the cookie plate, his greedy little fingers dancing from cookie to cookie. And there stood her sister, encouraging him in his gluttony.

"Oh, my gosh, he's fingering every one of them," Susan moaned. "And if eats any more I just know he's going to be sick."

"Oh, he'll be fine," said her father. "Let the kid enjoy himself. Where's your date?"

I don't know. He was here a minute ago."

I thought I saw him leave with Todd."

"Maybe they're bonding."

"Hmm," said her father noncommittally. "You know, he looks familiar, but I can't for the life of me figure where I know him from."

"He probably came into the hardware store at some time," said Susan.

Hank nodded. "Probably. He seems like a nice man, honey."

"I think I'm in love with him, Dad."

"Good. It's about time you found someone."

"And how are things going with you and your new lady friend."

"She's a great lady. I think your mother would approve."

"So, are there wedding bells in your future?"

"Don't be surprised."

Susan smiled and hugged him. "It looks like this is going to be a very memorable Christmas for both of us."

The words were barely out of her mouth when she saw Nicole leading Willie across the room toward them.

"Uh-oh," said Hank. "Willie looks a little green around the gills."

"Mommy, my tummy hurts," he said.

"I think he had too many cookies," said Nicole helpfully.

Susan frowned at her sister. "Oh, really? And who was over there helping him gorge himself?"

Conversation came to a sudden halt as Willie erupted, causing a flurry of squeals, movement, and sounds of disgust from several little girls.

"Mommy," cried Willie.

"Oh, dear," said Susan. She searched the foyer frantically for Nick, but saw no sign of him.

"I want to go home," wailed Willie.

"Oh, Dad. I don't see Nick anywhere."

"Come on," said her father, scooping up the child, "we'll take my car."

Susan looked at the mess on the floor, uncertain what to do. She saw a woman approaching with a fistful of paper towels and felt she should be socially responsible and help clean it up since it was her son who had made it.

"Mommy," he called.

"It's okay," said Nicole. "We can get this cleaned up. Just go."

"Nick . . ."

"I'll explain what happened. He'll understand."

Susan thanked her sister and hurried after her father. She only had time for a cursory glance around the parking lot as they piled into her dad's car, then her attention was fully occupied as they started moving and Willie threw up again.

"Once I get the money together to replace what I've spent of Rawlins's loan I can pay him back. When that's done, I'm out of this. I've got my lawyer standing by to take my name off all the papers. You can check with him and confirm that if you want."

"Don't think I won't," said Todd. "This is all pretty hard to swallow."

"Well, it's the God's honest truth, I swear."

Todd shook his head in amazement. "You have got to be the biggest bozo I ever met."

If Todd had said that to him two weeks ago, Luke would have let him have it, but things had changed in two weeks. Less than that, actually, and he'd gone from a businessman whose every move was logically thought out and whose life was perfectly planned and controlled to . . . bozohood.

He sighed and rubbed his freshly aching forehead. "I should never have listened to my brother. All his ideas are harebrained. But there was something about Susan.

I just had to get to know her better, had to prove to her I wasn't the villain you painted me out to be."

Todd let out a long sigh and laid his head back on the headrest. "You realize you've just cost me a job at a bigger paper?"

"Yeah, but I've probably saved you from messing up more than one set of lives."

"What do you mean?"

"Well, I just found out today that my mother has been seeing Susan's father."

Todd sat up and stared at him, bug-eyed. Then he let out a low whistle. "Man, we've got a real soap opera going here. If you can fix this mess it really will be a miracle."

"Tell me about it," said Luke. "Now, if you're done raking me over the coals, I'd like to get back in there. Susan's probably looking for me, and the sooner I get her home the sooner I can start damage control."

Todd nodded. "You've got tonight, buddy. But if I don't hear anything by tomorrow morning, I'll know this was all a bunch of crap, and I'll turn this story in tomorrow afternoon and watch you squirm like a sorry bug."

"Don't worry," said Luke.

"Hey, I've got nothing to worry about," Todd retorted.

Luke left Todd's car and headed back to the church, Todd following behind like an undercover cop. Inside the church, he couldn't see Susan or Willie anywhere. He finally caught sight of Nicole, bent down on the floor with another woman. What on Earth were they doing?

As soon as Luke got within sniffing range, he knew. "Nicole, where's Susan?"

Nicole was still busy mopping, a look of extreme distaste on her face. "Willie had too many cookies and got sick. Dad took them both home. Susan said to tell you she was sorry."

Not half as sorry as he was. Strike two. But he wasn't out. And he was at least safe from the morning paper.

He'd go over to Susan's house with croissants and Starbuck's coffee first thing tomorrow and tell her everything. And tonight he'd go home and try to get a decent night's sleep.

It was eight-thirty at night when Larry wandered into the office of the *Clarion*. He stopped by to talk to Cyd at the copy desk and see how things were shaping up on Todd's story. "I haven't got anything of Shelburne's here," said Cyd.

"You should have," said Larry. "With my picture of old Scrooge. Without the shades."

"Sounds great, but I haven't seen anything."

Larry frowned and headed for the news editor's desk. He got the same response. He finally went to the city desk, what would have been the first stop for Todd's story, thinking Todd had gotten it in late, but turned up nothing. What was that little weasel, Shelburne, up to?

Larry stalked over to Todd's desk and began to rummage through the piles of notepads and papers. Nothing. He got onto Todd's computer, and began to play guess the password. He tried Todd's birthday, the lucky number he used when he bought lottery tickets, his girlfriend's first name. Nothing. "Hey, Joe," he called to a man at a nearby desk. "What's Shelburne's girlfriend's birthday?"

"How the hell should I know?" snapped the guy.

Larry rubbed his chin thoughtfully. It hadn't been all that long ago that Todd had been trying to scrape up the last ten bucks he needed to buy the girl flowers. November? No. It had been earlier. October? Yeah, that was it. Early in the month. He'd taken her out to dinner, too. The sixth? That sounded right. Now, what year would the chickie have been born in. How old did she look? Larry experimented for another ten minutes, then hit pay dirt.

Once in, he opened the folder marked Scrooge, and there it was, in all its glory. His eyes grew wide as he read the first sentence, and he let out a low whistle. "What have you been sitting on, Toddy boy?" A gold mine, that was what. An Angel Falls gold mine. Larry grinned as he started the printer, then went to his own desk to get the extra copy of Scrooge's picture.

Once this all landed on the city desk it would jet to Cyd faster than lightning, and Larry would see his triumph on display tomorrow morning.

He went back to Todd's desk and plucked the papers from the printer tray. Then he turned off the computer and left a note for Todd: "Got your work done for you. See you in the papers."

He stopped by the city desk and dropped the pile in front of the frazzled-looking young man sitting there. "Here's the latest on Scrooge, and it's hot."

The guy practically pounced on the stuff. Larry left the office whistling.

Thirteen

"This is amazing," said Nicole, as Todd pulled into the parking lot of her apartment complex.

It had taken him the entire trip home to retell Luke's story, and she felt like she'd only begun to process the whole, incredible tale. "So, he's been waiting all this time to tell her who he really is so he could prove to her he's not a jerk?"

"That's what he claims."

"It's going to take more than driving her around town to deliver singing telegrams to convince Suz of that," Nicole predicted. "And I don't care how nice his mother is. She could claim he's Saint Francis of Assisi, but what would that mean? Everyone knows mothers are prejudiced."

"If he unhooks himself from Rawlins, it will go a long way toward proving his point," said Todd.

"That's a big 'if.'" She turned in the seat and smiled at Todd. "But I'm proud of you for giving him the chance. It can't be easy for you, sitting on such a big story."

"It's not," Todd admitted. "A story like this would open doors at any paper I chose. Not that that's the reason I was doing it. I was also doing this to protect your sister. But hey, if you're right about Susan being in love with him, and if it turns out he loves her, then I don't want to screw things up. After all, she's going to be my sister soon and family sticks together."

Nicole pounced on the most important word in Todd's speech. "Soon? How soon?"

He grinned. "Sooner than you might think."

"Like, by Christmas, maybe?"

"Maybe," said Todd, looking smug.

Nicole let out a squeal. "Oh, Toddy! Is it that ring I was drooling over last week?"

"Could be," he said. He was trying hard to look mysterious, but after a year and a half together, Nicole could read him like a book.

She threw her arms around him and pressed her lips to his.

When they finally came up for air, he said, "Don't take forever planning the wedding, baby, okay? I've taken about as many cold showers as I can stand."

"Valentine's Day would be nice," she mused.

"Perfect," said Todd. "Now, come here."

She came, and Susan and Luke and their problems were completely forgotten.

Luke left a message for Martha that he'd be in the office in time for the Christmas party, then drove to the Angel Falls bakery and picked up fresh croissants to bring to Susan for breakfast. He saw the school bus roar by him as he drove down the street. Good. He'd have her all to himself. Every nerve in his body was twitching now, and his shirt collar seemed to be gripping his neck more tightly with every block he drove. She'll listen, he told himself. She'll understand. She has to. She's my Christmas angel, my only hope.

•   •   •

Still in her bathrobe, Susan took the paper from her front porch and padded back to the kitchen to grab a cup of coffee. Once she had her morning java in hand, she sat down at the table and spread the paper out in front of her. The headline jumped out at her like a jack-in-the-box and she read the opening lines of the article in stunned disbelief: "Since the denial of the request of Luke Potter and fellow claimant, Don Rawlins, for a temporary injunction against Susan Carpenter that would force Mrs. Carpenter to take down her Christmas lights, Mr. Potter has been seen squiring Mrs. Carpenter around town. It is still unknown why he has chosen to see Mrs. Carpenter under the name of Nicholas Claus."

Susan blinked and read that last sentence again. She felt a stab of pain deep in her chest and pushed away from the paper. But that didn't make the damning evidence go away. There was Nick's picture next to the article. Her Nick, a fraud. Motives unknown, but strongly implied: There's more than one way to strip a house of its Christmas lights.

The doorbell rang and she jumped. She wouldn't see anyone. Didn't want to see anyone, ever again. She stayed rooted at the table, staring at the paper, watching Nick's picture blur as the tears filled her eyes. No, not Nick. Luke. Luke Potter. Mr. Scrooge. Mr. Deceitful, Make-A-Fool-Of-Her Scrooge.

Susan buried her face in her hands and sobbed, and the doorbell rang on. She was still sobbing when she heard a gentle tapping at the sliding glass door off her kitchen.

There he stood, the Scrooge of Angel Falls, the sneakiest, most deceptive, rotten man in the world, wearing an expression of fake innocence. She could hear his muffled voice through the window, "Susan, can I come in?"

Right. In two quick strides, she was at the window. She gave the curtain cord a vicious yank and the fabric charged across the window, obscuring him from view.

"Susan!" Now the polite knock was a bang.

"Go away!" she cried. "I never want to see you again."

She bundled the paper under her arm and stalked off, back through the house and upstairs. She marched to her room, and jerked clothes from her dresser drawers. Now she could hear him at the front door again. The doorbell was clanging, and he was banging on the door, shouting her name. She snatched up the paper and stalked to Willie's room, then threw open the window and leaned out. "Go away!"

He stepped off the porch and onto the walkway and looked up at her with that beautiful face, that beautiful, deceptive face. "Susan, please let me in."

Let him in? That was exactly what she had done, fool that she was. She'd let him into her house, her life, her heart. "Never!" she shouted, and hurled the newspaper down at him.

She'd liked to have hit him on the head. Unfortunately, the paper came apart and fluttered downward like a flock of birds and she had to settle for slamming the window shut.

"Susan, please!" His muffled shout seemed to thump against the window. Well, he could shout all he wanted but it wouldn't do him any good.

Susan marched out of Willie's room and back to her own, snatched up her clothes and headed to the bathroom. Then she turned the shower on full force, so all she could hear was water beating against tile.

Luke picked up the paper with dread in his heart. It couldn't be, it simply couldn't be. Shelburne had promised.

But there it was, his picture, and next to it the headline: TWO FACES OF CHRISTMAS. Under the picture it read, LUKE POTTER, ALIAS NICHOLAS CLAUS.

Luke felt like someone had rammed a stake through his heart. No that was vampires, not Scrooges. What did they do to punish Scrooges? He looked up at the tightly shut window and saw his answer. Rage and disappointment wrestled inside him, and he felt like his chest was going to burst. If he could have had a chance to explain, then maybe he could have made things right. Yes, Susan hated Luke Potter, but she loved Nick. If only he could have gotten to her to prepare her for the shock of learning that Luke and Nick were one in the same; if he could have had time to argue his case, fall to his knees and beg forgiveness, explain that he was a changed man, she would have listened. Instead, here he stood, past his nose in misery and drowning.

And there was only one person to blame. Luke strangled the paper with his hands, then shredded it. He hurled the pieces to the wind and marched toward his car. He didn't know how many years he'd get for manslaughter, but it would be worth a lifetime in a jail cell to feel Todd Shelburne's neck between his hands.

"Great story, Todd," called a fellow reporter as Todd made his way to his desk.

"Thanks," said Todd, then wondered, what story? He hurried back to the front of the office and picked up a paper from the stack. There it was, his story and Larry's picture. Larry! Todd would kill him. Who was he kidding? He'd never live to get the chance. As soon as Nicole saw this, he was a dead man.

He consulted his watch. Not quite nine. She'd be on her way to work. He hurried to his desk and dialed her cell phone number.

Her hello sounded wary, like she was afraid it would be him.

"Nicki . . ."

"You! How dare you call me after what you said to me last night!"

"I can explain."

"You don't need to explain. I'm not stupid. You used

my sister to further your career. You'll get a job at a big paper now. But you stomped on Suz's heart to get there, and I'll hate you forever for that!"

She punctuated her sentence with a dial tone, and Todd hung up feeling sick. How had this happened? It didn't take him long to get from Point A to Point B. "Where's Broom?" he bellowed.

His phone beeped at him, its intercom button flashing. He snatched up the receiver and snarled, "Yeah?"

"You've got a visitor," said a sweet female voice. "He's . . . Just a minute, sir! Well, he's on his way to you."

Todd looked up to see Luke Potter tearing across the room like a locomotive. Todd could almost see the steam coming from his ears. He got up, holding up a staying hand. "This is not what you think, Potter."

Potter shoved him, sending him toppling back into his chair so hard the thing tilted and fell backward, taking Todd with it. "Give me a chance to explain," he said, kicking like an upended turtle.

Potter's fingers closed around his shirt and yanked, pulling Todd up so fast he got dizzy. He felt his foot catch in the chair and fell against the guy's chest. He didn't stay in that position long, though, because the next thing he knew, he was nose to nose with a mask of rage.

"You promised me today," roared Potter.

Todd had never before considered himself a coward, but now he wondered. His heartbeat sounded in his ears like a raging storm, and he felt the sudden urge to cry for his mother. Well, who wouldn't, facing Dirty Harry, Superman, and the Terminator all rolled into one? "This is not my fault," he choked.

Potter let him go with a force that sent him staggering backward on weakened knees, and demanded, "Then whose fault is it?"

"Larry Broom, the photographer. He must have gotten into my computer, found the story."

"And ruined my life!" Potter exploded.

"Hey, he hasn't done anything for me, either," snapped Todd. "Nicole accused me of climbing to the top over her sister's broken heart and told me to take a hike. And I've already bought the engagement ring."

"You made this mess, you've got to fix it."

"Wait a minute, turkey. I'm not the one who went around with a phony name. Nicholas Claus, for crying out loud. Of all the stupid . . ."

"I told you, that was my idiot brother's doing," barked Potter.

"It looks to me like there are two idiots in your family," observed Todd.

Potter let out a sigh and sat on Todd's desk, shoulders slumping. He looked like a blow-up beach toy that had just had the air punched out of it. He combed his fingers through his hair. "I can't even get near her." He turned to Todd, his eyes wild. Todd took a step back, ready to run in case the guy grabbed for him again. "What am I going to do?" Potter asked.

Todd picked up his chair and sat heavily in it, shaking his head. "I don't know."

"You've got to write a retraction," said Potter.

"What the hell am I going to retract? Everything in that article you did, you lunkhead."

Potter stared straight ahead. "What am I going to do?" he repeated in wooden tones.

"Get that money fast," advised Todd. "At least if you get the money and get out of the lawsuit you've got a chance. Not me, I'm ruined. I can't get this article out of the paper. Nicki's never going to speak to me again." Todd felt his voice catch, felt the tears prickling the back of his eyes. He blinked furiously to drive them away and squared his chin. He would not break down and cry. Instead, he growled, "You've made a real Merry Christmas for us, Potter. Thanks a lot."

•   •   •

The shower hadn't helped. Susan wandered around the house, sobbing as she went. Her Yours-For-A-Song line rang and she ignored it. But she couldn't ignore the memories it triggered. She closed her eyes against the insistent image of Luke's happy face that day she'd sung to him. Now she knew why he'd been smiling. He'd been thinking what a great bit of irony it would be to make Suzi Christmas fall in love with him, Angel Falls's biggest villain.

What a fool he'd made of her! She remembered their many conversations about his "boss." His loyalty had seemed misplaced. Now she knew why.

She looked over at the tree he had brought her, resplendent even with its lights turned off. And there hung the little angel ornament. She turned her back on the tree and went into the kitchen and could almost see him standing there, eating gingerbread boys.

She buried her face in her hands and wept. So cruel. He'd been so cruel to trick her like that. She felt sick thinking of his kisses, his loving looks, his thoughtful gestures. And him taking her to see his mother, making that poor woman aid him in his nasty, little charade. How low could a man get! Susan took a deep, shaky breath. She was well rid of Luke Potter.

So said her mind, but her heart couldn't seem to agree. She could feel the tears welling up again. She flipped on her favorite FM radio station, then went to sit on the couch and let the Christmas music wash over her.

The phone rang and she ignored it. She heard the answering machine click on, heard her father's voice.

"I'm sorry, sweetheart," he said. "Real sorry. How about letting your old dad take you and Willie out for dinner tonight?"

Willie. Susan felt a wave of nausea. What if some child at school showed him that horrible story or teased him? How would he take it? He liked Nick . . . no not Nick, Luke. Susan felt a sudden overwhelming desire to hunt Luke Potter down and punch him in the nose. But that would only make more headlines, and Willie didn't need that. She had to think of her child. She had to get him out of school. She'd keep him home for a couple of days. But under what excuse?

Of course. Her father. Maybe Willie could begin winter vacation early by spending the day with Grandpa. She went to the phone and called her dad, who was happy to go to the school and pick up Willie and keep him through dinner. Then she called the school, and tried to make her voice sound as sane and matter of fact as possible as she talked to Mrs. Bartle, the principal.

"I think that would be an excellent idea," said Mrs. Bartle. "And Mrs. Carpenter."

"Yes?" said Susan warily.

Mrs. Bartle, a normally competent woman of great logic and crisp speech, stumbled over her tongue. "We're all, that is, I'm terribly sorry."

"Thank you," murmured Susan and hung up to find she was breathing rapidly and her whole face felt fevered.

That was it. She couldn't talk to another person. Not now, not ever. She turned off the ringer on her phone and fled back to the couch to hug a pillow.

Her answering machine clicked on, and she could hear Nicole's anxious voice. "Suz, I know you're in there. Are you all right? Please call me. I'm so worried about you."

She couldn't. She could only stay curled up on this couch, listening to music, pretending she hadn't been betrayed and made a fool of.

The office party should have been in full swing by the time Luke got to Bad Boy Enterprises, but no one looked very merry. "Luke, I'm so sorry," said Martha.

"I screwed it up big time, didn't I?" said Ben miserably.

"Yeah." Luke sighed heavily. "No. I brought this on myself. I went along with it."

"I could go see her, explain," offered Ben.

"Explain what? That your brother has a cash register for a heart?"

"Well, here, open the present from your staff," said Martha, shoving a beribboned box at Luke.

"No," yelped Ben, making a grab for it.

"Don't be silly," said Martha, moving it out of reach. "Your brother needs cheering up. This will help."

"No, it won't," said Ben.

"Ben was the one who bought it," Martha explained.

"And you won't be getting the bill for it," put in Roxy.

"That's some good news," said Luke, listlessly taking the present. He tore off the wrapping and opened the lid. As he pulled out the black T-shirt, the smile he'd been forcing fell completely away when he saw what was on its front. There stood a dopey looking sheep, wearing an old-fashioned, red nightcap. In big letters under it were the words "Bah, humbug."

Ben's face was the reddest Luke had ever seen. "Jeez," he said, sounding as sick as Luke felt. "I told you not to give it to him," he said, looking accusingly at Martha.

"Well, if you'd told me what was in it, I wouldn't have," she retorted.

"I didn't think about it until you dragged the thing out." To his brother he said, "I'm sorry, man. I thought things were going so good with you guys. I . . ."

Luke nodded, let the box and the shirt fall on Martha's desk, then turned and headed for his office, only vaguely aware of Martha's scolding voice saying, "Ben!"

And Ben's answer, "Everything was going so good when I bought it. I thought it would be funny."

Going so good. Going, going, gone.

Luke's day didn't improve with his visit to the bank. His friend, Keith, promised to do his best. "But it might take some time."

"How much time?" asked Luke.

"Well, it's the holidays. I wouldn't expect much until after Christmas. Probably not until after the first of the year. You know how it is this time of year."

The first of the year. Keith might as well have said wait fifty years.

His friend rested his elbows on his desk and leaned forward. "What's going on Luke? How did you get yourself into such a stinking mess?"

Luke tried to think of an answer that wouldn't make him look like a either a fool or a villain. None came, because he was both, He stayed mute and shook his head.

"This is probably not the best time in the world to be going for a loan with all this bad publicity," said Keith.

"This publicity has nothing to do with my business," insisted Luke, "and you know it. My stores don't have my name and they're both doing great."

Keith cocked an eyebrow. "I heard you had to delay the grand opening of your new one."

"It will be open after the first of the year."

"And your rental place. Got any renters yet?"

Luke scowled. "What are you trying to do here, Keith?"

"I'm trying to point out to you that right now this loan is going to be a hard sell. I can't approve it by myself. That would be career suicide. And you'd think the same way if you were in my shoes."

Luke rubbed his forehead. "Yeah, I know. Just see what you can do, will you?"

"You know I'll try," said Keith, rising.

They shook hands and Luke left the bank knowing he wasn't going to get the loan. So, here he was, still tied to Rawlins. He had to get free. But with every turn he hit the same roadblock: He was overextended with no decent liquid assets to dump.

The rental property. Selling it wouldn't give him instant cash, but a sold sign in the yard might at least give him a chance of floating a loan pronto. With all her fans, there had to be someone who would love to live next to

Susan. His jaw clamped in determination, he climbed into his car and headed for Angel Falls Realty.

The smile on Harrison Banks's double-chinned face faltered at the sight of Luke, but he shored it up and stuck out his hand. "Mr. Potter, nice to see you."

"Yeah, I'll just bet it is," said Luke. "I've come to throw you some business."

Banks perked up. "Oh? Well, sit down."

"I've got a house I want to sell, and I want to give you the listing."

Banks had settled himself in his chair and was trying to flatten the wrinkles out of his waistcoat. As those wrinkles were the result of puckering material, straining to hold together against the pressure of too much gut, it was a hopeless job. At Luke's words, Banks stopped his hands and looked warily at Luke. "Oh?"

"I want to sell my rental house."

"The one . . ." Banks faltered.

"The one next to Susan Carpenter's house," Luke finished for him. "The one you sold me."

Banks cleared his throat. "I'm afraid real estate doesn't move very fast this time of year."

"Especially a house next to Suzi Christmas's?" asked Luke pleasantly.

"Well.

Luke jumped out of his seat. He planted both palms on Banks's desk and leaned over it menacingly. "You sold me that place knowing what a circus it was. Now you'd better help me unload it before you get a letter from my lawyer."

"Mr. Potter, please," said Banks, his eyes wide with fear. "Calm down. Take a load off. Of course I want to help you sell your house. It's a charming place, and I'm sure we can find a buyer for it."

"Good," said Luke, his blood pressure settling back to normal. "Let's do the paperwork."

"But you're not going to get anyone looking at a house

four days before Christmas," protested Banks. "Especially . . ."

"One next to Suzi Christmas's house?" finished Luke.

"If you just wait until after the first of the year."

"I don't have until after the first of the year," Luke growled.

"Well, you won't sell that turk . . . er, house now," said Banks.

"You mean, you won't sell it," said Luke coldly. He stood. "I guess I'll take my offer to Happy Homes Sales."

"You'll never sell it," Banks called after him.

"You'd better hope I do," Luke shot back over his shoulder. "Otherwise, you'll be hearing from me—via my lawyer."

Still scowling, Luke got in his car and slammed the door. As he sat, reliving his conversation with the realtor, his head began to throb. Ben had gotten him the perfect present. Just because his life was in the toilet, did he have to go careening around town, trying to put everyone else's in there, too? He and old Scrooge really were soul mates, heartless, humankind-hating scum.

His cell phone rang and he answered it with a curt hello.

"Hello, son," said Luke Senior.

"Hi, Dad."

"You don't sound so good."

"Yeah, well, even Scrooges can have a bad day."

"It looks to me like you've been having a bad month," said his father. "I've been talking to your mom."

Mom. Luke had been so caught up in his own misery, he'd forgotten his mother. Fresh self-loathing stirred the sourness he'd been carrying around in his gut all day, and the little demon throwing the sledgehammer against the back of his head got in another good lick. He should give his whole family a break and leave Angel Falls. "Look, Dad. Maybe I'd better take a raincheck on Christmas. I don't think I'm going to be very good company."

"No," said his father, and Luke was surprised by the old man's strong reaction. "I want to see you, Luke. I've got something special for you that I think will make your life easier."

"A gun?"

"Not funny. Now, promise me you'll come."

"Sure, Dad. I'll try."

"No. I've made those kind of promises myself. You know it—half of them were to you. And believe it or not, I made them because my heart felt just as sick as yours does right now. But I want to see you, son, no matter how miserable you are."

"Okay," said Luke, resigned. "I'll stop by for awhile."

"Good," said his dad.

They said their goodbyes and hung up.

"Well, look at it this way," Luke told his reflection in the rearview mirror, "at least somebody wants to see you."

"Go away! I don't want to see you," said the love of Todd's life, turning her back on him.

He laid the bouquet of red roses on the counter. "Nicki, you've got to let me explain. It wasn't me who put that story in the paper."

"Oh, I suppose it was a ghost writer," said Nicole. She glared at him over her shoulder, then turned to an approaching customer.

"Nicki! You've got to listen to me."

"Mr. Shelburne," said a voice at his elbow.

Todd knew the foundation-encrusted face and Bride-of-Frankenstein hair that went with that voice. He turned to see Miss LaFleur, Nicki's supervisor, frowning disapprovingly at him.

"Hi, Miss LaFleur," he said. "You're looking"—*Don't say scary!*—"lovely today."

"Thank you," said Miss LaFleur, and pressed her very red lips together primly. She looked first at Todd's floral peace offering, then turned her schoolmarm glare back on him. "May I help you with something?"

"Yes. You can let Nicole go on break so I can talk to her. We've had a terrible misunderstanding, and . . ."

"There was no misunderstanding," shot Nicki from the other side of the counter, and she ran the customer's charge card through the machine with vehemence.

"Mr. Shelburne, I'm sure I would love to oblige you," said Miss LaFleur, "but in case you hadn't noticed, we're very busy here today." She held out her hand like Vanna White displaying the letters on *Wheel of Fortune*.

Todd nodded, acknowledging the beehive of females swarming around the cosmetics counters. "Yes, but . . ."

"And I'm afraid Nicole has already taken her break. Maybe you can catch her after work."

"Don't bother," said Nicki from the other side of the counter.

Miss LaFleur smiled at him, the makeup in her deep smile lines looking like clay. "Goodbye, Mr. Shelburne. Merry Christmas."

Todd pressed his lips tightly together, holding back the smart-ass remark he longed to hurl at the old bat, and nodded. He left, and went to a nearby department, skulking among the purses and watching until he saw Miss LaFleur move off to harass some other poor worker. Then he moved quickly, making his way back to Nicole's counter.

"What are you doing back here?" she demanded.

"Trying to explain to you what really happened," said Todd.

I know what happened, Todd Shelburne. You got greedy. You took out your little scales and weighed a job at a bigger paper against my sister's happiness and Suz lost. I don't want someone who doesn't understand family loyalty."

A new customer arrived. This one wasn't your typical fat, old, married man, making his yearly foray into feminine territory to find a present for the woman in his life and looking dazed. Todd took in the guy's Armani suit, silk shirt, highly shined black shoes, and suddenly felt very conscious of his own jeans, T-shirt, and old, cracked-leather bomber jacket, and he moved to hide his tenny-runner clad feet behind the counter.

He wouldn't feel so second-rate had the guy just been a good dresser, but he was good-looking, too. No, not just good-looking. He was what Nicole would call drop-dead gorgeous. He looked like Pierce Brosnan. Todd eyed the guy's black hair and swarthy complexion, and hated his own fair skin and freckles with a new zeal. With those deep-set, blue eyes and black brows, the newcomer looked like he could hypnotize a woman in sixty seconds flat. He had too much height to be a hulk, but Todd could tell the guy had muscle. And he was just old enough—late thirties, probably—to make Todd feel like a kid. Between the suit and the body, the newcomer had an aura of power that nearly knocked Todd off his feet. What would he do to Nicole?

No need to ask. Todd saw her straighten and give her hair a toss. "May I help you find something special?" she purred.

"I think I just have," said the newcomer.

Todd made a feral smile at him. "He'll have to wait. I'm not done yet."

The man shrugged. "I don't mind waiting." The look he gave Todd in return was nothing short of a dare: Just try and distract her from me. He stood there on the other side of the counter, biding his time, like some kind of tiger, waiting, sure of his prey. No, not a tiger. A jackal.

Nicki looked over her shoulder long enough to glare at Todd, then turned back to the jackal, saying, "I'm finished with that man."

"You are not," said Todd.

Nicole ignored him. "Here's something nice." She

picked up a bottle and spritzed some perfume on her wrist, holding it up to him.

The man bent to sniff her wrist. His fingers touched Nicole's hand. "That is nice."

Todd's hands clenched into fists. Nicki had done that same routine on him the first time they met. "Nicole," he rumbled.

She turned around and hissed, "Can't you see I'm working here?"

"Working at what?"

"Buy something or get lost."

"Okay," said Todd, fishing in his back pocket for his wallet. Whatever she wanted. He'd charge it and pay it off later. "I want to buy something."

Her lips turned up in the familiar sweet smile, but the expression in her eyes was anything but. "You'll have to wait, sir," she said. Then she turned her back on him to flirt with 007's twin. Picking up a small glass bottle, she said, "This fragrance is new. It's called Remembrance."

"Remembrance, hmm?" said the jackal. "I'd be willing to bet you don't need that to make a man remember you."

Remembrance. Todd didn't want to spend Christmas alone, remembering all the good times he'd had with Nicki. He wanted to be with her.

"Aren't you sweet," she was saying.

She spritzed the perfume on her other wrist and held it up to the guy again, and Todd felt his insides twist. She was doing this to torture him. It was working. "Larry can tell you the story was his fault," he said, heedless of the creep on the other side of the counter.

"Don't bother," Nicki called back over her shoulder. Then, returning her attention to her faux customer, she picked up another bottle. "I like this one. It's called Embrace."

"I could go for that," said the jackal. "Can you show me what that smells like?"

"Sure," said Nicole.

The jackal reached out, tapped behind her ear, and said, "Put some here."

Todd growled. "I don't have to take this," he informed Nicole's back.

"No, you don't," she agreed, not bothering to turn around.

"I'm not going to crawl anymore," he said.

"I don't care what you do," she returned lightly. "Crawl, jump, skip. Just so you leave."

"Fine. Merry Christmas," snarled Todd, and stalked off. Merry Christmas. What a joke! He'd never smile again.

Nicole watched Todd go and blinked furiously, hoping to stop the tears from flowing. It was useless. They spilled out anyway.

"An old boyfriend?" asked her customer.

She nodded, unable to speak.

"Would it help to talk about it? I'd be happy to buy you a drink after you're done with work."

What had she done? Nicole watched until Todd vanished in the crowd. She'd done what she had to do, she told herself. Todd had showed his true colors and betrayed her family. But she still loved him.

She turned back to look at the beautiful specimen of manhood standing in front of her. There was only one thing that kept him from being perfect. He wasn't Todd.

"I'm sorry." She shook her head, unable to say anything more. She was sorry about a lot of things.

When Celeste heard her son's dejected voice, she knew the news wasn't going to be good.

"I couldn't get to her in time," said Luke. "My real name made this morning's *Clarion*, and she won't even see me to let me explain."

Celeste felt the pain building up in her throat, but she managed to say, "I'm so sorry, dearest."

"It's my own dumb fault. Mom, I . . . Oh, God."

The sentence stopped, and Celeste longed to be having this conversation in person so she could take her son in her arms and rock him. "It's all right, darling."

"Thanks, Mom," he said, his voice tight, and hung up.

Celeste hung up the phone, and went to her writing desk. She brushed away the tears and pulled out her prettiest stationery. If only Luke's father had acted sooner, maybe this could have been averted. But now it was too late. Hank would never forgive Luke for publicly humiliating his daughter, and she couldn't blame him. If the shoe were on the other foot, she knew how she'd feel.

She didn't labor long over her letter. She didn't need to, since there was nothing to say except that she was sorry. And goodbye.

After she finished, she walked slowly to the post office. Maybe when Hank got this letter, he'd jump in his car and drive down, sweep her in his arms . . .

She stopped the reel. There was no sense letting that fantasy play out, because that was exactly what it was. A fantasy. She was sure he wanted to strangle Luke, and once he learned that Luke was her son, she would never hear from Hank again.

At the mailbox, she almost didn't put the letter in. But no, that would be cowardly. She laid the envelope on the blue, metal door and let it fall back to an upright position, sliding the letter into the box's blue belly. There. It was done. She blinked back tears and walked home, her shoulders bent like a woman carrying a great weight.

Luke paced his living room floor, rubbing the knotted muscles at the back of his neck. This day had been one miserable failure after another. And now he was out of ideas. But he couldn't just stay here, doing nothing. His condo had turned to a jail, and its walls were closing in on him. He had to break out, had to try and see Susan again. But how? She wouldn't even let him in. . . .

Of course! Luke remembered the one thing Shelburne had done right and smiled. "For those Angel Falls residents who still haven't had the opportunity to see the house that started all the fireworks this Christmas, Mrs. Carpenter's house, at 201 Sylvan Boulevard, will be lit up through December thirty-first," the article had said.

With a grim smile, Luke grabbed his coat and headed out the door. The show must go on, and even if her heart was breaking, Mrs. Santa would be out there, passing out candy canes, easy prey for Scrooge.

Fourteen

Larry Broom and Ed Banner pulled out of the parade of cars moving down Sylvan Boulevard to park six blocks down from Angel Falls's hottest tourist attraction. They popped the tops off their coffee cups and settled in to wait for opportunity to knock.

"Too bad Shelburne can't finish what he started," observed Ed, with a greedy smile that showed just how sorry he felt. "You really think there's going to be fireworks at Suzi Christmas's place tonight?"

"Hey, you were at the paper when Potter stormed in today. What do you think?"

Ed chuckled. "Poor Toddy-O. I wouldn't be in that boy's shoes for anything."

Larry nodded. "Talk about a mess, making his girlfriend's sister look like an idiot."

"I don't see what good taking himself off the story is going to do now—not that I'm complaining."

"A man who's in deep shit with a woman will do anything to get out," said Larry, and shook his head sadly. What a dork Shelburne had been, holding back that story just for his girlfriend. And Larry had told him that, too, when Shelburne came after him with clenched fists. Well, that was what love did to a man, it made him stupid. Larry looked out the window and caught sight of a little turquoise Toyota crawling by. "Hey, that looks like the girlfriend," he said, pointing to it.

"We're not interested in her," Ed reminded him. "We want Scrooge."

Nicole pulled into Susan's driveway and saw her sister on Mrs. Santa patrol, handing out candy canes to a bevy of preschoolers. The ground was crusted with a thin layer of leftover slush, and the air was nippy with the promise of more snow. Nicole pulled the collar of her fake fur more closely about her neck as she made her way across the lawn toward Susan.

Susan was talking to the children. "If you hold the candy cane like this, it looks like a shepherd's staff. Now turn it upside down. What does it look like?"

"A 'J,'" piped one child.

"That's right," said Susan. "And the 'J' stands for Jesus, and it's his birthday we celebrate. See him over there in the manger? Wave hi."

All the children waved and called exuberant hellos to the baby doll. Mary and Joseph waved back.

The children moved on. Susan turned and gave her sister the saddest smile Nicole had ever seen.

"How are you doing, Suz?"

"I feel numb," said Susan. "I just can't believe this is happening. How did Todd find all that out?"

Nicole felt her cheeks growing warm. She had to force the words out of her mouth. "I was worried. I told him where Nick, er, Luke worked and he checked it out." That wasn't going far enough with her confession and she knew it. "Actually it's worse than that. It was me who sicced Todd on Luke in the first place. Gosh, I'm so sorry, Suz. It's just that I was worried and . . ." Her voice broke, and she pressed her gloved fingers to her lips in an effort to get control of her emotions.

Susan put an arm around her and said, "It's not your fault I was stupid."

"You weren't stupid. You were tricked. Men, they're all rotten to the core!"

"Not all men. You got a good one."

"Mine's the rottenest of the bunch. We're through."

Susan stared at her in shock. "What!"

"It's true. We broke up."

"Oh, Nicki. Why?"

Nicole stared at her sister in disbelief. "Because he used you."

"Used me? I don't get it."

"Susan, that story should never have gotten in the paper. He promised. He was going to give Luke a chance to work things out. But he just couldn't wait to break his big story." Nicole pressed her lips together and blinked furiously. Her sister was still staring at her, looking confused. "He used you to make his career. I told him to take a hike," she finished on a sob.

"Oh, Nicki," crooned Susan. Nicole broke into serious tears, and Susan hugged her and let her get out a good deal of gusty wailing, then strolled her toward the front door, saying, "Willie just got home from Dad's a little while ago. Why don't you go inside and keep him company. He's eating popcorn and watching a special about Rudolph the red-nosed reindeer, and he'd love the company."

Nicole sniffed and nodded and let herself be ushered inside the house. Willie was parked in the middle of the sofa, a bowl of popcorn in his lap. No lights were on, but the lights from the Christmas tree washed the child and couch in pastel colors, and the beam from the television added its own otherworldly glow to the room. The scene looked like something that should be on a Norman

Rockwell plate, and Nicole found it comforting. She had lost Todd, but at least she still had her family.

Willie looked up and, at the sight of Nicole, his whole face brightened. "Hi, Aunt Nicki. Did you come here to watch Rudolph with me?"

I sure did," she said, her voice only slightly wobbly. "You're not going to eat all that popcorn by yourself, are you?"

"Nope," said Willie.

Nicole went and joined him on the couch, trying not to think of all the times she and Todd had curled up together on her own couch to eat popcorn and watch TV.

"You know how this movie ends?" Willie asked in a conversational voice.

How many movies had she missed the end to in the last few months, because by the end of the movie, she and Todd were too engrossed with each other to care about what was happening on the small screen. No, we're not thinking about that, she told herself. "How?" she asked.

"Happy ever after," said Willie, then turned his attention back to the screen.

Happy ever after. Sighing, Nicole dove her hand into the popcorn bowl.

Luke inched his way down Susan's street. It seemed even more crowded than the first time he'd driven it, if that was possible. The progress was even slower, due not only to the traffic, but the fact that it was now snowing. He couldn't find anyplace nearby to park and had to drive his Lexus three blocks beyond Susan's place and walk back.

There she was, that perfect body hidden under yards of padding, her incredible, golden hair tucked under that stupid wig. She was leaning over the fence, handing a candy cane to a little girl, and looking like an angel. Luke hurried through the front yard gate and came around to where she stood. "Susan."

She turned and looked up, her eyes wide. "Go away," she ordered. Then she turned her back on him, returning her attention to the child. "And if you turn the candy cane upside down, what letter does it make?"

Luke felt like he was going to climb out of his skin as he waited patiently for Susan to finish talking to the child. Behind her was another one inching up, waiting for her turn. At this rate, he'd never get a chance to talk to Susan. The first kid left and Luke took Susan by the arm. "Susan, you've got to let me explain."

She jerked her arm free. "The paper did that just fine. Now, go away."

"The paper didn't explain anything."

"Go away!"

"It didn't explain that I love you."

Susan stared at him with horrified eyes, as if he'd just threatened to kill her. "How dare you, after the way you used me, humiliated me!"

Out of the corner of his eye, he could see Joseph approaching, rolling up the sleeves of his robe, pushing back the sleeves of the long underwear beneath. Luke reached for Susan's arm. "I can explain, really. Can we just go in for a minute and talk. Please?"

"I told you I have nothing to say to you," she said, dancing away.

"Is this guy bothering you, Susan?" asked Joseph.

Now Luke could see that Mary had followed Joseph over, and was looking at him, chin out, hands on hips. Great. Mary, too. Who was minding the baby? "This is a private matter," he said stiffly.

"Well, it looks to me like the lady doesn't want to talk to you." Joseph's eyes narrowed. "Hey, wait a minute. I know you. You're the jerk with the fake name. You're Scrooge."

"Listen, you," shot Luke. "I suggest you trot on back to your stable and quit butting your nose into other people's business."

"Oh, yeah?" said Joseph, leaning in toward Luke, chin thrust out. "And who's gonna make me?"

"It's okay," Susan told him. "I can handle this."

Luke smiled, happy that he'd gotten his way. He reached to take her arm.

She jerked it out of reach and snarled, "Get off my property before I call the police."

Luke blinked, then squared his chin. "I'm not leaving until you talk to me," he said, his voice rising in volume.

"I am talking to you," she responded, her voice going up also. "And I'm telling you to get out of here."

"You heard the lady," said Joseph, laying a big paw on Luke's sleeve.

Luke shook him off, and the guy invaded his space again, so Luke shoved him, warning, "Back-off."

"Hey, you can't do that to him," said Mary.

One of the kids on the other side of the fence cried, "Mama, what's that man doing to Joseph?" just as Joseph pushed Luke back.

The next thing Luke knew, he and Joseph were throwing punches while someone hollered, "Call the cops!"

One of the candy cane scrounges burst into tears and Luke was aware of a small voice calling, "Nick!"

"Go back in the house, Willie," called Susan.

Luke turned to see Willie standing on the porch in his stocking feet, Susan's sister behind him, and caught a fist on the chin. He was vaguely aware of Willie screaming out his phony name again, and acutely aware of the flash of a camera practically in his face. Another flash put spots before his eyes as he staggered backward, or were those stars from the impact of Joseph's fist?

The world was spinning, and Luke shook his head to clear it. He looked up and saw the same photographer who had tracked him to his place standing on the other side of Susan's fence. "You," he roared, and pushed himself off the slick ground, lurching forward. The photographer and his accomplice took off at a run. Luke vaulted the fence and went after him. He caught the guy in three strides and tackled him, landing them on the sidewalk with a bone-jarring thud.

"Hey," protested the guy. "My camera. Ed, help!"

Luke grabbed a fistful of coat and hauled the man to his feet. "Worry, instead, about your head, because if you don't help me explain to Mrs. Santa how that story got in the paper, I'm gonna crack it like a melon."

The photographer's accomplice and another man closed in on them and began attempting to pry Luke off.

The reinforcements gave the creep courage, and he said, "Hey, you're news, Scrooge. You're a celebrity now, and you're public property."

"And you're dead," growled Luke, pulling back his arm to deliver a punch.

"Help!" squawked the photographer. His accomplice and the other volunteer each jerked on one of Luke's arms.

As he struggled, he could hear sirens in the distance. Their sound increased and the photographer grinned and taunted, "This will make a great picture. I can see the caption now: CHRISTMAS PRESENT FOR ANGEL FALLS: SCROOGE GOES TO JAIL."

"You're printing libel," said Luke, shaking his fist. "I'll sue!"

"What are you gonna do," taunted the photographer, "sue everyone in Angel Falls?"

The people standing nearby found that funny. The policeman striding up to them didn't.

Luke's heart sank when he saw who it was. "Oh, no."

"Not you again," said the officer. "Don't you have a life?"

"I'm trying to get one," retorted Luke. "But nobody will give me a chance."

The policeman took him by the arm, saying, "I've had it with you, guy. I'm running you in for disturbing the peace." The next thing Luke knew he was wearing hand-

cuffs. He looked down at his wrists in shock. This was
a dream. He was with the Ghost of Christmas Past, learning how to be a warmhearted human being. He'd wake
up any minute and everything would be fine.

He looked to where Susan stood, staring at him in
frozen horror, soft snowflakes drifting around her, bathed
in the gentle glow of Christmas lights. Mrs. Claus in her
Christmas yard. She looked like a figure in a glass globe,
a childhood dream under glass. And totally unreachable.
Luke felt sick.

The cop started to march him off. "You have the right
to remain silent, which I hope you'll do, and you can call
your lawyer when we get to the station. We all know
you've got one."

"Willie, come back!"

"Nick!"

Luke turned to see Willie barreling toward him, Susan's
sister in hot pursuit. Willie crashed into Luke and clung
to him like a limpet, crying. Luke wanted to cry, too. He
looked up and saw Susan rushing toward him, not to forgive, but to pull her child away.

"Don't take my friend to jail," Willie pleaded with the
cop, tears streaming down his face.

Luke blinked as the flash in his face signaled yet another attack by his tormentor. "One more picture," he
snarled at the jerk, "and I'll own your paper."

"I've got enough," said the guy. His friend stood next
to him, scribbling frantically on a small tablet. Luke
ground his teeth in helpless rage.

"It's okay, kid," said the cop, patting Willie on the
head. "He's just coming to visit me at the station."

Susan had joined the circle and now stood with her
hands settled on Willie's shoulders. The look she gave
Luke said, This upsetting scene is your fault, too.

"But why did you put those handcuffs on him?" Willie
was demanding.

Luke squatted down in front of Willie. "Because I wasn't acting very nicely."

"But he hit you," protested Willie, pointing to Joseph.

"Yes," said Luke, "and I deserved it." He looked up at Susan. "I deserve a lot of things. I probably don't deserve to be forgiven, but I was hoping for a chance to explain."

What was that he saw in her eyes? She didn't look at him long enough for him to be able to read her thoughts. Only to guess, and to hope.

"Are those really necessary, officer?" Susan asked the cop.

He looked like a kid who had just been told he couldn't go outside and play. "I guess not," he said, and unlocked the cuffs. "But just remember I'm doing this for Suzi Christmas and not you," he informed Luke. "So no funny stuff," he added, patting his night stick menacingly.

"What about my car?"

The officer smiled sweetly at him. "You won't need it. You get to go for a ride in mine."

Willie turned to his mother. "Is Nick in trouble?"

"No, dear," said Susan, taking a firm voice for her own sake as well as her son's. "He'll be fine." Willie was hopping from one foot to the other. She suddenly realized he was shoeless and gasped. "William Carpenter, where are your shoes?"

"I didn't have time to put them on," said Willie. He wiggled his toes. "My feet are awful cold."

"I should think so," said Susan. She tried to pick him up, but couldn't get her arms around her padded middle and Willie, too.

"Here," she said to Nicole, "Take him inside and stick him under a blanket and give him something hot to drink." To her son she added, "That was very foolish to come out in the cold. You'll be lucky if you're not sick for Christmas."

Nicole had Willie in her arms now and was trudging back to the house. Over her shoulder, Willie called, "I don't want Nick to be in trouble, Mommy."

"He'll be fine," called Susan.

She watched the police car edge its way through the traffic, blue lights flashing, and realized that if the people out there in the street could see inside her head, it would look much like those flashing lights, with a million thoughts whirring around. There went the night he kissed her on the couch, followed by a whole string of newspaper headlines, then the flashing camera bulbs, and his last words: "I probably don't deserve to be forgiven, but I was hoping for a chance to explain."

What was there to explain? He was suing her. The same man who had kissed her so tenderly was suing her. Maybe he had a split personality? Susan set her jaw. Well, both of him could rot in the Angel Falls jail with her blessing!

Officer Lewis was the cop's name. Luke read it on his badge as they walked into the police station. Police station, thought Luke scornfully. He'd been in bathrooms bigger than this place.

A woman with straight, gray hair, no neck, and shoulders like a fullback, wearing a blue police uniform sat at a desk, squinting at a computer. Officer Lewis called to her, "We got a live one, Hildy."

She looked up, a scowl on her face. "Well, don't expect any help from me. This demon-possessed computer is at it again."

Officer Lewis shook his head. "Bill Gates is going to take over the world someday, mark my words."

"I know a little about computers," said Luke. "Maybe I can help."

His companion frowned. "Don't get cute. You're a prisoner."

Luke shot him a look of disgust. "Would you mind cooling it with the insults?"

The cop blinked and looked shocked, then recovered. "What would you know about computers?"

"I own PC Edge," said Luke loftily. Actually, he knew more about selling computers than fixing them, but he was willing to bet the problem was a simple one.

"Humph," said Officer Lewis. "You don't look like a geek."

"I'm not an expert, but I do know a little."

"That's more than Lewis," said Hildy. "Come over here."

Luke sauntered over, Officer Lewis following behind, saying, "He's under arrest Hildy."

"What did he do?" cracked Hildy. "Insult your sister?"

"Oh, ha-ha. You took the call. You should know."

For the first time, the woman looked at Luke. He watched her eyes widen in surprise. "You're the guy who was making all the trouble at Suzi Christmas's house?"

"That's the one," Officer Lewis answered for Luke. "You know who this guy is? He's Scrooge."

Hildy made a face and shook her head. "What a shame, and you're so cute."

"Ha!" said Officer Lewis. "He's a pri—"

Hildy cut him off. "Watch your language, Lewis. There are ladies present." She studied Luke for a moment. "You don't strike me as the kind of man who would go over to someone's house and start a riot."

"He's stalking Suzi," put in Lewis.

"I am not stalking her!" snapped Luke. "I'm in love with her."

"That's what all those stalkers say," said Lewis. "I'm going to go talk to her tomorrow and suggest she get a restraining order against you."

Luke looked at the ceiling and counted to ten.

"Lewis, shut up," said Hildy. She nodded in the direction of a nearby desk chair and said to Luke, "Pull up a chair."

Luke obliged, rolling the chair next to hers.

"Now, tell me why I can't get into this file."

"I don't believe this!" protested Officer Lewis as Luke assessed the problem. "This man is a prisoner. What do you think the chief would say about you having him out here messing with our computers?"

"If this got fixed, he'd say, 'Good job, Hildy. You deserve a promotion.'" Luke could feel Hildy's assessing gaze on him as he worked. "I read that story about you in the *Clarion*," she said. "What in the hell did you think you were you doing going over there?"

"I was trying to prove to Susan that I wasn't a jerk," said Luke.

"Why?"

"I think I've found your problem."

"Never mind my problem. Yours is more interesting. Are you in love with her?"

"Oh, for Pete's sake," said Lewis. "That's enough." He took Luke by the arm and started to pull him away.

Hildy grabbed the other arm. "He hasn't explained my problem yet."

"Your problem is that you read too many romance novels," said Lewis.

"Yeah, well, if you'd read a few maybe you'd still be married," shot back Hildy.

Lewis frowned at that remark, but he let go of Luke's arm. He even went so far as to perch on the edge of the desk and eavesdrop as Luke walked Hildy through her high-tech maze. "Hey, that's pretty impressive," he said.

"Now, if you could just take care of your problem with Susan that easy," put in Hildy. "Too bad you can't get somebody to write an article telling your side of the story."

Luke stared at her in amazement. It had been so simple. Why hadn't he thought of it? "Hildy, you're brilliant!" he said. Then, to Officer Lewis, "I'm ready to make my one phone call."

"Here," said Hildy. "Use my phone."

"Why don't you see if he's going to want room service while you're at it," grumbled Lewis.

"Why don't you go see if you can find some real criminals to arrest," retorted Hildy.

"Here in Angel Falls? Ha."

Luke let their bickering wash over him as he waited for Ben to pick up. Wonder of wonders, the little turkey actually was home. "Ben, it's Luke. I'm at the Angel Falls jail."

"You're not at it, bud, you're in it," corrected Officer Lewis.

"What are you doing there?" Ben asked.

"I'm learning firsthand about our criminal justice system," said Luke. "Look, I need your help. I need you to take one of your buddies and get over to Sylvan Boulevard and pick up my car."

"What's it doing there?"

"Never mind. I'll explain later. Just go pick it up, and see if you can get it home in one piece."

"Okay, sure."

"But before you go, I want you to call Steve. Tell him I need him to help me with something tomorrow, and I'll be over at his place by ten." Luke looked at Officer Lewis. "I will be out of here by then, won't I?"

"Yeah, I guess."

"You do remember his wife just had a kid, don't you?" said Ben. "I don't know a lot about that stuff, but it seems to me . . ."

"Just do it," said Luke between gritted teeth. "My future is riding on this. Tell Steve if he can help me, I'll get his wife maid service for the next month, and I'll give him a raise. Oh, and he can have the next few weeks off, with pay, of course."

"Okay, sure. Anything else?"

"Yeah. Two more things. Call Martha and tell her to find a Mrs. Santa outfit somewhere, then to stand by to make a special delivery for me tomorrow afternoon. If she pulls it off, I'll give her the next week off with pay."

"Did those cops beat you in the head?"

"Are you getting all this?" snapped Luke.

"Yeah, sure. Hey, how about me? If I do all this stuff can I have the next week off?"

"You've already had your two weeks and then some. If you can do all this without screwing up you'll still be employed come the New Year."

"Thanks," grumped Ben. "What's the other thing you want me to do?"

"Call Todd Shelburne—he's in the phone book—and tell him to get down to the jail right away."

"Shelburne!" came the shocked echo.

"Just do it, Ben. Okay?"

"Sure, but I still don't get what's going on, or what you're doing in jail."

"A case of false arrest," said Luke glaring at Officer Lewis. "Which reminds me. Call my lawyer."

"Cute," said Lewis as Luke hung up the phone. "You should be a comic."

"Maybe I will," retorted Luke. "Maybe I'll do a routine about life at the Angel Falls police department."

"Yeah? Well, you can practice it in your cell," said Officer Lewis.

The cell was a pitiful little cage perfumed with eau de toilette and decorated with graffiti, but it was big enough to pace, which was what Luke did until Todd Shelburne showed up.

"It's about time you got here," said Luke.

Todd stood on the other side of the bars, staring at him.

"Let him in," Luke said to Officer Lewis. "I need to talk to him."

"Is he your lawyer?" asked Lewis in a snotty voice that made Luke's hands clench into fists.

"No, he's not my lawyer."

"Then I ain't letting him in," said Lewis with a sneer.

Luke glared at him, then hollered, "Hildy!"

"All right," said Lewis, unlocking the door. "But I'm staying right here, so don't try anything."

Luke gave a snort and rolled his eyes. "Barney Fife."

Todd stepped inside the cell, still wearing a look of confusion. "What are you doing in here, Potter?"

"Waiting for you to help me write a story."

"Well, don't plan on seeing it in the *Clarion,*" said Todd. "I'm not covering your story anymore."

Fifteen

"You're not covering my story?" repeated Luke.

"I told the chief I had a major conflict of interest." Todd fell onto the cell's thin, metal framed bed and the springs gave out an ear-jarring screech of protest. "I wish I'd never heard of you, Potter."

"Well, my life would have been a lot easier without you, too," said Luke. "You screwed it up real good."

"Hey, you screwed yourself. I just reported it," said Todd. "And the only reason I'm here is because I've got this gut feeling that helping you will somehow help me."

Luke rubbed his aching forehead. "You're right. I've got no one but myself to blame for this mess. It was like a snowball, you know? That one little lie when I first met Susan, it just kept growing until I wound up with the Abominable Snowman."

"Frankly, I'm not sure what you think I'm going to be able to do to help you," said Todd. "The only thing that will get you two back together is if Suz gets amnesia and forgets your real name."

"No, that's not the only thing. That's why I need you to help me write this story."

"I told you, I'm not covering you anymore."

"Yeah, I know. I think I've seen your replacement."

"What? When?"

"I met him earlier. He was at Susan's when I got arrested."

"Oh, jeez. Look what you've done to me! All this mess with Nicole is ruining my instincts."

"What are you talking about?"

"Here you are in jail, and I haven't asked you one single question about why you're here."

"Well, I appreciate your consideration," said Luke.

"That's not consideration. That's sick. How did you land here?"

"I went over to talk to Susan, to try and explain. Your friend, the camera bug, was there. He got lots of great pictures. I don't know which one they'll want to use, the one where I get punched out by Joseph or where Barney Fife there has got me handcuffed."

"Hey, watch it," snapped Officer Lewis.

"Probably both," said Todd.

"Great," Luke muttered. "A new low for Luke Potter."

"So why did you bring me here, to write an account of your darkest hour?"

"No. I want to write a confession and give it to Susan in some kind of book form."

"The story of a stalker," sniped Lewis.

Luke ignored him, watching for Todd's reaction instead.

Todd raised an eyebrow. "Isn't it a little late for that?"

"I want to explain why I did what I did, what I was trying to do to get out of this mess before everything blew up in my face. But I'm not a writer. I need someone who's good with words to help me get my thoughts in order."

As Luke was speaking, Hildy showed up, bearing two mugs of steaming coffee. "Hey, if you're going to write something to win a woman's heart you'd better let me help. You need a feminine point of view."

"Where?" said Officer Lewis.

Everyone ignored him.

Luke's own doubts regarding Hildy's femininity must have showed on his face, because she drew herself up and said, "Hey, just because I wear a uniform doesn't mean I have no heart."

"Don't either of you have duties to perform?" asked Luke hopefully.

"Not me," Hildy said, handing the mugs through the bars. "It's real dead tonight. But Lewis, here, needs to go write a report. Now that the computer's up and running, you've got no excuse," she informed him. "And as long as it takes you to write a report, I suggest you get started pronto."

Lewis shrugged as if to say the company he was keeping was boring him anyway, then ambled off.

Hildy returned her attention to Luke. "So, how do you see yourself, Potter? Misunderstood?"

Luke gave a snort and turned his head toward the wall. How did he see himself? He certainly hadn't started life with the ambition to turn into Angel Falls's resident villain. He shook his head. "You know, I used to have a heart," he mused. "Somehow, when my folks split up, I don't know, I just lost it somewhere in there under all the anger. And it's been lost for years. That is, until I met Susan. She made me see what I'd become, made me want to change." He sighed. "I don't care if I never make another penny my whole life. I don't want to be a success if it means I've got to be a miserable failure as a human being. If I could, I'd haul every Christmas present I've ever gotten in my whole life up to the North Pole and tell old Santa, 'Take 'em back. Just give me Susan, and I'll never ask for anything else again.'"

"That's beautiful." Hildy sighed.

"And there's your hook!" said Todd, snapping his fingers. "That's it, that's it. Oh, I'm so brilliant I scare myself. Hildy, get me a pad of paper. Quick! We're going to write a book."

By the time Hildy went off duty, the three collaborators were in a writing fever. She decided to stick around and help finish the project. By nine A.M., they had written a novella. Luke's eyes were scratchy, and his brain felt stuffed with cotton. The bed in his cell was looking good, but he had no time for sleep.

His lawyer showed up and Hildy walked Luke through the good-bye process. He bid her a fond farewell, promising to name his firstborn child after her if it was a girl, then Todd took him home, driving over snow-crusted streets. Angel Falls looked like a fairy kingdom. Looking around, Luke saw both his town and his life with the fresh perspective of a man who had found hope.

Back at the condo, he showered and shaved and made himself a cup of instant coffee, then made a phone call. Finally, carrying his precious manuscript, he headed for the garage. He saw Ben had gotten the Lexus back. It bore a scratch and a lovely dent in the right rear fender, and while such a discovery would once have sent Luke into a paroxysm of rage, he now merely noted it with a grunt and climbed into the Bronco.

Steve was waiting for him, looking as red-eyed as Luke, with coffee and the morning paper and the observation that Luke was becoming more notorious every day.

Luke looked at the pictures in disgust. As Todd had predicted, the *Clarion* had used both. There he was, captured forever being attacked by the stepfather of Jesus Christ. Maybe he could change his name, get plastic surgery.

"Have you had breakfast yet?" asked Steve.

Luke shook his head. "Only caffeine."

"We've got some Danish in the kitchen. Come on out and explain to me what you want me to do."

Over coffee and Danish, Luke walked his store manager through the manuscript. "I want this to look as good as anything you'd find in Barnes & Noble, something cloth bound, not shoved in a notebook with a plastic cover. I remembered you saying you helped your wife with something like this."

"Yeah, it was a family history book. She and her sister made it for her mom last year for her fiftieth birthday. This artsy craft stuff is right up their alley."

"I know you guys are busy these days, but if you could help me out you would save my life," said Luke. "And I meant what I said about the maid service and the raise. And you can order all the take out you want. I'll pick up the tab."

"That's an offer we'll find hard to refuse. Jen was just stirring when you came. Let me see if she's dressed."

Steve wandered off toward the back of the house, and Luke leaned back in his chair and smiled. In the eyes of Angel Falls residents he was still a Scrooge, but the crusty, old shell was crumbling away. He could feel it.

Steve came back, followed by his wife, Jenny, a petite, brown-haired lady wearing baggy, pink sweats and moving slowly. "I'm a mess," she announced. "Hi, Luke."

Luke thought she looked kind of cute, lost in all that pink, with her hair caught up in a ponytail. "You look great," he said. "A lot different than the last time I saw you. Anyway, I'm the one who should be apologizing for my appearance."

"You don't look bad for a man who spent the night in jail," she said.

He shook his head. "I hope your neighbors will still be speaking to you when they find out you were harboring a Christmas criminal."

"I'll take my chances," she said. "Steve tells me you've written your first story."

"It was a collaboration: me, a reporter, and my jailor."

"I can see the acknowledgment page now," said Jenny. " 'I'd like to thank my jailor.' "

"This is not for publication," said Luke. "There's only one person I want to read it. And believe me, I wouldn't be bothering you right now if it wasn't really important that I get it into readable form as soon as possible and have it look good. Like I told Steve . . ."

Jenny smiled, a beatific expression that said she knew more about the matter than she was telling. "Relax," she said. "I had a pretty easy delivery, and my sister just happens to be coming over today. We'll take you up on that offer of meals, though. Steve's an awful cook and my mom won't get here until the twenty-sixth."

"I can't tell you how much it would mean," said Luke.

"You don't have to," said Jenny. "I can see."

"Thanks," said Luke.

"Thank Steve," said Jenny. "He's got the hard part—all that typing." She sat down at the table and pulled the manuscript toward her and nodded. "I like the title."

Encouraged, Luke grinned, then took a sip of his coffee. He watched Jenny's face while she read, watched as her eyes began to sparkle with the hint of tears. The bloom of hope in his heart opened wider. Maybe, just maybe, Susan would have the same reaction.

Jenny finally turned over the last handwritten page, saying, "It's wonderful." She looked to her husband. "You'd better get started."

He nodded and rose from the table.

"How long will it take?" asked Luke.

Steve looked to his wife. "What do you think, hon? If we're aiming for Christmas Eve, it gives us almost two full days."

"With all three of us working on it, hopefully, maybe we can have it ready by then. If the baby cooperates."

"That would be great," said Luke. "He shook Steve's hand. "This is the most important work you'll ever do for me."

"We'll do our best to see you have it in time to give to her for Christmas."

"Thanks," said Luke. Now he just had to beg his delivery person to make a run on Christmas Eve. "Can I use your phone?"

"Sure," said Steve.

Luke hurried to dial his secretary. She answered the phone with her usual air of efficiency, "Bad Boy Enterprises."

"Martha, it's Luke."

"The king of bad. Where are you, and what's this errand I'm supposed to be running?"

"Did you find a Mrs. Claus outfit?"

"Lucky for you, I just happen to have something. I wear it every year when I take cookies to the old folks at the nursing home."

"Great," said Luke. "Any chance I can get you to wear it on Christmas Eve and make a special delivery for me?"

"Christmas Eve!" Martha squeaked. "I have got twenty coming for dinner, and there is no way . . ."

"Okay, okay," said Luke. "It's not in your job description. I was just asking as a favor."

Her voice softened. "Luke, you know I'd do it. I love you like my own son. But I just can't manage it."

The old Luke would have ranted, the new Luke said. "I understand."

"I tell you what, though. You can borrow the outfit. I'll leave it here at the office."

Just who did she think he was going to get to wear it? A sudden vision of Hildy, the cop, sprang into his mind. "Okay, thanks," he said, his voice taking on new energy.

"Are you going to be in today?"

"Probably not. I've got too much to do."

"Yes, you are a busy boy these days, aren't you?"

Luke knew she was referring to his latest moment in the spotlight, but refused to let her teasing bother him. "Is Ben in?"

"Yes, he's at his desk working, like a good little bunny. Do you want me to put you through to him?"

"No. Just tell him thanks for his help."

"Okay."

"Oh, and Martha."

"Yes?"

"Tell Ben to take the next week off, too."

"Okay. Merry Christmas, Luke. I hope next year is a better one for you."

"I think it will be," said Luke. He hung up, feeling great. Now, to find Hildy.

Hank pulled the mail out of his mailbox. Two bills, three catalogs, and a pink envelope. He looked at the delicate handwriting, then the return address. Celeste. He felt his heart clench, then ripped open the envelope and read.

Dearest Hank,
How can I begin to tell you how sorry I am? I had no idea when we were first seeing each other that your daughter was the lady my son was suing. I should have told you the last time we were together, but I couldn't bring myself to confess it. Luke really is a good boy who has made some very wrong decisions, but I know, as it is your daughter who has been affected by those decisions, you will find it impossible to understand or forgive. Frankly, if the shoe were on the other foot, I'd feel the same way. I'm so sorry things have to end like this between us. You were my Prince Charming, and I'll be forever jealous of the lucky woman who gets you. Please remember me with kindness.

Love,
Celeste

Hank stared at the paper and blinked. Celeste Knight was Luke Potter's mother? He read the words again, but even after a second reading his mind refused to accept them. This couldn't be happening. It just couldn't be.

He stood there at the mailbox and slammed his eyelids down to dam back the rising tears. And he saw Celeste. His eyes flew open. He stiffened his jaw, biting back the sob that wanted to escape and settling for punching the mailbox.

The first woman he'd even looked at since Bethie, the one woman he thought he could spend the rest of his life with, and look who turned out to be her kid! No wonder Celeste had felt sick the other night. When she heard who his daughter was, she had put two and two together and knew it would never add up. It couldn't, because if Hank ever saw that sneaking kid again, he'd rip him limb from limb.

He looked at the note again and crumpled it in a rage. This wasn't right. He loved Celeste, wanted her in his life. But how was that going to happen now?

Wait a minute. What was he saying? They weren't Romeo and Juliet. They were adults who needed only to answer to themselves.

He marched into the house, ready to get his car keys and head for her place, but by the time he'd gotten inside, grim reality had put a staying hand on his shoulder. Celeste was right. When you married a person, you married their family, too. There was no getting around it. Right now, his family and Celeste's weren't a match, especially with the latest development between Susan and Luke.

Hank picked up his paper again and reread the story. What to make of it? Why had the guy been on Susan's doorstep every day for almost two weeks, and why was he trying so hard to see her now? Was he Angel Falls's biggest jerk or just a holiday turkey?

Hank remembered what a turkey he'd been when he'd been chasing after Bethie. When she'd gone out with other guys, he'd followed her and managed to coincidentally turn up at the same movie or the bowling alley. He'd let the air out of Tim Schumann's rear tires and then been conveniently on hand after the dance to give Bethie a ride home. And that time they'd broken up for a week, he'd been completely obnoxious, calling all the time and camping out on her front porch. He supposed today they'd call him a stalker, but he'd just been a guy in love. And if Beth's mom hadn't put in a good word for him, they might never have gotten back together.

Maybe Luke Potter wasn't a total jerk or a crackpot. Maybe he was a guy who needed a chance. If that was the case, there was hope for Hank and Celeste. Maybe Susan could be persuaded to at least talk with Luke.

Hank's thoughts were interrupted by the phone ringing.

"Mr. A., it's Todd. Have you talked to Nicole lately?"

"No," said Hank and thought, uh-oh.

"She's not speaking to me."

Great. Here was another turkey who needed pulling out of the oven. "Why's that, Todd?"

"Because of that article in the paper."

"You mean today's?"

"No. I didn't write that one," said Todd. "The one before. Look, can I come over? You weren't busy or anything, were you?"

"No," said Hank. *I have no life at the moment thanks to Luke Potter.*

"Great," said Todd. "I'll be right there."

Hank hung up and poured himself a cup of coffee. Well, one turkey at a time. First he'd deal with Todd. Then he'd see what could be done about Luke.

Fifteen minutes later, Todd was sitting on Hank's living room couch, giving Hank a blow by blow account of his breakup with Nicole. "She thinks I went ahead and put that article in the paper after telling Potter I'd give him a chance to make things right with Susan, and I can't get her to shut up and listen long enough for me to explain. Jeez, Mr. A. I love Nicki, and Suz, too. I was just trying to protect Suz. Why else would I start a legal defense fund for her, for crying out loud? And it was Nicki who asked me to check out Potter in the first place. So how did I get from Todd the Hero to Todd, King of the Dung Hill so quick? That's what I'd like to know."

Hank felt the coals of hope bursting into flame. This might not be so hard, after all. If Todd had his facts straight, Potter was trying to straighten things out and prove himself worthy of Susan. And if he could, then Hank wouldn't have to knock his teeth out, and Celeste wouldn't have to worry that their children would come between them.

"Mr. A.?"

Hank recalled himself to the problem at hand. "Well, maybe she felt you were more interested in advancing your career than protecting her sister's feelings."

Todd's cheeks took on a guilty flush. "Well, it was a good story. But I was protecting Susan, too. Potter was taking advantage of her. At least, I thought he was."

I can see how you'd think that," agreed Hank. I was ready to rip the guy limb from limb after reading about what he'd been up to."

I think he's really got it bad for Suz," said Todd. I spent last night with him in his jail cell, writing a story he's going to have printed up to look like a book and delivered to her. I figured when Nicki hears that I helped him write it, she'll forgive me, but . . ." He let the sentence trail off, unfinished.

"But what?" prompted Hank.

"But I really wanted to give her that ring tomorrow night at Christmas Eve dinner, with you and Suz and the grandmas all together. I had it all planned: I was going to have Suz slip it in Nicole's piece of cake."

Hank sighed. How well he remembered those burning, urgent dreams of youth. Wasn't he experiencing some of the same feelings, himself, these days? "I tell you what,

Todd. The girls will be over at Susan's tonight, baking that cake and God knows what else to lug over here tomorrow. Let's you and me pay them a visit."

Todd's eyes lit up like a kid at a toy store. "Oh, great. Hey, thanks, Mr. A."

Hank smiled. "No problem."

He watched Todd go bounding down the walk to his car and smiled. He knew just how the kid felt. At the rate things were going, his kids' problems would be fixed before Christmas was over, and he and Celeste would be ringing in the New Year together.

Susan had tried to resist the temptation to open the newspaper, but she hadn't been able to, and reading this latest story and seeing those awful pictures had left her feeling sick. She'd burned the paper so Willie wouldn't see it, but the pictures and every word of the article had stayed on the screen in her mind, and she couldn't lose it.

All day, two warring thoughts had battled in her heart. Every time she thought of how her dreams of happiness had died as, for the second time in her life, she'd lost someone she loved, she felt a heavy sickness. She'd think of that picture of Luke in handcuffs and want to weep. Whatever he'd intended with his Nicholas Claus masquerade, she was sure he hadn't intended it to escalate to this. He couldn't have. Could he?

And every time that question came back into her mind, it brought along the thought that turned her despondency into anger. Luke Potter may not have meant his little plan to go awry like this, but he had intended to trick her, probably for the express purpose of getting her to take down her lights.

I was hoping for a chance to explain," he had said. What explanation was there for that kind of perfidy?

She was glad when her sister finally showed up at

eight, for although Nicole was miserable, too, at least it would help to have someone to talk to.

"Thank God most of the streets are clear," said Nicole, shedding her coat as she breezed in. "You don't have very many customers tonight."

"I had a steady stream up until about seven-thirty, even without the live manger scene. By now I imagine people are busy getting ready for their own Christmas."

"Yeah, you're right. I just thought after . . ."

Although Nicole stopped herself, Susan knew exactly what she'd been about to say. After the latest article in the paper, her house should have been swamped with curious people. She was glad the crowd had thinned quickly tonight. She'd smiled for enough gapers and suffered enough nosy questions in the last hour and a half to last a lifetime.

"I've got the whipped cream for the fruit salad, the mints for the chocolate-mint cookies, and the marzipan for the Christmas pastries," said Nicole, quickly moving on to safer conversational territory.

"Did you remember the red food coloring for the red velvet cake?" asked Susan.

Nicole's face puckered as she nodded, then she burst into tears.

"Nicki, what is it?" asked Susan, alarmed.

"That was Todd's favorite cake," Nicole wailed.

It was going to be a long night after all, thought Susan, putting an arm around her sobbing sister.

"Aunt Nicki!" whooped Willie, running down the stairs.

Nicole swiped at her tear-sopped cheeks and forced a smile for Willie.

"Why are you crying?" he asked.

"Never you mind," said Susan. "Now, kiss Aunt Nicki goodnight, then back up the stairs to bed. Tomorrow is Christmas Eve, and you want to be able to stay up for the whole party, don't you?"

"But I'm not sleepy." Willie protested.

"You go lie down and Mr. Sandman will come and make you sleepy, and you'll be in dreamland before you know it. Now, how about a goodnight kiss for Aunt Nicki? And I'll take another one, too, while you're handing them out."

Willie obliged, then reluctantly went back upstairs. The sisters headed for the kitchen, Nicole sniffling all the way.

"Why don't you call Todd?" Susan suggested gently. "I think he's suffered enough."

"Susan, he betrayed you, made you look like a fool. What kind of loyalty is that? A man like Todd Shelburne would publish my bra size if he thought it would make a good story. You can't trust a guy like that."

"He didn't betray you," said Susan. "He never lied to you and strung you along." She realized she was thinking of Luke Potter again—and strangling the whipping cream carton. She loosened her hold and put the container in the refrigerator where it would be safe from mutilation.

"I already told him I never want to see him again," said Nicole stubbornly.

"And did you mean it?"

Nicole's lower lip began to wobble. She shook her head.

"Oh, this is silly." Susan picked up the phone and handed it to her sister. "Call him."

"But that latest article," protested Nicole.

"He didn't write that."

"What? Let me see."

"I can't. I burned it. But believe me, every word is burned into my brain. And I distinctly remember seeing some other name on the byline. Ed somebody."

"Ed Banner?"

"Yeah, I think that was it."

"Then he's taken himself off the story," said Nicole in amazement.

"Um-hmm," said Susan knowingly. "Why would a dedicated newspaper reporter take himself off a hot story? Family loyalty, maybe?"

Nicole sat down heavily on a kitchen chair, ignoring the phone in Susan's outstretched hand. "It's too late. He won't want anything more to do with me."

"What makes you think that?"

Nicole told her sister about the episode at the perfume counter. "I just wanted so bad to punish him, to make him suffer."

"Oh, for pity's sake. He can't be suffering any more than you are. Call him and talk this out," Susan commanded, shaking the phone at her sister.

Nicole, crying in earnest now, took the phone and dialed. "It's the answering machine," she wailed.

The doorbell rang. Susan left the kitchen as her sister said, "Toddy, are you in there? Pick up the phone. Please."

Susan opened the front door to find her father and Todd standing on the front porch. "Is Nicki here?" asked Todd anxiously.

Susan nodded toward the kitchen. "She's talking to your answering machine."

Todd rushed past Susan, and a moment later she heard her sister squeal, "Toddy!"

She smiled at her father. "Daddy, you're a genius."

He mirrored her smile, saying, "It wasn't too hard to figure out where you two girls would be an the night before Christmas Eve."

"Well, come on in. You may as well wash your hands and roll up your sleeves, because I suspect Nicole is not going to be much use to me now."

They walked into the kitchen and found Todd and Nicole glued together, kissing as if he were a soldier shipping off to war.

"You can come up for air now. You've got company," said Hank.

Nicole pulled away, blushing. Todd grinned. "Thanks, Mr. A."

Hank shrugged. "For what, giving you a ride here? It looks like my daughter had already made up her mind to forgive you."

Nicole was looking at Todd with shining eyes. "I guess that's what love is all about."

Her words didn't sit comfortably on Susan's heart, and she decided it was time to change the subject. "If we're going to have anything to eat for our party tomorrow, we'd better get baking."

The evening passed pleasantly enough, Susan's kitchen rapidly filling with good smells and laughter. But once her company had gone home, she was left with a fading smile and the memory of Luke looking at her and saying, "I was hoping for a chance to explain."

She shook her head and turned off her lights. "No, Luke Potter. You had plenty of opportunities and you said nothing. I hope you're still in jail and they have every bar strung with a hundred blinking Christmas lights."

"I should have given you a chance to explain," sighed Nicole after she and Todd had surfaced from another very long kiss. Back at her apartment, they sat cuddled together on her turquoise, fake leather love seat, two goblets of half-consumed wine on the glass coffee table sitting ignored.

"Yes, you should have," agreed Todd, twining a strand of her hair around his finger.

"You've got to admit," she added, "it did look like you hadn't been able to resist temptation."

"There's only one temptation I can't resist," he said, then kissed her again.

"Oh, Toddy, I'm so happy," she said at last. "Let's not fight like that ever again. I was so miserable without you."

"Well, you sure did a good job of hiding it," said Todd. "I was the one who was miserable. I couldn't sleep, couldn't work. I just kept thinking about you with that guy."

"There was something wrong with him," said Nicole.

"Yeah? What?"

"He wasn't you."

"I don't deserve you," said Todd simply.

"I know," she said, and grinned. Then she sighed happily. "I just hope Susan and Nick, er, Luke can patch things up. I'd hate to be so happy when my sister is so miserable. She deserves to be happy."

"She will be," said Todd. "Don't worry. That story I wrote for Potter was brilliant."

"It will have to be more than that," said Nicole. "It will have to be magic."

"This is the season for miracles," said Todd. "Now," he murmured, "where were we?"

Susan went to her dad's the next morning and put the turkey in the oven. She set out her presents for the family under the tree while Willie excitedly explored the pile of red and green and gold wrapped boxes for the ones with his name.

He held up a rectangular one wrapped with paper bearing cartoon characters wearing stocking caps and riding on sleds. "Look at this one, Mommy."

"Mmm, that looks like a game," said Susan.

"Oh, boy!" Willie grabbed another rectangular box, this one from deeper in the pile."

"That looks like clothes," said Susan.

Willie immediately dropped the box, mining the pile for more precious gifts.

"Did you find anything from Santa under there?" teased his grandfather.

"Grandpa, you know Santa doesn't come until tonight."

"Oh, that's right," said Hank, with a wink at his daughter.

"And he'll come to my house, not yours," added Willie.

"But what if I want something?"

"Grandpa, what would you want?" said Willie.

"Maybe a certain lady?" teased Susan.

"Maybe," said her father and his smile seemed a little less assured than it had just a moment before.

Susan studied him. "Maybe? You're sure singing a different tune than you were a few days ago."

"We have a few things to work out."

"Like what?"

"Never mind me," said her father. "Let's talk about you."

Susan felt her face shutting down. "Daddy, these days everything you need to know about me you can read in the papers."

"My dad always said you can't believe everything you read in the papers."

What kind of a thing was that for her father to say about the man who had made a public fool of his daughter. "Who's side are you on? I can't believe after the way this man tricked me, you're not making plans to send him a bomb in the mail."

Her dad went to put an arm around Susan. "You know I'm on your side, honey."

"Well, you sure don't sound like it."

"You know better. I want to see you happy."

"Then you should be glad I'm rid of that man."

"I just think you should hear his side of the story. Todd told me . . ."

Susan felt herself on the edge of a very emotionally charged conflict, the kind she and her father had engaged in when she was sixteen and not into curfews. "Daddy, please! I don't want to talk about this. Come on, Willie, we have to go." She started marching toward the door.

"Susan," pleaded her father.

Susan stopped. She turned to him with an apologetic smile. "I'm sorry," she said. "It's just that this man has made my life miserable the last few days. I don't want my family Christmas ruined, too. And it is my life, Dad," she added gently.

Her father pressed his lips together and nodded.

She ran back to him and gave him a quick kiss on the cheek. "I'll see you tonight, okay?"

He nodded, still not speaking.

"And don't forget to baste the turkey," Susan added as she went out the door.

Hank stood by the window and watched his daughter drive off. He should have let the storm break, had that fight with her, should have made her sit down and listen to everything that Todd had told him. He sighed. Susan was right. She was a grown woman now, with her own life to live, her own decisions to make.

Just like he was a grown man with his own life, came the thought. This was stupid. He didn't have a grudge against Luke Potter anymore, so what was he doing here, moping around, feeling miserable? He grabbed his coat and car keys and headed out the door.

Sixteen

Celeste juggled the grocery bag and her purse and got the key turned in the front door. The scent of bayberry greeted her as she entered her house. Her living room looked like a magazine shot with her Queen Anne-style, blue velvet couch, its corners piled high with velvet pillows, and matching chairs next to it. By the window stood her tree, with its Victorian ornaments and wine-colored bows, gold beads, and white twinkle lights. Garlands of roses trimmed with gold ribbon looped across the fireplace mantel. Everything looked perfect, like an empty stage, waiting for the actors.

Weighed down by more than the grocery bag, Celeste headed to the kitchen. How many Christmases had it been since real life had measured up to her decorations and the fantasy that accompanied them? Too many. And this Christmas had started out with such hope!

The boys will be here Christmas day, she reminded herself, and found no consolation in the thought. It actually made her feel worse, because one of her darling sons was the cause of her present misery. *Oh, Luke, you learned all the wrong things from your father.*

Her thoughts were interrupted by the insistent ring of the doorbell. She left the bag sitting on the kitchen counter and went to answer it. When she opened the door and saw him, her heart constricted, and she felt suddenly breathless. "Hank? What . . . ?"

He answered her unfinished question by taking her in his arms, stopping her words with his kiss.

When he finally loosened his hold and smiled down at her, she looked up at him, tears in her eyes. "Oh, Hank. This can't work."

"Yes, it can."

"But my son . . ."

"Is a turkey," said Hank. "But I don't have any plans to wring his neck. He and Susan will have to work things out between them. If they can't, we'll just have them over on alternating holidays."

Celeste was laughing now, tears spilling over. "You crazy man, this isn't practical."

He walked her into the living room and to the couch. "It is, Celeste, believe me. I've given this a lot of thought. I wouldn't have come here if I hadn't."

"But your daughter hates my son," Celeste protested.

"She thinks she does. Isn't that what everyone thinks when they're mad at someone?"

Celeste remembered the early days before she and Luke Senior divorced, then that year after, when she was struggling with Luke Junior and Ben, trying to make their lives normal and well-adjusted. How she'd hated her ex-husband then. Or so she had thought.

She nodded. "You're right."

"I think our kids are in love with each other, but they're adults, and they've got to find their own way. They have their own lives to lead. So do we. Do you really want to throw away what we've found?"

Celeste had thrown away happiness when she'd sent her first husband packing. She'd never found it in that disastrous second marriage. This was her third chance.

She might not get another. Still, if things remained the way they were between her son and Hank's daughter . . .

She shook her head sadly. "It won't work, Hank. You know it won't."

"Okay, if everything got resolved between Susan and Luke, and they became engaged, would it work then?"

Celeste had a sudden vision of her living room filled with laughter and grandchildren, a happy, united family celebrating the holiday together, instead of the fractured event she'd experienced for so many years. "Oh, yes."

"And let's say that, after a few years, the kids had problems and broke up."

Celeste's happy vision vanished with an almost audible poof and her heart felt leaden, "I'm right. It won't work."

"No," said Hank firmly. "I'm right. Real life doesn't come with any happiness guarantees, especially when we make ours depend on the happiness of others. We can't live the rest of our life through our kids. We can't depend on them to make our lives good. Think of the pressure that puts on them. This is about you and me, Celeste. Nobody else, Now, I'm asking you, and I want an honest answer. Do you love me?"

God help her, she did. She loved everything about this man: his honesty, his solid dependability, his smile, his kisses, and his persistence. Bless his stubborn persistence! "Yes, I do love you."

"I feel the same about you. Now, make my Christmas merry and bright, and kiss me again."

Half an hour later, they sat snuggled on the couch. "Happy?" asked Hank.

"More than just happy," said Celeste. "Content."

"No matter what happens with our kids?"

That did rub a little of the shine off the contentment. "I have to admit, it's hard for me to be as deliriously happy as I'd like when I think of what Luke and Susan are going through. If only Luke hadn't let his godfather snare him into that lawsuit."

"They'll work it out," said Hank softly.

She looked up at him. "Do you know something I don't know?"

He grinned mischievously. "I might."

"Well, spill."

"I don't know a lot, except that your son is going to superhuman efforts to win my daughter. I believe he's trying to get together the money to pay back Rawlins. From what my other future son-in-law tells me, he and Luke have cowritten a book that may not make the best-seller list, but could go a long way toward taking him off Susan's black list."

"Oh, Hank, that would be so wonderful!"

"It would be, but we're not balancing our relationship on theirs. That would be like trying to stand on a chair with only one leg on the ground."

"I know, but it would be so wonderful if they could work things out. It would make everything perfect."

"Everything is already perfect. We've got each other."

Celeste smiled. Yes, everything was suddenly perfect. Here she was on her beautiful couch, looking at her perfect tree and the garlands on the fireplace mantel. The scent of bayberry wrapped the whole scene like a ribbon, but what made the scene complete was Hank. She only wished she could keep him with her to celebrate Christmas Eve, but she was sure he had family obligations. And she, too, had things to do. She'd visit her mom in the nursing home, have dinner, and stay for the nondenominational service afterward. Then she would come home to an empty house. Not so empty anymore, she reminded herself, but full of hope for the future. Still, it would be nice to have Hank with her.

I just wish we could be together tonight," he said, as if reading her thoughts. "But I've got my whole family descending on me. Can I come over late tomorrow afternoon?"

"Of course," she said. "The boys will be here."

"Good. That will give me a chance to shake your son's hand and say no hard feelings. And who knows? Maybe by tomorrow afternoon, he'll be able to shake mine and look me in the eye."

"Oh, my," said Celeste, feeling suddenly nervous.

Hank took the hands she was wringing and held them firmly between his. "It'll be all right. I promise."

"The boys will be gone by eight," she said. And having Hank come then would be better. Hank would be forgiving, certainly; but the encounter would be agony for Luke, and for her, too.

Hank seemed to understand. He nodded and said, "Save me some . . . What do you eat on Christmas Day?"

"Ham, scalloped potatoes, homemade rolls, eggnog punch." Eggnog punch with ice cream, which was melting in a bag on her kitchen counter. "The ice cream!" She yelped and jumped off the couch.

In the kitchen, she dug into the grocery sack and pulled out the half gallon of ice cream, fortunately residing in a plastic bag. The bottom of the bag was a lake of ice cream. Hank had followed her into the kitchen. She held it up for him to see. "So much for my eggnog punch."

He laughed heartily for a moment, then looked at her with wide, panic-stricken eyes. "The turkey! I'd better get home. If the kids show up tonight and find I've ruined the bird I'll be in big trouble."

"It's pretty hard to ruin a turkey," she told him. "They can cook fine all by themselves for hours."

"For my sake, I hope so."

She walked him to the door, and he gave her a hug and kiss. "Try to miss me," he murmured.

"I won't have to try," she said, which produced a broad grin on his face. "Merry Christmas," she added.

"It is. Now." He headed down the walk, and started

whistling. The strains of "We Wish You a Merry Christmas" came floating back to Celeste, and stretched the smile on her face even wider.

Susan opened the back door and called, "Willie, we're ready to go.

"Okay!" Willie crawled out of the door of Ralph's doghouse. As he ran across the lawn, Susan could see the large, wet, muddy spots on the knees of his pants.

"Oh, Willie. Look at your pants."

"Ralph wanted me to be in the doghouse with him," said Willie.

"Well, congratulations. You are. Now, come on," she said, hurrying him through the house. "We'll have to go upstairs and put on your corduroys."

"I like those better, anyway," said Willie cheerfully.

"I'm so glad," said his mother.

"Ralph doesn't want to be in the doghouse."

"Well, he'll have to be. The last time we left him in the house on Christmas Eve, he ate three packages and two sofa pillows and went potty on the carpet." By now they were at Willie's room. Susan went to his closet and pulled out a fresh pair of pants. "Now, hurry and get these on. I want to be at Grandpa's house by five."

They were halfway to the car when a maroon-colored compact car pulled up at the curb in front of them and let loose a short, square woman in a red skirt with a pom-pom trimmed hem and a shirtwaist blouse like Susan's great-grandmother might have worn. A bright, red shawl was draped around her shoulders, and a Santa hat topped her gray hair. She started toward them like a woman with a mission.

"Mommy, she looks like you when you pretend to be Mrs. Santa!" cried Willie. "Are you the real one?" he asked the woman.

"I'm just one of his helpers," she replied. "Are you Susan Carpenter?" she asked Susan.

"Yes," said Susan, a question in her voice.

"I have a special delivery present for you," said the woman, and held out a book-shaped package wrapped in silver foil and trimmed with gold ribbon.

"You really need to read this," the woman added, her eyes misting. "It's beautiful."

Susan saw no card on the package. "Who's it from?"

"Santa," said the woman as she turned and started back to her car. "Merry Christmas."

"What is it?" asked Willie.

What indeed? wondered Susan. A mysterious present delivered by some woman she didn't know. This had the earmarks of a Luke Potter trick. "Just a book," said Susan, opening her car door and tossing it in the backseat. "Let's go."

Susan tried to put her mysterious present out of her mind, but all the way to her father's house she was conscious of the thing riding there in the backseat. Maybe it wasn't from Luke. Maybe it was from one of her friends, or one of her employees trying to be clever and surprise her. Susan loved peeking in her presents, and anything she got from friends she always considered fair game for opening on the spot. But if she opened this one and it was from Luke Potter, it would probably make her miserable and ruin her Christmas. So, this particular suspicion-clouded gift could just sit in her car until after tomorrow, she told herself. And if it was from Luke, it would go instantly in the garbage.

Even after her lecture to herself, though, Susan found her curiosity over the present in the back of her car following her up her father's front walk like a lost puppy. Not interested, she told herself firmly.

The aroma of turkey wafted out to her as soon as her father opened the front door. The house was warm, Dad had the tree lights on and the Christmas music playing. Everything was perfect, just like it should be on Christmas Eve. Susan suddenly felt comforted as she entered and kissed her father's cheek. "Merry Christmas, Daddy," she said.

"The same to you, daughter."

She studied his jubilant face. "You seem especially merry. Does it have anything to do with a certain mysterious woman?" she teased.

He just shook his head. "We'll talk about it after Christmas. Right now we've got a table to set and a bird to carve."

As she took her mother's fine china from the china cabinet, Susan remembered the visions she had once entertained of eating Christmas dinner with Nicholas Claus seated next to her. It had been a wonderful dream. Until she awoke to grim reality.

The table was half set when the grandmas arrived, bundled in coats and bearing bowls of salad, dinner rolls, and Christmas cookies. With her red knit cap and her matching scarf, Grandma Appleby, the younger of the two, looked like a fat snow lady. She dwarfed frail, little Grandma Wilson. "Where's our boy?" she asked, looking around.

"He's in the kitchen," said Susan. "Sampling turkey."

Grandma Appleby headed for kitchen with her tossed salad, calling, "Willie."

Grandma Wilson lingered. "How are you doing, dear?"

Susan nodded, smiled. "I'm fine, Grandma."

At eighty-six, Grandma Wilson wasn't much more than a thin stick with a face crisscrossed by wrinkles, but there was nothing wrong with her mind. The old woman studied Susan with her sharp, blue eyes, and in that moment Susan remembered her own mother looking at her with those same blue eyes and that very same look. "Your mouth is smiling but your eyes aren't," said Grandma. "What happened to that nice young man you told me about?"

Grandma, obviously, hadn't read the paper. Susan felt

the prickle of tears at the back of her eyes. "He turned out not to be so nice."

Now the other grandmother emerged. Willie had her by the hand and was towing her toward them. They reminded Susan of a small tugboat pulling a great ship out to sea. "Willie tells me you got a mysterious present from one of Santa's helpers before you came," said Grandma Appleby.

"It's nothing," said Susan.

"I don't know. It certainly sounds intriguing."

"Grandma, I really don't want to talk about this."

"I suppose you don't want to talk about that latest story in the paper, either?"

"Oh, what story was that?" asked Grandma Wilson.

"That man Susan was dating came to her house and started a brawl," said Grandma Appleby. "Can you imagine such a thing?"

"No," said Grandma Wilson. To Susan, "Why would he do a thing like that?"

The Christmas from hell. She was living the Christmas from hell.

"It's a long story, Grandma," said Susan.

She was spared from having to explain further by the arrival of Nicole and Todd, Nicole, as always, blowing in like a strong wind. "Oh, Grandma," she said to Grandma Wilson. We were going to pick you up. I tried to call after work to tell you I'd be late, but you'd already gone."

"Oh, dear. I thought, perhaps, you'd forgotten me. Anyway, I was right on Nan's way."

"You scared me half to death. I thought maybe you were dead in there. I banged on the door for twenty minutes and we looked in all the windows."

"Why didn't you use your fancy new phone to call me from the perfume counter?"

Nicole's expressive features morphed into a picture of disgust, and Todd burst out laughing. She elbowed him in the stomach, and the laugh degenerated into a cough. "I don't have it anymore," she said.

Everyone stared at Nicole. "But that thing was like your third hand," Susan protested. "I've hardly seen you without it since you got it."

"Nicki didn't quite get the part about being charged extra when she used up her alloted air time," explained Todd. "I hope you were all planning to give her money for Christmas. She'll need it to pay her bill." Nicole turned her scowl on him, and he said, "Sorry," looking anything but.

"Well," Nicole said briskly, shedding her coat and draping it over Todd's head to hide his smiling face. "What needs to be done in the kitchen?"

"Plenty," said Susan. "Come on."

As the sisters and their grandmothers worked, the women chatted easily—until Nicole casually asked, "Did you get any interesting deliveries today?"

Susan could feel three pairs of eyes studying her, and felt her back stiffen in response. "What do you mean?"

"Mean?" hedged Nicole.

That confirmed it. The mysterious present out in her car had something to do with Luke. But why would her sister be involved in anything having to do with that villain? "What do you know about all this?"

Nicole looked at her wide-eyed. "Know? Er . . ."

"Nicole. What's going on?" demanded Susan.

"If you just read the book, it will explain it," said Nicole.

"There was no card with the present. Who was it from?" Susan drilled her.

"I don't think you should prejudice yourself," began Nicole.

"I think I've already guessed who it's from and that's enough to prejudice me against ever opening it."

"But you need to!"

Susan's self control broke, and she slammed down the

bowl of mashed potatoes she was holding. "What are you doing to me? Now that we both know what he turned out to be, you want me to get excited about a present from him?"

"Suz . . ."

"Just butt out," said Susan firmly.

"You are so stubborn," said Nicole between gritted teeth.

"I'm also old enough to know what I'm doing, and I don't need help from my baby sister when it comes to deciding what Christmas presents I want to open," answered Susan, her voice rising.

"Now, girls," said Grandma Appleby. "It's not right to quarrel on Christmas Eve. Anyway," she added, scooping up the bowl, "the potatoes are getting cold."

As the family gathered around the table, Susan saw Todd shoot a questioning look to Nicole, and noted the quick head shake he got in return. So, whatever this latest scheme was, Luke had roped both Todd and Nicki into it. That laid the tombstone on any inclination she might have felt to be generous and forgive Luke Potter. He was nothing but a manipulative sneak. How she hated the man!

As the various steaming bowls made their slow progress around the table, the men and the two grandmas found things to talk about to fill the void left by Susan and Nicole. They scrupulously avoided, not only the topic of Susan's mysterious present, but all her other Christmas adventures as well. She felt like a person with an incurable disease that no one knew quite how to talk to anymore. This too, she could lay at Luke Potter's door, ruining her Christmas with her family.

After dinner, the sisters cleared the plates, and began taking orders for dessert. "We have banana cream pie, almond pastries, or red velvet cake," announced Susan.

"Pie for me," said Hank.

"I believe I'll have the cake," said Grandma Wilson.

"I'm going to have to have a little sliver of each," said Grandma Appleby. "But just a sliver."

"Pie," piped Willie.

Nicole had already left her chair and headed for the kitchen to start filling orders. Susan was about to follow when Todd grabbed her hand and slipped something into it, whispering, "Can you slip it into her cake?"

Susan tightened her hand around the ring. The big moment had finally come. Well, someone would be happy this Christmas, so maybe the holiday wasn't totally ruined after all. She smiled and nodded.

Out in the kitchen, Nicole was already setting slices of pie on their mother's green Christmas plates.

"Go ahead and take those out," said Susan briskly. "I'll carry on with the cutting."

Obviously, still feeling hurt, Nicole took the plates and left in silence.

As soon as her sister was out of the room, Susan cut a generous, Nicole-sized piece of cake and shoved the ring deep into the frosting between the two layers. She quickly smoothed it over, then set the piece aside. Nicole came back for more desserts, and Susan handed her another couple of plates, hiding a smile.

A bittersweet ache settled in her chest as she remembered how Bill had given her ring to her. It had been a week before Christmas, and he'd taken her driving to look at Christmas lights. They'd gone to a neighboring town and he'd pretended to get lost and asked her to get the map out of the glove compartment. There had been the little, black box with her engagement ring. The tears that came with the sweet memory were light and easily blinked away, but the ones that came with a heavier thought refused to leave so easily. *You'll never find another man like Bill, and you'll never find the joy you knew with him. What happened to you this year proved that.*

"Okay," said Nicole. "That's it except for you and me."

Susan wiped at her eyes and reached for the plate. "Here's yours. I'll be right out."

Her sister stood by her side, and Susan could feel Nicole studying her. "Suz, I'm sorry. Are you okay?"

She nodded and cut herself a piece of cake. "It's nothing a little sugar can't cure."

For a moment Nicole continued to hover, as if she wanted to say something. Instead, she sighed and headed back into the dining room.

Susan took one more swipe at her eyes before following her sister out to the table. The casual talk helped settle her wild emotions, and she stole a glance at Nicole, hefting a bite of cake to her mouth. Susan caught a glint of diamond and grinned.

Nicole shoveled in the cake, took a chew, then stopped and blinked. As she ducked behind her napkin, Todd asked, "What is it, Nicki? Did you lose a filling?"

Nicole pulled out a ring with a diamond solitaire. "Toddy!" she breathed. "Oh, Todd!" She threw her arms around him as the grandmothers cooed and her father chuckled. Susan felt fresh tears stinging her eyes.

"I take it that means yes," said Todd.

"Oh, yes, yes," cried Nicole. "You know it does!"

Everyone applauded, even Willie, who had no idea-what was going on, but was still happy to help celebrate.

Nicole wiped the frosting from the ring, then slipped it on, and stuck her hand out to examine the effect. "It's gorgeous."

"Just like the woman wearing it," said Todd.

"It will look even better once you've cleaned off the frosting film," observed Susan. "I should have just tucked it under the cake."

"No, this was great," said Todd, eyes shining. I just wish we had it on video."

"Ourselves eating dinner? That would have definitely given away the surprise," said Nicole.

"Aw, you weren't surprised, anyway. You knew it was coming."

I was still surprised," Nicole insisted, taking his hand.

"I guess it's time to dig your mother's wedding gown out of mothballs," said Hank, wiping discreetly at a corner of his eye.

A little ping of jealousy struck Susan. Ashamed of herself, she looked down at her cake to hide any betraying sign that might have surfaced.

"Oh, yes," she'll look lovely in it," agreed Grandma Wilson. "Another wedding in the family. How delightful! When would you like to get married?"

"Next month," said Todd. Everyone laughed. "I was serious," he protested, raising his hands.

"I always wanted to get married on Valentine's Day," said Nicole dreamily.

"But that's only two months," protested Grandma Appleby. "How can you plan a wedding in two months?"

Susan couldn't stand any more. She let them talk on while she gathered the dishes. Once in the safety of the kitchen, with the dishwasher running, she pressed a hand to her face and indulged her hurting heart, trying to keep her crying quiet.

She nearly jumped when she felt the hand on her shoulder, the hand wearing the diamond engagement ring. "We could make it a double wedding," said Nicole softly.

"Nicole, just drop it. Okay?"

"Don't be mad, Suz. I just want to see you happy. And I'm only trying to give you the same good advice you gave me. Give the guy a chance to explain. You've got nothing to lose. Look at you, you're miserable. And it's Christmas Eve."

Susan hugged her sister. "Not half as miserable as I was, thanks to Todd. I'm so happy for you."

"Hey, you guys," said Todd from the doorway. "Your dad's showing the video from last Christmas."

"Okay," said Nicole. She gave Susan's arm a squeeze and left the kitchen.

Susan lingered, wary of taking her sour self out to the living room where she might curdle the others' happiness. Todd was still standing in the doorway. She turned her back to him, picked up a sponge and began to wipe down the counters.

"I know Potter was a real jerk," he said softly. "But most of us men are, sooner or later. I helped him write that book. He poured his guts out, and I think it explains a lot."

Susan didn't say anything, and he left.

She stood for a moment, looking out the kitchen window at the Christmas lights winking from a neighbor's roof. Then she left, too, and went to the hall closet to grab her coat.

Seventeen

Susan started her car and turned on the heat, then she flipped on the dome light and fished her controversial present from the backseat. She removed the pretty wrapping paper to unveil a slim volume bound in red brocade. The title, *All I Want for Christmas*, was embossed in gold. She ran her fingers along the satiny fabric. Someone had gone to a lot of trouble to produce this. It was probably too much too late, but her curiosity forced her to open the book. Feeling like she was about to step off a cliff, she began to read.

PART ONE

He was a small kid, but he could dream big. In his dreams, he was the greatest pitcher the world had ever seen. Thanks to him, the Yankees had won the pennant three years running. Every season his parents sat in the box seats he had bought for them and cheered their lungs out as he struck out batter after batter. Yep, the kid could do anything. Except bring his father back home.

The boy could remember every detail of the night his dad left for good, every anger-driven word that floated up to where he had crouched at the top of the stairs, every shadow in the hallway, every beat of his heart. The thing he remembered most vividly was what he'd seen when he caught that quick glimpse of his father's face—the mask of rage that so often haunted him at night and kept him too scared to get out of bed or even cry out for Mom.

These days, the boy's biggest dream was that his dad would move back in, that they'd be a family. Then he knew he wouldn't see the mask anymore. He was doing everything he could to make that dream come true. He worked every angle. Tried God: "Please God, make my dad come back." Even tried Santa, although he really didn't believe in Santa anymore: "All I want for Christmas is my dad to come back home." But Dad didn't come back home, and the kid stopped believing.

Susan felt the tears welling up in her eyes. What was it like to be someone who stopped believing?

She read on, following the exploits of the growing, unnamed boy who was so obviously Luke. Although some of the incidents were humorous, underneath them ran the river of one little boy's misery. Part one of the book ended with the boy standing on the pitcher's mound the first game of the Little League tournament and searching the crowd in the bleachers in vain for his dad.

Susan sat for a moment, looking out the window and chewing her lip. She could hardly identify with this child. Her mom and dad had stayed together, and they'd been at everything in which she ever had a part, every piano recital, every talent show. Heck, they were even there at the ceremony when she "flew up" from being a Blue Bird to become a Camp Fire girl. What was it like to grow up with the kind of yearning Luke had known?

Still, lots of parents divorced and their kids didn't turn out like Luke. They didn't set out to ruin other people's lives and make fools of them. She threw the book down on the passenger seat next to her. What was the purpose of this little masterpiece, anyway? To win her sympathy? Manipulate her into taking down her lights?

She drummed on the steering wheel, then snatched up the book again and turned to part two. She read and felt increasingly more sick as she watched Luke turn from a lovable child into an angry, selfish teenager.

> The kid couldn't stand to watch his girlfriend crying, so he looked out the car window instead. The park looked spooky. Listening to the girl's sobs, he felt like he couldn't tell where the blackness of the night outside the car ended and his own soul began. Breaking up the night of their senior prom had been a rotten thing to do.
>
> Too bad, he reasoned, she should be glad I still took her to the prom. Even that had been torture. He had been right to dump her. She'd clung too tight. Like ivy. She'd been choking him, talking about going to the same college, planning their whole future together. It was just too much pressure. "Nothing lasts forever," he had informed her. His dad had told him that, and Dad should know. Anyway, he had plans. College and an MBA. He'd make his mark in the world. Dad would be impressed.

Susan shut her eyes on the ugly picture. What had it cost Luke to show himself so heartless?

She returned her attention to the story, watching Luke enter adulthood. It was all there. His unwillingness to commit to any woman, his frustration with his family, and his attempts to help all of them, in spite of the fact that he himself needed help. And there, skirting around the edge of the picture as Luke went through his adult life, was Don Rawlins. Every time Susan read his name she gritted her teeth.

The man knew his godfather was rich. His dad had told him so. You'd never know it to look at Don. Granted, he drove a new car, and he smoked Havana cigars. He had a beach place down in Virginia, and he traveled wherever and whenever he liked. But he didn't dress rich; and his house was nice, but not pretentious. Still, something Don said had impressed the man. "I can do anything I want, buy anything I want. I can take any business I want. That means I have power, not only over my own life, but over other people's. Power's the ticket, kid. And it's more fun to use when people don't suspect you've got it." Yes, Don was a man who knew how to make things happen, knew how to grab fate by the throat and make it hand over success. Yeah, thought the man. Don knows how to take life and turn it into something. All I want is a chance, and I can do that, too.

"Oh, Lord," moaned Susan, and turned the page.

PART THREE

She was different. He knew it the moment he saw her. She was the sun. She was joy and hope, and he wanted her. Then he learned her name and knew he couldn't have her. But that just made him want her all the more. So here he was again, right back to where he'd been as a kid, wanting something he could never have, determined to get it, somehow.

Susan read on, a lump forming in her throat. It was all there, every meeting they had ever had, every conversation, seen through Luke's eyes. The story flowed on to its climax, and farcical scene in her front yard. She still remembered the look on Luke's face as the policeman towed him away. She bit her lip and read on.

> Now the man sat in jail, caged like a beast, and realized he was right where he deserved to be. But not where he wanted to be. And all he could think as he looked around him was, oh God, I want a second chance. I want Susan and everything she represents. All I want for Christmas is a chance to become a new man.

Susan was sobbing now, barely aware of the hot tears stinging her cheeks. She turned to the final page and found a handwritten note:

> Dear Susan: I owe Don Rawlins money, but as soon as I've gotten together the funds to pay him back, I'm dropping out of the lawsuit. I was a fool. I don't want to remain one. Can you help me give this story a happy ending?

"Save me, Sabrina, fair," Harrison Ford had said to Julia Ormond in the movie, Sabrina. Susan had watched him (at least six times) and thought, yes, save that man. Anyone can see he doesn't want to be like he was. All he needs is a good woman.

Help me. If this were a movie and women were watching her, Susan knew exactly what they would be saying. She was the only one who could save Luke's heart.

The knocking at the window on the passenger side of the car made her jump. She turned to see her father's concerned face peering in at her. His words came through the sheet of glass, muffled but understandable. "Mind if I join you?"

"Oh, Daddy," she cried and opened the door.

He got into the car and held her until her sobs subsided, then said, "You've been out here an awful long time."

"I was reading." She handed over the book, and he examined the cover. "A real tearjerker, huh?"

"I was wrong about Luke Potter."

"Oh, probably not entirely," said her father.

"No, I mean I was wrong not to give him a chance to explain. I think he's a different person now than he was when I met him. People do change, don't they?"

"They can, if they want to badly enough."

"And do you think Luke does?"

"Well, I don't think he's going to all this trouble, and making his own life miserable, for the fun of it." Her dad held up the book. "Do you mind if I look inside?"

"Please do."

Looking over her father's shoulder while he scanned the pages, Susan reread the book. When he had finally finished, he handed it back to her and said, "My future sons-in-law make a pretty good writing team."

"Then you think Luke means what he says in there?"

"No man in his right mind would write this stuff unless he did," said her father. "And no woman in her right mind would let a man like that get away."

Susan hugged her father's neck and whispered, "Thank you, Daddy."

He patted her shoulder. "Now, what do you say to going back in the house? It's almost time to leave for church, and I'll bet you're going to want to wash your face."

"Oh, yes," said Susan, imagining the mascara tracks marching down her cheeks.

She walked arm in arm with her father back into the

house, beaming through her tears. Once inside, she hurried up the stairs to repair her makeup.

As she went, she heard Nicole's worried voice, asking "Is she all right?"

And her father's reply. "It looks like we're going to have a lot to celebrate this Christmas.

Dad was right. Susan did have a lot to celebrate, the biggest thing of all, the return of hope. Maybe she would be able to find love again, after all. She knew she'd made a good start: She'd already found forgiveness.

Twenty minutes later, the Appleby clan piled into two cars and headed off for the Christmas Eve service.

Back at Susan's house, Ralph, the Houdini dog, trotted around the side of the house toward the front yard, his collar and chain laying stretched out in front of his doghouse like resurrection remains. One of the older strings of lights along the roof gave a pop. Ralph jumped and barked up at it. He cocked his head and whimpered, watching while a wisp of smoke squeezed out of the wire like a ghost. The wire popped again and burped more smoke and Ralph yapped, but no one came from the empty house next door to tell him to be quiet.

Luke watched while his teenage stepbrother and stepsister casually tossed aside boxes of designer label clothes and computer games. Andrew got a new boombox and said, "Cool. Thanks, Mom."

Andrew's mother, an exercise-addicted, bleached blonde in her middle forties, said, "Don't thank me. Thank your stepfather."

"Thanks," said the boy with a little less enthusiasm.

"You're welcome," said the old man, smiling with forced jollity.

Andrea plucked an envelope bearing her name from the tree boughs and tore it open. She pulled out some sort of tickets, and her face lit up. "Oh, Mom, Luke, thank you! Four of them."

"We figured you and Rob might want to go with another couple," said her mother.

"I've gotta call Tina," gushed Andrea, and disappeared into her room.

Luke looked to his father. "Rock concert tickets?"

His dad nodded. "Mangy Butt. They're Andrea's favorite group, and with the boyfriend she's got, I'm not surprised. It looks like he's got a mangy butt, himself."

"Darling," scolded his wife.

"It's true," said the old man. "If I had a daughter dating a guy like that I'd lock her in her room."

"But you don't have a daughter," said his wife in tones that told him to mind his own business.

Luke watched the hurt surface on his father's face, watched the old man catch it and stuff it back down, deep, where no one could see it. Sometimes he wondered how happy Dad was in his marriage.

Andrew popped a tape in his boombox and cranked the thing up to an earsplitting level.

"Does he have to do that in here?" shouted Luke Senior.

"He's just trying out his new gift," his wife shouted back.

Luke watched this latest exchange between Dad and his quasi-youthful bride. He'd seen their skirmishes before and he knew who would lose.

Dad didn't disappoint him. He stood, plucked another envelope from the tree, then motioned for Luke to follow him out of the living room.

Luke followed as his father led the way down the hall to the spare bedroom he'd converted to an office. Even in there, with the door shut, they could still hear the muffled thump, thump of the bass coming from Andrew's new boombox.

"Looks like you had a good year," observed Luke.

"I did," admitted his dad.

Luke knew he shouldn't say it; it sounded rude and

spiteful. But he couldn't help himself. "Too bad you wasted it on those two."

He half expected his old man to tell him to mind his own business, to defend the monsters, say they weren't really such bad kids, list their many attributes—what those would be Luke couldn't imagine, other than to point out that they both bathed regularly.

Instead, Dad nodded. "I know. I keep trying to make out of them what I had with you guys: a family."

Luke could only stare at his dad. The shock of the old man's words robbing him of speech.

Dad shook his head. "I had that when you guys were little. I was Ward Cleaver, and you guys were Wally and Beaver. And your mom, she was great—better than June. But I just had to have more, had to get a better house, a newer car, make something of myself. My dad always said I never would amount to much, and I had to prove him wrong. I don't think I did," he added, his voice breaking.

"Dad, don't say that," said Luke, alarmed by this sudden display of emotion.

His father shook his head, unable to speak for a moment. When at last he got command of his voice, he said, "I know I blew it with you and Ben. There were so many times when I should have been there for you, and I wasn't because I was out trying to make something of myself. I wanted to do better the second time around, but . . ." He let the sentence trail off. Both men sat silent, the thud, thud of Andrew's boombox pulsing into the silence like a heartbeat.

The old man forced a smile. "Well, anyway, what's done is done. I can't rewind the tape and fix the past, but I can at least be there for you in the present." He held out the envelope to Luke. "Here's a little something to help you out of the mess you've gotten into." Luke looked questioningly at his dad. The older man shoved the envelope at him, saying, "Just open it."

Luke took it and slit it open with his thumb, then pulled out a check. The numbers swam before his eyes. He blinked and checked again to see if he was hallucinating. He wasn't. It was the exact amount he needed to repay Don. He looked at his father in amazement.

"That should square you with Don," said Dad.

"How did you know?"

"Ben told me. He had to do some snooping around to get the exact figure. I think the boy's a natural-born detective. What do you think?"

Luke was shaking his head in amazement. "That you're incredible. Dad, are you sure you can afford this?"

"I told you, your old man has had a good year."

"Dad, I can't . . ."

His dad cut him off. "Of course, you can. You're my son. You can thank your brother, too. Half of that was his, but he wanted to donate it to the cause."

Luke felt tears prickling the back of his eyes. He pressed his lips together in an effort not to look like a fool in front of his father.

"Merry Christmas, son."

Luke still couldn't trust himself to talk. Silently he leaned over and gave his dad a hug, the first one he'd given him in twenty years.

"Dad, I don't know how to thank you," said Luke at last.

"Just don't turn out like Rawlins. Or me. That will be thanks enough. Make things up with that young woman, start a family, and enjoy it. And take time to enjoy the Christmas lights."

Luke smiled.

Dad consulted his watch. "Don's probably home right now."

Luke nodded. "Thanks Dad. Merry Christmas."

Luke left his father's house and headed for Don Rawlins's place. He'd pay back Don tonight, and tomorrow he'd be on Susan's doorstep.

•   •   •

Don Rawlins ambled out to the living room while the women cleared the table. His wife's sister and her old-maid niece had made pleasant dinner companions, nice and meek and, as always, agreeing with everything Don said. Yes, he'd make them happy and leave that little niece something someday. He'd been planning on leaving something to Luke Potter, too. The boy had been like the son he never had; ambitious and energetic, and possessing a sharp business mind. But he'd turned traitor, and Don would be damned if the kid would see so much as a penny from him now.

The thought of Luke's betrayal pulled out one of Don's ever ready frowns. The boy deserved every bit of public humiliation he was enduring now. Who did he think he was, some movie hero fighting the town bad guy? If he hadn't met that little dingbat across the street . . .

Don looked out the window. Those lights of hers seemed especially bright tonight. Had she added extra wattage just to torment him? He squinted his eyes for a better look. No, not more lights. A flame. By God, she'd gone and put her house on fire!

A corner of Don's mouth turned up. Well, well. We do reap what we sow, don't we? The little fool had sown her foolishness in spades, and now it looked like she was about to reap an appropriate harvest.

Don shut the drapes, took up the remote and turned on the television. No need to report the fire. Someone had probably already called the fire department.

Eighteen

As Susan sat in church and sang Christmas carols, their words took on a new meaning. She sang, "Peace on the earth, goodwill toward men," and realized that although the joy and wonder and merriment were all a big part of Christmas, they weren't the most important part. That was forgiveness. Christmas was about forgiveness from "heaven's all gracious King."

And that forgiveness meant peace and goodwill toward all men, even the ones who scorned her Christmas lights, even the ones who, because of their wounded hearts, couldn't see past the pain to the enjoy the light and laughter of the season.

But all that was about to change for Luke Potter. She was going to call him as soon as she got home and tell him just how to write the ending for that story of his. Together, they would nurse his heart back to health.

Now the lights in the sanctuary were being dimmed. Susan's favorite part of the service was at hand. She held the small candle she had been given on entering and waited with anticipation while an usher lit the candle of the person sitting at the end of her pew. That person turned to the woman next to him and lit her candle, and she lit the candle of the person on her other side, and so the little dot of light moved on down every pew until the whole room was filled with the soft glow of many candles. Susan's father touched her candle with his lit one, bringing it to life and whispered, "Merry Christmas, daughter."

The soft glow blurred as Susan's eyes filled with tears and she turned to Todd, seated next to her and touched her candle to his, whispering, "Merry Christmas, brother."

He smiled, and with one hand holding Nicole's, he touched his candle to hers, a foreshadowing of the wedding ceremony to come.

The congregation was singing now, "Silent Night, holy night. All is calm, all is bright."

Susan was so into the moment, it took her a while to notice that the singing was dying away, replaced by a buzz of whispering voices. She turned and looked over her shoulder. She could see an usher hurrying down the aisle toward her. Like a background figure in a painting, she caught a glimpse of police uniform through the glass window of the sanctuary door. What on Earth?

The usher stopped at her pew. "Susan, there's a policeman to see you."

Willie! But Willie was here in the pew with them, seated between the two grandmas. What else could it be? A robbery, perhaps? With her father following she left the pew behind her, thinking, please don't let the burglar have stolen Willie's present.

She got to the foyer and now the policeman wasn't some vague background figure. He was large and thick, and the leather on his belt creaked as he moved toward her.

"Mrs. Carpenter?" he asked.

She nodded. "I'm Susan Carpenter. What's wrong?"

"Maybe you'd like to sit down," said the man.

Susan fell onto the nearest chair and felt rather than

saw her father's hand on her shoulder. She was vaguely aware of Todd and Nicole, standing by her side, and of Grandma Appleby demanding, "What's going on?"

"I'm afraid I have some bad news for you," said the policeman. "There's been a fire at your house."

Susan's family gave a collective gasp, and she felt the world suddenly spinning around her. There was an earthquake happening in her stomach, making her Christmas dinner roll and weave. "Oh, God," she whimpered.

"It's not totally destroyed, but the damage is significant. If you like I can take you there in my squad car."

She shook her head. "No, no. I . . ."

Silver bells, someone was ringing tiny, silver bells. She could hear them, see glints of silver at the edge of her eyes. So dark, she wasn't in her body anymore. It was falling . . .

When Luke first saw the smoke, he thought it was snow clouds moving in. But no, these clouds were tinged with black, and there was an unnatural glow underneath them, right about the spot where Susan's house sat.

His heart hit high speed, and he pushed down on the Bronco's accelerator. From six blocks away, he could see the fire engine, its hose gushing water like some gigantic faucet. He could see the firemen rushing about and the cops trying to keep back the gawkers.

He parked as close as he could get, then ran to the scene. The firemen had the fire under control now, and its flames were diminishing, but the house was half consumed. There, next to it, stood his empty rental, unscathed and mocking. He felt sick.

"Looks like there's no more need for a lawsuit," said a voice at his elbow. He turned to see his gloating godfather. Don was wearing the kind of smile Luke had seen on kid's faces after a football game. *We won, we kicked butt!*

It was all Luke could do not to plant his fist in Don's

gloating face. Instead, he dug into his overcoat pocket and pulled out the check from his dad that he'd endorsed over to Don. "There never was. This squares us."

Don took the check, looked at it and nodded. "I'd say it does."

Luke returned his gaze to the smoking house.

"That house should be a lesson to you, kid," said Don. "Act like a fool, get a fool's reward."

Luke turned on him. "Oh, and you're so smart. What kind of reward have you earned? Everybody in town hates your guts, including me, probably even your wife."

Don's face purpled. "You watch your mouth."

"Or what, you'll sue me?" retorted Luke. "You can't sue me for libel. I'm telling the truth, and we both know it." Luke looked at him with contempt. "And to think I thought you were so cool when I was a kid. What happened to you, Don? How'd you get to be such a sour, old lemon-sucker?"

"You're a fine one to talk," spat Don. "You're just like me, kid. Just like me. And nothing's going to change that." He turned on his heel and marched off toward his house, throwing over his shoulder, "And don't come crying to me next time you need money. I've got better things to invest in than losers!"

Luke watched him go, rage roaring white hot in him. Why couldn't it have been Rawlins's place that got burned?

Two cars edged past Luke. He recognized Susan's father at the wheel of one of them. He moved away to the opposite side of the street, feeling like an unwanted family member at a funeral, and watched Suzi Christmas and her family assemble on the sidewalk to stare at the charred ruin of her house.

The place hadn't burned to the ground, but Luke could imagine the smoke damage was horrific. Inside, he could see the black skeleton of her Christmas tree and could imagine her wondering how she was going to explain it to

Willie when Santa didn't bring him that *Star Wars* toy he'd been dying for. Maybe she hadn't even thought of that, maybe she was wondering if any of her pictures had survived. His mom had always said if her house were on fire that would be the first thing she would rescue. And Susan hadn't been home to rescue anything. Maybe she was wondering what to do next, or maybe she wasn't thinking at all. She looked stunned.

Luke watched in frustration as her father put an arm around her shoulder, and wished it was him standing there with her. No, it was more than a wish: He ached to run across the street and take her in his arms. But he didn't have that right. Not yet.

Something wet and cold touched his nose. Then another something. He looked up. Snow. Big, fat flakes drifting down. Where was that snow a few hours ago when it might have done some good? The same place he was. Nowhere to be found.

They all stood there, like so many statues, just staring at the house. No one crying, no one saying anything.

Nicole was the first to break down. Susan could hear her sister's noisy weeping, but she couldn't cry. She stood there, numb. A fireman came up to talk to her. She just stared at him, unable to follow anything he was saying. She was vaguely aware of her father talking to the man. She heard the pop of flashbulbs, heard more voices, saw Todd talking angrily to two men—men from the *Clarion,* most likely, since one of them was pointing a camera at her. She stared at it, unseeing, and watched her past going up in smoke.

It seemed like an eternity before her father was bundling her back into his car, saying, "Come on, honey. Let's go back to my house."

Luke felt like crying as he watched Susan and her family mourning. He wanted so much to be a part of it, wanted to help her, but he couldn't. This was how Ebenezer Scrooge felt as the Christmas ghosts squired him through his life: past, present, and future. It was a terrible thing for a man to stand so near those he loved, to reach out and be unable to touch them.

He watched Susan's father help her into a car and drive off. The newsman Todd had been talking with went off to shadow a fireman, and Luke hurried across the street to catch Todd just as he was about to get behind the wheel of his car. "What's going on?"

Todd looked at him in surprise, then anxiously over his shoulder toward his fellow reporter. "What are you doing here? Are you crazy?"

"I came to pay Rawlins the money I owed him," said Luke. "Day after tomorrow my name will be off that lawsuit."

"Well, that's good news, but it's old news now."

"How's Susan?"

"In shock."

"Did she read the book?"

Todd nodded. "Loved the thing. It made her bawl like a baby. But it looks like she's going to have other things on her mind for awhile."

Luke chewed his lip, looking at the charred structure. "I want to help her."

"Unless you can rebuild her house overnight, there's probably not much you can do. Too bad you can't turn back the clock."

Todd's car window rolled down and Nicole's voice drifted out, "Come on, Toddy. We've got to get back to Suz."

"Yeah, you're right." He opened the door. "Sorry, man."

Luke nodded and stepped away. Todd gave him a salute and drove off.

Luke returned to his car and sat there for a long time, letting the snow fall around him, watching the firemen clean up the mess, and all the while Todd's words kept rolling around in his mind. *Too bad you can't turn back the clock.*

He kept staring at the two houses, Susan's burned one, and his perfect, unharmed, empty one. As he sat there looking at them, an idea came. He looked at his watch. It was only eight-thirty. Could he do it? With help, yes. And he knew just the two elves to recruit.

Susan's father drove her back to the home of her childhood, the place where she'd be staying for the next few months. Willie was there with the grandmas and several people who had come straight from church. Everyone wore concerned expressions and spoke in hushed voices.

Except Willie. He came bouncing up to his mother. "Can we open our presents now?"

What should she do? Keep him in happy ignorance and let him enjoy himself? She'd have to break the news to him when they were done, because normally, after the family opened their presents, and took their holiday pictures, she and Willie would go back to their own house to wait for Santa to come. Willie would want to know why they weren't going home. The tips of his ears were already tinged pink, a sure sign he was getting tired. If she waited until he was completely worn out, how would he take the news?

She looked helplessly at her dad, who simply said, "It's your call, Susan."

With a deep sigh, she knelt down in front of her son. "We're going to open our presents in just a minute, and have a wonderful Christmas together because we have something to be very thankful for." Willie was looking at her curiously, his head cocked to one side. She steeled herself and went on, "You see, there was an accident at our house while we were gone. I'm afraid it caught fire and part of it burned up."

Willie's eyes grew big. "Did Ralph's doghouse burn?"

Ralph. She hadn't even thought about the dog. "No. He's fine."

Willie looked around. "Where is he?"

"He's back guarding the house," said Susan, hoping it was true. "We're going to spend the night at Grandpa's because our house is all smoky smelling, and it would make us sick if we slept in it."

"Oh, boy!" exclaimed Willie, and Susan breathed a sigh of relief. But his sunny expression quickly clouded over, and he asked, "How will Santa know where to find us if we're at Grandpa's?"

"Well, he might get a little lost," said Susan. "But he'll find us eventually."

"Tomorrow? Will he find us by tomorrow?"

"Well, if not tomorrow, probably the day after," promised Susan, determined to drive clear across the state for Willie's present if she had to. "And tomorrow Grandpa will probably make us pancakes for breakfast," she added, hoping to distract him from the thought of Christmas morning and an empty tree.

"Oh, boy!" exclaimed Willie. "Can we open presents now?"

She nodded and turned her son loose for the grandmas to watch. Grandma Appleby handed her a cup of coffee and patted her on the shoulder. She sank onto a chair and tried not to cry. At last she couldn't hold it back any longer. She slipped away to her old bedroom, laid down on her old bed, and sobbed.

The phone rang downstairs, and Hank answered it.

"This is Luke Potter," said the caller. "Is Todd Shelburne there, by any chance?"

Luke Potter. This was all they needed to top the day, more emotional upheaval. "Mr. Potter, I realize you're anxious to push your suit, but this is not a good time."

"I know about the fire, sir," said the voice, "and I don't

want to bother Susan. I imagine she's not in any shape to talk to anyone right now."

"That's right," said Hank, preparing to hang up.

"And I'm sorry to bother you," continued the pest, "but I think I can do something to help ease some of your daughter's pain."

"That would be something, considering how much you caused her in the first place," barked Hank, losing his patience. "Unless you can rebuild her house overnight and restring her lights, I seriously doubt there is anything you can do right now."

Nothing seemed to offend the guy. "Please, Mr. Appleby, if I can just talk to Todd. I promise this won't be anything that would hurt your daughter further, and for what it's worth, I knew about the fire because I saw it. I'd gone over to Don Rawlins's house to pay him back some money I owed him and tell him I'm dropping out of the suit."

Hank grunted. "Not that it matters now."

"That's what Rawlins said, but it matters to me, and it would matter to Susan, too. Look, I know your family needs to be left alone, but if I could just talk to Todd for a minute . . ."

"All right," said Hank grudgingly, and then called Todd to the phone.

"Who is it?" asked Todd.

"The other holiday turkey," said Hank, handing off the receiver.

He watched while Todd listened, his son-in-law to-be growing more chipper with every passing second. "Sure," said Todd. "I'll meet you at the paper." He hung up and said, "Gotta go, Mr. A."

"Hey," said Hank, "what's this all about?"

"A holiday surprise," said Todd mysteriously, pulling his coat off the coat tree.

Nicole was in the entryway now. "Toddy, where are you going?"

"I've gotta go help Santa," he said, and gave her a quick kiss.

"Help Santa? What are you talking about?" demanded Nicole.

Todd was already heading out the door. "I can't tell you, babe. You'll just have to wait and see. See you to-morrow."

"But what about your present?" she called after him.

"Save it for me," he yelled back as he hurried toward his car.

Nicole turned to her father. "Daddy, who was that on the phone?"

"Luke Potter."

"Luke!"

"I guess he's still trying to win himself a real heart," said Hank with a sigh. He put a hand on his daughter's shoulder and steered her back toward the living room. "Let's get this present opening done so we can go to bed. I'm bushed."

Luke met Todd in front of the *Clarion* and passed off a piece of paper. "Here's what I want it to say. I don't care what this costs, I want a whole page. As soon as you get that squared away, meet me at the house."

"Okay," said Todd, "I'll see what I can swing," and hurried inside.

Luke got back in his car and headed for the Angel Falls Mall. The place was a zoo, packed full of snarling, tired, last minute shoppers. Fortunately, the toy store wasn't full of them. All their customers were home by now, and trying to put together toys that taunted "some assembly required," looking for the Part A that inserts into Part B.

Luke walked in and the lady at the counter smiled at him—surely a good sign. "I called earlier," he said, "about the Luke Skywalker's X-Wing. Were you able to find one?"

"Our other store had one left and they brought it out," said the woman. "It's a good thing you called when you did though. I had another man call right after you, frantic to get one."

"I guess Santa likes me better," joked Luke, handing over his credit card.

He saw the woman's eyes widen when she saw the name on it. She looked at him with recognition, and he knew she was seeing Luke Potter, jailbird, and wondering why Santa would favor him over one of Angel Falls's good little boys. He felt his cheeks warming and shrugged. "Even Scrooge changed."

"I guess," she said doubtfully, and turned to the register to ring up the purchase.

Luke's cell phone rang and he flipped it open. "Yeah."

"We're here," said Ben. "Lights, Santa suit, and sleeping bags."

"Good," said Luke. "Go ahead and start. Shelburne should be there soon. Tell him to go next door and dig out Susan's photo albums. That should keep him busy until I get there."

"Okay," said Ben.

"And Ben?"

"Yeah?"

"I owe you a lot, man."

Luke could almost hear his brother's embarrassment. "Hey, bro, that's what families are for. I guess it's time I paid you back for all those baseball pointers you gave me when I was in Little League."

Luke grinned. *Pretty expensive baseball lessons.* "Well, thanks."

"You're welcome. Does this mean I get another week off?"

"No."

"Didn't think so. Hey, when, exactly, are you going to get here?"

"As soon as I buy every last string of lights to be had in this mall."

"Oh, boy," moaned Ben. "I have a feeling we're not going to get a chance to use those sleeping bags."

"Not if you stand around talking on the phone all night," agreed Luke.

"Bye," said Ben, and the phone went dead.

Luke thanked the clerk, took his toy, and headed for the nearest department store in search of Christmas lights.

By the time he arrived at his rental place, Ben and Celeste had managed to make an impressive start. Luke opened his car trunk and hauled out the first armload of lights.

Susan woke at five A.M. on Christmas morning with a monster headache. The presence of her son next to her bed, saying, "Mommy, Santa didn't come," didn't help.

She had to fight hard to throw off the longing to burrow into the bed, pull the covers over her head, and never come out. Instead, she sat up, saying, "Sweetie, remember I told you he might get a little lost?"

Willie nodded, then burst into tears, and Susan found herself crying, too.

She took her son into bed with her and rocked him in her arms. "It's okay," she crooned as the tears ran down her cheeks. "It's okay. Santa will find us eventually."

"But what if he doesn't?" cried Willie. "I've been good, Mommy."

"Yes, you have, darling."

"I want to go home," the child sobbed. "Maybe Santa left our presents there."

Susan's throat constricted. She couldn't face seeing her half-burned house. "We can't go home to stay for awhile. Our house is all burned and icky-smelling, and has a big hole in the wall. We'd be awfully cold."

"I want to go home," Willie repeated, as if she'd never spoken.

She hugged him tighter. "I know, sweetie. But for right now, this is home."

"This is Grandpa's house," he protested.

"And we're together, here with Grandpa. And home is wherever people who love each other live together. That can be at our house or here, at Grandpa's. The important thing is that we're together." Which one of them was she trying to convince?

"Ralph isn't here," pointed out Willie.

"Well, after breakfast we'll send Grandpa to go get him, and he can stay here, too." Susan scooted back down under the blankets. "Now, here. Let's cuddle up and take a little snooze before breakfast."

Willie snuggled down under the blankets with her. "Are you sure Santa will find us?" he asked.

"I'm sure," she said. "Santa and I are good friends. He'll find us sooner or later." And sooner or later she'd deal with that issue, but not now.

Willie began to hum quietly. Susan held him and tried to will the tears to stop flowing.

Long after her son had drifted off to sleep, she lay in bed looking out the window at the gradually lightening darkness. Words she had blotted out last night when they talked with the firemen began drifting into her conscious mind. *Lights . . . possibly a worn string . . .*

Her lights, the Christmas lights she had so loved and fought to keep had betrayed her. Was there some irony here, or what? Fresh tears made their stinging presence known on her cheeks. She had taken such pride in those lights. Maybe too much? Had she reached a point where being Suzi Christmas, local celebrity, had given her more joy than the simple pleasure of enjoying her decorations and contributing something good to the community? Had she reached the point where she saw herself more as "Saint Suzi" than as Susan Carpenter, a woman who simply loved to celebrate Christmas?

If she was seeing herself like that, she certainly hadn't

lived up to the image during the last few days as she'd nursed a grudge for Luke Potter.

Saint Suzi, it would appear, wasn't so perfect herself. Some saint! Even so, she surely didn't deserve to have her house turned into a smoke-deformed ruin. She had always believed that things had a way of working out for good, but what good could possibly come out of this?

You're alive and your son's alive, she told herself. There's something good.

Great. Now she was turning from Saint Suzi to Pollyanna, playing the glad game. But she wasn't glad, and she didn't care if her house ever got rebuilt. She was tired of starting over, tired of coping with raising a child alone, tired of hoping.

She shut her eyes. It felt safe to lie here under the warm covers. Dad could entertain Willie today. And if anyone showed up wanting to see her, he could tell them she wasn't feeling well, which would be the grossest understatement uttered since the *Apollo-13* astronauts said, "Houston, we've got a problem." No matter what, she wasn't leaving this bed, not even for another fire.

True to her word, she stayed in bed, leaving her dad to cope with Willie. Maybe she would stay here forever.

By late morning she could hear their voices drifting up to her from the front lawn, and knew that Dad was helping Willie build a snowman from the freshly fallen snow. Normally she would have been out there with them, breathing in the crisp air and reveling in the pure, white beauty and the hushed atmosphere that only a blanket of snow could provide; happy to not have to drive in it, thrilled by the opportunity to play with her son. Today, as she lay in her childhood bed, she wondered if she'd ever be able to get excited about anything again.

Mid-afternoon brought Nicole, who came with fresh clothes for Susan. She perched on Susan's bed and tried to coax her to come downstairs. "Todd's mom sent a

Christmas pudding," Nicole added, as if pudding could substitute for a lost house.

Susan shook her head. "I'm just not up to it, Nicki. Tell Todd hi for me."

Nicole plucked at the bedspread. "We went by the house. It's really not so bad, Suz. Only one side is damaged."

Susan felt sick to her stomach. "Oh, Lord."

Nicole hurried on, "And some of the men from church went over and covered it with that thick plastic that builders use, so the snow can't blow in."

Susan burrowed deeper under the blankets.

"Grandma Wilson called today to say she found a bunch of pictures of Willie as a baby."

Pictures. A fresh wave of nausea washed over Susan. All those pictures of her first year with Bill in the house. Were they gone?

Who knew? What did it matter, anyway? What did anything matter? When it came right down to it, life sucked and only fools refused to see that. Only idiots insisted on running out into the storm to search for rainbows and silver linings.

"Suz?" prompted Nicole.

Why did her sister keep verbally poking and prodding her? "I don't want to talk about this," she said. "I just want to be left alone."

"But don't you think you'd feel better if you came downstairs?"

Susan gave a snort of disgust. "Just exactly how would that make me feel better? How would that change my life?"

Her sister seemed impervious to Susan's rudeness, and determined to hang around, like a doctor in a psycho ward, making sure the patient didn't do anything to hurt herself.

"It might make you feel better to talk about it," said Nicki.

"I don't want to talk about it," said Susan. She didn't want to think about it, either. All she wanted was to be left alone. "I just need to sleep." Forever. Sleep and dream.

"Suz, I don't think . . ."

Susan's patience snapped. "Will you just get out!" To further reinforce the message, she rolled over onto her side and faced the wall.

"Okay," said Nicole, finally admitting defeat. "Maybe you'll feel like getting up later."

Susan said nothing. She listened to her sister's retreating footsteps, waited for the bedroom door to shut. Then, when she knew she was truly alone, she buried her face in her pillow and sobbed in a vain effort to purge the blackness balled up inside her.

The sky outside Susan's bedroom window stayed gray all day. She lay on her bed and watched it darken as the twilight gave way to the early dark of winter. The sky matched her mood, and the approaching sound of jingling bells felt like an intrusion.

The jingling grew closer, and the sound of voices from downstairs grew louder. She heard the front door open, heard the voices downstairs crescendo with excitement. Then came Willie's whoop, and his cries of "Mommy, come quick!" preceding him as he ran up the stairs. Susan steeled herself for a fresh invasion into her cocoon of misery.

The bedroom door burst open, and Willie thundered into the room. "Santa's here, Santa's here!" Just in case she might not have heard him the first time, he jumped onto the bed, grabbed her arm, and began pulling in an effort to get her up and moving. "Come on, Mommy. Santa's here!"

"Willie," she began, trying to calm him down.

"It's true," insisted Willie. "He's parked his sleigh right outside our house."

Susan sat up. "What?"

"Come quick!" answered Willie. Then, unable to wait for his pokey mother, he let go of her arm and ran out of the room yelling, "Santa!"

Susan was out of bed now. She looked out the window at the snow-covered world, and sure enough, there beside the parking strip sat a sleigh. Well, a sleigh of sorts. What stood on the street below was a horse-drawn carriage, decked out with cedar boughs and red ribbons and tiny lights blinking every color of the rainbow. Some sort of draft horse stood in the jingle-bell trimmed harness, his mane and tail braided with red ribbons.

Who could have dreamed this up? Another member of their congregation? One of the neighbors?

"Suz!"

Susan turned to see her sister striding into the room. "You really do have to get up now. Santa is in our living room, and he's not giving Willie his Christmas present until you come down."

Susan gave the bed a longing look, then sighed. If someone was being kind enough to go to all this trouble for her child, then the least she could do was go downstairs and thank him personally. "Okay," she said. "But I'm not staying more than five minutes."

Nicole picked up the pile of clothes she'd brought earlier. "That's fine. But meanwhile, you'd better get dressed. There's a lot of people down there and more coming every minute. If you come down looking like that you'll embarrass all of us."

Susan snatched the clothes from her suddenly bossy sister, muttering, "All right already." She supposed Nicole was right. She probably looked like her life: a wreck.

Nicole nodded briskly. "Good. And don't forget to brush your teeth."

"Yes, Mommy," Susan retorted.

Her sister started for the door, then turned, ran back, and hugged her. "Oh, Suz. Everything is going to turn out wonderful. You'll see."

"What's that supposed to mean?"

Nicole's only reply as she rushed out of the room was, "Never mind. Just hurry up."

Susan moaned and shook her head. She'd rather be in bed, but her sister's excitement was contagious enough to resurrect a spark of curiosity. Nicole had brought her a pair of jeans and a white, beaded sweater that looked like it had cost an entire paycheck. She climbed into the jeans and pulled on the sweater, then dragged a brush through her hair while she slipped her bare feet into the pumps she'd worn the night before.

Willie's voice drifted up to her from the stairs. "Hurry up, Mommy."

"I'm coming," she called, and rushed to the bathroom to give her teeth a quick brushing.

She barely had time to get toothpaste on the toothbrush before her son was at her side, tugging on her sweater and urging her to come.

She followed him down the stairs to find a crowd gathered in her father's living room. She stopped and blinked in amazement. There was her dad and Nicole and Todd, of course, and the two grandmas, along with Todd's mother and father. She saw Buddy with his wife and kids, and wondered vaguely when he'd arrived.

He came over to give her a hug and a kiss on the cheek. "It's about time you got up. We've been waiting for an hour to see you," he said. Then added, "Any money you need for rebuilding the house, we'll make sure you get it."

Susan, knowing her brother had just paid off a home-improvement loan, felt her eyes stinging with fresh tears, turning the rest of the people present blurry. In spite of her impaired vision, she recognized friends from church, and several of her father's neighbors.

In the middle of the gathering stood a man in a cheap Santa suit, Willie kneeling at his feet, playing with an excited, yapping Ralph, who was looking especially festive with a big red ribbon tied around his neck.

At the sight of Susan, the dog wiggled excitedly, broke away, and ran over to greet her. She scooped him up and discovered that he smelled like soap. Holding the dog, she came slowly into the room. This Santa looked very familiar. She studied the eyes, the nose. Could it be?

"Can I open my present now?" asked Willie eagerly.

Santa nodded, and unslung his bulging bag. "Here you go, young Willie. Santa's sorry he was late, but it took a while to find you."

Willie tore off the wrapping and lifted the box with a shriek of triumph. "My Luke Skywalker X-Wing! Oh, thank you."

"You're welcome," said Santa, looking at Susan, who was staring at him, dumbfounded. He grinned, and bent back to his sack. "Let's see, we have something for Mr. Appleby here, and for Nicole. And some fruitcake. Oh, and here's something for Mrs. Carpenter." He pulled out a pile of photo albums and scrapbooks, all tied with red ribbon. "Santa brought over your photographs, just so you'd know they're okay."

Susan felt the tears spilling from her eyes. She set Ralph down and took the precious albums.

"Oh, and Santa has one more thing," he said, and pulled a newspaper out of the near-empty sack. He held it out to her. "You should find something of interest to you in Section B," he said, forgetting to use his phony Santa voice.

Still shocked, she handed the albums over to Nicole who stood next to her, practically buzzing with excitement, and took the proffered paper.

"Page twenty-two," he said.

Susan turned to the page and stared at the huge, bold print:

DUE TO TECHNICAL DIFFICULTIES, SUZI

CHRISTMAS'S LIGHT DISPLAY HAS BEEN MOVED TO MR. SCROOGE'S HOUSE.

There was the address of the house next door, Luke Potter's house. She looked up at him in amazement.

"Santa would be honored if you would let him escort you to see the display," he said softly, offering her his elbow.

"I don't understand."

"You needed some Christmas cheer, I needed to change. Would you like to come see if what I've done will do the trick?" said Santa Luke.

Susan stood there, nearly dizzy from the myriad of thoughts racing around her mind, unable to speak.

"Just go with him, Suz, " urged Nicole, and Susan was vaguely aware of her father stepping up and holding out her coat. "He has some important things to tell you."

"Please?" added Luke.

"We'll be right behind you," Nicole added as Susan's father slipped her coat up her arms.

Every face in the room was looking at her expectantly. She took Luke's arm and the group broke into applause and cheers.

She felt almost like a bride leaving the church as family and friends clapped and hooted and waved them on their way. At the end of the shoveled front walk, Luke pointed to her feet. "I don't think you're going to want to wade through the snow in those shoes." Before she could say anything, he'd swept her into his arms and was starting down the snowy street, making everyone cheer all the more loudly. He lifted Susan into the carriage, climbed up beside her and covered her with a blanket. Then he stood and slapped the reins on the horse's rump. The animal plodded off down the road, the echo of her family and friends' whistles and catcalls following them.

As soon as the commotion had died down behind them, Luke spoke, "Todd was right when he called me a Scrooge, but I'm not the same man I was when you first met me. I'll do anything to prove it. I want to start by covering whatever repair costs your insurance doesn't. I'll get a home-improvement loan, sell my place, do whatever it takes to get the money you need. You can redecorate, do whatever you want."

"Luke—" she began.

He stopped her, saying, "Let me finish. I owed Don Rawlins money. It wasn't why I said I'd go in with him on the lawsuit in the first place, but it was why I found it hard to pull out. It was like some sort of emotional blackmail. Don gave me my start in business, and when I needed quick cash to expand, he was right there. I thought that meant something. I . . . don't know. It's hard to explain."

Susan laid a hand on his thigh. "You already did. Eloquently."

"I paid him back last night. It was like . . . breaking a spell. But I broke the spell too late to save your house. I'm hoping I'm not too late to save what we were building together."

He stopped the horse and turned to her, his expression earnest under all those fake, white whiskers. He looked so endearing, she felt herself smiling for the first time in almost twenty-four hours.

"I really have changed, Susan. I don't want to go back to being the man I was before I met you. It's a lot to ask right now, when you've got problems of your own, but please give me another chance. Help me keep sight of the meaning of Christmas. I need you."

Susan's throat was too constricted for her to speak, but her kiss served better than words.

The parade of cars forming behind them began to honk, and more cheers filled the winter air.

They pulled apart and smiled at each other. Luke put the horse back in motion, saying, "I don't deserve you."

Susan smiled. "I'll try in the future not to remind you that you said that."

"Remind me as much as you want."

By the time their carriage finally arrived at Susan's house, the neighborhood was crawling with people. The sight of her charred house lurking in the darkness made the tears spring to her eyes, but after taking in Luke's glowing peace offering next to it, she found herself crying and laughing at once. A myriad of lights jeweled his rental house, and a wicker sleigh and reindeer sparkling with white lights sat in the front yard. Mary and Joseph were there, too, waving at her.

Cars already lined the snowy street curb, with more pulling up. Susan noted that the Channel Six news truck was there, too.

"I thought it would be good to make a public declaration that I'm a changed man," said Luke, nodding in the direction of the TV truck. "I want to marry Suzi Christmas, and the only way this town will allow me to do that is if I prove myself worthy."

"You already have," said Susan softly, and squeezed his hand.

This crowd, like the one at the Applebys, was in a party mood, and they cheered as Luke lifted Susan down from the carriage and carried her up the walk to his house. They walked past her big food donations box. It was freshly repainted, and looked like it would probably leave any food-bank contributors with a reminder of their generosity on their coats. Susan noticed the box was already half full and looked at Luke in amazement.

"How did you do all this?"

"I had help," said Luke, nodding to his front porch.

Out the door came his brother and a woman dressed as Mrs. Santa, a basket of candy canes slung over her arm. She smiled and waved at Susan.

"Come on," said Luke, hurrying Susan to the front porch, where the two stood waiting.

"You've already met my brother," said Luke. "The one who . . ."

"Started this mess," finished Ben amiably.

"And I think you remember my mom, the woman your dad has been seeing."

Susan found herself incapable of speech.

But Celeste wasn't. "I hope you'll forgive my earlier deception. Luke was trying so hard to prove to you that he wasn't all bad. It's a terrible way to begin a friendship, I know, but I certainly want to be friends. You have a wonderful father," she rushed on. "I hope you'll share him with me."

Susan could only laugh, cry, and shake her head as she offered Celeste a hug.

As the two women embraced, Susan was aware of the flash of a camera and turned to see Todd and Nicole and a photographer.

"How about a kiss for Santa?" called Todd.

Susan obliged, and the crowd broke into applause.

A small body wiggled between Luke and Susan breaking them apart. Luke scooped up Willie, holding him in his arms. Then he signaled for quiet. The TV cameras rolled while, in a loud voice, Luke said, "I'd like to announce that I am not dropping out of the legal battle over Susan Carpenter's lights." A collective gasp rose from the crowd. He held up a hand for attention, then, smiling down at Susan, added, "I'm just changing sides."

After the wave of applause and cheers subsided, Luke continued, "I've learned a lot about the Christmas Spirit this year. The message behind the holiday is well worth celebrating, and I hope that from now on, like Scrooge, I'll be remembered as a man who knows how to keep Christmas and keep it well."

The crowd went wild, and Susan felt as if her heart would burst.

"Hey, bro," said Ben. "That was a pretty cool speech. Maybe you should go into politics. They love you."

As if to prove his words, someone in the crowd started singing, "We wish you a Merry Christmas," and others took it up until the still growing crowd was a huge chorus. "We wish you a Merry Christmas and a Happy New Year."

Susan's father had now joined them, and stood with his arm around Celeste. Willie was singing for all he was worth, perched in Luke's embrace like a little bird.

Luke continued to smile at the crowd of serenaders, and only Susan heard him mutter, "Great. All we need now is Jimmy Stewart."

Well, Rome wasn't built in a day. Anyway, she knew they didn't need anyone's good wishes. They had found their Merry Christmas, and the New Year lay before them like a lovely present tied with red ribbon: full of promise and waiting to be opened.

Merrily Ever After

Luke Potter, the new mayor of Angel Falls was holding an open house, and cars were lined up bumper to bumper along the circular drive of his white, colonial home on the outskirts of town. Set atop a knoll, the house, with its amazing display of lights could be easily seen from the highway, and his wife wondered if the music and excited laughter carried that far as well.

Probably, but it didn't matter. This time of year everyone expected the domain of Suzi Christmas to be a highly visible presence in the community, and as Don Rawlins had moved to New York after losing his legal battle against her two years ago, there was no one left to object.

With Baby Nicholas on her hip, Susan moved among her guests, keeping a wary eye on Ben's latest girlfriend, a tall, strawberry blonde with an impressive bustline and a very full mouth that showed long, horsey teeth and emitted an equally equine laugh—a laugh that was growing louder with every cup of eggnog she consumed. Watching the woman teetering on her three-inch heels, Susan decided she had better go steer the lady away from the Christmas tree.

It looked like Nicole had the same idea. Susan could see her break away from Celeste and their dad, who were plying Willie with Christmas cookies, and start waddling toward Miss Tipsy as fast as her pregnant condition would allow.

Neither sister could reach the woman in time. She threw back her head to laugh at something Ben said and lost her balance. Arms outstretched in a hopeless attempt to regain her balance, she pitched backward—sending eggnog onto a startled Mrs. Murphy—then fell into the tree. It cradled her with loving boughs as it tipped over, relieving one elderly guest of her wig and burying Ralph, who set to yapping indignantly.

Susan and Luke arrived at the tree at the same moment, and while Susan rescued their guest's wig, Luke helped Ben dig his girlfriend out of the broken tree.

"Jeez, Chloe," said Ben in disgust. He turned to his brother. "Man, I'm sorry."

Luke just smiled and shrugged. "'Tis the season. I wanted to get a bigger tree, anyway. Old Jake needs the money, and he'll love to see me coming."

As Susan watched Luke, still smiling, prop up the damaged tree, she felt sure that old Saint Nick was cruising somewhere nearby in his sleigh, and giving a mittened thumbs-up.

Dear Reader.

With the holidays right around the corner, I thought Suzi Christmas would approve of my giving away an Advent table runner. You can see a picture of it on my Web site (sheilasplace.com). My husband picked it up for me in Germany, and although it is so gorgeous I'd like to hang on to it, in keeping with the spirit of the season, I want one of my readers to have it. So, if you're interested, please send me a postcard with your name and address to the post office box listed below. If you'd like to be included on my mailing list, you may indicate on the same card. I'll take the entries up until November twenty-fifth. The winner will be notified by mail, but look for an announcement on my Web site, also.

Best of luck and happy holidays!
Sheila

Send contest entries to:

Sheila Rabe
P.O. Box 4573
Rolling Bay, WA 98061-0573

NATIONAL BESTSELLING AUTHOR
JILL MARIE LANDIS

Experience a world where danger and romance are as vast as the prairies and where love survives even the most trying hardships...

☐ **Come Spring** 0-515-10861-8/$6.99

☐ **Until Tomorrow** 0-515-11403-0/$6.99

☐ **Last Chance** 0-515-11760-9/$6.99

☐ **Day Dreamer** 0-515-11948-2/$6 99

☐ **Just Once** 0-515-12062-6/$6.50

☐ **Glass Beach** 0-515-12285-8/$6 99

☐ **Blue Moon** 0-515-12527-X/$6.99

☐ **The Orchid Hunter** 0-515-12768-X/$6.99

Prices slightly higher in Canada